Catch my drift

# Catch my drift

GENEVIEVE SCOTT

GOOSE LANE

Edited by Bethany Gibson.
Cover and page design by Julie Scriver.
Cover illustration by JaySi, Shutterstock.
Printed in Canada.
10 9 8 7 6 5 4 3 2 1


Library and Archives Canada Cataloguing in Publication

Scott, Genevieve, 1978-, author
Catch my drift / Genevieve Scott.

Issued in print and electronic formats.
ISBN 978-0-86492-988-4 (softcover).--ISBN 978-0-86492-989-1 (EPUB).--
ISBN 978-0-86492-990-7 (KINDLE)

I. Title.

PS8637.C68615C38 2018          C813'.6          C2017-906115-1
                                                C2017-906116-X


We acknowledge the generous support of the Government of Canada,
the Canada Council for the Arts, and the Government of New Brunswick.


Goose Lane Editions
500 Beaverbrook Court, Suite 330
Fredericton, New Brunswick
CANADA E3B 5X4
www.gooselane.com

RECYCLED
Paper made from
recycled material
FSC® C103567

To Gillian, my sister.

# The Best Time

Lorna stepped to the edge of the pool and stared down at her toes. Though the evening air was thick and warm, her nail beds were purple. Somewhere through the pool fence, she could hear the bell of an ice cream truck.

The pool was closed for the evening, but Debbie, Lorna's roommate, was the lifeguard in charge of Wednesday lock-up. She and Lorna had planned this session back at the beginning of August.

"Just say when," Debbie said. The stopwatch swung casually from her narrow wrist.

Nerves contracted in Lorna's stomach, bunching into the shape of an apple. She looked up and ahead. Across the park, men and women strolled in pairs or stretched out together on the dark green grass. *Focus,* Lorna told herself. *Fukiss.* She shook out her hands and wiped them across her nylon-plastered ribs. "Yeah," she said. "Ready."

Debbie whistled; Lorna leapt. She felt the tidiness of her dive, the satisfying surge of water against her forehead. She tore across the twenty-five-metre pool, legs pumping, sucking air deep into the branches of her lungs. At the wall, she turned with a hard kick and began to visualize her next target: the delicate, tanned knobs of Debbie's knees. As she reached Debbie's end and turned again, Lorna's mind jumped to her own lumpy knees, now motoring her through the water. Focus, her brain shrieked. But the thing was, they really were potato knees: thick, draggy things laced right up the middle like footballs. Focus, focus, *fukiss*.

At the end of the four laps, Lorna slammed her hand on the deck, splashing Debbie's shorts. Her breath was scorching, ragged. She tried her best to look unruffled.

Debbie nodded as she stared down at her watch. "You're getting there," she said. "That's for sure, definitely."

Lorna couldn't bear to look at Debbie's crinkled, earnest face. She looked instead at the concrete deck, the grey puddles becoming shiny in the dropping sun.

"You slowed down in the middle there. Just a little, huh?" Debbie said.

"Time?"

"One minute eleven."

Lorna slapped her bathing cap on the deck and ducked below the surface. Water tingled across her scalp. Debbie was training to be a teacher. When Lorna came back up, she'd say, "Chin up, you!" She'd say, "Don't sweat it. You're getting better every day!" She'd suggest doing something "fun" to take Lorna's mind off things. Lorna needed her mind on this and this alone: varsity tryouts were two weeks away. She kicked off the tile and swam underwater to the other side of the pool.

...

One year ago, Lorna had been a shy freshman from Albany, New York, and the fastest newcomer to the varsity swim team. She chose the University of Toronto, six hours from home, because the school had sent two girls to Munich two years earlier. The Montreal Olympics were just around the corner. At her very first varsity meet, Lorna missed the first-place spot by just tenths of a second. Her speed caused a stir among her teammates. Climbing back to her seat in the stands, a boy named Kenneth tossed her a clementine. He was a senior, an engineer, a butterflyer. In the showers, she'd heard a teammate describe his body as a perfect swimmer's V. Across a crowded campus, it was always easy to make out his shape, and all the swimming girls wanted to slide in next to it. A week after that meet, Lorna dropped her time to match that of the missed first-place spot. The next week, she and Kenneth were dating.

Normally Lorna cut through campus to get home, but tonight, after dodging Debbie's invitation to someone's back-to-school barbeque, Lorna walked to their apartment alone, the long way. In the last day or two, the university grounds had become crowded with hugging, squealing students. Lorna wasn't ready for all of that; she wasn't ready for the summer to end. Her best time — in a short pool with extra turns — was still two seconds behind last year's qualifying time for the women's varsity team.

Halfway home, Lorna's left knee began to click and she slowed her pace, stopping for a moment in front of a bus bench. She put her leg up and pressed two fingers into the soft hollow under her kneecap. *Come on*, she whispered. It was always the left knee that bothered her at night: an ache that felt like a toothpick pressed deep into the meat beneath the skin. The right knee was more of a problem in the rain. Neither hurt much in the water. In June,

Lorna's physiotherapist said that she could start training again. His office had a lemony smell and a framed poster of marathoners on the wall with the caption "Keep on the Sunny Side." "Just see how it goes," he told her. "One day at a time."

It was *going*, but it wasn't going great. And Lorna felt sure it wasn't just her knees holding her back. Not completely. In high school, her coach stressed that focus was job one. *"Fukiss!"* was the thing Coach Heli repeated to her swimmers again and again in her quick Estonian accent. Lorna was always proud of her ability to jam her mind shut in the water; her brain was just another body part, doing its bit to coordinate with her heart, her arms, legs, and lungs. She pitied the undisciplined swimmers who couldn't focus. What Lorna liked best about swimming was *not* thinking. Thinking slowed swimmers down. But in the last few weeks, Lorna's mind wouldn't shut all the way. There was always a crooked gap left open: thoughts slipped inside and burrowed like moths. "Broken," they whispered. "Spoiled legs." For the first time in her life, Lorna's mind was making her lose her rhythm.

Lorna had been a swimmer since the seventh grade at Greensides Junior High. The pool was brand new and anyone could be on the team. Lorna joined because her father said she needed a hobby. He explained this while she helped him stake tomatoes on a summer afternoon, a forced break from the many hours she spent watching TV in their cool, dark basement. "What *you* need, Lorna, is a stake," he'd said, spearing a liver-coloured stick into the ground. "A skill or an interest to stop you from sprawling out of control. Give you something to aim for." Lorna's father was a widower and a commercial real estate man with very few indulgences. He believed a good life came from finding what you did well and doing it better than other people. He drove

Lorna to practices every morning, and she swam at a steady, respectful distance from the pale feet of the boy or girl in front of her.

Lorna didn't stand out until her first competition: the whistle blew, her mind shut down, and her body shot forward with blurry speed. There was no one beside her when her fingertips slammed the deck. Up in the stands, she could see her father and teammates shouting hard and waving their arms. Until the other girls came, splashing and gulping behind her, Lorna was sure she'd had a false start. She had never had good haircuts or a huge group of friends. Her grades were middle-high, not exceptional. But that day in the pool, she understood who she was.

Alone in the apartment, Lorna got in the shower and let the hot water pound her shoulders until they itched. She always preferred to shower at home, even during varsity training. The spray from the locker room showerheads was too sharp, and an older clique of girls — girls with broad shoulders and nicknames like Fin Lizzy — screamed popular songs and joked about the shape of each other's tits like it was nothing. They asked Lorna crude questions about Kenneth and laughed without waiting for her answer. In her bathing suit puffed with soap, Lorna was always lonely in the showers. When she thought about the upcoming varsity season, she tried not to think about those girls.

Feeling her body relax under the spray, Lorna rinsed her plastic razor under the water and ran it over every reachable hair on her arms and legs, weaving carefully around the scars on her knees. The tickly movements near the tender skin made her body shudder. She thought of Kenneth's fingers, brushing her knees under the tablecloth at last year's fall athletic banquet. The pads of his fingertips had been rough as pencil erasers. She wondered, then, if the other girls could tell where his hands were and hoped that they could.

Lorna snapped the thick rubber band on her wrist. She'd been doing this all summer—it burned like hell, but it was the only way to keep her focus, to "Keep on the Sunny Side." She rinsed the razor and left it on the edge of the tub. Later, she'd ask Debbie to shave the downy patch on her nape.

Lorna snapped off the warm water, got out of the shower, and towelled off in her bedroom, staring at the distant view of the city's grey lake, massive and forgettable. The sun was gone now, vanished into the water. Lorna imagined a pile of sunken summer suns at the bottom of Lake Ontario, lost forever like pennies in a well.

The apartment she and Debbie shared was on the eighteenth floor of the Northway, the tallest in a string of white and beige 1960s towers east of the university. Debbie was an easy roommate because she was often out. She had her job as a lifeguard, a sick mother an hour away, and countless girlfriends in identical buildings on the same street. Still, it wasn't exactly luck that brought the two of them together. From February until May, Lorna had lived with Kenneth on the first floor. On the afternoon that Kenneth left, he had given her the handwritten ad for the room at Debbie's place, torn from the lobby bulletin board. She'd stared hard at the googly-eyed double *o*'s on the word *roomie*, trying to understand what she'd done to make them enter her life.

Kenneth was behind the wheel during the accident the January before. He was driving too fast, annoyed by his fifth-place finish in the first meet of the new year. On the highway, Lorna held the door handle tight and didn't say anything: she'd placed first on the women's side. They were only minutes from her dorm when he slammed the brakes to avoid a burlap-wrapped Christmas tree that had rolled off the sidewalk. Kenneth steered the car onto the curb and right into a newspaper box. Lorna didn't have time to brace herself, and both of her knees slammed into the dash. Kenneth was fine.

After the two surgeries, the doctor said it would be a month or more before Lorna could walk without help, several months before she could swim. Lying in her hospital bed, fingering the hot, bandaged lumps under the sheets, Lorna couldn't imagine who she was. She thought of her father, who'd wanted her to swim so that he wouldn't have to worry. She thought of her mother, Marion Kedzie, a talented pianist and popular music teacher, invited once to play at the governor's mansion. She died a week after Lorna was born, a case of post-partum septicaemia, but Lorna had one photograph from the hospital: a new mother in a frilly, collared nightgown, peering at a tiny baby in what seemed to be a large Pyrex tray. The expression was hard to read, maybe because Lorna had never known her mother's face, but she thought of the look as one of hope. Lorna wept for the person she wouldn't become, now that she had nothing to aim for.

It took Kenneth four whole days to visit the hospital. When he did, he brought a ficus tree wrapped in a yellow bow with decorative foil. His wet hair had frozen during the walk over. In the cracked vinyl chair next to Lorna's bed, he jiggled his leg up and down and avoided looking right at her. She hadn't wanted to, but she started to cry again. He put the tree down next to her meal tray. He didn't say he was sorry; he said, "Here." When she told him what the doctor said about swimming, what the dormitory said about not being able to accommodate handicaps, what her father said about coming home and finishing her degree at the community college, Kenneth got up to look out the window. He told her that if she wanted, she could probably just move in with him at the Northway Apartments. He only had a bachelor, but it was on the first floor, so she'd be fine. Lorna said her father would never let her, but then Kenneth said that maybe, depending on how things went, they could get married after his graduation in the spring. They could take off somewhere with sun and salt water that would fade her scars.

Living in Kenneth's apartment, sharing his bed, Lorna found with relief that she didn't miss the five a.m. practices, the five p.m. practices, or never seeing the sun. She didn't miss the constant hunger, the itchy skin, or the apple-shaped fear that sprouted in her gut before every time trial. It was astonishingly easy to focus on her new goal: she was a wife-to-be. She didn't want Kenneth to feel guilty about what he'd done to her; she wanted him to know how lucky she felt to be with such a clever, V-shaped man. She made Kenneth's mother's Ukrainian recipes and grew tomatoes on their tiny balcony overlooking the dumpster. She researched places they could escape with sun and salt water. When the physiotherapist told Lorna she was strong enough to swim again, it was only the honeymoon she thought about. Kenneth took her to dinner when she told him the news, and afterwards they made love in his quick, jabbing way. A week later, Kenneth put his hands on Lorna's shoulders and said he was sorry, but it sounded like she'd be OK. He said that if he were ever back in Toronto, the Northway — quite possibly the whole block — would remind him of her. She pulled away from him then. Minutes later, Kenneth and a rented van full of books, records, and swimming trophies were making their way to an oil field in Alberta.

The streetlights were coming on now outside Lorna's window. She turned on her desk lamp and stretched out on her single bed to start her physio routine. She pulled one knee up to her chin and listened for pain. Quiet. As she pulled on her second knee, Lorna found herself wondering if there were any Olympic-size pools in northern Alberta. She snapped the rubber band on her wrist again.

The next day was cloudy and everyone said it would rain, so Lorna had the two-hour lane swim at the public pool pretty much to herself. She was practising dives when she heard her name and looked up to see Alex Ketchum, gripping the diamonds of the pool's chain-link fence. Since July, Lorna had been tutoring Alex every Sunday evening at the Burger Shack across from the park. All freshmen needed to pass English 100 to complete the year, and Lorna, who'd gotten an A in the second semester, tutored jocks and foreign students for rent money during the summer repeat session. Alex wasn't foreign or an athlete, but he was an actor and that distracted him. He played the teenaged son on *Dog Daze*, a local TV program about a suburban family with a talking sheepdog. He was the curly-haired hero for the preteen audience. On the show, he always wore the same expression: sweet and slightly dumbfounded. But when he smiled, you could see his incisors, and it made Lorna think of some rascally storybook animal. A good-natured fox or wolf. He was cute, if a little goofy, and Lorna liked to be seen with him. She often fantasized about being spotted by one of the swim team shower girls: the girls who pitied her, or at least pretended to pity her as a way to preface their gossip.

Lorna and Alex always met at eight, just after lane swim, but when he called her name it was still before seven. "Thought I'd find you here!" He had to shout across the deck.

Lorna knew she should get out of the water and speak to him, but she felt self-conscious in her bathing suit: an old one, a little see-through in the back. The wind was also picking up, blowing Alex's hair and the leaves of the poplar trees behind him. She closed herself into the corner of the pool. "You're early."

He leaned into the fence. Alex was short for an actor, although you couldn't really tell on TV. "Ballantyne's is having fifty-cent drinks till nine," he said. "Want to go?"

Lorna had never been to Ballantyne's, a smoky bar frequented by graduate students and artists, not athletes. "Right now?"

"Whenever you're done." He squinted at her. "It's shitty weather for swimming, isn't it?"

"Give me a minute." Lorna dipped back underwater and pushed off the side. She glided way out and then began her strokes, reaching forward with arms elegantly curved. Lorna always swam better when someone was watching. She wanted to show Alex what she did out here, shitty weather or not. When she looked up after six laps, he had wandered away. She hauled herself out of the pool.


All of the windows were open at Ballantyne's. Alex and Lorna sat right up at the bar on stools. Being in a bar, much less sitting up at one, was not something Lorna was used to. She felt awkward, on display, and she hoped Alex didn't notice.

A barmaid leaned over to kiss Alex on both cheeks. She had the small, bra-free breasts and shaggy short hair of a French pop star. She poured Alex a rum and Coke, and then turned to Lorna, her head cocked as though to say: *Realize, of course, that you don't belong.*

"I'll have the same," Lorna said. She looked down at her own clothes and supposed she made surprising-looking company for a minor celebrity like Alex. Tonight she wore old jeans, a thin white sweatshirt, and canvas sneakers. Her wet hair pressed cold, heavy circles onto her breasts. No makeup. Though in fairness, she hadn't expected to be *out* out. Over the last couple of months, tutoring Alex had involved reading *To the Lighthouse* aloud at the Burger Shack for five dollars an hour. He said he couldn't follow the story in his own head.

Alex finished his drink in two long gulps and ordered another. Lorna sipped her rum slowly; felt its warmth spread through her core.

"Did you bring your paper?" she asked, though it was clear he wasn't carrying anything. Alex had another week to turn in his final essay for a passing grade. They had planned to review his rough draft.

"Nah." Alex shook an ice cube into his mouth and crunched. "Student services opened today. I dropped out." He said it casually but without looking at her.

Lorna blinked. "Out of school?" That was crazy: the paper was so easy to do. She'd practically written his whole introduction herself.

"Don't take it personal."

"I'm not." Although she was.

Alex rolled back his shoulders. "I'm going to make for LA."

"What for?"

"TV, what else?"

Lorna didn't know much about the TV industry, but "make for LA" sounded starry eyed and nutty. Alex wasn't that big of a star. "What about *Dog Daze*?"

"Actually, that's wrapping up."

"Oh. I'm sorry."

Alex shrugged, like *c'est la vie*. "Makes it a good time to go." He pushed his glass forward to be noticed by the barmaid. A drizzle was starting outside and brought a stuffy, wet pavement smell into the bar.

Lorna wasn't sure quite what to say. "Do you have a lot of auditions down there?"

"Not yet."

"If you pass this year, at least you'll have options."

Alex shrugged.

Lorna shrugged back. "So what are you going to do there?"

"Don't know. I'll see what flies my way." He gave her a helpless smile that was really a fake helpless smile. "I don't expect everyone to understand."

The last time Lorna heard that kind of line was the day Kenneth left her. She could still see his Marantz record player strapped into the passenger seat, *her* Paul McCartney album on the turntable. "We need to figure out who we are," he said. It was so unfair because Lorna *had* known who she was. She'd been a great swimmer with times around the one-minute mark and dreams of the Olympics. She'd been nearly a fiancée. He ruined everything.

Lorna snapped the band on her wrist. Alex didn't notice: the shaggy-haired barmaid was pouring him a fresh drink. She peeled the lid from a can of peanuts and shook some into a small bowl.

"Actually, I thought you might understand." Alex tossed up

a peanut and caught it with his mouth. "Being an athlete." He looked straight at her in what seemed like an actorly way. A wise old man, sitting at a bar. "You know about having a path to follow."

Lorna considered the phrase. It was the kind of corny thing you could find printed on a bookmark at a church bazaar or on the wall of her physiotherapist's office.

"Writing papers, getting a degree, none of that means shit to me. I'm an actor. An actor acts," Alex continued.

Lorna nodded. "But you don't have to go all the way to LA to do that."

"But why wouldn't I? LA's the top. Wouldn't you go to the top if you could?" Alex nudged her glass toward her; it was still almost full.

"If I were ready."

Alex shook his head. "I'm as ready as I'll ever be."

Lorna lifted her drink. "I read this thing once about how thousands of people move to Hollywood every year and wind up homeless and living under bridges. Maybe you should have some sort of plan."

"You can't plan everything."

Maybe you couldn't plan everything, but Lorna thought it was naive, even lazy, to look at life that way. She wanted to admire Alex's nerve in the way he clearly wanted her to, but real success took focus, preparation. You couldn't just walk out your door, no plan at all, and expect to net opportunities like butterflies. She felt suddenly very worried for him. "And what if nothing flies your way?"

"Then I'll do something else." Alex turned his glass around slowly on the counter, drawing a wet pattern of circles that looked like Olympic rings. "I'm not afraid of life, right? I'm the kind of guy who takes chances." He said this much louder than he needed to, glancing at the barmaid. Lorna knew that Alex was used to women listening to him, and because he was an actor on an actual TV show, some women assumed that what he said was thoughtful or deep. This probably made him believe the same things about himself. Lorna, on the other hand, had long disliked "I'm the kind of person who" statements. They were almost always self-flattery disguised as unalterable fact, like having brown hair. But Alex looked back at Lorna, his eyes greedy for approval, which made her feel slightly sorry for him.

"I guess that's cool," Lorna said

Alex's incisors flashed with his smile. "Haven't you ever just done something without knowing what would happen?"

Lorna examined the wrinkled pads of her fingers. "Sure," she said. "But I regretted it."

Alex didn't say anything, and the silence between them felt too heavy for Lorna not to continue. "OK," she said, "so when I was thirteen I read all about these women who were swimming across the English Channel. I wanted to be like them, so I signed up for this swim-across-the-lake thingy over the summer. I had no idea what I was doing; I was way younger than everyone else. Some local reporter even came out to take pictures of me, and I told him I was going to win the whole thing." He was a grey-haired reporter dressed in an itchy-looking fisherman's sweater. He'd said to her, "Let's hope you're stronger than you look."

"Did you? Win it?"

"I didn't even finish the race."

Open water always intimidated Lorna, but Sugar Lake, just outside of town, was particularly eerie. The shore was a slimy bed of rotted leaves. Pontoon boats and water-skiers zipped recklessly on the surface all summer long, while muskies, catfish, and broken clams lurked in the silty sludge below. The two-and-a-half mile distance across was twice as far as Lorna had ever swum, then. But she still thought she could win. Because of what happened earlier that year when the whistle blew, Lorna believed she could do anything she wanted.

"So you regret bragging?"

"I made it pretty close," Lorna said. "Maybe a quarter mile left." She had started off fast, but her arms grew shaky after the first half-hour. Within thirty or forty minutes, it seemed everyone had overtaken her, their white backs and colourful caps disappearing into early morning mist. She made it far enough to see a blur of people standing at the opposite shore, waiting around for the last place, show-off kid. Eventually Lorna flipped onto her back and cried, quietly at first, and then loud enough for the volunteer paddlers to notice. They hauled her into the canoe by the armpits, her shins bumping against the gunnels.

Alex flipped ice around with his mini straw. When he appeared to register that she was no longer talking, he asked, "So that's it?"

"Yep." And truly, that was it. Afterwards, her father took her for a club sandwich at a hotel restaurant. They ate quickly, quietly, and then she was sick in the parking lot. Her father was almost cheerful then, assuring her that nothing more than a flu bug slowed her down.

"And ever since then?" He held three fingers to his forehead in a Boy Scout salute. "Be prepared."

Lorna shrugged. "I'm a sprinter, not a distance swimmer. I should have stuck to that."

Alex let out a low whistle and shook his head. "If that's your biggest regret—"

"I never said it was. That was just an example."

Across from them, the barmaid was rushing to close the windows. The rain was coming harder now: fast, straight-down drops that bounced off the pavement. Pedestrians ran with newspapers over their heads and took cover under awnings. Streams of red and yellow car lights flowed together in the wide, wet street. Lorna thought it was beautiful, but she didn't know how to point this out to Alex. It would seem like she was trying too hard to change the subject.

After a moment, Alex swatted the air in front of them, erasing her story and whatever weirdness it had caused between them. "Let me get you another drink," he said. "To say thanks for everything."

Lorna's cheeks were heavy and warm from the first rum, but she didn't interrupt Alex's gesture to the barmaid. She had lost count of what he was putting away.

They left Ballantyne's a couple of hours later, during a pause in the rain. An earthy-scented breeze seemed to lift from the ground; the street was quiet and anything beyond the sidewalk was soft-focused to Lorna now. Alex smoked and whistled as he walked her home. There had been a lot of talk in the bar; on the street Lorna couldn't think of a thing more to say.

In front of the Northway, Lorna searched her gym bag for keys. "Thanks for the drinks," she said.

Alex leaned against the door's rippled glass panel, relaxing into it like the walk had been exhausting. "And now what?"

"Now I guess you go to LA."

"Yeah."

"They say it's nice down there." Lorna's fingers found her cold metal key ring. A fresh raindrop smacked down on her wrist.

"I could write that paper," Alex said suddenly. "If that was the best thing for me right now."

"I understand," Lorna said. But she didn't believe it. Alex was sweet, but he wasn't a focused person. Or maybe he was, maybe that was the lesson here. She pulled out her keys with a jangle.

Alex dipped his chin and looked up at her. She noticed his eyelashes for the first time. Thick and girlish. "I'm sorry if you think you wasted your time."

Lorna shook her head, came up with a polite smile. "Really, it's fine. You paid me."

"You're a good teacher," Alex said. "You could probably be one, if that's what you wanted to do with your life."

"Thanks," Lorna said. "It's not, but thanks for saying that."

It was like he was waiting for something from her. Did he want her to invite him in for a drink? She wasn't sure there was anything to drink in the apartment. She had to swim early the next morning. Plus Debbie could be home. But Lorna just kept standing there. She wondered what it would be like to kiss him. She'd only kissed two people before: Brett, her cousin, behind a row of transport trucks at a motel during Expo '67. Then Kenneth, of course. More rain spattered onto the concrete steps. She unlocked the door. "Thanks for the drinks," she said again.

"Raining again." Alex put his sneaker in the gap of the door. His wild grin gave her a tugging feeling below the belly button.

Debbie was not at home. Lorna found a bottle of sherry, fuzzy with dust, in the cupboard above the stove. A granny's drink, probably given to Debbie as a gift, but it would do. She poured them each a shallow glass and set his on the trunk by the couch.

Alex sat and took off his shoes. She leaned against the window ledge across from him.

"Wait," he said, leaning forward. "You don't have a boyfriend, do you?"

Lorna blushed and brought her glass to her lips. "No."

He relaxed into the couch. "I didn't think so. Not that you're not cute."

"I don't have a lot of time for dating."

He looked around the apartment as though trying to discern what had such a grip on her time.

"Varsity season's coming up."

"Right, right," Alex nodded vigorously. "Your path." Lorna pictured a bright blue swimming lane that never ended.

"You wanna come sit here?" Alex patted the spot on the couch next to him.

Lorna felt her pulse everywhere. She pressed the glass to her mouth, buying time.

Alex's glass clicked down on the trunk. He crossed the room, took her drink from her, and put both his hands on her face. His mouth felt cool. She put her hand up against the window, felt the rhythm of the rain rushing against her fingertips as he leaned his body into hers. Alex held her lower lip between his teeth for a second or two. When he let go, he tilted his head toward the closed door down the hall. She let him lead her there.

Sex turned out to be unexpectedly easy. With Kenneth, Lorna had always wondered if she was doing it right, if there was something else he wanted her to be: stiller, faster, wetter, tighter. Alex's expression, when she opened her eyes to check, was greedy then grateful. He fell asleep immediately afterwards, his warm forehead pressed into her shoulder. Lorna pulled the sheets over her scarred knees, the smell of chlorine rising from her skin. She wished she could find her clothes, but she didn't want to disturb him.

The next morning, Alex walked Lorna to the pool and they hugged goodbye. She began her warm-up feeling giddy and modern. Blue skies had taken over the city, and she could feel the sun on every surface of her skin. Sleeping with Alex was the proof that she was finally over Kenneth. If Alex called, fine. If not, that was fine, too. They had their paths to follow. Now she could focus.

In the week that followed, the last before the start of school, Lorna doubled her efforts at the pool, swimming three thousand yards or more every afternoon. She charged across the water with nothing whatsoever in her mind. There was no doubt that she was swimming faster. Perhaps faster than she'd ever swum. In the evenings, Debbie encouraged Lorna to go out, to take a load off, but Lorna declined with the same acid mix of jealousy and smug satisfaction she felt the year before when she returned from early practices to find the girls still asleep in the dorm. Must be nice, Lorna thought, just to while away the time, but that wasn't who she was. Lorna's time mattered.

On the Thursday before school started, Lorna arranged for Debbie to time her. She arrived at lane swim at six to find the gates locked and the water being drained. There was a chemical issue, Debbie explained, and the pool would be shut down until Sunday at least.

Debbie said a few days of rest would be good for Lorna, but Lorna felt on edge without her routine. She tried another pool across town, but the lanes were too short and the children were too noisy. She considered the pool at the university athletic complex, but she couldn't face the girls she might run into until she was sure she was ready. So Lorna did try to rest. She tried to shop for new clothes but found that she couldn't focus on the task, only wandered the department store, touching fabrics, deciding on one item and then putting it back. Cleaning the apartment was even more bewildering. Hair and dust were everywhere. She bought a sports magazine and brought it to the park, as she'd seen other girls do, but the sun made the pages too bright and she could never find the right casual position. She managed to read one story about four mountain climbers who'd gone missing somewhere in Washington, the likely victims of an ice avalanche. "They didn't know their own limits," the brother of one of them said.

At the laundromat down the street, Lorna was dumping clothes into a washing machine when she heard a familiar voice. The season finale of *Dog Daze* was playing on the wall-mounted TV. Lorna sat down to watch Alex hug his TV family goodbye, the show ending with the ironic premise that Alex's character, Marty, was going away to university. Harvey, the family sheepdog, was stretched out at the end of the driveway in protest. The laughing family managed to lift the beast out of the way, but he took off after the station wagon, pink tongue flapping from his mouth. An eruption of "aww" came over the audience track as the car slowed and the door swung open to let the dog hop in. There he goes, Lorna thought as the station wagon disappeared down the shady street. The summer is over. Alex is off to Hollywood; swim trials are just a few days away. The washing machine shuddered and then stopped, dropping towels with a heavy slap. Lorna filled with dread for both herself and Alex.

When the park pool reopened, the water was bluer and colder

than before. Lorna crashed through her lengths, eyeballs and nostrils stinging. Worst of all, she was struggling to find her rhythm. Her mind and body would not work together. It started with jingles. Radio commercials pinged up and down in her head, her body adapting too easily to their breezy pace: *Back-to-school shirts! New slacks and skirts! Come on, get ready at Thrifty Threads first!* She tried to lock her mind to her breathing but thinking about how to think made her concentration worse. Loose thoughts squiggled in and got stuck, stubborn as hair on the bathroom tile. She thought of the people in the ice avalanche. She thought of Alex getting off an airplane into blinding sunlight and palm trees, that sweet but dumbfounded look on his face. Her fastest strokes came from a breathless sort of fear, a sense that she was being chased. Rather than somersault at the end of those panicked lengths, she grabbed for concrete, swallowing air and trying to calm down. She'd hold on to the edge for a long time, watching her shadow grow longer on the deck.

On the Sunday before school began, Lorna stopped several times to look over at the pool fence. She wondered if Alex had changed his mind, if he'd become suddenly realistic. She had some idea that if she only just saw him, if he returned, if they slept together again, she might get her rhythm back. Things would be in place. But when she looked up, there were only fallen poplar leaves, dull and yellow, pressing up against the fence.

Before Debbie said a thing that evening, Lorna knew her time wasn't good. Debbie's voice was too chirpy. "One minute thirteen. That's better, isn't it?"

"I'll go again," Lorna said.

Debbie shook her head. "I have to close the pool."

"Come on."

"It's getting too dark to read this thing." Debbie slipped the stopwatch into the pocket of her shorts. "Let me close up and we'll go to a movie."

Lorna didn't want to spend time with Debbie, but she didn't want to be alone either. She suggested Ballantyne's.

Sitting up at the bar, Lorna ordered a rum and Coke and Debbie had a 7-Up. The windows were closed and the music pounded and crashed. While Debbie talked about a swim school for little kids at a new community centre, Lorna scanned the bar for Alex.

"Are you looking for someone?" Debbie asked.

"No," Lorna said.

"You seem distracted."

"Sorry."

"That's OK, it's really noisy in here." She leaned in. "But does that sound good to you? I mean, do you like little kids?"

Lorna tried to smile at her friend. Were they friends? "Sorry. Does what sound good?"

"Teaching with me! Like I said, Marianne wants me to find another girl and I think we'd be a good team. Just Saturday and Sunday afternoons. Maybe after school, too, if there are enough kids enrolled."

"You want me to teach swimming with you?"

"Yeah!" Debbie nodded eagerly. "I told Marianne I'd ask. I didn't promise anything, but what do you think?"

Lorna felt the heat underneath her sweatshirt creep up into her face. "Debbie," she said. "The team has practice four hours a day. Saturday and Sunday mornings, too. The whole school year."

"Sure," Debbie said. "But in case—."

Lorna swallowed. Even doe-eyed Debbie didn't think she was going to make the team. "In case what?"

Debbie looked up, but her gaze didn't quite meet Lorna's. "I think you're training too hard, Lorna.

"I'll be fine." Debbie had no idea. No idea how Lorna could surprise people when the whistle blew. Her body and mind worked together; they did impossible things under the right kind of pressure.

"Even if you do make the team," Debbie said, "Are you sure you really want all of it? All those practices, all that strain?"

"I've been doing this since the seventh grade."

"I know it," Debbie said, although Lorna was quite sure she didn't understand it. "But I just wonder if it's making you..." Debbie didn't finish her sentence. She smiled warily at Lorna.

"What? Faster?"

"I was going to say happy."

Lorna picked up her drink and sucked it through her teeth. The cold clipped the back of her molars. "Don't worry about it."

Debbie crinkled her wide, freckled forehead. "You're still healing."

"My knee hardly hurts at all."

"It's not just that."

"If you mean Kenneth, I don't even miss him." It came out so easily. Lorna looked at Debbie, emboldened. "As a matter of fact..." But she decided not to say anything about Alex. Debbie would want to know too much. "As a matter of fact," Lorna repeated, gulping the rest of her drink, "I'll be fine."

"We could have such a fun year," Debbie said. "We could have parties..."

Lorna thought of repeating what Alex said about following your path, but Debbie wouldn't get it, she couldn't relate. Debbie would just float on ahead; she wasn't good at anything. She would become a teacher, marry a teacher, have three kids and a two-car garage with a basketball hoop. Lorna was different. She was a swimmer. "We can have a party if that's what you want," Lorna said finally, to shut Debbie up. "Later in the month. After tryouts."

Debbie wiped the counter in front of her with a napkin. "Well. You're doing really, really well."

"Thanks."

"You're doing so well, Lorna." Debbie frowned. "It's good enough. You don't need to prove anything."

On the first day of school, Lorna searched for Alex's name on class lists, but there was nothing. She tracked down a drama seminar and crossed campus after lunch to watch a British professor with tea-stained teeth demonstrate how to faint. She considered staying late and asking the students about Alex, but what would she even ask? What reason could she give for wanting to know? What would she do with what she found out?

On the night before varsity tryouts, Lorna couldn't sleep. It was the idea of not sleeping that kept her wide awake, the fear of being too groggy to swim fast in the morning. She was up to pee every half-hour, and each time she returned to bed, she tried to do it with a clear head. *I will think of nothing. There is nothing at all to think about.* But her mind spun, seeming to search for something to hook on to. She jammed her eyes closed and tried to picture a calm blue surface. She liked to encourage dreams about water.

For a few thick seconds, Lorna drifted into the same nightmare she'd been having since the seventh grade. It was set on a misty pond she'd seen once in a library book on the Salem witch trials. In this version, Lorna was floating on a raft, her body bound by a burlap sack. She felt the familiar, heavy push on her chest: a rushing, then rapid sinking underwater. When Lorna coughed herself awake, her hair and skin were damp.

At four thirty, Lorna gave up on sleep. She put her best race suit on under her clothes and pulled the band from her wrist to tie her hair into a tight, scalp-searing ponytail. She did her stretches on the bathroom floor and then moved quietly out the door, trying her best not to wake Debbie.

In the dark, Lorna hurried down the sidewalk, shivering from the mix of morning cold and nerves. Despite an early start, somehow she was running late. The apple had returned to her stomach; it rose and pressed against her sternum then her throat as the athletic complex came into view. She walked around to the side of the building where the pool doors were opened up to the outside. Humid, chemical air rolled into the morning dark. She could hear the echo of girls' voices, the slapping and forcing of water. She thought of her nightmare and tried to push it out of her mind. Lorna heard Coach Vicky's brash, dirty laugh. She leaned against the brick, her arms hugging her mid-section. She was all twisted up; her body wanted the apple out.

Inside, a few girls were still in the change room but most were already out on the deck. The change room was bright and overwarm, and chlorine caught the back of Lorna's throat. She hurried past the strewn gym bags, warm-up suits, and towels. On a corkboard across from the bathroom stalls, a single mimeographed sheet pinned to the wall said "Varsity Qualifying Times: '75-76 Season." She didn't stop to scan the paper; she really couldn't stop.

Lorna slammed into a toilet stall and knelt over the bowl. She coughed hard, trying to dislodge the apple, but produced only a mouthful of bitter saliva. Out on the deck, she heard Vicky's three short warning blasts. It was time for the girls to assemble, to receive instructions, to focus. Lorna spat and spat.

Leaving the bathroom stall, Lorna tightened her ponytail in the smudged mirror. She splashed water over her mouth and face, pink and puffy from lack of sleep. She did not look at the corkboard. She did not take off her clothes. What she really needed was air.

Outside, the sun was beginning to push up in the east, making the sky as peachy and confident as a juice commercial. Lorna hauled the cool air deep into her chest. Then she began to walk south, away from the athletic centre. She passed vendors out in Chinatown, sweeping the sidewalks and setting up white plastic tables for displays of fruit, perfume, and underwear in plastic packages. In a dusty window, a man was stringing a line of bright, barbecued chickens. Lorna nodded at him and kept on following the road, sweat gathering under her swimsuit, the sun rising against the side of her face. She passed joggers, dog walkers, and street cleaners. Buses roared by. Lorna kept moving forward, reaching downtown's loud grey construction. Her right knee began to click, then her left, but she didn't stop. She continued under a dingy expressway underpass, holding her breath against the sharp smell of urine.

It was full morning when Lorna reached the end of the street and the lake from her bedroom window. She headed west along the painted guardrail, such a meager separator from the cold water's lapping edge. She looked over at the scratchy swathe of the island airport. Not too far to reach.

Lorna peeled off her nylon jacket, the breeze waking the damp skin under her swimsuit. A few feet away, a man sat slumped against the rail in an oil-stained sleeping bag, a squash-coloured dog cuddled next to him. She looked down at the foam clinging to the lake's concrete retaining wall, the ribbons of gasoline. Below the lake's surface, concealed from swimmers, were rusted car parts, broken furniture, dogs tied to concrete, birds that hadn't made it across. Everyone knew this about the lake. But at the surface, the blue water sparkled. She took a deep breath. She laid her jacket on the rail.

A little plane took off from the airport, low and shaky in the sky. Though the plane was headed east, she imagined Alex was up there. She put her hand out toward the plane, as though to wave at it or shield it from view.

"Beautiful," the man with the dog said.

She looked over and smiled politely. His gaze was on nothing in particular; he closed his eyes.

Lorna thought of the passengers looking out the plane's tiny windows. Would they see her? A girl standing at the edge of a guardrail, knees slightly bent? *Let's hope she's stronger than she looks.* For a second, they might wonder who she was, where she was heading. In another second, they'd be too far away to see.

# Wise

**D**ad is sleeping at our house tonight, but he's not coming to the play because he's three sheets to the wind. Mom told us that, frowning in the way that makes her chin red and lumpy like a spoonful of Zoodles. But Dad doesn't look like sheets to me. Sheets are what I'm supposed to wear for my Shepherd in Blue costume. They're rolling in the dryer downstairs. Mom had to wash them after Dad knocked the gravy pot onto my lap at dinner.

Before we leave for church, I find Dad watching TV in the den with Jed. "Mom says we're going without you."

He glances back at the kitchen. "Boss's orders."

I sit on the ottoman, smelling Dad's socks. "My part's stupid, anyway," I say. "All I do is shout 'O come let us adore him' and then stand there staring at Jesus." Dad was an actual actor on a real TV show once. If he came to our play, he'd see that I'm the only shepherd with a line.

"O come lettuce adore him. O come cabbage adore him. Who's next, the artichokes?" Dad laughs. I laugh because that's what he wants me to do.

"You should be Mary," Dad says.

"Impossible. She's nine. Mary's gotta be at least twelve." Jed talks without moving his eyes from the TV.

Dad pulls his cigarettes from his front pocket. "Who says?"

"That's how old the real Mary was when God knocked her up," Jed says.

"Jesus Christ," Dad says.

"Why did God pick someone who was only twelve?" I ask.

Jed turns and grins. "Still had her V-card. Virgin Mary, right? Girls those days were easy."

"You hearing this, Lorna?" Dad calls to the kitchen.

I think about Angela D'Souza, the twelve-year-old playing Mary. She cried at the last rehearsal because someone accused her of farting. There's no way anyone would want to do it with her. The easy girls are in eighth grade at least, like Cindy Springgay who will show a guy anything for five bucks.

Mom sticks her head in the door. She doesn't answer Dad. "We're late."

I look back at Dad and he smiles at me kind of dopey. "Go on, Care Bear," he says. "Break your legs."

Driving to church, Mom asks us if we're nervous and we say we're not. I am a little bit nervous, but not about the play. I'm nervous because Mary had a baby when she was only twelve. That's just a little more than two years away.

"How old were you when you had us?" I ask Mom.

"Too young," Mom says. "Twenty with Jed. Twenty-two with you." Twenty-two is ten years older than Mary.

"Do you think God will ever decide he wants to have another baby?" I ask.

If God wanted another kid, I wonder if he'd pick me or

Angela D'Souza to be the mother. Angela smells like onions, but at least she's twelve.

Mom looks at me in the rear-view. "Not likely."

Not likely, but maybe. What if it did happen again? What if God chose me?

"Mom, if I had a baby in junior high, would you be really, really mad?"

When mom gets annoyed, she makes her lips all thin and mashes them together. Jed calls it bitch mode. I can see bitch mode in the rear-view.

"I'd be very disappointed," she says. "It would ruin your life."

"Except what if the baby was God's?"

"Cara, that's ridiculous." She is scanning the church parking lot. We are late. The lot is almost full.

"Even if God did get you preggo? Everyone would just think you were lying," Jed says.

"Jed, don't say preggo," Mom says. "Please."

"I bet most of Bethlehem thought Mary was just making up a story to cover her butt." Jed elbows me in the arm and puts on a squeaky voice. "'We only did it once, Joseph! How did I get to be such a fatty?'"

Mom drives into a parking spot that says Authorized Vehicles Only. She breathes hard out her nose. "It's Christmas, what are they going to do?" She glances back at me like I have any idea what they'd do or not do then looks irritated when I don't answer her.

I press my belly as hard as I can with the seatbelt. I do feel something. Something lumpy, like a knot or a baby. I tell myself it's just dinner in a ball, but there's always a chance. If it happened once, it could happen again. That's why it's important to be good, but not too good. If I'm too good, God could pick me next. I'd be preggo with Jesus II, and no one would believe me.

By the time we get down to the parish basement, Shepherd in Red and Shepherd in Yellow are already dressed. The mothers are putting pink powder on their cheeks. When Mom lays out Jed's costume, I realize we forgot my sheets.

"Why are you just standing there?" Mom says.

"We need to go home," I whisper. "You forgot the sheets."

Mom's lips are thinner than ever. "*I* forgot them? For Christ's sake, Cara."

I stay quiet. Good, but not too good.

"Ask if anyone has extras," Mom says.

"But I'm Shepherd in Blue. I need blue sheets!"

Mom peels off her powder blue ski jacket and shoves it at me. "Wear it back to front." The jacket makes me look more like a hippo than a shepherd. I'm about to tell her this, but her eyes are across the room. Jed is standing in front of the mirror, smearing black gunk all over his face.

Mom marches over and I follow. "What the hell—"

Jed grins and holds up a small tin. "Shoe polish," he says. "Balthazar's a black guy."

"Where did you get that?"

"Everyone knows Balthazar's black."

It's true. Most of the illustrations in our catechism book are red and brown, but there is an exception on the nativity page: Balthazar, the second wise man, is definitely black.

"I mean the polish," Mom says.

"From Dad. He polished his shoes for this, you know."

Mom breathes out all heavy. "You have to take it off."

"No way."

"Yes way." Bitch mode.

Mom turns to Father Oliphant, who is coming over to join the excitement. "I'm sorry, Father. Jed didn't tell me about this."

Father Oliphant's face is pink and sweaty. Little kids call him Papa Elephant. Jed and I call him Garbage Breath because his breath reeks like the alley behind Mandarin Mansion. Mom says he's suspicious of our family because we don't go to mass on Sundays. We only go to the Catholic school — Our Lady of Fatima, or Fat Lady's — because a kid at the public school got curb-stomped a few years ago.

Garbage Breath dabs Jed's cheek with his thumb. "I'm not so sure this will come off." His stink reaches my nostrils even from a few feet away.

Jed backs away. "Balthazar's black!"

"Yes, we know." Mom grabs Jed's elbow, steering him toward the bathroom. "But it's racist to paint your face like that."

"Why?" Jed jerks away from her, looking at me with this question. I want to help, but I have no idea.

"Right now, Jed." The vein in Mom's forehead sticks out like a strand of blue spaghetti.

"Fuck you!" Jed says.

Mom slaps Jed's face. It happens so fast that I think it's my imagination, but the palm of her hand is streaked with black polish.

"Lorna, easy," Garbage Breath says, putting a hand on Jed's shoulder. When I notice him again, I notice everyone else. A mom with a makeup brush has her hand over her mouth. The other Wise Men stare at the floor. They have small triangles drawn on their chins for beards, so it doesn't seem fair that Jed's not allowed to paint his own face.

Garbage Breath picks up Jed's gold and red gown. "Take your brother's costume," he says to me. "We need a Balthazar."

I stand backstage with the other Wise Men. We don't get to come on until the very end, after Jesus gets born. It's freezing backstage. I pull my arms into the sleeves of Jed's gown and hug my ribs. I wish I were still Shepherd in Blue, under a warm bundle of sheets.

As the play starts, I think about whether God heard what Jed said to Mom. If God did hear, it probably means Jed's going to hell. But there's a good chance he didn't catch it. If God is everywhere, if he's spread across the whole entire world, it's pretty unrealistic that his ears are anywhere near us. Here in this church, we probably just get a tiny slice of his toenail or his anus. I try to erase that thought. I don't want God to know I'm thinking about his anus — the little *x* Mom showed me in the diagram of privates that came with the *My Changing Body* book she got at our neighbour's garage sale. Then again, if God knew I was thinking about his anus, he probably wouldn't choose me to be the one to have his baby. *Anus, anus, butthole*, I think.

Through a space in the thick, dusty curtains, I watch Mary and Joseph circle the stage, rapping at innkeepers' doors and getting turned away. Each time Mary and Joseph get refused, Angela says, "Do not despair, Joseph." She was only supposed to say that line after the first no, after that she's supposed to act like she's losing hope. I wonder if the real Mary lost hope. Did she know that having a baby was going to ruin her life?

After a while, the chubby narrator from Jed's class says, "But even after everything seemed hopeless, that night, in a humble manger, the Lord Jesus Christ was born." A spotlight shines on Mary and Joseph. They huddle under a papier mâché ledge, surrounded by kindergarten cows and sheep. Everyone is smiling at the doll in Mary's arms, the kind with a cloth middle and dangly plastic limbs. It's definitely supposed to be a girl. Angela wraps it up in a white tea towel and looks at the shepherds coming her way. There is a silence where I was supposed to say, "O come, let us adore him!"

It's almost Jed's part. I pick up my gift for Jesus: a shoebox, spray-painted gold and silver. My hands are shaky. Someone must have opened the door because a blast of cold air eats right through my gown. A spotlight moves to stage left and Melchior gives me a hard kick in the ankle. "Go!"

I stride toward the manger. "We are the three kings," I say, trying my best to sound like a boy. "Of Oriental." I lay the gift down by Jesus and then pull my arms back into my sleeves. Jesus is warm and bundled up inside the manger. Lucky Jesus.

The lights dim and a group of long-haired teenagers play "What Child is This?" on guitars. Cindy Springgay sings a solo. Tonight she is wearing a red velvet top that laces up with a bow at the front. I can see the naked bulge of each tit from where I'm standing. I heard she got sent home from school last month for wearing white jeans with handprints drawn on the butt and the words: "Dan M. Only."

Joseph holds Jesus up for the crowd to see, and the audience laughs when the tea towel slips right off. Mom and Jed are in the fourth row, but neither one of them is laughing. Instead of watching this, I wonder what Mom would be doing right now if she never had Jed and me. I know she used to be a swimmer. Maybe she'd be going to Seoul this summer.

The lights come on again at the end of the song. That's when I see Dad, standing at the side door, his hair wet and pressed flat against his forehead. He is holding a bundle of blue sheets. He looks lost and I wonder how long he's been there. I can't tell if he recognizes me.

After the play is over, there are star-shaped cookies and chocolate milk for us in the church basement, but we don't stay. Mom grabs her jacket and heads straight for the exit where Dad is standing.

"You walked here?"

Dad nods.

"Christ, Alex."

Mom heads toward the doors and Dad wraps the blue sheets around my shoulders.

"Guess you didn't need these," he says.

"That's OK. Did you see me?"

"'Course, Wise Lady," he says. "You any smarter?"

"I don't know."

"But what happened to you, Jedi?"

Jed doesn't answer. He kicks a pile of slush, the same grey as his scrubbed face.

"Forget it, Alex," Mom says.

On the drive home, "Silent Night" comes on the radio. I can see a bump in Mom's cheek from where she's mashing her teeth. The song was her dad's favourite. Usually she says so whenever it comes on, but tonight no one says anything at all.

Raindrops freckle my window and I hold my hand up to the cold glass, following the trails of water with my fingers. At a stoplight, a woman in the next lane looks over. I like that she just sees a regular family on Christmas Eve. She must think I'm waving because she smiles and waves back. The heater purrs its hot breath, and for the first time in hours, I feel warm. I lean my head against the window and close my eyes. I am surrounded, huddled-in, just like Jesus.

# Anything
WINTER, 1988

orna didn't want to go to Derek Wiggins's party, but she was making an effort. According to Alex, part of their "whole problem" — they never called it anything else, always their "whole problem" — may have had something to do with Lorna's incuriosity about his work. Alex said he loved his new job in the credit department of a large bank, felt valuable in it, and really wanted Lorna to be proud of him. Lorna thought it was whiny of Alex to need her to be interested in his work. But going out, getting dressed up: she saw how it could be good for them.

Derek Wiggins's townhouse was in a new, cheap-looking complex near the entertainment district. Lorna had dropped the kids off once in December when Alex was staying there a few weeks, but tonight was her first time inside.

Derek answered the door and threw a thick arm over Alex's shoulder. "What's happening, brother?" He was a puffy, pinkish guy, maybe twenty-five, dressed in khaki shorts and a T-shirt that said "Co-ed Naked Surfing." He had one of those very low voices that made talking sound like it hurt.

Lorna handed Derek a bottle of Merlot. From what she could see past him, guests were drinking beer from clear plastic cups.

"Keg's on the balcony," Derek said, leading the way to the living room. He turned, holding the bottle of wine like a club. "Or want me to crack this?"

"Beer's fine. Thank you, Derek." Lorna forced a smile.

"Coats go up in the spare," Derek said. "Ketch knows the way."

Lorna followed Alex through the living room and up the stairs, watching as he waved hello to young women in short dresses and very high heels, guys wearing running shoes and T-shirts like Derek's. Alex frequently talked about work "buddies," and Lorna pictured squash-playing men in their forties with belly laughs and vigorous handshakes. It was a hopeful image, she realized now, because this was a crowd of twenty-somethings. People at the beginning of their careers were young.

"They call you Ketch?" Lorna asked at the top of the stairs.

"Oh, yeah. Didn't tell you that one." Alex grinned and pushed open a door with the word *Gynecology* stencilled to the outside.

So this was the spare. This was where Alex had spent the three weeks before Christmas. There was a small TV and a collapsed futon covered in jackets. The two windows were stacked high with empty beer cans. A movie poster for *Porky's Revenge!* brought a splash of colour to primer-white walls.

Alex chucked his coat on the bed and rolled up his sleeves, ready for action. Someone had cranked the music, and Lorna felt the vibrations through her stockinged feet. The theme of the party was Stupid Cupid. Lorna had no idea what the dress code for Stupid Cupid was, but her black slacks, cream-coloured blouse and beige stockings now made her feel like someone's mother. She'd agonized over what to wear but evidently with the wrong crowd in mind.

Lorna thought about the young, dancing bodies downstairs

and it occurred to her, then, that these young people might know—very likely did know—about Jenny. Back when Alex's colleagues were older and thicker-necked in Lorna's imagination, she felt safe assuming that what happened between Alex and Jenny was discreet and carefully carried out. But why wouldn't Jenny have told these gals downstairs what she and Alex were up to? Girls killing time in a career, yearning for office gossip over lunch at Romeo's Pizza. And surely Derek knew. What evidence was there that Mr. Porky's Revenge would keep it to himself?

Coat still on, Lorna turned to Alex. "Who here knows?"

He looked around dramatically. "What?"

Lorna squinted. "Does everyone know? About half?"

"Oh," Alex said. "You're talking about...?"

"For Christ's sake."

"Nobody." Like a child, he crossed his heart. "I promise. Everyone's dying to meet you, Loo."

Downstairs, Alex got them each a cup of beer. Lorna sipped hers at the end of a corduroy couch, a wild fern partially obscuring her. Across the room, a couple of boys listened to Alex as he fanned a Stones album in the air, the one with the pink cake on the cover. Lorna could see that Alex was the old-but-cool guy, "Ketch." She squinted at his rosacea-tinted face and receding hairline. If they were strangers, would she find him attractive?

The last time Lorna asked herself that question was after surprising him at a ski resort cafeteria in 1975. From a guy in his drama department, she'd learned that he was not in Hollywood after all but working as a chairlift operator two hours north of the city. In the second week of December, she drove out in Debbie's Datsun to tell him she was pregnant.

Lorna picked cinnamon hearts out of a bowl and crunched

them into her back teeth. Someone had made an effort at party decorations: a clothesline of red and white panties, a mirror covered in lipstick kisses, pink balloons inflated to various levels, nipple markings drawn on the tops. Lorna angled her head to look at herself in the mirror. Her chin and forehead were oily and red. Her hair, smooth enough in her own house, now seemed to poke up on top like a daddy-long-legs. She no longer had the hair of youth, she just had to admit it. At thirty-two, dressing for a night out could make Lorna feel quite young, even cute, but this party, these people, were destroying that feeling.

Girls had joined the group around Alex now. The one standing closest to him was baby-fattish with a wide, eager face. As far as Lorna knew, which perhaps wasn't much anymore, she was not Alex's type. The other girl—darker skinned, short dress, big breasts—was more of a concern, but a skinny boy kept a hesitant hand perched at the small of her back.

Lorna scanned the other faces in the room. What if Jenny were here? Alex said she was only a summer student, but if these were her friends, she could show up, couldn't she? Lorna had never seen Jenny, but she didn't picture a beauty. What beauty with her whole life ahead of her, earning a degree in business, would want a married thirty-two-year-old with two kids and, let's face what was becoming clear, a twenty-one-year-old's job?

When Lorna found Jenny's notes in October, the worst part was not that they existed but how they existed. Over fifty pink Post-its piled neatly in Alex's old cigar box at the top of his closet. Notes written in open bubbly script, the *W*s like buttocks, the kind of penmanship that girls Cara's age worked really hard to cultivate. Lorna had opened the cigar box in search of a prop for Jed, who was downstairs at the time, preparing a history skit with three girls from his class. He was playing Winston Churchill and the girls were his "secretaries." The first note Lorna opened said only, "Thanx for the *Mmm*uffin!" Lorna knelt in the closet, fingers cold and shaking. She moved only when she smelled frozen pizza burning in the oven.

Finding the notes did not produce the kind of shock Lorna might have expected. In some deep, stomachy way, Lorna already knew. Never once did she consider that she'd misunderstood what the notes implied. She'd seen the looks Alex gave himself in the bathroom mirror as he dressed for work — the smirky, slitty-eyed looks she'd seen on men her age in the windows of the Irish pubs around her office. For months, maybe even years, she'd had a kind of awareness that Alex wasn't faithful. But it was like being aware of the smell of rot somewhere in the house that was persistent yet mild enough to put off looking for. Why search for something you don't quite have the energy to fix? It wasn't laziness exactly, but maybe related. The hardest part about finding the notes was that now she knew, and she had to do something.

Lorna didn't confront Alex right away. She didn't know how. If she were hysterical or even weepy, maybe it would have been easier. But she was just tired. She didn't tell friends. Friends would be outraged. Adultery wasn't the sort of thing women tolerated quietly anymore. You were supposed to scream and sue, and then, with the passage of time, become some kind of one-woman entrepreneur. It was exhausting. Lorna didn't want to pack her bags; she didn't want to yell or get advice. She wanted time to think about it. Later, there would be more time.

So Lorna slept, it seemed, for a month. She woke for work. She woke for Alex's birthday, serving ice cream cake and posing for family photos in the wet autumn leaves. Cara had an operation for her lazy eye, and Lorna slept and slept while Alex sat up in a rocking chair in Cara's bedroom. She slept while Alex joined a fitness club, getting himself in tip-top shape for, no doubt, more betrayal. But as time passed, Lorna knew less and less what to do. She wondered what the point was in doing anything at all. So he'd had sex with someone else, possibly many someone else's. Big deal. They rarely had sex anyway. After a few weeks, it was as if she had forgotten.

But eventually the subject did come up on a drizzly Sunday afternoon in November when the kids were both out. Alex had promised to fix the dishwasher but announced he needed to head out for a few hours first to help a buddy install his winter tires. Lorna didn't believe in unnamed buddies. Unexpectedly, she burst into tears. Even more unexpectedly, so did he. In the low light of the kitchen, he told her that his "thing" with Jenny was over, but Lorna had the distinct impression that he was only at that moment deciding this. Alex explained that Jenny had been a summer student at the bank and "things just got a little chummy." He admitted that he was on his way to see Jenny now because she was home from college for the weekend, and he wanted to end things "like a man." He said this so solemnly it made Lorna laugh. Did he think this earned him points? Ending it like a man? She imagined him picking the girl up around the corner from her parents' house, driving her out to the beach or somewhere terrible, telling her he needed to rein it in while she cried onto his new bicep.

Lorna drained her cup of beer and watched the semi-circle of guests widening around Alex. He seemed to be in performance mode, scratching his head, making his stunned Marty face. Jenny's generation was only about ten years old when Alex played

Marty on *Dog Daze*. These were Alex's long-lost adoring fans. The show was taken off the air before they could outgrow it and see how truly dreadful it was.

Alex put on his breaky, teenage voice. "Doggonit, Harv! Why do you gotta have the last word?" This was the standing line that preceded the show's ending credits, always followed by a cheerful bark, which someone in the group now supplied.

Back when Alex was living in Derek's spare, Lorna found Cara watching a ten a.m. rerun of *Dog Daze* while she was home sick from school. On the third day of Cara's sore throat, Lorna realized she was faking sick in order to watch her father. She phoned Alex and invited him for Christmas. Just three days.

Derek appeared in the group now with a tray of Dixie cups clumped with red Jell-O. He passed them around to Alex and his little circle.

"Stayin' out of trouble?" Derek called to Alex.

"Tryin' my best, man."

"That's a load of crapola!" Derek toasted Alex with his Jell-O cup.

After seeing the job in the paper, it was Lorna who'd suggested Alex apply to the bank. At the time, he was working the graveyard shift for a cable customer service line, keeping his daytime free for auditions. In the years since *Dog Daze*, he'd been cast in a hardware store commercial and an in-flight safety video. Suggesting daytime work hurt Alex's feelings, but he agreed to try it on for a few months. Somehow it stuck. Earlier that evening, Alex told Lorna he hadn't connected with a group like this in a long time.

Lorna rose to collect her Jell-O cup, but Derek was already crossing the room. She moved over to Alex's circle and put a hand on his arm. He turned to her, grinning, but his eyes didn't seem to settle on her face.

The darker girl was talking. "I'm definitely going to see Jim Morrison's grave. That's like number one."

"That's really amazing," Alex said.

"He's, like, a god."

"His death was kind of...senseless," Lorna said, feeling herself redden with this entrée to conversation. The girl looked at Lorna blankly. Nobody seemed like they were dying to meet her at all.

"This is Kavita," Alex said. "Kavita's leaving our team in Jan to bum around Europe."

"Oh," Lorna said. She wasn't sure if she should say her own name or wait for Alex. "On your own, or...?"

Lorna wondered how Alex fucked a girl this age. Not why, but how? Certainly not in the adamant, purposeful way he fucked her on Boxing Day. Fucking with the determined expression of someone moving a piano across a room.

"Yeah," Kavita said. "I have friends, like, all over though."

"Goddamn," Alex said, grinning into his cup. "I'm jealous." When had Alex ever wanted to go to Europe? Did he have any clue what he'd do there?

"You should come!" Kavita exclaimed, smacking a hand over her tits. "Kiera and Mo are coming for a week, too. We're meeting up in San Sebastian." She nodded, thrilled with her own idea. "Because Mo knows a guy who basically owns a hostel."

What did it mean to basically own something?

Alex laughed. He didn't say no. He didn't turn to Lorna and wink and say, "What do you think, hon?" He just grinned again and licked the bottom of his Jell-O cup.

Not sure what else to do, Lorna smiled idiotically at Kavita, too.

"Five days just for the *playa*!" Kavita shook out her hair. "I totally need that."

Alex chuckled as though she'd said something hilarious. "Man," he said. "I'd give anything to be your age again. Seriously, anything."

"Yeah," Kavita said. Clearly she also thought it was stupendous to be her age.

Alex held up his cup. He looked only at Kavita. "Who needs another dose?"

"I'm going to go find the Ladies," Lorna said.

On her way up the stairs, Lorna passed a couple in black, hands entangled, lips and chests pressed together. She had to cough to get them to move. Was that the sort of thing Alex did with Jenny? Press her up against a wall? Lorna tried to think of the last time she'd been pressed to a wall. It was quite possible that the answer was never.

The upstairs bathroom was small with a stained shower curtain and a nappy peach cover on the toilet seat. Lorna filled her plastic cup with water and gulped it down. Behind her, in the mirror, she could see a shelf of products lining the tub and recognized Alex's special brand of psoriasis shampoo. That shampoo cost seven dollars a bottle. She turned and put it in her purse, wondering what else of his was still here. He'd packed a shockingly large suitcase when she asked him to go. She hadn't specified a time frame, imagining about a week or so of punishment to start, but the suitcase showed he was thinking longer. At first this disturbed and frightened Lorna, but in time she adjusted to his absence. She came to like the added quiet, how clean she could keep the kitchen and bathrooms. She joined an adult swim club at the community centre and began racing with a co-ed (non-naked) house league. Her times were laughable, but it gave her something else to focus on. She felt proud of her adaptability. Jed and Cara didn't like it, but it was hardly torture: half of their friends at school had divorced or separated parents. Plus she and Alex weren't even married; the detangling would be simple enough, though it wouldn't be easy.

At the end of Alex's Christmas visit, Lorna was preparing to drive him back to Derek's when she found him in the kitchen, eating from a glass bowl of leftover stuffing. He was wearing his old sheepskin coat, a coat he'd left behind the first time. Every day that Alex was gone, Lorna had noticed that coat folded over the chair in the bedroom and meant to hang it up. Seeing him wear it, ready to leave with it, Lorna was forced to admit that all this time, the sheepskin on the chair had been a small comfort. She wasn't ready for it to go. She put her hand on Alex's back. She thought she could feel his heartbeat through the worn fabric. By the time they were upstairs, she suspected that touching him was a mistake. But in bed, Alex cried. He shuddered and clung to her. He apologized until it began to embarrass her.

Lorna checked her watch. It was still three hours before they said they'd leave. She drank another lukewarm glass of water. It was the first time she'd left Jed and Cara home alone at night. Jed would be watching *Saturday Night Live*, and Cara would be doing god knows what. She'd become strange lately. The night before, Lorna had found Cara hunched over her desk, writing punch-out Valentine cards to her father, signed "Lorna" or "Loo." In a nervous sputter, she said it was just for fun.

A sharp rap on the door startled Lorna as she reapplied her lipstick. "Just a minute!" She blotted her lips, flushed the toilet, and then ran the tap for several seconds. She emerged to a queue of four or five women and hurried past them, the shame of a too-long bathroom visit blooming in her cheeks. She paused at the top of the stairs, her fingers on the metal rail. Laughter burst up from below. Her face burned. She really, really didn't want to go back down.

Lorna crossed the hall and tucked herself into the spare room. She examined the pile of coats on the bed: some leather, some wool, but mostly the neon ski jackets that were so trendy now. She had a sudden urge to slide right under the tangled sea of strangers' outerwear, to be completely buried in cool pinks and greens. She hadn't been sleeping well. Late at night, she would look at the easy *O* of Alex's sleeping mouth and couldn't understand it. He was the betrayer, so why was she the one awake with guilt? Perhaps *guilt* was the wrong word.

Alex's sheepskin coat was sliding off the bed. She sat and pulled it into her body, the pilled collar rubbing against her chin. Who was Alex talking to now? Did he wonder where she was? Would he look for her? Did she want him to?

Since returning home, Alex had become good at hanging his clothes. He bought a rowing machine for the basement, did occasional groceries, and was doing his best to quit smoking. But they hadn't had sex since Boxing Day. This reality pecked at the back of Lorna's mind. Riding the bus home from work at night, she would think: *OK, today's the day. Tonight we'll get back on track.* But once home, Lorna was quietly grateful when Alex, exhausted by the efforts of being well-behaved all day, fell asleep in front of *Night Court*.

Lorna lay back on the bed and stared up at the ceiling fan, a thick layer of dust visible on its slanted blades. *Anything?* she thought. *He would give up* anything?

On one level, Lorna understood this. She and Alex hardly had the chance to be kids like the ones downstairs. At twenty years old, they'd become parents. They'd done it all over again two years later with some vague idea that another baby would prove — to whom, exactly? — that nothing had been a mistake, that they were living the lives they wanted to. But, of course, they'd always known it was a mistake. They'd agreed to that much in the ski hill cafeteria. Alex was earning money to go back to California. Lorna had a degree to finish. His eyes on the hill of skiers through the cafeteria window, Alex told Lorna he could get the name of a doctor, someone who'd helped out a co-star on *Dog Daze.* But they never made any calls.

Mainly Lorna blamed herself for what happened after the ski hill visit. Her father's stroke, one week later, made time seem stiller than it was. In the Albany hospital, when he told her that his life's real joy had been his daughter, it was such an out-of-character thing for him to say that she wondered if she'd been missing something all these years. Teachers and other people's mothers had always told Lorna how fortunate she was to have such a wonderful father, and it surprised her, because there wasn't anything she thought of as exceptional about her dad. Her father was a responsible man, which she supposed now was really what people meant, but he'd never been affectionate or warm. So when he said that thing in the hospital, she wondered if, through some eerie near-death means, he actually knew something he wasn't saying. She thought he might be giving her a sign and let herself wonder. Maybe she and Alex could get used to a baby: just love the thing and be happy. She thought of the hopeful photo of her mother at the hospital. Then, after her father died, after the funeral and the month of bewildering lawyers' meetings, after she'd decided it was crazy to look for signs from a dying man, it was too late for any doctor worth his salt to do anything for her and Alex.

Lorna heard girls laughing in the hallway. Or wait? Was it crying? She hoped they wouldn't come in. Lorna swung her legs up onto the bed and began to cover herself in jackets.

There was a time when Lorna felt more bitterly about her choices, about the life she missed out on. Washing a week's worth of dishes at midnight, the kids finally asleep, Lorna would fantasize about the many ways she could have — should have — rebuffed Alex that night in the rain after Ballantyne's. When Jed was born, people told Lorna she was lucky that Alex had stuck around, but he wasn't really there. He was never home enough, especially for someone who didn't exactly work, and whenever he was home, he just felt in the way. It annoyed her the way he watched the kids eat, sleep, and stumble with the same look of amused expectation as a six-year-old in front of Bugs Bunny. *They're real!* She wanted to scream. *They're real, and they shit!* Ten years ago, if a little genie had turned up with the offer, she would almost certainly have gone for a do-over of her life. She had devoted serious thought to the moment she would go back to in time — sometime before the accident, obviously, but sometime before Kenneth? She would run through the possibilities — the pros and cons — as though this were an actual real decision she would someday get to face. She lay in bed in the morning, waiting for her children's fussing to turn serious, stealing time to consider the question.

But listening now to the weeping girl in the hallway, Lorna felt sure you couldn't pay her to be nineteen again. Of course there was romance in the idea of having it all ahead of you, but she couldn't pinpoint much from her early twenties that she particularly wanted back. It would be too risky—so much could go wrong. She'd miss her children. She had a good job at a top market-research firm, even without her degree, which was something considering the economy. She'd pieced together a decent if not spectacular life from a one-night stand. Plus, she didn't particularly want to go to Europe.

Lorna dug her hand deep into the worn pocket of Alex's jacket, gritty along the seam. She felt a few pennies, a lighter, and a folded square of paper. Her first thought was that she was touching a note, but as she pulled it out, she saw an ordinary receipt. She scanned for illicit items: cologne, flowers, condoms? The first thing was potatoes. The second, honey-baked ham. Lorna folded the receipt. Ham and mashed potatoes was her favourite. As a child, ham was the only roast her father could make. Alex knew that. She had a vision now of Alex bent over the oven, his face flushed with heat. Tomorrow he'd play the dutiful husband on Valentine's Day, and she would act delighted by his generosity. She wanted to feel touched, even relieved by the receipt and the fantasy, but she did not.

Lorna rolled over on top of the coats. This was the guilty feeling she couldn't put her finger on. This was what kept her up at night. They were pretending again. Pretending they were living the lives they wanted. They could go on this way, but the real truth was, Alex would do anything to be young again. When the chance came—and sooner or later, with some woman or other, it would—he'd take it. She knew too much to believe otherwise. Lorna refolded the receipt and slipped it back inside the pocket. It would be easier if it had been a note.

About ten minutes passed before the doors opened with a soft swish. Lorna froze on the bed, half her body covered in coats. She heard Derek's sandpaper voice. "Is that her?"

"Loo?"

Lorna sat up fast, blood rushing too quickly to her temples. She blinked at the two men standing in the door, backlit by the hall.

"Everything OK?" Alex asked.

Lorna looked at Derek. "I'm sorry. It's a nice party," she said. "I'm just not feeling well."

"Not a problem." Derek clapped Alex's arm, leaving them alone to deal with their boring, thirty-something issues.

Alex took a step into the room. "You're not feeling well?"

"I just got tired."

He sat down at the edge of the bed. She could smell beer not just from his breath but his pores. "I thought you'd like to meet everyone."

"I know," Lorna said. "I'm just not up to it. I thought I was, but I guess I'm not."

"So. You want to leave?"

She knew he didn't want to go. "I can take my own taxi."

Alex rubbed his chin. He looked over at the beer cans lining the window. "I'll come."

"Really, I'll be fine. Stay as long as you want." Lorna stood and searched for her own coat, finding it in a small pile that had slipped to the floor. Gratefully, she put it on.

"I'll walk you out at least."

"If you like." Lorna grabbed Alex's coat off the bed and

handed it to him. She thought about the receipt. She should have taken it, a memento or something, but it was too late now.

Alex took the coat and then gave it back. "That's not mine," he said. "I wore the Sunice."

Lorna remembered now. The cab they had taken to Derek's turned sharply onto his block; she'd fallen against Alex's shoulder, the rough neon shell crunching against her cheek.

Alex moved Lorna aside to rifle through the spread of winter gear, spilling more coats onto the floor. He found his turquoise ski jacket and gave it a spank to straighten it out.

The sheepskin in Lorna's hands smelled of loose tobacco and melted snow. She held onto it just a moment longer.

# Ernie Breaks

## SUMMER/FALL, 1988

At the end of every school year, Mom gets Jed and me a passing present. This year we asked for skateboards or a puppy, but Mom suggested goldfish and the conversation was over.

Mom picks me up at three thirty to take me to the tropical fish store that some guy in her Quit4Life group owns. It's a long drive, she says, but worth it because we'll get a deal. Jed has a pool party, so he doesn't get to be part of it.

There's a thick tangle of plants in the window of the store, and inside it's dark and wet, like walking into someone's mouth.

"Yoo-hoo!" A short, chubby man comes up and smiles so big I can see the gold wrapped around the back of his teeth. He kisses Mom on the cheek.

"Isn't Gary's store neat?" Mom says all loud and chirpy, like I'm six years old. It drives me nuts when Mom changes her voice to make people like her. To make people give her a deal.

"We're looking for a passing present for Cara and her brother," Mom says. Mom doesn't tell Gary that Mrs. Connelly said my progress in math over the last year makes me a borderline candidate for Room 12. Jed calls it the retard room.

Gary rubs his hands together. "Very nice, little lady," he says. "Very, very nice." And then for no reason that I can see, he says, "Shall we go fishing then?" in an English accent.

Gary shows Mom and me a tank full of white fish with black lines running through them like prison uniforms. "Angelfish," he says, drawing a line on the glass with his finger. "Graceful, huh?"

"No, not an angelfish," I say. "Jed won't like them. They sound gay."

"Cara!" Mom's neck turns the color of a ham.

"Well, now," Gary says, giggling.

"I'm so sorry, Gary," Mom says, practically falling over. "I think we might have meant something different there."

"That's all right, Lorna. I can see that." Gary wipes his fingers on his shirt. "Have you ever thought about a turtle? Turtles can be a lot of fun."

The turtles at the back of the store have red ears and are smaller than Oreos. Gary grabs one from the tank and drops it in my palms. I squeeze my arms together and let it waddle up the pale alley of skin, its bobbing head like a mushy green marble. A turtle's not a puppy, but it's so ugly that it's cute.

"I don't know," Mom says. "Turtles sound like a lot of work."

"Do they bite?" I ask.

"He may snap at you if he feels threatened," Gary says, "but you almost never see that. They're peaceful. Not like those pretty angelfish. They're mean bastards when they fight."

Mom laughs in a stupid sounding way, not even noticing that Gary's saying bad words, too.

The turtle yawns and looks up at me. "He likes you," Gary says, tilting his head at us. "He knows you'll take good care of him."

It takes a hundred years to pay for the turtle. While Gary and Mom drift around the store looking at tanks and filters and gravels, I hold the turtle outside in a clear, water-filled plastic bag. Mom's always saying she'll just be a minute and then takes a thousand. When Dad still lived with us, Mom ran into a shop at the Santa Claus Village once and didn't come right back like she said she would. Dad banged the steering wheel and said, "Goddammit! Your mother will never come out of that store!" I cried until he made me get out of the car. Now I feel like Dad probably did then. I don't want to be in charge of the turtle all by myself. It's cute and everything, but I don't know what I'm supposed to do with it.

When Mom and I finally get back to the station wagon, the sun has made the car so hot that I burn my belly on the metal seatbelt.

"Whew! Watch that bag," Mom says, rolling down her window. "After spending sixty dollars, I'm not in the mood for turtle soup." She lights a cigarette. Jed says Mom's only in Quit4Life to meet boyfriends. He says all the divorced moms do it. I wonder if she likes Gary, if he's going to be her new boyfriend.

"Did we get a deal?"

Mom doesn't answer. Then after a moment she says, "Cara, when you said that angelfish were gay, what did you mean exactly?"

"I don't know. They sound girly. Like kittens and ponies and stuff."

Mom crinkles her eyes as she sucks in the smoke. "It's an adult word." For some reason, I think of the back section of the video store with the cut-out panther and the purple curtains.

"He said bastard."

She lets smoke out through her nostrils. "We don't make references to people's sexual preferences."

I jiggle the turtle in the bag and watch it bob up and down. "Do you think Gary is cute?"

"You need to think before you just say things, Cara," Mom says. "And for Christ's sake, stop moving that bag around. You'll make the turtle seasick."

At home we have our passing party with cake and ice cream. Jed thinks the turtle is the best. We call him Ernie because he looks and moves like Ernie Sherman, the guy at the drugstore where Mom buys cigarettes because she knows she won't run into anyone from Quit4Life there. Jed wins the coin toss to keep Ernie in his room but lets me spend the first night in a sleeping bag on the floor. When we were little, Jed let me sleep in his bed whenever I got scared. I like the way he breathes when he's asleep: low and slow and in circles. I wake up to Jed dangling Ernie over my face.

We play with Ernie all summer. We bring him to Dad's new apartment for a weekend and make obstacle courses out of toilet paper rolls and playing cards. We flood Mom's rock garden to build a natural habitat with mudslides and drowning Barbies for Ernie to rescue. Jed makes a comic book about an Ernie with two different heads tucked inside his shell: Normal Ernie and Evil Ernie. He lets me make photocopies of the book at the library so we can sell them some day.

When school starts again, Jed's in the new wing for seventh and eighth graders. I don't get to play with Ernie so much because Jed stops letting me into his room after school. His friend Toby comes over every day so that they can play bloody knuckles and ignore me. Jed never helps with my math homework like Mom made him promise.

After Thanksgiving we have a math quiz on fractions, and I can't remember how to put the numbers together. Everyone around me is scratching things down like it's a race. I look at what Valerie is doing to my right, but her arm is covering her paper so I can't see. Valerie Calorie. We call her that because she's fat. She also thinks she knows everything. Whenever she explains stuff, she sighs really loud and talks with her eyes half-closed so that you can see the purple veins in her lids. She already has boobs, but not in the way that is cool.

I stare at the blank page and remember Mrs. Durant saying something about fractions being like a pizza that you cut into pieces. I draw a circle at the top of my page and cut some lines through it. I don't understand why we have to learn about broken numbers. If something is broken, it's wrecked and useless. If it's not your fault, you usually don't need to care about it.

"Two minutes," Durant says. I stare hard at the pizza, trying to remember. I draw some more lines. Then I attach a little neck, a small head and some feet. I draw a little flower for Ernie to eat. Then Durant says to trade our papers for grading. I take Valerie Calorie's from her, but I don't give her mine.

"What's your problem?" she says, hands on her hips.

"What's yours?"

"You're supposed to give me that!" She tries to grab my paper from me, but I hold it down with my fist. She pulls harder and it rips in two. She gets the chunk with the picture of Ernie and laughs with her mouth open wide. "You're the one with the problem," she says. "You're retarded."

I grab the black magic marker from inside my desk and swipe it across her yellow sweater. She squeals and jumps backwards, eyes blinking like crazy and searching for Durant. I put the tip of the marker on my own sweater and draw a faint line so I can say she attacked me first, but Durant sees me do it.

I get sent to see Ms. Del Degan, the new principal with the powdery face. She is away at a dentist appointment, which is lucky, but the secretary makes me stay anyway. She gives me a piece of foolscap and tells me to write a letter of apology to Valerie. She doesn't care that Valerie said I was retarded. She gnashes a piece of gum and laughs into the phone. I can't think of anything to write to Valerie except that she should be more like a fraction and get skinnier.

"You didn't get very far," the secretary says when the bell finally rings. "Not too bright. Now you'll have to do it for homework."

After school I jump whenever the phone rings because it might be Mrs. Calorie or Durant calling Mom to complain about me. I sit on my bed and try writing the letter again. *Dear Valerie, I'm sorry I got mad today and drew on you. I shouldn't have done it. Hope we can still be friends.* The last part is definitely a lie, but it's what Durant and the secretary will want. I decide to ask Jed what he thinks because at least he'll think it's cool that I got in trouble. He got sent to Ms. Del Degan last year for poking little pins through the skin on his fingertips and chasing after Mandy Mahon, who actually has cool boobs.

I hear music coming from Jed's room down the hall. He has a special knocker on his door that's been there since Halloween a million years ago. When you pull the handle, a cowboy voice says, "Dodge, Kansas, leave your guns at the door!" I try it, but no one comes. When I push the door open a crack, I see Jed and Toby looking down at his record player. Jed is holding Ernie over the turntable. He puts him down shell-first. "Watch this," he says. "He'll go flying."

I look at Ernie's tiny, twitching legs. "You'll hurt him."

Jed turns around, hair hanging over his eyes. "Private property."

"Don't do it."

"Turtles don't feel anything. They have shells," Toby says. "Don't be gay."

"Don't make references to people's sexual preferences."

Toby squints at me like this is the stupidest thing he ever heard anyone say.

"Ignore her," Jed tells Toby. "She's a retard."

"He's my turtle too."

Jed turns up the volume on Amazulu's "Montego Bay" and takes his finger off Ernie's pale yellow belly. Ernie spins around slowly at first and then faster when Jed flips the player to chipmunk-speed. I watch Ernie drift closer and closer to the edge of the record. My heart is pounding like crazy, but I'm afraid I'll start to cry if I say anything. After a few seconds, Ernie flies off the turntable and lands right on his feet on Jed's bed. *Thank you God*, I say in my head.

"Fuckin' A!" Toby picks Ernie up off the bed and lobs him to Jed. Jed catches him and slams the door.

I'm still standing in the hallway when Mom comes around to tell Jed and Toby to get ready for hockey practice. She asks if I want to come along with them and have hot chocolate, but there's no way I'm going. Now that I'm in fifth grade, she lets me stay home by myself for up to two hours. It's enough time to save Ernie.

I go back to Jed's room after they leave. It smells like dirty laundry and vinegar, and I have to step around shiny, naked records to get to the tank. Ernie is asleep on a big plastic rock.

"Hey there, Ern!" Ernie jumps from his rock and swims down to the gravel. "I'm sorry that Jed's mean now." The back of the tank is coated in brown slime and it gets on the sleeve of my sweater when I reach in to pick him up.

I put Ernie on the palm of my hand. He feels heavy, almost as big as my whole hand now. I stroke Ernie's shell with my fingers, tracing his waxy lines. "I'm going to save you, OK? I'll tell Mom what Jed did to you and how your tank's all sick." When my fingers get close to Ernie's head, he opens his mouth up wide like he's going to yawn, but instead of yawning, he lunges at my finger. I jump backwards like Valerie Calorie and Ernie flips from my palm and crashes off the edge of the tank and onto the floor. His head, arms, and legs all go sucking back into his shell.

I watch to see if Ernie will move, but nothing happens. I'm afraid to touch him, so I poke his shell gently with my toe. "Come on, Ernie. You're OK." Ernie has never snapped before. Jed has made evil Ernie come out.

Ernie stays completely still. I kneel down and scrape him up with one of Jed's records. Two legs wiggle a little, but his head stays scrunched in. I slide Ernie off the record, back into the tank. He doggy paddles on one side, but his body keeps dipping underwater. I pick him up carefully and drop him on the rock where he'd been sleeping. "Just stay there," I whisper.

I close the tank and leave the bedroom as fast and controlled as I can. *Please let Ernie be OK. Please let Ernie be OK.*

Back in my room, I pick up my note to Valerie Calorie. When I read it again, I see that the printing looks sideways and stupid. Durant always says my printing is clumsy, at least two years below grade level. I rip up the letter. Rip it into tinier and tinier pieces until it's like snow covering my comforter. When I hear the slam of the car door outside, I scoop up the scraps and toss them under my bed.

I don't see Ernie dead. Jed finds him. I hear Mom in the hall telling Jed that it was probably an infection that killed Ernie. "You took good care of him, sweetheart," she says. "Nothing lasts forever."

Mom says there is sad news and asks me to come down to the kitchen to talk. While she explains about Ernie, Jed keeps his eyes on me.

"Did you notice anything unusual about Ernie?" Mom asks. "Anything that was different today or yesterday?"

"I don't know." I look at Jed. His neck and ears are bright pink.

Mom asks if we want to have a funeral for Ernie or do anything special to say goodbye. We both say no. She takes the chocolate ice cream out of the freezer and scoops out two large bowls. "Well," she says, "Christmas is coming." She tugs my ponytail gently. "You both loved Ernie. Should we talk about another kind of pet?"

Jed and I stare at our melting bowls of chocolate ice cream. When the phone rings, Mom waits a few seconds and then goes to answer it. I think that if it's Mrs. Calorie or Durant, I really don't care. But it's just Ian, her boss. She sounds all cheerful on the phone, not like someone whose turtle just died.

The next day at school, my desk gets moved up against Durant's. It's the first time she's done that, and I can't turn around and look at the class without my whole face burning. At recess, Durant makes me stay inside to do extra math sheets, which is fine because no one wants to play with me anyway. They think I'll get them in trouble or ruin their clothes. Erica B., who has the best clothes, said I made the stuffing come out of her ski jacket, and then Valerie sucked up to her by saying she saw me pull it. I get disinvited from Kathleen's birthday party, which is supposed to have a lip-synch contest.

After a week, I get my old desk back, but the situation is actually worse. I'm switched to Room 12 for one hour of math every morning with Ms. Graham.

The retard room is big and sunny with round tables instead of desks. There's only about five kids in there at one time, so mostly I get Ms. Graham to myself. Ms. Graham wears big felt hats and says weird things like "Rootin' tootin'!" whenever I do something right, but at least Valerie's not there. We play Connect 4 and Mastermind, and on Thursdays she gives me ten minutes of *Math's a Blast!* on the computer. She says if I get perfect on the fractions test before Christmas, I can have pizza to celebrate.

After school, I study alone in my bedroom, doing each question on my practice sheet over and over until I know the answers by heart. The day before the test, Jed stops by my door and stands there watching me.

"What?" I ask.

"Mom says maybe you want help." He stares at the carpet while he talks.

"Well, I don't."

He takes a step in. "It's fine if you do. Did you know that four out of three people have trouble with fractions?"

"I told you I don't need help!"

Jed backs out of the door, his palms held up. "Whoa! Sorry!" It's only after he leaves that I realize he was trying to tell a joke.

Anyway, I really don't need help because Ms. Graham's Christmas fractions test is so easy. I get all ten questions, plus the two bonuses. It turns out that everyone is getting pizza, but Ms. Graham specifically ordered Hawaiian just for me. All the other retards wanted pepperoni. When she brings it in, I think we're going to eat it together at the round table, but she has her own bagged lunch. "I'm on a diet," she says, patting her stomach. "Plus it's for you, kiddo! You earned it."

"I can't eat the whole thing." I've never heard of a teacher giving a kid a whole entire pizza before.

"Share it with your friends in the lunchroom." She holds up ten fingers. "If you give three friends two slices, how much of the pizza will you have left?"

She should know that question is too easy for me. "Four out of ten. Four-tenths."

"Good." She nudges the pizza box toward me. "I won't even bug you to reduce it this time."

When the lunch bell rings a minute later, I step out into the hallway with the pizza box, but I don't feel hungry anymore. I don't want a retard treat that not even Ms. Graham will share with me.

While everyone else is having lunch inside, I head for the playground and the bench furthest away from the doors. It's almost cold enough to snow, but the pizza box is warm on my thighs. I gobble the first two slices so fast that I don't taste a thing.

"You're eating a whole pizza all by yourself?"

I close the lid and look up at Valerie Calorie's greedy face. She must have finished her lunch inside in one minute flat. Piglet. She puts her hands on her hips. "Give me a slice?"

"No."

"I'll tell Durant."

It's not worth it. Durant already hates me. I give her the smallest slice and watch her flick the pineapples onto the ground.

"Who let you have a pizza?" she talks with her mouth full.

"Ms. Graham."

"Aw. She feels sorry for you because you're stupid."

"No she doesn't."

"Wanna bet?"

In another minute, all of Valerie's dorky friends start crowding around. I give out more warm slices, just wanting the dumb pizza to disappear.

When Toby comes up, there are only two slices left. Seventh and eighth graders don't normally get the same lunch period as us, but Toby and Jed have yard duty on Fridays. They're supposed to push little kids on the tire swing and break up fights and show good citizenship, but mostly they just hang off the fence and talk about hockey and *Saturday Night Live*.

"Where did you get the pizza?" Toby puts his basketball shoe up on the bench next to me.

"None of your beeswax."

"Yeah, it is." He licks the silver inside of a chip bag with his fat tongue. "I'm on duty. I need to know everything."

Valerie Calorie has sauce on her chin. "Ms. Graham gave it to her."

"Ms. Graham from the retard room?" Toby snatches my last slices. "What's two minus two, retard?"

I don't answer him. I don't care.

Toby waggles the slices in the air. "Oh my god. You don't even know two minus two!"

Valerie squeals and claps her hands. "She doesn't. She really doesn't."

"Yeah, I do." But I'm only looking at Valerie. I guess it makes Toby mad because he shoves me hard on the shoulder. I fall over the bench and land on my butt. I expect people to laugh, but when I scramble up, no one is even watching me. Everyone is looking at Jed. Jed, who came out of nowhere but now has Toby in a headlock. The pizza slices he stole are face down on the asphalt.

"Get the fuck off me!" Toby swings his arms. Jed grunts with the effort to hold him in place. Valerie and her stupid friends make a circle around them.

When Toby manages to get free, he goes for a punch, but Jed tackles him easily down to the ground. I see Valerie running off to get a lunch lady.

"What's your problem, Ketchum?" Toby's voice comes out high and everyone laughs.

Jed doesn't answer, he just keeps panting in Toby's face.

"Teacher's coming!" someone yells.

When Jed gets up, he doesn't look my way at all. He just dusts off his knees, gives Toby the finger and walks away.

A round, red-faced lunch lady comes rushing high-speed

toward us like some kind of tomato on wheels. She blows a whistle from a chain on her neck, which gets even more people staring. The fight really should be over, but Toby's too pissed. He rushes up behind Jed and kicks him in the butt. Jed trips forward but doesn't fall; he swings around and punches Toby bam on the mouth. By the time the lunch lady arrives, wheezing and pressing her hands to her knees, Toby is bleeding. I hide the pizza box under the bench.

When Mom comes home that night, there's a call from Ms. Del Degan, of course. Jed gets grounded for the Christmas holidays, and I expect him to drag me down too, but he doesn't say anything about the pizza. I'm glad Mom doesn't have to find out I'm a loser at school now on top of being dumb at math. Mom's always worried about what I'm good at and whether I have friends. In October, I lied and told her I was going to be the lead in a version of *Cats* that my class was putting on. On parent-teacher interview night, I asked her three times not to mention the play to Durant. If they talked about it, if she found out I was a liar, she never said.

It does nothing but rain for the first holiday week off school, so Jed doesn't really miss anything and just hides out in his room. Sam Grossman from down the block, my only friend these days, and probably because she isn't from school, gives me a bag of chocolate Hanukah coins that I slip under Jed's bedroom door. He pushes the coins back.

The first day there's snow, Jed works on a comic book at the kitchen table while I get ready to go tobogganing with Sam. Mom obviously feels sorry for Jed because she suddenly says she'd be perfectly happy to reduce his punishment if he can offer a good explanation for his actions. "Violence is never the right answer. But if I understood—"

"Toby's a dick," Jed says.

Mom crosses her arms. "What does that mean to you?"

"Same thing it means to you."

"So why now? Why hit him all of sudden. I'm curious to know."

"I'm a bully, OK? Ms. Del Degan already told you."

"That's not what she told me, exactly." Mom turns to both of us. "Toby is no weakling. If he were, this would be a different conversation."

Jed stares at the window. Mom keeps her eyes on him a moment, then goes back to the sink. "Suit yourself," she says.

When Jed turns around, I give him a small smile. He squinches his eyes and shakes his face at me like "*What? What's your problem?*" Then he gathers his pencils and goes back to his room.

# Vacancy

**W**hen the doorbell rang, Lorna was in front of the fridge, eating peanut butter directly from the jar. She'd been at the Y pool the last couple of hours while her real estate agent, Brenda, another single mom from Quit4Life, showed the house. Now the showings were over, the kids were still at friends' homes, and Lorna had a moment's peace. She wanted badly to ignore the bell, but the chance it could be her neighbour's seventeen-year-old daughter, locked out again, made her answer it.

Lorna fluffed her bangs and unlocked the door. A woman stood smiling in a damp coat. She scrunched up her nose, apologetic. "I know the open house ended a couple of hours ago." She glanced over her shoulder at the lawn sign. "But is there any way? My husband and I are just here for the weekend."

Lorna didn't know how to show a house, but there wasn't much to lose. Brenda said business had been slow. It was a wet, early March weekend and, according to Brenda, only five couples had come through earlier and none of them struck her as "real serious." Lorna managed a wide, Brenda-esque smile for the woman. "Lorna Kedzie. I live here," she said. "But come on in. I'll show you around."

"I'm Amanda," the woman said, removing her coat and shaking rain onto the foyer floor. "My husband's just parking." She looked behind her. "This is a cute block. Is it always hard to park?"

"Once you're a resident on the street, you can get an annual pass," Lorna said. "It's easy." She had no idea if it was easy; Alex had taken care of it every year. She took Amanda's coat, noting a rounded bump underneath her sweater.

Amanda was attractive in a way that reminded Lorna of a morning TV news anchor. Thirty at most, with a smooth layer of baby fat still in her face. Her brown hair sprung cheerfully off her scalp. She bent down to remove her leather boots.

"Oh, you don't need to do that," Lorna said. "We wear our shoes all the time."

"But they're dirty." Amanda looked up at Lorna with a tilted, prudish expression. "And wet."

Chastened, Lorna batted her hand. "Right, I'm sorry. Go ahead."

Amanda lined her boots neatly against the radiator while Lorna backed up to the rug in the middle of the small foyer, conscious of the squeak of her running shoes on the linoleum.

"May I?" Amanda gestured toward the living room.

"Absolutely."

Spacious and south facing, the living room was, in Lorna's opinion, the house's finest feature. She watched Amanda look from the old fireplace, still ornamented with original turn-of-the-century tile, up to the domed light fixture on the ceiling.

"It's really quite something in here when the sun's out." Lorna strengthened her voice, trying to sound warm and credible.

Amanda nodded toward the piano nestled in the nook of the window. "Do you play?"

"No," Lorna said, walking toward it. "I keep meaning to learn." She hadn't yet figured out what she'd do with the piano in an apartment. It had been Lorna's mother's, and Lorna was attached. Twenty-five years ago, her father showed her how to play the "Heart and Soul" duet, and Lorna had taught herself the melody of a few Beatles songs with her right hand, but eventually she grew bored by her limitations. She asked her father for lessons, but they were never arranged. Lorna wondered now if her father thought it would be disloyal to have another piano teacher in the house.

Lorna ran her finger along the music rack, feeling the salty sting of dust on her chlorine-chapped fingertips. She was pregnant with Cara when she and Alex moved the piano out of her father's storage and into the house. She'd fantasized about a daughter in a crushed-velvet recital dress, cheeks flushed, chubby little fingers on the keys. She still had flashes of this happy fantasy when she glimpsed the piano after the doors to the living room had been closed for a while. She needed to remind herself that her kids were big now. That Cara, who still couldn't read music after two years of lessons, had begged and begged to quit. Being brought back to reality could feel to Lorna like a kind of death.

Amanda twisted her gold rope necklace. "We could probably just knock this room out, right? Open up the foyer?"

Lorna took the suggestion like a kick in the spine. This was, of course, another reason agents took charge of showing a house.

"More modern, right? For entertaining?" Amanda said.

Having had enough of the living room, she was heading toward the staircase.

"Whereabouts do you live now?" Lorna asked, trailing behind, as though Amanda were showing her the house.

"Alberta now. But we've lived everywhere. Alaska, Texas."

"Oh," Lorna said. "How exciting." She blushed at her flat delivery. She'd never been good at this sort of chat.

"Always the middle of nowhere. My husband's in oil," she said. She touched her belly gently. "We're going to try something more urban for a while."

"This house is very central."

Amanda shrugged. "I'm not so sure that I'm a Toronto gal."

Lorna considered what defined a Toronto gal. Perhaps some brutish individual who didn't take off shoes, like herself.

"My husband went to university here," Amanda said.

"I see," Lorna said vaguely.

"So he knows the vicinity."

"It's a terrific . . . vicinity."

"How long have you lived here?" Amanda looked around the room.

"A little over ten years." They'd begun renting the place from Alex's father when he moved to Florida in 1979, then inherited part of the house when he died two years later. Alex was still buying the rest from his older sister. It was a creaky midtown Victorian with knob and tube, poor insulation, and a roof that leaked. Over the years, they had spent most of Lorna's inheritance on the house's upkeep. This was a point of some contention because Alex's parents had also owned a run-down lake house on an enviable chunk of land up north, a property Alex inherited outright and the sale of which would have allowed Lorna to hang on to her money. But Alex, irritatingly, was sentimental about the old place. Lorna was sure no one, not even Alex, had been up there in over two years.

Lorna was about to offer to take Amanda upstairs when the doorbell rang again.

"That'll be him," Amanda said.

"Good timing." Lorna strode toward the front door, but she didn't open up right away. There, on the other side of the bevelled glass, was Kenneth Kravchuk. Kenneth, just standing there, huffing on his glasses. Lorna's throat contracted; she turned the knob slowly and managed to smile as Kenneth looked up, but a flicker of panic in his face stopped her from greeting him by name. His eyes moved quickly across her. Then he looked over his shoulder, like he might just take off.

"Took you long enough," Amanda said, coming up behind Lorna. "But listen, apparently if you live here you can get a parking permit or something."

Kenneth set his glasses back on his face. He looked only at Amanda.

"Can I take your coat?" Lorna was surprised by the smallness of her voice. As she reached for the coat, her hands were shaky.

"I'm fine." Kenneth's voice was deeper than Lorna remembered, but even through his beige raincoat, she could see that he'd kept his swimmer's V. His face was still thin, all points and angles.

"This is Laura. She's the owner," Amanda said. "But she's going to show us around anyway. Isn't that kind of her?"

"It's really no problem." Lorna tried again to catch his eye.

Kenneth did not remove his smooth leather shoes. He brought his fingers to his mouth and rubbed his nail against his tooth.

She knew this gesture. She wished he'd never told her what a comfort it was to feel the smoothness of a nail against a tooth. It was a habit she'd picked up herself way back when. "Actually," he said. "We don't have a ton of time."

Amanda sighed. "Where do we need to be? We can be late, Ken. This might be it." She turned to Lorna. "Kenneth's got this eye. He could have been an architect." She brought her hands together and then broke them apart. "We want a place we can just crack into. Really reveal what's there."

Lorna moved out of the way. "Please," she said. "Go forth and conquer." She attempted to laugh, felt a prickly redness spread across her face.

Kenneth nodded, swallowed. That sharp glug of his Adam's apple. Lorna always marvelled at how he managed to shave over it. Did Amanda think about that? Did she sit on the edge of the tub and talk to him while he shaved? Did he tell her secrets? The names of his exes?

"Want to look upstairs, hon?" Amanda said.

If Kenneth was behaving out of character, Amanda didn't appear to notice. With a hand on his back, she steered him past the living room, waving the fact of it away. Lorna kept a few paces behind, watching the back of Kenneth's head as they climbed the stairs. Sometimes she thought about running into him downtown. In these fantasies, she would be with Ian, her tall, handsome boss. She'd be wearing an important black skirt and jacket combo, the new green pumps she hadn't yet felt bold enough to wear. They would be walking and laughing, their head tossed back in sheer *joie de vivre*. Kenneth would stare as she strode off, knocked out by her apparent life success and general beauty. About six or seven years back, she actually thought she did see him once in a hot dog line outside City Hall. She'd been skating with the kids, had a cold sore, and was feeling Christmas fat, so she hadn't approached.

Amanda ran her hand along the banister, her ring scraping against the wood. The diamond looked sharp and pointy. "What's the square footage?"

"About fifteen hundred."

"Bigger than it looks," Amanda said, smiling in Kenneth's direction.

"More if you count the yard," Lorna said.

Kenneth's first floor bachelor at the Northway was four hundred square feet. Lorna hadn't minded the smallness. It was back when she believed that making sacrifices automatically meant better things to come. When she moved in at the end of January, her legs still in casts, he told her the little cement balcony would be great extra space in summer. She told him she knew how to grow tomatoes. The whole thing was romantic.

As Lorna followed Kenneth into the den, her eyes seemed only to find the things that had once been theirs: the trunk of high school trophies and letters they'd used as a coffee table, her mint table lamp, the ficus tree. On the TV stand, there was a photograph of Debbie, Cara's godmother. Would Kenneth remember the freckled girl who lived seventeen floors above them? The girl whose roommate ad he'd handed to her the day he left? He probably wouldn't know that she was dead now. A winter car accident, like the one that did in Lorna's knees, only far worse.

Kenneth paused at the built-in bookshelf, touching the wood, looking at the rows of books and magazines. He put a knobby finger on a 1973 world atlas, tilting it gently toward him.

"This is nice," Amanda said from the other side of the room. "Cozy."

Lorna moved closer to Kenneth. "You want that?" Her throat clenched. She waved at the bookcase and swallowed. "I'm getting rid of a bunch of this, so..."

Amanda let out a nervous laugh from across the room. "What? No. Ken totally does that. He thinks he can just touch everything."

Kenneth pulled the atlas out and stared at the cover. He knocked it gently with his knuckle. "Thanks," he said.

It had been a long time since Lorna had looked at that atlas. The page she'd shown Kenneth on Sierra Leone—a destination of sun and seawater, just like he said he wanted—was surely still folded. She pitched Sierra Leone as somewhere he could use his engineering degree to build water pumps while she taught English. She was sure they could be happy there. But in any case, other pages were folded now. The kids used the atlas for school projects all the time. She'd buy them a new one.

Looking embarrassed, Amanda drifted out of the room, leaving Lorna and Kenneth alone. Let him make the first move, she thought. She wished she wasn't carrying the extra fifteen pounds. Her waist, when he held it fifteen years ago, had been so narrow.

"You need to see this, Ken," Amanda called from down the hall.

Kenneth cleared his throat, still examining the bookshelf. Lorna ran her hands down the sides of her jeans. Could he smell the chlorine in her hair? Was he curious if she still swam?

"Excuse me, " Kenneth said, and he walked out of the room.

In the master bedroom, Amanda paused at the school photos of Cara and Jed on the dresser.

"Two children?" she said.

"Yes."

"The boy's handsome," Amanda said.

"Thank you." Lorna knew it. Still in middle school, Jed already looked seventeen. He was tall, his hair was long, and he dressed cool, seeming to have a natural instinct for what that required. Lorna looked at the picture of Cara. Did anything about her daughter strike people? She had Alex's flecky brown eyes, his thick lashes, but Lorna's thin lips. Jed had inherited Alex's even complexion, but Cara's skin lacked decision: pink and white, sometimes half and half, and getting oilier with age. Her hair was also losing its childhood blond. Now that Lorna looked at the photo, at her daughter's hair pulled thinly over one shoulder, she could see that it was almost completely mousy. But she wasn't a bad-looking girl, was she?

Lorna glanced at Kenneth, who had wandered over to the windows facing the street. Thin winter rain scratched at the glass. Did Kenneth find it interesting that she had two children? Was he even a little curious what they looked like? She thought he might already have kids, too.

"Do you need a bigger place?" Amanda was looking at Lorna with a pucker between her eyebrows, an abrupt disruption to her smooth face. She glanced around quickly. "I mean, can I ask why you're selling?"

Lorna looked from Amanda back to Kenneth, who glanced her way now, too. Did he suspect a marriage gone awry? To Lorna, it became desperately important for him not to think this.

"Actually, it's a funny story." Lorna's voice quickened with the lie. "We've inherited something. Quite unexpectedly, to be honest."

Amanda's face relaxed. "Wonderful." Then she clapped her hand to her forehead. "I mean, I'm sorry. For the death. I'm guessing it was someone close."

"Thank you." She looked over for Kenneth's reaction, but he'd disappeared into the ensuite. "It's really fine."

Lorna watched from the side of the bed as Amanda and Kenneth explored the bathroom. She felt tense watching Kenneth slide open the shower curtain. She knew tiles were missing in three places in the tub: bare squares of putty lined with black threads of mould that she'd tried to hide with carefully arranged shampoo bottles. There were also stains on the enamel sink, scribbled over with a whiteout pen. Kenneth was always obsessive about hygiene. Once, early on, he brought her home a bouquet of new toothbrushes because hers, he said, had become too ratty. The gesture shamed rather than touched her.

Kenneth slid the curtain closed and moved on to inspect the cabinetry under the mirror. "Nice storage," he said, opening and closing one of the drawers.

"Thank you. Husband did that." She felt a heavy flush in her cheeks again. She was sure she'd never used the word *husband* like that before, without a possessive pronoun.

He squinted up at her. "You've had a lot of interest?"

Lorna turned slightly. "Quite a bit."

The three of them moved quickly through the kids' rooms. Cara's pink walls were covered in pin-ups from *Teen Day* magazine: squatting, smiling young men with baggy pants and blousy shirts, their hair shaved at the sides and slicked back on top.

"Your daughter's into the New Kids!" Amanda said.

"I guess so!" Lorna really didn't know what Cara thought of

these glossy teenaged boys. The magazine said "pin-up," so that's what she did. At parent-teacher interviews, Lorna had learned from Mrs. Durant that Cara was struggling socially. She clearly wanted friends, but she was a hanger-on, a follower, easily bullied by the girls whose attention she was trying to secure. It was unsettling. Cara did have one close friend, Samantha Grossman from the down the street, but Lorna wasn't sure that Sam's influence was helpful. Sam was an eerily polite girl who seemed to know too much for her age. Once Lorna found Sam and Cara wearing sheets and bathing caps, preparing to go door to door as fake Hare Krishnas. Sam got Cara reading V.C. Andrews, prompting a list of creepy bedtime questions about incest and the afterlife. But if Cara wasn't with Sam, she was alone in the yard, beating a balding tennis ball against the side of the house for hours. In winter, she did it in the laundry room in the half-dark, the dull thuds spreading through the house. For the coming summer, Lorna had decided to enrol Cara in competitive tennis. It might turn out to be her "stake": something to lift her up, to provide camaraderie and direction. At Cara's age, Lorna needed the same thing.

Amanda centered herself in the middle of the room. She looked dreamily at Kenneth. "This would make a perfect nursery, don't you think?"

Lying next to Kenneth in bed, Lorna could never resist asking what he was thinking. "You just want to know if I'm thinking about you," he'd snapped. "I'm not always thinking about you." Lorna had told him of course not, of course he wasn't, she was just interested in *him*. But was she? What Lorna recalled now was only how desperately she needed to be on his mind.

"It's a little dark," Kenneth said.

"Helps baby sleep," Lorna said. "Mega quiet."

Mega? Another word Lorna was certain she'd never used before. *Don't blush again*, she thought, but she did anyway.

"Maybe a little dark," Amanda said. *Don't give in to him*, Lorna wanted to say.

Kenneth scratched his neck and pointed at the door. "Let's have a quick look on the main floor."

They were beginning their way down the stairs when the telephone rang. Lorna squeezed past, brushing Kenneth's shoulder. "I'll see you in the kitchen."

It was Ruthie Grossman on the phone, Sam's mom. She wanted to know if Cara could stay for dinner. Lorna looked around for Amanda and Kenneth, but they weren't right behind her. She assumed they were in the living room, where Amanda would outline her plans to crack it open.

"Larry's out of town and we're going to be bad and order Chinese," Ruthie said. "We'll get everything! You know how much Cara loves Moo Shu!"

Ruthie was always very eager to show off whatever she knew about Cara. The other night after the girls' swim class, she'd asked if Lorna was concerned about the state of Cara's eyebrows. When Lorna asked why, Ruthie looked at her with such stagy shock it was embarrassing for them both. "They've practically disappeared!" she said. "Sammy's too. I spoke to her, and she said that boys like them that way! And now she's asking for a sports bra. Can you imagine it?" But there was a gleam in Ruthie's eye, like she'd been waiting her whole life for these woman-to-woman moments with her daughter. On the drive home, Lorna tried to raise the matter of eyebrows with Cara, but her daughter turned scarlet and said her body was her own business, a message they were drilling hard at school these days.

"I'm sorry, Ruthie, I'm just in the middle of something—"

"Well, it's no extra hassle, if that's what you're worried about. Cara's so polite. It's truly never a hassle!" The *never* was rankling, whether or not Ruthie intended it. Cara ate at the Grossmans' a hell of a lot.

Lorna watched Amanda and Kenneth enter the kitchen. She smiled vaguely and fluttered her hand — *go ahead!*

"You come, too," Ruthie said. "As a matter of fact, don't you dare say no!" Lorna had every intention of saying no. The thought of Chinese food with Ruthie, creepy Sam, and Cara—who would doubtless hate to have her there—was frankly the last way she wanted to spend the evening.

Lorna watched Kenneth open the pantry door. Again, she tensed. At their apartment, he'd stored everything in glass jars. She kept her sugar, flour, and years-old chocolate chips all slumped in the bags they came in.

"I'm going to call you back in a minute," she said to Ruthie.

Clicking off, Lorna turned to find Amanda with her fingers perched over the stove. She snapped the gas on and jumped back when the flame roared up like an eager orange genie. "We don't cook much," Amanda said, laughing.

At nineteen, while Lorna slaved to recreate Kenneth's mother's meat aspic, did he already know this was the kind of "gal" he wanted? She'd tried so hard to guess at what he wanted. Bow in the hair? Short hair? Permanent? Kenneth seemed to want everything a particular way — hot breakfasts, no radio while studying, toothpaste squeezed from the bottom only — but on the matter of Lorna, his preferences always felt hazy. He'd be happy for her to join his crowd at the Grad Club after class one night, but the next week the suggestion would make him furious. For years, Lorna wondered what she'd finally done to push him the wrong way, to make her life plan teeter and topple like a game of Jenga. But at thirty-three, it was easy enough to see what had happened. He'd made a rash decision out of guilt and didn't want his whole life consumed by it. When that physiotherapist told Lorna she could swim again, he believed it meant his penance was over, that he could finally get on with his life. It was understandable, although he could have been much kinder.

Amanda cast her beaming face toward Kenneth, who was now half in the pantry. "Don't you love the wallpaper in here, hon? It's so yellow!"

Kenneth didn't answer. He seemed to be keeping his distance from both women.

Amanda approached the sliding doors leading out to the snow-patched yard. She pressed her hands and face up to the glass. "Not a ton of space out back, but such a cute garden."

"Just a rock garden."

Amanda yanked the sliding door open, letting in a wet sweep of air. The sound of giggling drifted over from the yard next door. The seventeen-year-old, Elena Costas, no doubt.

Amanda wrinkled her nose. "Are those skunks?"

Lorna sniffed and shook her head. "Just dope, I think." She pointed her chin at the neighbour's yard. "Teenagers next door."

"Oh," Amanda frowned, a complete reassessment of the neighbourhood visible on her face. "But no critters back here?"

Lorna glanced at Kenneth then; she couldn't help it. They'd

had raccoons on their balcony. That May, she and Kenneth would get down on the apartment's thin grey carpet and watch through the glass door as the raccoons climbed out of the building's dumpster and onto their first-floor balcony with a mix of blunder and grace. There were just a couple small ones at first, then they multiplied. Lorna joked that it was like a raccoon nightclub—sometimes ten or eleven of them fighting and fucking until sunrise. In the morning they'd find them asleep, nipples up to the sun, trampled mounds of toxic shit everywhere. In the end, Kenneth and Lorna couldn't even open the doors to let a cross-breeze through. Her tomatoes, which he blamed for the invasion, spoiled in the sun. When they washed their clothes at home to save money, they had to hang them inside and swipe through a jungle of humid pant legs to cross the single room. Lorna got a heat rash that needed thick expensive cream that made her itchy and unfuckable.

Amanda seemed to have forgotten the matter of critters and was scratching around inside her purse. "Can you give me your agent's name?"

"Let me find you a card." Lorna moved to the kitchen drawer. She knew she wouldn't hear from them and felt honestly sorry for Amanda's disappointment. Which of the house's imperfections would Kenneth focus on? After the fight, would Amanda feel stupid and unsure of herself? What had she already given up for his good opinion?

At the door, Lorna handed the card to Kenneth. "I should be honest with you," she said. Kenneth looked up, a nervous twist in his lips. She turned to Amanda. "We do have critter problems from time to time. Raccoons, mainly. Nothing serious."

Amanda tucked her hair behind her ears. "That's the city

though, right?" She looked at Kenneth for confirmation, but he was facing away, his hand already on the doorknob.

Amanda bent down to deal with her boots, steadying herself with a manicured hand on Kenneth's arm. Kenneth's eyes met Lorna's. "Appreciate that," he said, then he turned the doorknob. "Thanks for the tour."

Lorna watched them walk away from the house: the atlas tucked under Kenneth's arm, Amanda's fingertips on his elbow.

Back in the kitchen, the sliding glass doors were still partly open. The old leaves on the rain-flattened lawn ticked up with the breeze. Lorna stuck her head out into the cool, wet air.

In the yard next door, Elena Costas and a boy were huddled by the shed. The boy smoked the joint, pinching it between his fingers, his eyes on the ground. He resembled the boys in Cara's pin-ups: tall but baby-faced, slouched in a Raiders jacket. Lorna could see across the yard that Elena's desert boots were soaked through. Her tight jeans had a cloudy pattern, and she bent her knees over and over to keep warm. Elena was a pretty girl who wore far too much makeup. Cara, of course, idolized her.

The boy took a last puff and chucked the joint onto the muddy grass. He picked up his backpack and loped across to the gate. Elena watched him go, hands in the pockets of her open cardigan. Lorna's heart dropped low in her chest. Poor, pretty Elena. She didn't know where that boy was going, if she was invited, if he'd come back. She wanted to say something reassuring to Elena, but what?

Lorna stepped outside. The yard had an orchard-like smell, and she breathed it in with sudden appetite. In a minute, she would call Ruthie back. She would take Cara out for dinner, learn more about the New Kids, find a way to bring up sports bras. Cara wouldn't be polite, but at least she'd be close.

It was only after the boy was through the gate that Elena looked up in Lorna's direction. Lorna smiled gently, waved. Elena untucked the hair from behind her ears and let it fall to cover her face. She hurried, head down, to unlock her own back door.

# Bounced

**P**ractising for Wimbledon?"

I catch the tennis ball on the face of my racquet and look up. A blond woman in a pink suit is leaning on the gate to our yard, one hand on her hip.

"No," I say, embarrassed. "I'm just bouncing a ball."

"I can see that," the woman says. "Your mom's inside?"

"Yeah."

The woman is pretty much a flamingo — skinny legs, pointy pink shoes — and the biggest butt ever sticks right out under her jacket. She goes up to the door, and I go back to bouncing the ball against the side of the house. I imagine the flamingo is a tennis scout looking for kids to take to training in Florida. Right now she's saying, "I saw your daughter volleying out there, and I just had to pull over!"

To increase the chances of this actually happening, I stop bouncing for a minute to tap my racquet against the side door seven times. It's what I need to do to have good luck, or at least for nothing bad to happen. Before going to bed, I touch every window and every door in our house: seven taps each. This protects us pretty well. For example, when Mom tried to sell our house last month — because she doesn't seem to care that it's the

97

house I grew up in, the only house I ever want to live in — no one bought it. Even the sign is gone. Then I got a B+ on my oral book report, even though I made up the existence of the tennis book *Ace Age* pretty much on the spot. The best part is I've been Queen of the Court in tennis lessons three weeks in a row, and my instructor, Dan Bangor, smiled at me twice.

After a little bit, the screen door opens and Mom and the flamingo step out into the yard.

"Cara, can you cool it a minute?" Mom says. Her hair is blow-dried and she is wearing peach lipstick, which is definitely not normal. "I want you to meet Mrs. Needham." Tennis scouts have names like Sue or Carole-Anne. Not Mrs. Needham. We both say hi.

The flamingo walks around me in a circle. "So this is your yard, huh?" She writes something on a notepad and makes a sucking sound. "That changes things. You had me thinking annuals garden."

"I have a little rock garden. Stone cress, sandwort, candytuft," Mom says.

The flamingo jerks her chin at a rip in the screen door. "You'll want to patch that up before having anyone in." She looks at me like she knows it's my fault. "It's one of those small things that can really change an impression."

"Who's coming over?" I ask.

"No one today, honey," Mom says.

The flamingo claps her notebook shut. "Let's see the basement." She waggles a finger at me. "Go easy, Ms. Evert."

Chris Evert hasn't won a grand slam in like three years. "I like Martina," I tell her as she disappears inside.

When I hear the flamingo clacking away from our house later,

I don't stop bouncing to say goodbye. I only stop when Mom calls Jed and me for dinner. We're having a "summer dinner." Summer dinner means cold cuts on a plate with brown bread and vegetable sticks. I get a can of tonic water from the fridge and take a long sip. It's the only soft drink in the house.

"Have you ever wished we lived just a little closer to school?" Mom says. She sits down and unfolds her napkin.

"No," I say. School is the last place I want to live near.

"Well, that's something we can talk about." She puts her fingertips together and leans forward in her chair. "I've decided to put our house back on the market."

"What does 'back on the market' mean?" I picture a giant grocery store where houses sit nestled between pointy pieces of paper grass.

"It means we're selling it again, idiot," Jed says, his mouth rammed with mock chicken.

"That's why I wanted you to meet Mrs. Needham," Mom says. "She's our new agent."

"What happened to Brenda?"

"Mrs. Needham is different," Mom says. "Very experienced, very respected. She's married to Ian, my boss, so she's giving us a bit of a break. We're going to give this another shot—"

"I don't want to move," I say for the six hundredth time.

"This house is too big for three, don't you think?" Mom says.

I didn't think so in the winter; I don't think so now. "What if Dad comes back?" I ask. It's not like that's never happened. One Christmas he was gone for three weeks, and then he came right back.

"That's very unlikely," Mom says. "Besides, we have a whole yard we never use, a living room just for Christmas."

"So you want, like, an apartment?" Jed asks. He smears hard butter on a piece of bread, shredding it into pieces.

I look at Mom. She wouldn't. Apartments are for poor people. Petra Sokolov, my tennis enemy, lives in an apartment. I know because Mom made me go to her stupid birthday party. All the girls in my class were invited, but none of the good ones showed up. The Sokolovs' hallway stunk like boiled cauliflower and their balcony had bird shit everywhere. Mr. Sokolov gave her the set of ninety-nine earrings for ninety-nine cents that they sell at the back of *Teen Day Magazine*, and we each got a pair to take home. Mom usually says those kinds of earrings are junk that will turn your ears green, but she made me wear my dangly bananas to tennis the next week. "The Sokolovs don't have a lot of money," she said. "That was such a thoughtful thing for Petra's dad to do."

Mom looks at us with eyes all big and round like a kids' librarian. "Who knows where we'll land. Moving is an adventure. We're going to have fun with Mrs. Needham."

"That's very unlikely," I say.

When Dad moved out, it was hardly an adventure. He took me with him to steal milk crates from the A&P after dark. I watched for security guards while he piled the crates from the loading dock into the car. It was late February, and the wind smashed my face and made the tips of my ears feel poisoned. When he finally left, Dad tripped on the ice outside and dropped his stereo in front of the house. All the parts went springing everywhere. That was the only time I've seen him cry. I found some of the screws and stuff after the old snow melted. They're in a plastic baggie in my underwear drawer.

"Sick! Your meat has a rainbow on it!" Jed says. I look at the roast beef in my hands and see the shimmery strip through the middle. I fling it back on the platter.

"Cara!" Mom says. "Eat what you touch! Do you think meat is free?"

"It has a rainbow!"

Mom picks up the same piece and wraps it around a celery stick. She takes a bite and then hands the stick back to me. The celery is gross and raggedy where she bit. "Do you see me dying?"

At the end of the week, a sign goes up on our front lawn with a picture of the flamingo's face. She is resting her chin on her fist and smiling so wide it looks like she could swallow her head backwards. The sign says "#1 Sale: Here when you '*Needham*'!" I keep an eye out front while I'm bouncing my tennis ball after school, but nobody stops by to ask how much our house costs.

A few Saturdays after Mom's announcement, we have an open house again, which means strangers get to come over and look at all our personal stuff. I want to stay and see the people, but open houses are for everyone except the family who actually lives there.

I spend the afternoon at Sam's house, where I pretty much live on weekends anyway. Mom's always trying to get me to invite people from school over, but the girls in my class are either losers like Valerie Calorie, or too cool and pretty to be friends with anyone other than themselves. The fab five are the coolest girls: Erica B., Erica L., Ash, Jill, and Kyla. They all take gymnastics on Thursdays, wear Vuarnet, and pass each other fluorescent Post-it notes during class that Durant pretends not to see. Even she sucks up to them. I'm just waiting: eventually one of the girls will move away or get kicked out of the group for some reason, and they'll need a replacement to stay a fivesome. Until then, it's better to just hang out with Sam, whom no one knows, and just practise at being cool.

When Sam's mom is home, we usually bake or do crafts. When it's just Sam and me, we do the games that Sam makes up. Sometimes we pretend to be Jewish refugees and set up camps in the basement or the pool cabana. Sometimes we call people and tell them they'll win a cruise if they can guess Sam's teacher at Hebrew school, Mr. Leftin's, first name. It's Pinchus, so impossible to guess. We also have a band called *Scam*, which is our names put together. Our best song is "Pregnant again and just turned ten," even though I'm turning eleven in June. Today, Sam wants to have a séance in the basement while her mom is at Jazzercise.

The Grossmans' basement smells like damp cement and the whole space is rammed with junk: *World Books*, an old gerbil cage, Sam's baby furniture. Sam told me her parents are holding on to the baby stuff just in case, but their babies keep dying before they're born.

Sam and I sit cross-legged on a couple of dusty patio cushions next to the dryer. She sets her Mom's Shabbat candles in a circle around us, lighting each one with a mini pink Bic. We have to be pretty quiet because we're not totally alone. Violet, the Grossmans' Jamaican cleaning lady, is upstairs. Because of Violet, everything but the basement smells like limes.

Sam puts a white paper plate between us. With a black marker, she draws a star right in the middle. She calls it a pentagon. "Who do you want to bring back from the dead?" she asks. Her cheeks are orange from the candles.

I can't stop squirming around. I'm not exactly scared, just kind of nervous and excited to speak to ghosts. "I don't know."

"Do you know anyone who died?"

I think about Sam's mom's dead babies, but maybe that's too creepy. "What about Marcia Riley?" Marcia got kidnapped from her apartment building a few summers ago, and no one found her body. She went to swimming class at the same time as me, but she wasn't in my badge. The kidnapping was all over the newspaper for a while, and Mom practically wouldn't let me leave my room. By now it seems everyone's forgotten about her.

"I think it works better if it's someone we actually knew," Sam says. "Someone who'd want to talk to us."

I think for a minute. "My godmother died. I don't remember her that well, but she was my mom's best friend."

Sam's eyes widen. "Really? What was her name?"

"Debbie."

"Debbie what?"

"I don't remember. I was only like five when she kicked it." Most of what I remember about Debbie is the dying part.

"How did she die?"

"Car accident." Mom says her car broke down on the highway, and when she got out to flag help, some truck slid on the ice trying to stop and plowed right into her.

"Was she pretty?"

"I guess." There's a picture of her on top of our TV. She was a redhead with freckles. When I was a little kid, I used to draw her a lot because her hair was fat enough to use the whole brush of a Mr. Sketch.

"OK, let's do her."

Sam takes my hands and hers are sweaty. She scrunches her eyebrows together. "We're calling on the spirit of Debbie. Debbie, if you're there, give us a sign."

We sit for a minute, maybe more. Nothing happens.

I look at Sam. "What kind of sign?"

Sam glances around the room. "OK, Debbie. If you're here, make the flames flicker."

We keep our eyes open this time and try to concentrate on the candles, but it's hard to tell if they're flickering or not.

"Your turn," Sam whispers.

"What do I do?"

"Ask Debbie a yes or no question."

I don't know how Sam knows all these rules. "Is she even here?"

"Of course. Aren't you, like, way colder than before? It's the spirit passing through."

I can't tell if I'm colder, but maybe Sam's right. "Hi, Debbie…" I start to laugh; it's too weird talking out loud to a ghost.

"This is serious, Cara." Sam squeezes my hands.

I try to swallow the laughter. "OK, OK," I say, thinking hard. "Is Mom going to sell our house? Yes or no? Give us a sign."

We wait. I listen to the creak of Violet's footsteps upstairs. A toilet flushes somewhere and I hear the whoosh in the pipes. Was that a sign? I look at Sam, but she has her eyes closed tight. I concentrate on the flames, try to pay attention to everything around me. Upstairs, Violet is humming what sounds like Roy Orbison's "You Got It." Roy Orbison died last Christmas. I know because Mom was practically crying when she read it in the paper. "Somehow I thought he could never die," she said. I guess she was really into him when she was my age.

Violet's humming gets louder. *Are we selling the house?* You got it.

"Sam?"

"Shhh."

"It's the sign."

"What is?"

I let go of her hands. "Violet. The song." My heart is racing. Sam narrows her eyes. "What song?"

When the door swings open at the top of the stairs, Sam and I both scream. Like seriously scream, as if we were on a roller coaster.

Violet switches the light on. "What's going on down there?"

Sam rushes to blow out the candles, but Violet is already bumping down the steps with the vacuum cleaner. When she gets to the bottom, she looks only at me with her hand on her hip. Violet is a big woman with a permanent puddle of red in the corner of her eye. It's hard to ignore her. "We're just playing," I say.

"Playing at what?"

"Only a séance."

Sam looks at me like *shut up*. "A Shabbat," she says. "That's what Cara meant."

Violet grunts as she bends to pick the plate up off the floor. She looks back at me like everything's my fault. "Who teaches you to play games with the devil himself?"

"It's fine," Sam says.

"You silly, stupid girls." Violet pulls her gold crucifix out from her dress. She wraps her fist around the chain and holds the whole thing away from her chest. "Lord Jesus," she says, "please give these girls your white light of protection."

I glance at Sam. She turns her finger in a circle around the outside of her ear. She looks like she's trying not to laugh, but I don't think it's funny.

"Why do we need protection?" I ask.

Violet takes the necklace off and puts it on the laundry shelf, holding it down under a jumbo bottle of detergent. "The devil's always on your back," she says. "He's waiting for an invitation to your soul." She leaves the necklace dangling there as we follow her up the stairs.

Later, when Ruthie comes home, I expect Violet to tell on us but she doesn't. Ruthie invites me to stay for spaghetti bolognese, but I'm glad when Mom comes and takes me to Romeo's Pizza instead. She tells me there wasn't much interest in our house, which should make me happy, but I can't stop thinking about Violet's bulging fist clutching that crucifix away from her boobs.


It's hard to say exactly when, but a little while after the séance, I start getting scary thoughts. The sentence *Hell take my soul* starts barging into my head several times a day, right out of nowhere. I don't even know if I believe in hell or souls, but it doesn't matter, the thoughts still stick to my brain. It can happen anytime: when I see the picture of Debbie, if there's violence on TV, during the "Deliver us from evil" part of the Our Father prayer at school. Sometimes I think of my brain as a great big fishbowl. All my regular thoughts are little fish, spinning around and minding their own business. But the hell-thoughts are sharks. They eat up everything. I decide that if I do a little more door tapping at night—plus all the windows, plus everything in my room that's square—I might be able to save myself. But the sharks are vicious.

Mom smokes and smokes in the yard every night, even though she supposedly Quit4life and we even went to the sandwich party. I wonder what her fishes are while she sits there: does she miss Dad? Does she wonder what he's doing? Is she sad about the house? But every time I ask what she's thinking, she says that question never gets an honest answer. I know she's right. Once when she asked what I think about when I bounce my tennis ball against the house for hours and hours, I told her that I'm just practising to make it to Wimbledon. When Mom was around my age, she was already a major athlete, so I knew she'd like that answer. The truth is, though, mostly I make up stories about people I know. One of my favourite things is to make up stories about the kids in my class whose parents are divorced. I think about how their parents met and fell in love, and then I invent whatever went wrong. Usually when the parents meet in my stories, they have raincoats on and they laugh a lot and run hand-in-hand to catch buses or ferries or something. Then, ten years later, the father might disappear when he gets up to use the bathroom at the movie theatre. Or the mom might get caught with her boss in a hotel fire. Other times, I just think about Dan Bangor, my tennis teacher, which I'm not about to tell Mom. And I definitely wouldn't tell Mom about the hell thoughts. I'd have to explain everything about the séance and Debbie's ghost. She wouldn't like it. She never wants to talk about Debbie.

...

Mom says a family is coming back to see the house, so she makes Jed and me tidy everything. She bursts in while I'm brushing my hair in the bathroom. "There is toothpaste everywhere," she says. "It looks like a bird shit all over the sink!" She scrunches up a wad of toilet paper and rubs at the counter. "Your revolting stains can turn a buyer right off."

"Do you know who's coming?"

"Goddammit, Cara. What difference does it make?" She sighs and throws the tissues into the toilet bowl. "Just go get changed for tennis lessons."

"I am changed."

Mom looks up at my jean shorts and green tank top and rolls her eyes. Then she leaves me alone.

The flamingo has been at our house since before I woke up. She rolled big barrels of pink and white flowers into the yard and made a fan of magazines in the living room. Now she walks down the hallway blasting vanilla air freshener with two hands.

"I was just coming with these!" She hands me some fluffy yellow towels from under her arm. "It's amazing the difference some decent hand towels will make. Even in a bathroom that refuses to look clean!" She finishes spraying, sniffs, and then sighs like not even the whole can will get the house to smell good.

"Do people take showers here?" I ask.

"No, they do not. They just take a little boo. Test the bones—" I don't hear the rest of the description. It's just that word: bones. This morning I woke up feeling normal, but now the sharks are back.

"Well don't just stand there!" The flamingo takes the yellow towels back from me and hangs them in perfect squares on the rack. "There."

I tap the towels then chuck them in the bathtub as soon as she leaves.

Tennis lessons are always the best part of the week, but it's even better today because Petra Sokolov, my tennis enemy, is away. I've been worried lately because Petra told me Dan Bangor asked her out. I said there's no way that's true because Dan's twenty and she's only twelve. She said Dan doesn't mind how old she is because she has a lot of maturity. "Plus," she said, "he likes my hair. Not just the hair on my head." Then she burst out laughing.

The tar court is so hot it feels like it's melting around my running shoes. Dan Bangor invents a game called "Beat the Heat," where only the champion gets to play on the shady side. I am the champ every time. After a while, no one except me wants to play anymore so I get to hit alone with Dan while the other kids practise air band with his new portable stereo. Dan has skin the colour of chewy caramels and he plays with his T-shirt tucked into the back of his shorts. He has muscles like great big cables in his back.

"Your overhead's looking awesome," Dan says, taking a long sip of water from a bottle before dumping the rest on his head. "Most girls can't get any power."

"Thanks," I say, but quietly, because it's hard to talk in a regular voice around Dan.

"But you need to practise your groundstrokes."

I tell him that where I practise tennis at the side of the house there isn't much actual ground.

Dan shakes out his hair and water drops spray my T-shirt. "Find a brick wall or a garage door and just give 'er, you know?" I nod and he crouches to my level, pointing two fingers at his eyeballs. There's a strip of pink zinc on his nose. "Visualize, OK? See your opponent and just hammer the ball where she won't expect it."

At the end of the lesson, the other kids do a lip-synch using Dan's stereo. The guys stand in the back, holding their racquets like guitars. The girls put tennis balls underneath their shirts to make tits and use the ends of their racquets for microphones. They don't take tennis seriously like Dan and me. While they do Madonna's "Like a Prayer," I pick at the cracks on the court and pray that one day Dan and me will get married. Mom's always saying people shouldn't get married too young, but in eight years I'll be practically twenty and Dan will be twenty-eight. I won't ever fall out of love with him, so he'll never have to trip and smash his stereo and cry his eyes out.

When we get home from tennis, a man is standing on our front steps talking to the flamingo. At the slam of the car door, both of them turn around and I see the man's face. Mr. Sokolov.

Petra and her sister Marta come flying out our front door. "Hi, Cara!" Petra says. There are Cheezies in her braces. "If we move here, I'm getting your room."

"No. Stamped it!" Marta says. She has a long shiny nose and the same stickuppy bangs as Petra. I want to mash my racquet into her face.

Petra sits down on the stoop like she already owns the place. "Dan miss me today?"

"No."

I go past them through the yard with my tennis racquet. The ugly barrels of flowers take up all my space, so I dodge around them, smashing the ball. I realize that I didn't have a single hell-thought the whole time I was at tennis. The Sokolovs destroyed that. I let the ball land in front of me for a groundstroke and then whip it back up, spraying the stupid flowers out from one of the barrels. The ball bounces back to me and I spin around and smack it in an unexpected direction just like Dan said, but it hits the screen door. There's the quietest crack, then the glass crushes inward all at once. I run up to the gate to see if anyone saw, but the Sokolovs are jamming themselves into a car, and Mom is waving goodbye with a big dumb grin on her face. I go back and collect as many of the pink flowers as I can and squish the stems back into the barrel.

Mom comes over to the yard once the car drives away. I start to cry before she even sees anything. I can't help it.

"What is it, sweetie?"

I go right to her, burying my head in the crook of her arm. Her cool dampness feels good on my hot cheeks. "I don't like the Sokolovs."

She runs her hand up and down my back. "The Sokolovs are lovely people," she says. "Their family is growing." They're growing, but we're shrinking.

"This is our house." My teeth are jammed together. It's not fair that the Sokolovs get to live here just because their father is still at home.

"Cara, anything can be our house," Mom says. "We're lucky that way."

"They broke our door."

"They did what?" Mom lets go of my shoulders and I hold my breath and wait. She walks to the glass and pushes it gently with her sneaker: jagged pieces rain down like icicles. She stands back but shields her hands around her face to see in. "Where's your tennis ball?"

"I don't know."

She turns back to me. "I'm going to ask you one more time."

I can't even look at her.

"No tennis lessons this summer to cover the cost."

I smack my racquet down hard on the rim of a barrel. Mom comes over and grabs me by the shoulders. She squeezes so hard it pinches. "I know this isn't easy, Cara. But for Christ's sake, don't make it worse."

That night, I can't fall asleep even after three rounds of tapping. The hell-sharks are eating up every other fish in my brain. If I were little, I'd go sleep in Mom's bed, but I haven't done that in years. If I tried it now, she'd want to know what's wrong, but it's too much to explain. She'd think I was going crazy, on top of already being mad at me.

I get out of bed to see if Jed's awake and wants to do something, anything, but I hear him snoring through the door. I listen, like I used to when I was little, wondering if his breathing sound can still put me to sleep. I try to make my breath do what his does. Up and down, in and out. A little while later, Mom shakes my shoulders. "I think you were sleepwalking, sweetheart," she says. "Let's go back to bed."

After school the next day, Mom's on the phone with the flamingo non-stop. She keeps talking about "the number," like "What happened to my number?" and "That's not the number we talked about—" Jed and I listen from the kitchen where we're both pretending to do homework.

"The Sokolovs aren't going to buy it," I tell Jed. "They're too poor."

He shrugs. "Petra Sokolov says she got 896 on Breakout."

Breakout is my favourite arcade game. It's like playing tennis against a wall: you knock down as many bricks as you can with a paddle and ball.

"She's lying. They only have Dragon's Lair. I even went to her ugly apartment, so I know."

"She says they got a Commodore 64," Jed says. "So they can probably play whatever they feel like."

"Do you think we'll get a computer when we move?"

"No. Mom's cheap," Jed says.

When Mom looks over at us, it's like she forgets I'm supposed to be in trouble. She pulls a twenty from her purse and tells me to get an extra large with olives on half.

On my walk to Romeo's Pizza, I notice that a house on the end of our street has a "Here when you 'Needham!' sign, too. It's the same one we have on our lawn, except it says "Sold". I stop and examine the house. It's bigger than ours with a pretty row of trees out front. The car in the driveway looks more expensive than Mom's, but that's not the main thing. The main thing is the driveway itself, which is long and wide with a garage door at the end of it. It's perfect for groundstrokes. I run all the way to Romeo's. What if Mom wants to surprise us? What if we're getting a bigger house? A way better house with a huge garage door for bouncing.

That night, I wait until I see Mom's bright orange cigarette tip from my bedroom window. I take my wallet from the top of my dresser and go join her outside. She tries to hide her cigarette behind her back when she sees me, but it's too late. "I'm sorry, honey," she says. "I know I shouldn't do this."

"That's OK." I sit next to her on the grass in my nightgown, one of Dad's old T-shirts. Since I caught her doing something bad, there's a better chance she'll forgive me about the door.

"I'm going to miss the lilacs," she says, taking a deep breath in with her nose. "Don't you love that smell?"

I sniff hard at the air but all I can smell is the smoke whirling up from between her fingers. "Are you still mad about the door?"

She rolls her cigarette on the edge of her ashtray, shaping the burning end into a cone. "I'm disappointed you lied."

I put my wallet on her lap. "There's $12.19."

"That's thoughtful."

I take a quick breath. "Can I please do tennis this summer?"

She leans back and tilts her chin to the sky. "I don't know, Cara."

"I'll never play near glass again." I want to tell her about the hell-thoughts, that maybe I need tennis to stop thinking about hell, but I just can't explain.

Mom takes another big puff of her cigarette and blows the smoke out in a straight line. "I know this is a lot of change, Cara," she says finally. "A lot for your age. I'm sorry for that."

I hug my knees up to my chest and tap my chin against them seven times. I wonder if Mom remembers being my age. I've seen exactly one photo of her from around my age, and it was in a really old newspaper. In the picture, she's standing up to her knees in a lake, wearing a white bathing cap and a swimsuit with a strip of maple leaves down the side. "I don't mind change," I say.

Mom laughs then coughs. "Oh, really?" She crushes her cigarette into the ashtray.

I look around the yard. "Yeah."

Right in front of where we're sitting used to be a metal climbing dome that Mom and Dad built. When Mom took it apart, I cried seeing all the coloured ribs on the ground. I hadn't climbed on it forever, but I didn't want to be too old for it. I didn't want to get old. Mom said it was important not to think that way. "Not all the good things are in the past," she said. "Especially not for you. You just don't know what's ahead yet."

When we go inside, Mom tucks me into bed and I ask her to leave the door open. I feel like hearing Jed breathe while I'm falling asleep, even if I can't hear that much.


On the last day of school before summer holidays, Mom tells us to wait for her at three thirty because there's a place she wants us to see. When Mrs. Durant asks everyone what they're doing for the holidays, it doesn't even bother me when Petra brags about moving into my house.

Durant asks where my family is going to go and everyone looks at me. I want to keep the secret, I really do, but I can't hold it in. "Well," I say, turning my tennis racquet against the hard orange carpet, "pretty much a mansion."

"A mansion, Cara?" Durant says. "Seriously?" She bunches up her face like she doesn't believe me for a second.

I look at Petra. "Maybe you can come over." I give her a not-very-nice smile and look to see if one of the Ericas is listening. "It practically has a tennis court."

I'm hopping from foot to foot when Mom shows up in the parking lot at three thirty.

"What's up with you?" Mom says.

"Shotgun!" I walk to her car, but the passenger door is locked. I look up, but she's just standing there.

"We're only crossing the street," she says.

Jed and I look across at the apartment tower opposite the school. Dirty white, a million windows, disgusting. No one lives there. She can't be serious. I roll my eyes. "Funny."

"There's a stylish three-bedroom I'd like you to see on the seventh floor."

I point my racquet at the building. "There?"

"Yes, here."

"I'm not living there."

"Hey," she says. "We're just taking a look. There's a pool."

"Probably filled with Band-Aids." I know this will hurt her feelings, but I don't care. She should know how disgusting this whole idea is.

"When you see your new room, I think you'll change your mind."

"My new room? What happened to just taking a look."

I look at Jed. He shrugs. "I know a guy who lives there," he says. "They have Super Breakout in the tuck shop."

If people see me go into that building, they'll think I was lying about the house with the garage. They'll think we're poor. I shake my head.

Mom takes in a big breath and lets it out slowly. "You know, I thought you were starting to look forward to this."

I want to smack Mom in the shins with my racquet. "If you make us move there, I'll go live with Dad."

Mom laughs. "We'll see how that works out for you."

"I swear."

Mom sighs and hikes her purse up on her shoulder. "You have a choice, Cara. Come in with Jed and me, take a look, give your informed opinion—"

"Or?" I look at the white bricks, stained like the teeth in a denture commercial before the fizzy pill goes in. I want to Super Breakout the whole thing.

She squints at me. "Or you can stay right here, have no say whatsoever, and act like a big baby."

"Stay here."

"Fine," Mom says, turning toward the road.

Jed looks at me. "You're really not coming?"

"Not in a million years."

And then Mom and Jed leave me. They cross the street, climb the few steps to the building's main doors, and disappear. Mom doesn't look back for me once.

The schoolyard is almost empty now. I lean against the car's hot metal, squeezing the rough strings of my racquet. Across the street, an old woman in a grey coat waddles up the front steps with a bunch of plastic bags hooked to her wrists. I don't want to live near people like that; you shouldn't wear a coat in June.

A truck pulls up in the space next to Mom's, and some song about a highway to hell is blaring from the radio. I grit my teeth and jam my eyes shut, trying to build a wall around my brain, trying to stop hell from coming in. I walk around Mom's car, tapping my racquet on the doors and windows seven times each, but what's the point? The worst things are already happening. And what if I made them happen? My whole body feels sweaty and hollow. I want Mom and Jed to come back out and say, "Whoops! That was a mistake!" But they just stay and stay.

When I glance back at the building, I see Jed up on one of the balconies. He looks very small from here. I wave, but he doesn't see me. I jump up and swat my tennis racquet in the air.

A man gets out of the truck and looks at me. He says, "You got a problem there?" His eyes are red and watery and there's a blue tattoo of a dripping knife on his inside arm. I can hear a little kid crying in the back of his truck. He says, "Jesus Christ. Knock it off, Angelo." I rush across the street.

Standing on the sidewalk in front of the building, I look up at the balconies again, but I can't see Jed from underneath. I can't hear him breathe and my heart is hammering inside my chest. I try to count seven floors to where he is, but it's easy to lose count when everything looks the same. I take seven breaths, one for every floor. I can't hear the music anymore, and I try not to look back at the truck across the street. My heart calms down, but only just a little.

I don't want Mom to come out and see me in front of the building, so I move over to the quiet, shadier side where the windows don't start until high up. I pull a tennis ball from my backpack, take seven steps back, and whack it hard against the brick. Stupid building. The ball comes off the wall with a soft thump, and I slice it with a two-handed backhand, a loud grunt exploding from deep inside me. I'm at Wimbledon and the grimy brick is Petra with her ugly stick-up bangs. I smash the ball as hard as I can. A brown man in one of the high-up windows is looking down at me, his hand resting on his chin. I think of the applause and the British voices on TV: *"She's incredible! So small, so strong!"* My heart speeds up and I fly to the right, just in time to fire an unexpected return.

# Girl Friday

SUMMER, 1991

**B**efore driving home from Mississauga, Ian suggested dinner at the Veranda, a California-themed restaurant next to the Holiday Inn where he and Lorna had just held focus groups. The dining room at the Veranda had five extra large TVs showing extreme surfing and extreme skiing, but Lorna and Ian found a table outside on the actual veranda. It was a balmy evening in late spring; the strip of trees separating the restaurant from the parking lot was in pure green fluorescence.

Lorna ordered a glass of Chardonnay and a chicken caesar. Ian ordered potato skins and a diet ginger ale. He had been in alcohol rehabilitation once in his early thirties and then again, nine years ago, after his fortieth birthday. This was all before Lorna knew him. She was used to drinking alone, with him.

A delivery truck pulled up next to the veranda, and Lorna looked at their reflections in its large rear window. She did the thing she liked to do sometimes, which was to imagine she was someone else, watching herself and Ian out for dinner. *Now, see. There's a couple who stayed in love. Look how interested they are in each other's opinions. How respectful. Equals in every way.* Ian was married, and she and he weren't in any way *involved*, but

Lorna acknowledged that she'd like to, someday, meet a man *like* Ian. Distinguished, ambitious, tall: everything that Alex hadn't been; everything she hoped her children would become. Well, the tall was less important, though it might give them more confidence. When Lorna was with Ian, she liked running into people she knew, and she tended to avoid detailed introductions. "This is Ian," she'd say, mysteriously, letting her dentist or swim acquaintance draw their own conclusions. A smile, paired with an enthusiastic, "I'd like you to meet Ian!" produced the same effect. Nearly fifty now, Ian still resembled a youthful Burt Lancaster. Quick grey-blue eyes, plenty of hair, a straight nose that was only lightly spider-veined in the crevices. He had a habit of squinting that showed both how closely he listened and how neatly his eyelids folded at the corners.

Ian relaxed into his chair. "That went well." He started conversations when he was good and ready. Until then, there wasn't much point in saying anything at all.

"Sure," Lorna agreed. They'd been testing reactions to a political ad with an emphasis on service-sector job creation. Ian facilitated; Lorna sat on the other side of a two-way mirror and made sure the clients had enough bottled water. For years, she'd taken meticulous notes for Ian, but he rarely asked for these, so she'd stopped bothering. Ian drew his own conclusions. He often made things up, quite frankly, but they were usually clever, useful things. Lorna's forte, her reason for being there, was what Ian called "client effervescence." She was a terrific host, he said, and because clients felt so comfortable with her, they automatically trusted him. Hostessing wasn't something that came naturally to Lorna, but for Ian's sake she was happy to pretend. She did her best to recall clients' favourite sports teams, recent vacations, children's graduations. Hostessing made her feel like a whole other kind of woman, someone Alex and her children wouldn't recognize.

"They hated the fat woman," Ian said. "Put a beautiful woman in an ad and people get their knickers in a knot. Say they're being manipulated. Put the uglies in, they complain twice as much. And you can't just use a man." He sucked his drink to the bottom. "Not on employment."

"How about a woman who looks like a man?" Lorna said. "A handsome woman." But she didn't feel like working. A jaunty song was playing over the restaurant speakers. The Beach Boys, or a new group like them. She watched a little white dog with a pale pink tummy roll in the grass a few feet away.

"A handsome woman," Ian repeated, lighting a cigarette. He smoked with such physical animation that Lorna felt she could see the smoke descend to his lungs, catch, and turn over before coming back out again in a neat line. He looked better smoking than anyone she'd ever seen. Compared to Ian, everyone else looked like they were faking it. "I wouldn't know any of those."

Was that a wink? Sometimes it was hard to tell with Ian. Lorna glanced back over at the grass. "Maybe I'll get a little dog," she said quickly. "When the kids go to university."

Ian glanced vaguely at the dog and then looked back at Lorna. "So," he said. "I've been meaning to mention something."

"What's that?"

"A rumour at the office. Something very silly, actually." He knocked a fleck of ash off his shirt. "They're saying that you and I are, let's say, unprofessionally involved."

Was Ian now so good at reading people that he could tell what she'd been thinking moments ago? She felt heat pumping into her neck and face. Her certainty that the blushing would not escape Ian's notice made it all the more intense. "Sorry?"

She was relieved that Ian didn't repeat himself. "Like I said, it's silly. But I think you know what I mean. Marcus raised it with me last week." Marcus O'Connor, the *O* of OpinioNation Ltd. (Ian Needham was the *N*), was thought to be the most reliable pollster in the country. People said he could smell rain underwater.

Ian offered Lorna his cigarette across the table. She shook her head. She hadn't had a cigarette in nearly a year. He took another drag. "Because, apparently, we both extended our trip to New York last month by precisely one night."

"But that's not so strange."

They had both extended their trips, but for entirely different reasons. Lorna's high school swim team had a reunion. Ian was meeting an agent about a book proposal; she didn't know the first thing about his book.

Ian sighed. "I gather that people were just looking for proof," he said. "To make sense, I suppose, of our closeness."

"But we're a team."

Lorna was the office research coordinator. Ian was the top qualitative research guy in the city, an oracle for public opinion. But everyone knew he was lost without Lorna. In a game at the office Christmas party, Lorna was voted least likely to say, "That's not my job," and Ian was voted most likely to say, "Someone get me Lorna!" Privately, Ian referred to Lorna as his Girl Friday. This past Christmas, he'd given her a pen with this moniker engraved.

"So you told Marcus that's crazy."

Ian sat back in his chair, cigarette tipped up. "Is it? Crazy?"

"Silly, then." Lorna wasn't the least bit sure how to respond. As Ian leaned forward to tap his ash, for a heart-stopping second, she thought he might kiss her.

Ian leaned back and pushed the hair off his forehead. "Anyway, I think you ought to know what's being said."

"All right. Do you think I need to be concerned?"

Ian tilted his head to one side. "On a scale of one to seven, where one is extremely concerned and seven is not concerned at all, I'd suggest a four, maybe a five. Because the other reason to mention it, Lorna, is I'd like to promote you." He put the cigarette down on the little foil ashtray and folded his hands in front of him. "To be our new operations gal. I think it would be unfortunate for both of us if there were uncharitable speculation as to why."

"But what about Doug?" was all Lorna could think to say. Doug was currently in charge of operations: a huffy creep with a habit of picking his scalp and sniffing his fingers. Very likely, Doug was the source of the rumours about her and Ian. His job, which as far as Lorna could tell involved distributing timesheets and ordering telephones—tasks that seemed to make him furious to have to perform—did not include anything Lorna had ever expressed interest in.

Ian swiped the cloud of smoke in front of him, shooing away the idea of Doug. "I think you're the one for the job."

"I'm flattered," Lorna said

"I hoped you'd be pleased." Ian crossed one leg over the other, his feet jutting into the aisle between tables.

"I am. Pleased."

He glanced at the approaching waitress. "And I wonder, in that case, if we oughtn't to behave very professionally."

"Let me think about it," Lorna said.

Ian let out something between a snort and a laugh. "Oh?"

Lorna shook her head. "About the job, I mean." A new layer of heat sank into her face.

"Well, I hope we'll agree."

"Yes." Lorna agreed, but to what? The job? The end of dinners like this?

Ian smiled at the waitress, and she set down his food. He raised his empty ginger ale glass with a little shake. "Thank you, love."


Within ten days, Lorna began her new job in operations. She managed timesheets and reviewed the budgets. She reorganized the file cabinet and supply cupboards. She also got a small bump in pay. Her new office, an upgrade from the front desk, had a clear glass wall facing the corridor. To the people walking by, Lorna had the sense she was either too visible or completely transparent. Every morning, Ian tapped the glass with his fingertips, making Lorna feel like an oversized goldfish in a Chinese restaurant. This tapping was part of the shift to unnaturally distant behaviour between them, the sort of behaviour Lorna imagined you'd put on if you *were* having an affair.

This, Lorna had to admit, wasn't an entirely unwelcome idea. Since the conversation at the Veranda, she had turned the possibility of actual Ian, not someone *like* Ian, over in her mind. And why not wonder, if everyone else was wondering? When he drove her home from Mississauga that night in his red Saab convertible, she let the sun press down on her eyelids and pretended they were on their way to his house in the country: in her imagination, the sort of distant red barn she was asked to identify through a scope at her annual eye exam. But unlike at the eye doctor, Lorna wasn't sure how clear she wanted the picture to be.

If it weren't for Libby, Ian's wife, the spiky-haired woman responsible for selling Lorna's house above asking, maybe Lorna would allow herself to imagine things clearly. Libby was doughy faced in the way that spikey-haired middle-aged women tended to be, but she was the type people called "a firecracker": bright, energetic, not to be messed with. Funny, Lorna thought, how men were never called firecrackers. Ian, certainly, would never be called one. He was the most coolheaded person Lorna had ever known. Self-possessed, unflappable. He would never get carried away, and so he would never leave Libby. Still, when the office air conditioning was too intense, Lorna found herself holding warm photocopies to her ribs, imagining Ian's heat.

The very week Lorna moved to her new office, Lizbeth Kotsakos came on as Lorna's front-desk replacement and research coordinator. Chosen by Ian and Marcus, Lizbeth was fresh out of community college with a diploma in business administration. She would take over Lorna's role assisting Ian with focus groups, eating dinners in suburbia, riding in the Saab. As the staff gathered for her introduction, she explained that she was looking for a role where her people skills would shine. "To me, it's gotta be people before paper," she said and nodded at her remark repeatedly. She was a plump girl with a soft, smiley face and a preference for bright skirts and frilly blouses with elaborate clasping systems. In Lorna's view, Lizbeth laughed too much. Ian, for example, was hilarious, but it was the sort of humour that took truly knowing him to laugh as hard as Lizbeth did. And Lizbeth's laugh was truly awful; it sounded very much like an orgasm. That was the first thing Lorna didn't like about her.

The second thing that Lorna didn't like was Lizbeth's failure to observe the limits of what was appropriate for her role. Lorna noticed it first during Lizbeth's training. The girl nodded earnestly as Lorna went over the steps of how to book focus group facilities, how to read cross-tabulated data, and the little tasks that would fall to her, like where to order birthday cakes and flowers, but Lizbeth's mind wasn't focused on the task.

"Wow," Lizbeth said, combing her fingers through her bangs. Lorna smelt dewberry, the cloying scent also favoured by her thirteen-year-old daughter. "How long did you do this job for again?"

"Four years."

"Holy."

"Holy what?"

Lizbeth swivelled in her chair. "Nothing, sorry. But I think, for me, this will be like a one-year thing. I want to just sponge it all up. Next year I want to be, like, moderating focus groups, doing interviews. Really be in the guts of it."

Lorna shook her head. "I don't know, Lizbeth. Marcus and Ian – all the associates, actually – have very advanced degrees in psychology."

Lizbeth scrunched her lips to one side and shook her head. "No," she said. "Ian is self-taught."

"Sorry?"

"He told me he's not a book guy." Lizbeth laughed as though the memory was of a truly witty exchange. "He said there's nothing to it. Just smoke and mirrors."

"Well," Lorna said. "Ian's sort of a genius. Geniuses make the impossible look effortless; that's their trick."

"But he started pretty young, so I figure that—"

"Before you were born," Lorna interrupted. "Still, it's a very *Gordian* thing." Lorna was pleased with finding a word that Lizbeth most likely didn't know. She hadn't known it until she met Ian. "They say he can squeeze blood from a stone." A client had described him that way once. Ian would find a better way to describe his talents. Stones didn't have blood. Or was that the point?

"I can't wait to just sit and watch," Lizbeth said, starry-eyed.

"Well. You'll be pretty busy with the details. You need to keep the clients happy back there. Keep them fed and watered. Be useful and friendly." The chaste chirp in Lorna's voice reminded her of Mary Poppins: all spit-spot. She didn't even speak this way to her children.

Lizbeth nodded. "That also."

"That's the job." Lorna filled the silence with a throaty laugh that she felt made her sound about seventy-five. Lizbeth had a jaunty orgasm.

Laziness was the third thing that Lorna didn't like. Lizbeth let things slide. Ten days after she started the job, Lorna returned from a dentist appointment to find Lizbeth in the break room, eating and chatting with Pat and Cory, two of the younger associates. Lorna herself never took lunch in the break room, but that wasn't what bugged her. The problem was the kitchen.

Cupboards and drawers blaring open, cutlery and dishes stacked in the sink, smeared with all manner of sauces. Ground coffee was folded up in a sopping wet filter on the counter like a discarded diaper. Briskly, Lorna closed the cupboard doors and filled the sink. Cleaning up was everyone's responsibility, sure, but now it was really Lizbeth's.

As Lorna pulled up her sleeves to wash the dishes, Ian popped his head in. "Seen Lizzie?"

Lorna shook the dish soap and squirted it into the sink. "If you find her, I could use her help in here."

Ian looked around, not appearing to register anything out of place in the scene in front of him. "Apparently she was looking for me."

Why wasn't he telling her to put that dish down? They both knew she had bigger fish to fry in her see-through office. Lorna scrubbed the hollow of a glass, her bracelet knocking hard against the rim. The skin at the bends in her fingers looked baggy. Lorna clinked the glass into the drying rack.

"How do you think she's settling?" Ian asked.

"Lizbeth?"

"Yeah."

"She seems very comfortable."

"She has a great energy."

What did that even mean, Lorna wondered. That she was young? "She's young," Lorna said.

Ian leaned against the doorframe. "She was great with the cellular phone groups. She's developing your knack with clients."

"How is Howard?" Lorna's voice was coming out louder than she wanted. "Did his son get into theatre school?"

"I have no idea."

"Well do ask him next time. Tell him hello."

"All right." Ian paused. "I'm sure you don't miss all that."

"I do."

Lorna did miss focus groups. They were always full of surprises. She'd seen a grown man cry once over a proposed change to a sport team logo. Once, in a discussion about health insurance, a woman had removed her shoes and socks to show Ian a festering toenail. Others in the office complained about groups gobbling up their evenings, but it was hard for Lorna to know what to do now with her extra time at home. The kids had learned to get along without her after school. They had their TV programs, glossy magazines, friends to talk with on the phone. They made their own weekend plans and their own lunches for school. They cheered at pizza money on her nights at work, and rolled their eyes at whatever casserole she tried to cook the next night to make up for it.

"You should sit down with Liz," Ian said. "Let her in on some of your secrets."

Lorna turned right around to face Ian. "I'm sorry about the paper plates this morning, by the way."

"Plates?"

She shook her head. "I told Lizbeth we have perfectly good ceramic plates when we're having clients in. I'm not even sure where she found the paper stuff. Anyway, I'll remind her. Won't happen again."

Ian handed her his empty water glass. "Sure."

...

Ian and Lorna had scheduled their first budget meeting for the last day of the month. For Lorna, doing budgets was both tense and boring: she was paranoid about mistakes but impatient about checking her work. It was the worst part of her job, but she looked forward to the meeting. Perhaps they could make it a lunch thing? Would a sandwich together at noon really constitute grounds for "uncharitable speculation"?

On May 31, Lorna updated her reports and waited for Ian to tap on the glass. As May rolled into June, and then June became hot, she still waited. Every morning, she fixed the date on the top of the report and printed two copies. Around ten a.m., she made a point to run a brush through her hair and refresh her lipstick.

When Ian finally stopped in her doorway and motioned for her to follow him, Lorna found that she was nervous. The two of them hadn't sat down together since the evening at the Veranda. The utterance of "unprofessionally involved" felt a million miles away.

In his office, Lorna came close to delivering the tongue-in-cheek joke she'd been planning for a while: "On a scale of one to seven, where one is extremely likely and seven is not likely at all, how likely is it that they're whispering about us right now?" But from the moment she walked in, Ian was all business. He reached for her folder and put on his reading glasses. He read her report silently, chewing one of the mint-flavoured toothpicks he kept in a crystal shot glass on his desk. She sat across from him, nervously kicking her feet. She glanced around the office, noting, not for the first time, that there were no pictures of Libby. Not even the desk calendar she sent to her clients. Once at a cocktail party at the Needhams, Lorna had casually scanned the house for photo evidence that Libby had at least once been pretty – Ian's equal. She stopped short of entering their bedroom.

"Looks good enough," Ian said finally.

"That's it?"

"Well, let's see if we can't keep the summer party budget to twenty-five a head."

"I'll talk to Lizbeth about it."

"Her hands are pretty full, but it's a good thought. She could have some contemporary ideas."

Lorna's jaw tightened. "But it's her job. The research coordinator organizes the summer party."

"Ah," Ian said. "Is that written up somewhere?" He winked, but not in a kind way.

"I always juggled it."

"I trust you'll figure this out." Ian tossed out his toothpick and replaced it with a new one.

Lorna looked past him at the lake out his window. "Sailing started yet?" In the summertime, the two of them had a standing Friday date watching the sailboats race around Toronto Island. Anyone was welcome to come and watch, but Lorna was the only regular.

"Lorna," he leaned in. "I've been thinking..."

Lorna also leaned. The gurgle of his water cooler masked her sudden stomachy sounds. It had been so long since she'd heard him say her name.

Ian leaned back just as suddenly and jiggled his wrist, correcting the position of a gold watch. "You know what? I've taken enough of your time, and I need to give someone a call back at the attorney general's office."

Lorna didn't move while he reached for the phone receiver. He raised an eyebrow as he began to dial. The eyebrow said: *Why are you still here?*

The OpinioNation summer party was always at Anthony's, a tasteful after-work bar close to the office. Lorna relayed Ian's directive to Lizbeth, mentioning a range of favourite appetizers she could pre-order to keep individual meal costs down. But at the end of the week, Lizbeth sent out a memo that the party would be at the Latin Palace in the east end. The memo said "It's Time to Party Hardy!"

When Lorna approached Lizbeth's desk with the memo in hand, she found Lizbeth cutting a paper report into slips the size of fortune cookie messages. The mahogany front desk looked like an arts and crafts table.

"I checked into Anthony's," Lizbeth explained, "but Latin Palace has a happy hour, so it's a way better deal."

"Ian doesn't drink," Lorna said.

"He's not the only one. Plus he said it sounded terrific."

Lorna looked at her, an angry rhythm starting in her pulse. "Ian doesn't have time to get tangled up in these sorts of questions. Next time, come to me."

Lizbeth's face purpled. "He said you didn't want anything to do with it. Anyway, it's a totally good place. Swear."

"I'm sure," Lorna said. She looked down at Lizbeth's project. "So why are you slicing up Ian's focus group report?"

"Oh! It's my report," Lizbeth said. "We talked to these people about getting cell phones, right? For Celluphone? I'm looking for themes." She cupped her hands around a little mound of paper. "All of these quotes are about price. You know how people always say, 'No way, cellular phones cost too much,' right?"

"I have no idea, Lizbeth. I wasn't there."

"But then, see, that much bigger pile is what people say about convenience, like..."

"Interesting." Lorna said, her eyes moving down the hall.

Lizbeth wasn't discouraged. "Because, think about it. If you had a phone, your kids could call in an emergency. That kind of stuff really appeals to people in your age category. So even though we thought price was, like, too big a barrier? Well..." Lizbeth had a lazy way of talking, a mushy mouth. And was she too bored to finish her sentences?

"What exactly is my age category?" Lorna asked.

"Oh," Lizbeth said. "Moms, I guess?"

"Never mind. Why don't you just use two different coloured highlighters to separate the ideas? Seem easier."

"It helps to see the ideas next to each other," Lizbeth said. "Ian and I talked about it after the groups. And did you know he's colour blind?"

"Of course," Lorna said, although she didn't know.

"Actually," Lizbeth said. "I wanted to ask you. Ian said to ask you. I know I'm supposed to be here at reception all the time, but I thought maybe I could take this afternoon off and shadow Ian for his ride-alongs?" Lizbeth was practically honking with excitement. "We're going to watch how people use their phones in their cars in real situations!"

Lorna shook her head. She couldn't help it. "Marcus has two standing meetings on Wednesdays that need prep. You can't be out of the office."

Lizbeth nodded. "Sure. But I thought maybe you could cover for—"

Lorna's whole body tensed. "Unfortunately, Lizbeth, that's really not my job."

Lizbeth's face dropped, but only for a moment. It gave Lorna a guilty poke in the gut, but she relished it all the same. "I'm sorry," she said, softening her tone. "Maybe another day."

Lizbeth nodded. "Also, Ian thought maybe you could make me flashcards?"

"Flashcards?"

"Well, cards were my idea. But he thinks I need to learn the little things. Clients' wives names, that sort of thing."

Lorna shook her head. "I don't think that's necessary. They don't expect you to know that sort of thing yet. It's far too intimate."

On the first Thursday of July, the small gang of OpinioNation employees sat unsteadily on plastic patio furniture, drinking sangria and shooing mosquitos on the upper deck of Latin Palace. Calypso music bumped from mounted plastic speakers.

"Charming," Ian said, squeezing past Lorna to the head of the table. He dusted off his chair before placing his suit jacket around the back.

Lorna shook her head. "I didn't pick it."

"It's very youthful. Cheap, surely."

Lizbeth had gone home to change after work and was reappearing now in a strapless daisy print dress, so tight around the top that her breasts appeared to be packed down into sausages. "What do you think?" she asked, beaming.

"It's loud," Lorna said.

"Look at you, getting old!" Ian winked at Lorna and then turned to Lizbeth. "It's extraordinary." He glanced over at the far end of the table and lowered his voice. "But would one of you mind joining Marcus?" He looked specifically at Lorna.

At the far end of the section reserved for their group, Lorna saw that Marcus was, in his strange high-pitched way, asking a waitress to wipe the bird shit from the edge of the table. Marcus was impossible to have a conversation with. He either didn't speak, or spoke all at once and too quickly, without eye contact. You couldn't even ask about his wife and family without feeling like you were making him uncomfortable. Lorna sighed, not quietly. She was wearing her favourite green pumps and just had her streaks done that morning; it would all be wasted babysitting Marcus. "I'll do the first shift," she said to Lizbeth.

For half an hour, at the quieter end of the table, Lorna drank the sugary sangria, listening to Marcus speak, mainly to his fork, about a regression analysis that showed declining views of Progressive Conservatives. It was nearly impossible to imagine how he'd managed a conversation with Ian about "unprofessional involvement."

On the fun side of the table, which Lorna now recognized was the young side, with the exception of Ian, Lorna could hear Lizbeth laughing uproariously. "Crazyass!" Lizbeth nearly shouted. Lorna had heard Lizbeth use this expression before. It gave her the same shuddery feeling she got when she imagined running her teeth across a dry napkin. What bothered her wasn't the "ass." Lorna swore around her colleagues all the time. It was that, at twenty-two, or however old Lizbeth was, she felt entitled to swear, to wear bold things, and to assume she could do someone else's job. She was unapologetically herself, and Lorna believed her to still have the kind of unfinished self one should at least try to conceal and be quick to apologize for.

Renata, a middle-aged analyst with a terrible ducktail haircut, slid over next to Lorna. She wore rectangular hot pink earrings, which were clearly her idea of how to "party hardy."

"You pick this place? It's funky," Renata said. Lorna loathed the term "funky." It seemed to reside exclusively in the vocabularies of women over forty-five, trying to seem hip.

"Nope, not my job." Lorna kept her eyes on the far end of the table, trying to get Lizbeth's attention for the switch off. "Not anymore."

"Do you miss it?" Renata dunked her finger into a plastic pot of ranch dressing. "Your old job?"

"Parts."

"It's funny," Renata said. "I never really pictured you in ops."

Lorna turned toward her colleague. What did she mean? Was it possible that Renata was one of the uncharitable speculators? Did she think Lorna didn't deserve her new role?

"I've been here five years," Lorna said. "I know this place upside down and backwards, so."

Renata nodded energetically. "Right, I know. I just kind of thought he was grooming you for research." She jerked her chin in Ian's direction.

"He thought I'd be good in Ops."

"I'll bet you are. But don't you think we could really use more women analysts? And more women conducting the actual research." She looked across the table and sighed. "You know, the other day Pat said it was a waste of time to include Oriental women in focus groups because they never *say* anything. Can you imagine it?"

Lorna looked over at Pat and Cory, now attacking a plate of nachos. "He's young."

Renata crinkled her forehead. "He's sexist. And racist."

"But he didn't actually say that to the woman, did he? Or the client?"

"Still. Women are hardly to blame if they're not saying anything."

Was Renata a feminist? Nothing wrong with feminism, but it seemed like something from the history books. Lorna once heard a woman on the radio describe herself as an equalist, and she preferred that idea. It was best if men and women could get along, be friends. They were lucky to live somewhere that was even possible. She'd read about women in Africa being sold for their virginity. If you opened your eyes, there was no shortage of far-off places that Renata should worry about.

"We need people like you out there," Renata said, nudging Lorna with her elbow.

Lorna shook her head. "I don't have the qualifications."

"It's not like Ian has qualifications." Renata's voice was much quieter now. "I mean, not like, formal training. Not like Marcus. Ian didn't even finish his BA."

Lorna glanced Ian's way. He was sitting expansively, mid-explanation of this or that, his cigarette making slow illustrative circles. Lorna realized this was her second discussion in a month about Ian's credentials. Strange that she'd never bothered to ask about his training herself. Was it a secret? Or did everyone know? But what did it matter. He had a talent, a special genius.

Renata moved in closer; Lorna could smell the ranch on her breath. "Yeah, he worked for Marcus on an election campaign one summer years ago. Marcus needed a qualitative guy to stay competitive in the business. And you know Ian, all charisma. Marcus smelled an opportunity, but Ian's not formally trained."

"Are you?" Lorna asked. "Formally trained?"

"Master's in social research." Renata ran both her hands through her hair. "But I'm interested in technology now. You know about dial testing?"

"Cool." Lorna did not know about dial testing, but she didn't care, and she was distracted by a spot freeing up closer to the head of the table.

"Great little gadgets for getting a minute-by-minute reaction to a TV spot."

Lorna nodded. "Sure sounds like it. I'm sorry, Renata. Do you mind if I jump over there and have a smoke? I don't want to bother your asthma."

Renata glanced across the table and then back at Lorna, a sad, ditched expression on her face. "Go ahead."

"Thanks." Lorna smoothed her skirt as she walked around and squeezed into the vacant spot next to Lizbeth, one chair away from Ian. She reached for Ian's Vantages.

"Tsk, tsk!" Ian snatched the pack away from her, offering it first around the table. No one was taking. "Oh, you're all so healthy," he said. "It's disgusting."

"I want to live to a hundred," Lizbeth declared. Her silver bangle smacked loudly against the patio table as she put down her drink.

Ian winked her way. "Good chance of it."

"Well, not really," Lorna said.

They all stared at her.

Lorna forced a light-hearted smile. "Life expectancy is only about seventy-eight." She turned to Lizbeth. "But let's switch spots, OK? I don't want to smoke over you and wreck your chances." Only Lorna laughed. She got up and swapped seats with Lizbeth, landing her next to Ian.

"I thought you quit," Ian said. "Where's your willpower?"

"Tough week," she said.

"What is your job now, exactly?" Cory asked. He was a red-faced, twenty-nine-year-old associate. His unironed shirt billowed at the back.

"Exactly? Operations..." Lorna hesitated. "...manager."

"I didn't know we had managers."

"Neither did I," Ian said cheerfully. Lorna tried to catch Ian's eye, but his gaze was soft and over her shoulder, impossible to hook.

"So wait. You really have screws in your head?" Lizbeth said suddenly. Lorna realized that her arrival must have interrupted Ian's story.

Ian tapped his temple. "Yep. Real ones," he said. "You can feel them."

"Wow," Lizbeth said. "Crazyass."

Ian picked up Lizbeth's hand, dragging it in front of Lorna, and pressed her fingertips to his hairline. Lorna had felt the screws before. Tender pellets under Ian's warm, slightly oily skin. He'd been in a bar fight once in the early seventies. Loved to tell the story.

"Can you feel them?" Ian asked.

Lizbeth closed her eyes and bit her lip in concentration as Ian slid her fingers around on his skull. "Umm—"

"Jesus. They're right there!" Lorna said. "It's not hard."

"OK," Lizbeth said, crinkling her nose. "Maybe I can feel them."

Ian brought Lizbeth's hand back down to the table but paused to look at her electric blue nail polish. "Too cold in here for you?"

Lizbeth, of course, had an orgasm.

"Must be nice," Lorna said. "I wish I had the time to go for a manicure."

"I did this myself," Lizbeth said.

"Marvellous!" Ian said. "Then you could do Lorna's nails."

Lorna looked at her short, prim, and Protestant-looking nails. Neither woman had a reply for Ian. Lorna realized, then, that perhaps Lizbeth didn't like her, either.

"My grandparents own a nail salon," Lizbeth said. "Over on Yonge Street."

"Is that right?" Ian said. "I'll tell everyone about it."

"When I was a little girl I wanted to do nails so bad," she said.

"Well, you did say you were a 'people person,'" Lorna said. She felt bored and left out. Her cigarette was still unlit. "Hey, tough guy." She turned to Ian and placed her cigarette between her teeth. "Could ya offer a gal a light?" It came out more Mae West than Lorna wanted, completely embarrassing. In the silence that followed, she felt as though she'd farted.

Ian slid the lighter toward her. Lorna turned her head and lit the smoke she hardly wanted herself: she'd almost made it a year.

Lizbeth plucked the fruit out of the bottom of her sangria glass and sucked it in her mouth. "This stuff's good," she said, grinning. Her teeth were stained grey. Cory and Ian both reached for the pitcher to fill her glass.

For the next hour, Ian continued to tell stories, mostly things Lorna had heard before: the summer he spent working on a lobster trawler in Scotland (*I bet you had an amazing suntan!*), his colour blindness again (*How could you tell my nails were blue?*), the time he chased a purse snatcher with a picnic fork (*Crazyass!*).

When Lizbeth got up to use the restroom, knocking her chair over in the process, it occurred to Lorna that an advantage of her new role was that she had the corporate Visa. She could make this whole terrible party die. Quietly, importantly, Lorna turned to Ian. "I think it's time to wrap up."

Ian rattled his upper body in exaggerated surprise. "It's not even dark?"

"It's getting on." She glanced back at the restrooms. "I think some of our more impressionable colleagues may have over-indulged."

"Come on," Ian said. "I've seen a lot of drunks. Everyone's just having a good time."

"We should be a little responsible." Lorna's voice had the prudish edge again.

Ian sighed. "Oh, Lorna."

"What?"

"Just relax, will you?"

Lizbeth returned, newly lip glossed. She stood by the table and all three men turned toward her. She lifted one of her beige platform heels and fixed a strap on her shoe. Her feet were pink and squashed looking through the straps, like pig hooves. "I thought there was going to be dancing."

Lorna glanced at Ian. "Not generally."

"Unless," Ian said, turning to Lizbeth. "We're letting you down."

"I'll dance," Pat volunteered.

"There you go!" Ian said.

Pat, Cory, and Lizbeth made for the tiny patio dance floor. This left Lorna and Ian alone, at last. Ian faced the dance floor, a flickering string of coloured lights ticking across his forehead. Lorna took a large sip of sangria. "*Sooo.* You were going to ask me something?" she said.

"What was that?"

"That's just it, I don't know. But the other day in your office, you said you'd been meaning to ask me something?"

He turned slightly and frowned. "Why, then, didn't I just ask?"

Lorna opened her eyes wide—appealingly, she thought—and shook her head gently.

After a pause, Ian said, "Well, one thing I've been thinking about is getting you enrolled in a database management course. Maybe it was that. Lizbeth thinks we should be making our historical data easier to access, and it's actually a good idea."

Lorna followed his gaze back to the dance floor. Lizbeth was waving her arms over her head, a little belly poking out in that tight dress. Pat and Cory had their sleeves rolled up, faces shiny with sweat. They were both doing a sort of dance that involved glancing over their shoulders every ten seconds as though searching for their asses. They really were idiots. Asian women were brilliant not to speak to them in focus groups.

Lorna cleared her throat. "So," she said again. "Has our embargo been lifted?"

"Beg your pardon?"

She dropped her voice. "I don't think anyone's gossiping about us anymore."

Ian rubbed his chin. "I'm not sure this conversation makes sense."

Didn't make sense full stop, or didn't make sense now? After putting out her smoke, Lorna attempted a new conversation. "What a relief to have the kids away for the week," she said using her normal voice. "They're up at their father's lake house."

Ian didn't turn. The music was loud, though it was still possible to hear a person, Lorna thought, if you only just took a look at them.

Lorna tried again. "This must be what it feels like for you all the time, having a kid away at school. Like you're a whole new person, right? Free to do anything at all." What made her say these things? It sounded like a come on.

"Edie's home for the summer. We're all off on vacation next week," Ian said.

"Where?"

"North." Ian gestured vaguely over his shoulder and then looked back at the dance floor.

Lorna blinked back the sting of rejection.

"Funny how these guys don't know how to dance," he said after a moment.

"Should we show them a thing or two?" It seemed like the right response, though Lorna was not a very good dancer herself and did not want to get up.

He batted the air. "You never want to be the old guy out there," he said.

On the dance floor, Pat was buying drinks in test tubes from a mini-skirted bartender. Lorna felt a hand on her shoulder and turned to see Renata. "I'm going to get a taxi." Renata dug through her purse. "Do you want to come with?"

"Well." Lorna glanced over at Ian. "I was wondering if it

might be time. The children are going to drink up our entire events budget." She gestured toward the scene with the test tubes.

"Fine, Lorna, fine. It's a wrap." Ian picked up his jacket and called out to the dance floor. "Party's over, lads. Stay if you want to." Lorna felt a shot of victory. Ian was following her lead. If he'd just drive her home now, they could have a conversation—a conversation that made sense—in the car. Her apartment building was only ten blocks away from where he lived. She wouldn't say anything ridiculous about embargoes.

"We're going?" Lizbeth called back.

"*We're* going," Lorna said, drawing a circle around herself, Ian, and to some extent, Renata. "You're free to stay."

Lizbeth handed her test tube back to Pat and started toward them. Lorna actually felt her shoulders slump forward with disappointment.

"Lorna and I are grabbing a taxi, Lizbeth," Renata said. "You're welcome to join us." Lorna clenched her jaw. She hadn't actually agreed to taking the taxi with Renata. She wanted to drive home with Ian.

Lizbeth gathered her large white leather purse and looked at Ian. "Are you still good to give me a lift?"

Ian pushed his hands into his jacket pockets. "Of course."

A knot pulled tight in Lorna's gut. She stood numbly as Lizbeth waved to the abandoned-looking boys on the dance floor.

After quickly signing the bill, Lorna rushed to follow the group onto the sidewalk, the urgent clack of her heels startling against the pavement. Renata was hanging over the curb, trying to flag a cab. Ian and Lizbeth stood together under a spray of lamplight.

"Where do you live, Lizbeth?" Lorna asked, desperately.

Lizbeth looked from Ian back to Lorna. "East end?"

Lorna couldn't believe her good fortune. "Huh. Same as Renata. See, I'm just wondering if there's a better way to arrange ourselves. Ian has a wife waiting at home and I don't want to—"

Lizbeth shook her head. "Ian said he didn't mind."

Ian closed his eyes. Lorna could see his lids wrinkle, flutter. "You know what? Why don't I drive you all home."

Lorna laughed. "That's very generous, but really there's no—"

"Renata, want a lift?" He shouted.

But a taxi was pulling right up. "We're fine, Ian," Renata called back.

Ian didn't say, "Let the car go." He said, "Good stuff, then."

Lorna swallowed hard. She followed Renata dumbly into the cab. She felt dumped, the same way she had at her tenth-grade Valentine's dance when she emerged from the restroom to find her date slow dancing with Barb "School Tramp" Van Kamp. What could Ian and Lizbeth possibly have in common? Maybe it was flattering to be looked up to by someone so young, but could he not see that she was fattish with terrible style?

Lorna tried to smile at whatever Renata was saying in the taxi, but her mouth wouldn't quite stretch that way. Instead she said, "You don't think that was a bad idea, do you? To leave those two alone together?"

Renata looked at her. "No. Why?"

Lorna shook her head quickly. "It's just . . . Well, being in charge of operations now, how things run, I want to be conscientious. And you brought it up, sexual politics at work. I'm trying to stay one step ahead."

"She's cute," Renata said.

"She's hardly twenty."

"But she seems to have her head screwed on right," Renata said. "Plus, we know Ian. I doubt he would make that mistake."

"I'm sure you're right." Lorna faked a yawn.

"Just Ian's shiny new ball."

"What?" Lorna snapped.

"He's just looking out for her," Renata said. "He's paternal. Plus it's hard to be the new kid."

Was that all this was? At thirty-five, and three years into the job, did Lorna no longer need looking out for?

"Maybe she'll turn out to have a knack for research," Renata said.

"Really? No, I don't see it."

Lorna looked out the window. The summer night was thick with people buying ice cream cones, pushing bikes, lining up in front of brightly lit bars and restaurants. It was still early.

Lorna awoke the next morning, grateful to have the apartment to herself. She had the beginning of a plan that would make her feel better. She didn't want to take a computer course in database management. She didn't want to be left out anymore. As soon as she got into the office, she'd speak to Ian about rejoining the research team. She'd tell him how much she appreciated the opportunity to try something new, but research was where she belonged. They needed more women in research, as Renata had pointed out, and Lizbeth shouldn't beat her to it. Perhaps she'd never made it clear enough to Ian how much she admired what he did. Practising her speech, Lorna gestured at the mirror. "I want to be" — she managed only to find Lizbeth's words — "in the guts of it."

Lorna smiled broadly at Lizbeth as she breezed into the office. "Good morning!" Lorna said. "Feeling OK?

"Pretty good. I'm a little tired."

Lorna lowered her voice. "Don't feel like you have to keep up with the boys," she said. "It's a rookie error."

Lizbeth shook her head like she didn't catch Lorna's meaning.

"Drink for drink. It doesn't generally work out in a woman's favour." Lorna busied herself, picking the brown leaves off the plant in front of Lizbeth's desk.

"I know that." The slapping tone of Lizbeth's voice made Lorna look up from the plant. Lizbeth was sitting up straight now.

Lorna swiped the air in front of her, moving on. "Ian in?"

"Didn't he tell you? They've headed up north. Wanted to get a head start on traffic." Lizbeth brushed the bangs off her forehead. "I can give him a message."

"No need. I'll be in touch with him myself," Lorna said breezily. "I have all his numbers." But Lorna felt irritated. She'd have to wait for him to come home to activate her plan.

Lorna's message light was on in her office, but she was disappointed to find that it was a call from Alex. He said he was taking the kids to the bus station that morning and to expect them back at three that afternoon, a day earlier than they discussed.


Late in the morning of Ian's return, he asked Lorna for a minute before she found a second to speak to him herself. She headed cheerfully into his office, wondering if perhaps the embargo was, finally, gone. She took her regular seat across from him, began by asking about his vacation. The week had given Lorna more time to prepare her speech and she felt ready.

"Could you get the door?" Ian said.

"Sure." Lorna closed it, a spike in her pulse. It felt like old times: a confidential moment between Ian and his Girl Friday.

Ian tapped a paper on his desk. "Did Lizbeth mention to you she was resigning?"

"No!" Lorna wondered if Ian detected the private glee in her exclamation.

He rubbed his neck. "I'm not going to announce it broadly. I'm wondering if you could chat to her first."

"Me?" Lorna had barely spoken with Lizbeth in a week. "What do you want me to say?"

Ian sighed. "Ask her what we can do. Is it a question of pay? Is she feeling overwhelmed?"

"I doubt that."

"Just have a little chat. Find the bee in her bonnet. I think we'd all like to keep her."

"Actually," Lorna said. "I wanted to talk to you about staffing. I'm thinking that we could really use some more—"

"Could we just do one thing at a time?" Ian said, holding up his hand.

When Lizbeth turned up in Lorna's transparent office after lunch, Lorna was nervous. She wasn't accustomed to these sorts of delicate conversations nor did she have any genuine interest in changing Lizbeth's mind. She motioned for Lizbeth to shut the door and indicated the chair across from her, but Lizbeth didn't sit. She stood a few feet back, grasping her elbow.

Lorna managed to squeeze out what she considered to be a professional smile. "I'm sure you know what this is about."

"I think, yeah."

"Would you like to talk about it?"

Lizbeth took a breath. "Sorry if I'm putting anyone out."

"Don't worry, you're not. Not at all." Lorna wrinkled her nose in what she thought of as a companionable way. "Tell me, though. Is it to do with how you're paid?"

"Well, no." Lizbeth glanced at the hallway.

"Are you feeling overwhelmed?"

"No." Lizbeth flipped her hair to one side. "I wouldn't say that."

"Good. I wouldn't want to think we'd run you into the ground."

Lorna laughed but Lizbeth did not. Anyway, she was done now with Ian's checklist.

"It's kinda more like the opposite," Lizbeth said.

"Yeah?"

"Yeah."

Why was this so hard? Why wasn't Ian having this conversation? He always knew what to say to people. Could draw blood from a stone. Suddenly, the truth lodged itself in Lorna's throat. She'd been right to ask the question in the cab with Renata. Something had happened between Lizbeth and Ian.

Lorna sat forward. "Can you elaborate?"

Lizbeth shifted her stance a little. She looked at the chair but didn't sit. "I just think that personally I need to do a job that has more kind of..." Lizbeth's face began to redden along the edges. Appropriate to be ashamed, Lorna thought, if you'd screwed your boss. "I don't know."

"Well, we can't help if you don't know, Lizbeth."

"It's just like..." Lizbeth rubbed her wrists together as though she were about to sample perfume. "Maybe because I'm the only woman, or the only young woman, I mean...I don't know, I just don't feel like this is a place where I can really move up."

"Move up?"

"Like, get promoted."

"Lizbeth, you've been here for five minutes."

"Well a couple of months, anyway. But sometimes—well, most of the time actually—I don't think I'm doing anything important."

Lorna looked at the girl. "I'm just curious, Lizbeth. Did something happen?"

"What do you mean?"

Lorna felt a spurt of adrenaline. "You know what I mean," she said quickly. "Something inappropriate. An unprofessional involvement?"

"Like what? Like sexual?"

Now Lorna was blushing. "Well, however you want to put it. But yes."

Lizbeth shook her head. Lorna wondered if, perhaps, a bit too vigorously. "No."

"You're sure?"

Lizbeth looked down at the edge of Lorna's desk. "That wasn't what I was trying to say."

"No, but—"

"All I'm saying is that Girl Friday is not a serious job."

Lorna flinched. "Girl Friday?"

"Or whatever. It's a dead end."

Something had happened. It was so obvious.

"I understand," Lorna said. She stood to meet Lizbeth at eye level. "We'll make this your last day."

"I'm glad to stay the next two weeks. I don't want to put anyone out."

"You already said that, and you're not," Lorna said. "We'll make sure you're paid. I'll put out a memo."

Lorna shook the girl's small, sweaty hand.

...

Shortly after five, after Lizbeth and most everyone had cleared out, Lorna found Ian in his office. She held her notebook tight to her chest and tapped lightly on his half-opened door. Ian put his pencil down on a stack of paper. Lorna took a quiet step inside. "I had the talk with Lizbeth."

"I caught a word with her as well." Ian arched his shoulders and rolled them back. "It's a shame, isn't it?"

Lorna put her hands on the back of a leather chair across from Ian. "She said she thinks it'll be difficult to move up here."

"And what did you say to that?"

Lorna stared out at the lake. It had been humid all week, but today was the stickiest, the stillest. Only one small green sailboat stood on the water, and it was fixed in place. Square in the middle of Ian's windowpane. "She thinks it's difficult here for women. Specifically."

Ian looked at her. "But you were promoted, weren't you? Did you bring that up?"

Lorna tightened her grip on the back of the chair. "Did anything happen, Ian?"

"What sort of thing?"

Lorna gave him a sharp look. "You know."

Ian chuckled. "I do know one thing. You won't miss her."

"I hardly knew her."

"But you didn't like her. She knew it; I knew it."

"I wouldn't say that." Lorna wondered if this was what it was like to be a participant in Ian's focus groups. This was squeezing blood from a stone. "I mean she was a bit..." Lorna let that trail off.

"You could have been nurturing. Taken her under your wing."

Lorna dug the back of her left heel into the carpet. "I think she got plenty of attention from you."

"Is that right?"

"Everyone saw it."

"What, exactly?"

"I don't know, Ian. Anything is possible at this point."

"Jesus, Lorna." Ian stood up from his desk. "We had a talk once. Of everyone here, I would have least expected this kind of an accusation from you."

"If I'm wrong then I apologize." Lorna's voice was rickety.

"You're wrong," Ian said.

Lorna didn't apologize.

Ian picked up a toothpick then put it down again. "Lizbeth was clever, hard-working, ambitious. You felt threatened and she paid for that."

"So I made her quit?"

"You made her quit."

"That's a laugh!"

It was the oddest choice of phrase. Loudmouthed yet old fashioned. The kind of phrase Lorna associated with people like Ian's wife. She tried to think of another rebuttal, but right there, at the edge of Ian's brown leather writing pad, was a glob of spit. Her spit. Bubbly and shaped like an exclamation mark. He was looking at it, too. And now that they were both looking, it felt impossible to look away.

Ian slid his finger over the drop of saliva. He studied his moistened index for a long moment before slipping his hand into his pocket. Lorna looked quickly back at the lake.

"Look," Ian said after a moment. "Let's drop it. I'm sorry."

Lorna nodded but didn't look. She was not sure which thing he was apologizing for. Sleeping with Lizbeth? Accusing Lorna of insufficient nurturing? Touching her saliva?

Lorna heard Ian's footsteps move past her. Dignified of him, she thought, to leave and give her a minute. But he stopped moving before he reached the door. "Christ, Lorna. I want..." His hand was on her shoulder, pressure from his fingertips on her skin.

Lorna kept on looking at the window. The green sailboat was no longer in the middle of the pane; it had been moving, just very slowly.

"Lorna. I..."

Lorna closed her eyes. She smelled mint-flavoured toothpicks. Maybe there never were any rumours. She felt a shudder deep down and tried not to think of how she looked to Ian with her eyes closed. If she opened them, she would need to say something, give him a certain kind of look. It was too risky; any small thing and he could change his mind. Better just to stay like this, do nothing but wait. Wait for his hands on her face, the scrape of his stubble, the crude knock of teeth.

# Catch My Drift

SUMMER, 1991

A parasite is in the lake algae. Heike says the neighbourhood kids are breaking out in itchy red bumps. From the end of our dock, with my toes curled over, I can see the electric green blooms sway underwater. There is no point in being up here if we can't swim. I dip my tennis racquet into the lake and swirl the green muck around the racquet's face and neck.

The cottage belonged to my dad's parents once, and he spent all summer here when he was a kid. When I was little, we came up here, too: Mom, Dad, Jed, and me. But after Mom kicked Dad out, no one visited for a long, long time. You can tell because it smells like a wet phonebook inside. Dad moved in after losing his job at the bank a couple of months ago.

The lunchtime sun feels like needles at the back of my neck. I get this idea that I'm going to throw myself off the dock and into the algae, the green slime sucking against my mouth like hair in the drain. I step back from the edge and try to think of something happy. Even when it's daylight and the sun is out, even when I'm supposed to be having a good time on vacation, sometimes I get this scared feeling in my chest, same as when I hear a bang in the middle of the night. It's a little like the hell-thoughts I used to get, but there's no words attached. It's just a bad feeling that tunnels right through me. I try to knock the algae off the racquet, but it clings. I fling the racquet and watch it twirl onto the shore. I don't care what happens to it. No one will play tennis with me here, and the walls of the cottage are too uneven to bounce against.

The planks on the dock dip under my steps, so I walk carefully, balancing my weight and holding my arms out to the sides. *Step on a crack and you'll break your mother's back. Step on a line and you'll break your mother's spine.* I'm looking down so it takes me a moment to notice the boy grabbing my racquet, putting his hand right into the foam that rolls off the lake onto the shore. He looks my age but paler and bonier in a pair of orange swim trunks. His skin is covered in pink bumps.

"Don't touch," I say. "It has algae."

"I just want to borrow it." He jerks his long blond bangs off his forehead.

"What for?"

"Just wait."

I squint up at the yellow cottage to see if anyone's watching. Heike's busy pinning laundry up on the line outside. She's a recorder teacher from Germany who parks her camper van in the cottage driveway and uses all our stuff. She wears dresses with jeans underneath and has hairy armpits. Dad calls her "my friend Heike."

There's nothing else going on, so I follow the boy down the beach, trying to count the spots on his back, but there are so many and some of them are smeared together. We walk until we get to the spot that people call the lighthouse. There's no real house, just a pile of reeds and rocks around a silver pole with blue and orange lights on top.

The boy digs his foot into the wet sand. "What's your name?" he says.

"What's yours?"

"Simon." He flicks the sand at the rocks. "See that?"

A pale grey snake, thick as a fire hose, is twisted up against the rocks.

"Is it alive?"

"That's why I need this." He holds up the racquet.

"We should leave it alone."

Crouching, Simon goes right up to the snake, the racquet held out. He shovels it up and flips it over, splitting its skin like a rotten banana. A million white worms pour out from the middle; more worms than I've ever seen in my whole life.

I kick sand at it. "Sick!"

"We can't just cover it up. Say a dog comes and eats it."

"Do dogs eat snakes?"

"Eel," he says. He scratches a spot on his arm then licks his finger and scrubs the sore with spit. "I'll get a box from my house."

I don't know what we'll do with a box, but I stay while he jogs back, watching the worms spray across the sand like a spilled box of Minute Rice. I wait a long time but the scared feeling comes back, prickling up through my armpits. I draw seven X's with my toe in the sand. I want to go tap the rocks at the bottom of the lighthouse, but I'm trying not to tap stuff anymore. I read a story in *Teen Day* about kids who have this disease that makes them wash their hands a hundred times a day or turn the lights on and off all night. One girl wouldn't leave the house until she drew a perfect *O*, so she just kept drawing and drawing until she went completely crazy and had to get locked away in some hospital. I don't want to get that disease.

The worms can't hurt you, I tell myself without tapping. They're teeny weeny, and the eel is dead. But I can feel my heartbeat in both sides of my neck, and when the wind swishes the reeds, making the sound of one thousand knives, I take off down the beach.

Heike's making beet burgers for dinner. I sit on the counter while she chops the curled root tails and peels the dark skin so the beets bleed over her hands. It flashes into my head that the beet juice is real blood, that I stabbed Heike without really meaning to do it. I hop off the counter and move as far across the kitchen as possible.

Heike says, "That boy? He has the disease."

"I don't care."

"You like him?" Heike smiles down at her stupid beets.

"I just met him."

Jed pulls a hot dog out of the microwave. He won't eat Heike's beet burgers. "We don't care about the water disease," he says. "And just so you know, Cara's best friend Sam Grossman is Jewish."

"What does that have to do with anything?" Dad says.

Jed looks at me and rolls his eyes.

We eat out on the picnic table and barely talk. Dad asks what we did all day and I tell him nothing, there's nothing to do.

Jed says, "Hey, Heike? Can I call you Hike-a-mountain?"

Heike winks at Dad. "How's your joke going? Call me how you want, just don't call me late for dinner?" She makes a snorting noise.

"Oh my god," Jed says. He looks at Dad and me, smirking. "She actually laughed at that?"

"Your joke wasn't any better," Dad says, prying the cap off a beer.

Heike lets out a big breath and then smiles at everyone with cigarette teeth. "Who wants dessert?"

The cake she brings out looks like a yellow sponge and tastes like alcohol. I mash mine with my fork until it coats the bottom of my plate.

"Cara, you're thirteen years old. Don't play with your food for god's sake," Dad says.

"Is it supposed to be soaking wet?" This makes Jed laugh.

Heike smiles again. "This is special German cake."

"Is it made from ground up Jewish people?" Jed's cake is pushed aside and he's chipping at the table with the end of his knife.

"Jed!" Dad says. "What is with you?"

Heike puts her hand on Dad's hairy arm. "Perhaps Jed is wanting to discuss the war?"

"That's not what this is about." Dad glares at Jed and me. He picks up his fork and makes a big loop and one of those stupid cereal commercial *Mmm* faces as he pops the cake into his mouth. He puts his arm around Heike's shoulders when he's done chewing.

"I knew it!" Jed gets up from the table, a red stain spreading down the middle of his face. "She is your girlfriend."

Dad pulls his arm back. "Jed," he says.

"Your girlfriend's cake sucks the bag." He turns and heads toward the porch.

Heike pulls the cake pan to her chest. A lump slides in her neck. Dad doesn't yell or even get up. He puts his hand on Heike's. "Ignore him."

Why would Dad tell Heike to ignore us? We're the ones who are supposed to be here. I untangle myself from the bench and join Jed on the porch. Jed and I were always friends at the lake, and it looks like Dad and Heike are going to be their own team.

"See that?" Jed says now, his eyes narrow, practically spitting at the porch screen. "Laughing at her own jokes again." Heike's turned away from us, facing the breakwater. Dad's hand is between her shoulders. The fabric of her dress stretches with each tug of breath.


At breakfast Dad tries to be all cheery again. "Hotter than Hades," he says. "Who wants to go for a dip?" I look at him with slitted don't-be-stupid eyes. We're not supposed to go in the lake. Jed doesn't answer like usual. He has a wall of cereal boxes set up all around his place at the table.

"Cara'll come to the pool with me," Dad says. He slams his hands together like goody gumdrops. Dad used to make fun of people who went to the pool when there's a whole lake to swim in. "Why swim in a toilet?" he'd say. This year he makes the pool sound like Disneyland.

The pool is packed with kids and the concrete already burns at ten in the morning. Other girls my age sit in little groups without any parents. Dad and I lay our towels down and then

Dad goes, "It's been real!" and cannonballs into the deep end, splashing two teenage girls in bright bikinis. One of them says, "Manners much?" while he's still underwater. I lean back on my towel and let the sun push down on my face, wishing I were somebody else—and anywhere else but here.

When Dad surfaces, he waves from the middle of the pool, showing off his clumpy deodorant. "Come on, Care Bear!" he says.

The girls look over at me. One of them whispers to the other and they both laugh and paddle their toes, their nail polish shining underwater.

Dad heaves himself out of the pool making all sorts of embarrassing grunts. "Too sophisticated to go swimming, eh?"

"Why swim in a toilet?"

He stands over me and the cold drops of water are ice hitting my skin. "Heike's very concerned about the lake," he says. "She's a brainiac on plant biology. Not worth the argument, if you catch my drift."

Mom and Dad thought it was worth it to argue about everything. Where to park the car, when to clear the dishes, how to cut an onion.

"By the way," Dad says, streaking suntan lotion all over his face, "is Jed always this cheesed off?"

"Not really."

"Well, what does he like to do?"

"Watch the *Simpsons*. *Tetris*."

Over in the shallow end, a teenaged girl has her legs wrapped around a boy's waist, and one of her bathing suit straps floats down by her elbow so that you can practically see her boob.

Dad squints at her too, which is embarrassing. I wonder if he notices that I have boobs starting. The last time we went to a pool together, he could still throw me across the water. I pull at the towel to cover up my chest; boobs are weird for dads to see.

"My friend Heike bothers him." Dad nods, frowning.

"I guess."

"Why don't you let Heike give you a recorder lesson?"

I scrunch up my nose and draw a hangman with my finger in the wet drops on the deck. "Is she going to be here all week?"

"The thing is, Cara," Dad says, propping himself up with an elbow. "The thing is, it can be lonely up here without you guys. Heike's good company."

"Better company than Mom?"

Dad makes a click-click sound with his mouth like he's trying to get a horse going. "That's a complicated question, Care Bear," he says. "Things change."

I think about Mom alone in our ugly apartment building. It's idiotic for things to change and for everything to end up worse. Heike is a way worse girlfriend than Mom. She doesn't even shave.

Dad pulls a cigarette out from his sports bag and lights a match.

"I don't think you're allowed to smoke here."

"I mean, not everything changes," he says, shaking out the flame. "I love you and Jed more than anyone."

"Do you love Heike?" I trace five spaces into the concrete for her name.

"Come on." He narrows his eyes as he sucks the cigarette.

"Well?"

He pats my knee. "Don't worry about that too much, all right?"

Clouds move overhead and the jiggling blobs of sunlight fade all at once on the pool. Kids in the water are laughing, splashing, spitting. I get that scared feeling again. What if someone poisoned the pool? What if I poisoned the pool somehow and I don't even know it? I open and close the locker pin on my towel seven times. "Dad, do you ever think things you don't want to think about?"

But Dad's not looking at me. His attention is on the girls at the edge of the pool. The one in a purple bikini is speaking to him: "Got an extra butt?"

"Sure do," Dad says even though she's fifteen, max. He slides over and lights her cigarette while she dips her blond head. "Don't tell on me," he whispers. The girls giggle, which makes Dad smile all crinkle eyed. I wipe out my drawing and roll onto my other side.

The couple in the shallow end of the pool is still going at it; they don't care that everyone is staring. Then I see this sunburnt fat guy come crashing down the ladder and charge toward them shouting "Fuck!" and "Bitch!" Everyone goes crazy in the shallow end, scrambling to get out of the way. The fatty wraps his arms around the other guy's neck while the girl kicks herself free and staggers up the pool steps with her strap still down, her pink and white boob just hanging there. I check if Dad's looking, but he's watching the boys.

The lifeguard blows his whistle over and over but the boys don't stop. The fatty has the first guy by the bangs and punches him in the face. Now there's blood. Blood all over the guy's face and dripping into the pool.

Dad crushes his cigarette out on the deck. "There you go, Cara," he says. "Boys can't control their wieners. They ruin it for everyone."

Simon comes by later that afternoon while I'm lying on the picnic table, tanning, waiting for Heike to teach me stupid recorder because I promised Dad.

"You didn't tell me your name," Simon says.

"Cara."

"My mom says you guys are from the city."

"Yep." I look at his feet through the slats in the picnic bench. If I move my head just a little, I can make the shadow hide the spotty part of his foot.

"How come you didn't stay with the eel?"

"It was gross."

Simon sits down on the bench. "Do you want to play Battle-ship?"

"Can't."

He nods but he doesn't leave, and when Heike comes out with a brown box of music stuff, she asks if he wants to learn too.

Heike pulls three lawn chairs together in a circle and we all sit down with our butts sagging nearly to the grass. She gives us each a stumpy wooden instrument and blabs about the holes in the wood. When she says "high note" she makes her voice all squeaky and holds her arm up over her head so that I can see her weedy armpit hair. I try to give a look to Simon, but he's busy with the recorder on his mouth, flapping his fingers over the holes.

When Heike plays "Go tell Aunt Rhody" she closes her eyes and puffs her cheeks out like pink balloons. Just like that, I get an idea that I'm going to strike her across the face with my recorder. I press my tongue hard into the ridge behind my teeth. *You won't hurt her*, I say to myself. *You won't.* At least I don't think I will, but already I'm feeling the crack of wood on bone in my fingertips. I put my recorder down and hold it tight between my knees. I breathe in slowly through my nose. Everything smells like hot pine needles.

Heike stops playing. "Cara," she says. "You don't want to play?"

"Can't," I say.

"You can." She gives me that brown-tooth smile.

I try again, but my fingers feel cold and they tremble. I blow into the mouthpiece, but it's too loud. A glob of spit leaks onto my bathing suit top. I shake my head.

Heike looks at Simon. "And you?"

Simon brings the thing to his mouth and copies her sound, the notes coming out clear and sweet like real music. Heike sings along: "The old grey goose is dead. Yes, the old grey goose is dead!" Simon finishes and wipes his mouth with the back of his hand.

"Like an angel," Heike says to Simon. Then she looks back at me. "Now you again."

Squeezing the recorder in my sweaty fist, I tell Heike I'm not feeling well and run back into the cottage. In my room, I slam the recorder in the bottom dresser drawer, next to the sandwich bag with Dad's old stereo screws and springs. I brought them up, but I haven't given them back yet.

The screen door bangs and Heike calls my name. I go to the bathroom and sit on the toilet with my hands between my knees. There's a picture of a yellow flower beside the medicine cabinet, and I try to think about how pretty the flower is, how good and gentle. I breathe slowly.

When I come out again, Simon is gone and Heike is filling a glass with bleach. She slips Simon's recorder in it. "We can't take any risks," she says. "He has the disease."

Outside, Heike's laundry still wobbles on the clothesline. I rub a little dirt into the crotch of each pair of her underpants. Maybe if I do something a little bit bad, the very bad thoughts will go away.


Every morning, Jed disappears somewhere on his bicycle. Because there's nothing else to do, nowhere to go, and no one else to hang out with, for the rest of the week I go to Simon's place after lunch to play Ping-Pong or Battleship. On a Friday night, we find Simon's pretty mom Marie painting her nails at the kitchen counter, getting ready for a party down the beach. Two trays of devilled eggs shimmy in Saran Wrap on top of the running dishwasher. Marie spreads her hands out in front of a fan, and I think about what would happen if her fingers got sucked in. Flying pink skin, blood speckling the dirty white countertops. I suck in my cheeks and stare hard at the photos on the fridge, trying to memorize them instead: a wedding picture with Simon's dad in a blue ruffled shirt; Simon's mom with a pie on her face; the whole family holding a big striped fish.

"You want?" Marie says. She has a Quebec accent, and her voice is like a loud whisper. I look over and she waggles her bottle of nail polish. I do want coloured nails, but I shake my head. Can't get too close.

Marie nods at the plastic bag hanging on the arm of her chair. "There's something in here for your skin, too, Simon." Simon turns away, probably embarrassed.

The spots on Simon's body look less red to me, or maybe I'm just getting used to them. "Your scabs are better," I say, being nice. "The disease is from the water. The algae has little bugs that get into your skin."

"No, no." Marie waves her hand and shakes her head.

"But—"

"It's gonna rain," she says. Her forehead goes wavy when she looks out the kitchen window. "Better play outside before the afternoon's wrecked."

Simon and I each take an egg outside and sit on the breakwater under the thick smear of clouds. We sit quiet for a while, watching adults play volleyball lower down the beach, their feet making a million dents in the sand.

"Your mom's nice," I say.

"I guess."

"Where's your dad?"

"Oil rigs." He looks at me, and I notice his eyes are the same metal color of the lake. He takes a bite of the egg and yolk sticks like paste to his lips.

"Cool."

"I guess."

"You have egg on your mouth."

"Where?" He sticks his tongue out and jabs it left and right.

I put my finger on his lips and his ears go red. "It's gone," I say, even though it isn't.

"What's your dad do?"

"An actor," I say. Working at the bank is less cool, plus he got fired. "Did you ever see *Dog Daze*?"

"Nope." Simon kicks a flip fop down to the sand. "We should go for a swim. That's what we should do."

"In the pool?"

He shakes his head. "They won't let me."

"How come?"

"Because of the sores." He scratches his shoulder, making a tiny bead of blood pop. "Sorry," he says. "They itch."

The hairs on our legs are touching. It feels fuzzy like when you put your hand too close to a television screen. I feel a rain drop on my knee and another two on my wrist, but Simon doesn't move so I don't either.

"Sometimes the itching wakes me up in the middle of the night. I scratch everything until it bleeds. It's bad, I know, but I can't help it."

"I know," I say, rolling the rain across my wrist.

"How do you know? You don't have spots."

There's a grunt of thunder. The adults on the beach are collapsing their lawn chairs, putting bottles away in bright coolers.

"I do things I can't help too," I say.

"Like what?"

"Sometimes I think about stuff that I don't even want to, that I don't even try to."

"What stuff?"

"Bad thoughts."

"Huh," Simon says, but he doesn't ask what. He brushes his hands together, wiping away the egg bits. "Sounds like an itch in your brain." Then he reaches over and scratches the top of my head.

The rain really starts then, piercing holes into the sand. "Let's go in the lake," Simon says, standing up. "It's the best when it's raining."

"What about the algae?"

"There's none right here," he says. "Promise."

Standing up makes me dizzy. "I don't have a bathing suit."

"Who cares? You're getting wet anyway."

Simon jumps down to the beach and rips across to the water, sand coughing up behind his heels. He stands ankle deep, waiting for me. "Rain makes the water warmer," he says. "Really."

I follow him to the shore, jumping into his footprints. He jogs backwards, silver spray crashing up to his waist. I wade to my knees, breathing the lake smell, the same smell as always: tin cans and plants. I remember Dad grabbing my wrists when I was little, spinning me around: *Motorboat, motorboat goes so slow.*

I wade a little further and the cold water climbs up my legs, my stomach. The bravery hits me like a shove and I dive, cutting the surface of the lake and swimming down to its scalp-splitting colder layers. The water wobbles against my lips, and my hair swirls mermaid-like around my face. When I push myself back up, I'm gasping for air and feeling good, feeling like it's a long time ago. I float next to Simon on my back, letting the rain smack down on my forehead.

Jed sees me come in with my wet clothes. "You went in the lake?" he makes a barf face.

"Sick. No. Do you think I want the disease?"

"Why're you wet then?"

"Duh. It's raining." My hair is dripping down my back and onto the floor.

Jed narrows his eyes at me. "You were with that zitty kid, weren't you?"

"No."

"Touch his wang?"

"Gross."

Then he looks me up and down, stopping at my chest. "Nice tits," he says and cackles at himself. I fold my arms over my chest. *Look who's laughing at his own jokes*, I want to say.

"Hey, kids," Dad calls from the porch. "Come see the rainbow."

Jed rolls his eyes. "I'm good."

Sometimes it's like Dad doesn't know basic things anymore. Like that Jed and I are too old now to be interested in rainbows.

I change into dry clothes and go to the kitchen for a pop and handful of chips. Through the door to the screened-in porch, I see the rainbow he's talking about. Both sides of the arc are totally visible, something you only see on T-shirts and kindergarten drawings. I find myself wondering if Simon can see it; if we're both looking at the very same thing at the very same time. Dad has his arm around Heike's waist. She leans into him, her scratchy yellow hair smushed against his shoulder.

Later that night, Heike sets up Monopoly on the porch table while Dad taps his foot to the rock music wafting up from the beach. "Maybe we should drop into that party after all," Dad says to Heike, rubbing her shoulder. "Rain's gone."

"Oh, no, Alex. You know how it's going. Everyone bombed." She waves her hand in front of her nose.

"It's the friendly thing," Dad says. "Neighbourly." He flips a game piece from one hand to the other.

"You and the smell of booze," she says. "We should do something together, no?"

"You should definitely go to the party, Dad," Jed says, slamming a dart into the board across the porch. "I saw a woman go down there with some serious sweater meat."

"What's sweater meat?" I ask.

Dad laughs. "Like father, like son." He puts the game piece down and rubs his palms together. "One drink," he says to Heike. "It's Saturday night."

"We'll keep the game out," Heike says.

After they're gone, Jed and I throw darts together. He doesn't say anything, only "Yes!" and "Fucker!" but it's the first thing we've done together all week. I don't even really try to win because it feels like those old summers for the second time today, and that's good enough.

Through the screen, the sun is fat and low, spilling an orangey trail across the lake. I'm not ready for the day to be over, the best day we've had here so far, but the sun just does its thing, doesn't care what it's shutting down. When we were little, when it was too hot to sleep, Mom would take Jed and me swimming just before dark. The water was so still. Jumping in was like breaking glass.

"Do you remember going swimming with Mom at night?" I ask.

Jed squints at the oozing sun on the lake. "She never went in with us," he finally says.

After a while, there's a scratch on the porch screen and Jed coughs out, "Boyfriend!" before I even turn to see Simon. He's looking up at us, drinking from a can of Orange Crush.

"Want to check out the party? The whole beach is down there," he says.

I ask Jed if he wants to come, I even mean it, but he looks at me like I'm the stupidest person he's ever met. When I leave with Simon, I can feel Jed watching us from the porch.

Down the beach, the party house is lit up with coloured lanterns and blue mosquito grills that zap and hiss. Simon scrambles to the top of a pump shed on the edge of the property and pulls me up. There's a view of a hundred sweaty faces on the lawn and down to the bonfire by the water. We watch people dance, and I see Heike come out from the house and pick through the cans in an ice-filled baby pool a few feet away from us. She sits on a folding chair with a Coke and rolls her long finger around and around the rim of the can, her head tilted back at the stars. A few days ago I thought I would bash her in the face with a recorder. I shiver and pull my bare knees to my chest.

A sweaty-faced woman in a white button-up dress sways to the music, dancing by herself around the yard. She drifts in front of Heike who half smiles at her then looks away. The woman bumps up against the shed and we hold our breath, but the next moment she's falling, her hands crashing into the baby pool. Simon laughs and then I start too. It's the hiccupy kind of laughter that's hard to stop because you're supposed to be quiet.

Heike rushes over and helps the woman up, brushing the water off the front of her dress. "You need foods," Heike says, which for some reason makes Simon laugh even harder.

"Are those kids?" the woman's eyes roll up to where we're sitting. "Whose kids are those?"

Simon grabs my elbow and we jump down from the shed, tearing off across the beach. It's only when we get to the lighthouse that we stop running. Bent over, catching his breath, Simon says, "Let's go swimming again."

"Too cold." I finger the goose bumps on my arm. "Too dark."

"No, it's perfect." He gets so close that I can smell his Orange Crush breath. Back down the beach, adults are singing "American Pie" at the bonfire, too far away now to see us.

"I only brought two shorts. The others are already wet."

"You can take them off. It's dark."

I shake my head.

"OK," Simon says, but he grabs my hand, closing his fingers around mine. A funny feeling starts inside me, like scratching in my gut, only good. Then Simon squeezes my hand and points up at the rocks where a cigarette makes a bright orange spot between the dark lumps of two people. He steps back behind a clump of reeds. "Over here," he whispers.

Hidden by reeds, we both kneel in the sand and I think now he's going to kiss me. I try to remember if I'm supposed to keep my mouth open or closed. I don't know if I like Simon enough to french him. We only just met. He's not cute, exactly, but his eyes are good. Part of me doesn't care how cute he is; I can always make that part up when I tell Sam about it. My heart is springing back and forth. I run my thumb over Simon's knuckles, feeling the crust on his sores. I know exactly where the red parts turn dark pink, then paler, right up to where the color blends perfect with his skin. He moves his hand under the flap of my T-shirt and it's cold and dry against my bare stomach. I hear him swallow.

Up on the rocks there's a laugh I recognize and then the cigarette falls, sparks bouncing down toward the water. Simon pulls his hand out from under my shirt and leans forward on his knees. It sounds like Dad's voice. Dad, telling a story, but I can't hear too much. The other person, a woman, is laughing at whatever Dad's saying. What if it's Mom? It could be. She has a lot of different laughs.

Dad stands up and launches a bottle in the lake. Then he stretches his hands behind his head. "I'm going in!" He pulls off his T-shirt.

"You're crazy!" It's a loud whisper. Marie.

"Let's go," I say to Simon.

"Shhh." He crawls forward on his hands and knees.

The next thing I know, I'm staring through the reeds at my Dad's naked butt. Dad wades into the water slowly, stirring up the lake we're not supposed to touch. He gets to his waist and then turns to Marie. "Coming?" He combs the lake with his hands and water rises like silvery claws between his fingers.

Marie stands up all wobbly and shuffles to the end of the spit. She puts a foot in the water. "It's frigid," she says.

"You're frigid. Just hold your tits and run." Dad leans back into the lake and kicks his feet.

Marie pulls her dress up over her head and drops it on the rocks. Then with a little squeal, she splashes into the water. Her breath is loud over the lake.

Simon stands slowly. "Stay," he says. I want to ask where he's going, but I'm afraid of being heard. I keep my eyes on the water where Dad and Marie bob toward each other, giggling and naked. Marie makes cold, shivering noises, but when she and Dad join together, they're both quiet.

I can hear Simon moving behind the rocks. Suddenly, the pole light flickers on, spilling pale blue light onto Marie and Dad. Marie kicks hard, her head turning in every direction. "What's happening?" she says. I slide down onto my stomach.

Something dark flies out from the rocks and slaps the surface of the water right in front of Marie. She reaches for it then screams. She holds her tits and runs, just like Dad said, all the way to the shore. Through her wet, white underwear I can see the dark puff of her bush.

Dad swims over and lifts the dark thing. Then he coughs and jogs backwards, rinsing water like crazy up and down his arms.

"What is it?" Marie hisses.

"It's an eel," he calls back. "It's a dead fucking eel."

"Oh god, oh god," Marie moans. She stumbles over the rocks, looking for her dress.

Dad marches at the beach, his thing waggling in front of him. "Who the fuck threw that?"

The lights turn off then and everything goes black. My heart is pounding into the cold sand. I slide backwards, pushing off from my hands, moving faster and faster until it feels safe to get up and run. I bolt across the beach, the bright bonfires blurring my vision. When I get back to the cottage, Jed's still on the porch but there's no Heike. I come through the back door, tapping each piece of furniture seven times on my way to my room.

I wake up to the sound of the trunk slamming, my feet still rough with sand. Through my bedroom window, Jed and Dad load things into the car. Heike's on the grass outside her van, rolling up a plaid sleeping bag.

Dad finds me on my way out the door. "Ready to move 'em out?" He's grinning away like nothing ever happened.

"We're not supposed to leave until tomorrow."

"Is that right?" Dad scratches the back of his neck. "Well, Jed's all set." He looks back at the car. Jed's bare feet are up on the dash.

"I'm not."

"You need a hand?"

"No."

Dad holds his hands up like he's under arrest. "All right."

In front of Simon's house, Marie's dress from last night is folded over the clothesline next to his orange trunks. When Dad's out of view, I walk through the dewy grass and knock gently on Simon's window.

The front door opens and Marie slides halfway out, wearing just a thin pink bathrobe. Her hair is piled high in a clip, and it looks like she ran her finger along the bottom of an ashtray and spread the dust underneath her eyes.

"Is Simon home?" I come up to the door.

She scrunches up her face so that everything on it sucks into the middle. "So you just bang on the window, huh? Good morning to you, too." I don't know what to do. I never say good morning. Only people on the radio say that. I try to look past her through the door. She moves to block my view. "You need something?"

"We're leaving," I say, my voice sounding teensy and dry.

Simon's mom puts one hand on my chin and squeezes. I can see through the split in her bathrobe, but I can't move my head to look away. "The spots on Simon's body are not plant diseases," she says.

"OK."

"Simon has a condition. I don't like little snobs from the city who make up stories."

"I didn't make anything up."

"Simon was so upset last night," she says. "His arms and legs bleeding all over, telling me we have to move again."

"Not because of me," I whisper.

"Because why?" Her long nails press harder into my cheeks.

"Nothing."

When she finally lets go, I turn back and see Dad on our driveway. He smiles and waves but neither of us waves back. Marie lets the door slam behind her.

I rush back to the cottage and ram last night's damp, sandy clothes into my bag, feeling like I'm about to cry. In the bottom drawer, I find Heike's recorder and the baggie with Dad's stereo springs and screws. I slide the baggie into my pocket.

Outside, Heike sits in the open door of her van, her knees pulled up to her chest. She is eating from a cracker pack with bright orange cheese. A guilty feeling bubbles up from deep down in my stomach. We should have been nicer.

"Here." I cross the yard, holding out the recorder. "Are you leaving too?"

"I think so." She smears cheese on a cracker.

"I'm sorry I didn't learn more recorder."

She takes the recorder from me and shrugs. "Who says I wanted to teach you?"

I just stand there, sucking my lower lip into my teeth. My Dad is not my fault.

Heike nods her chin in the direction of Simon's house. "You say goodbye to your boyfriend?'

"He's not my boyfriend."

Heike's laugh is sharp. "For many weeks, you will think about him everyday." She snaps her cheese-dirty fingers. "And then this will stop. It's always like this." She looks right at me.

"Let's go, Cara," Dad calls.

Heike hands me her cracker wrapper. "Throw this out," she says. Then she gets up, brushes her hands together, and walks around to the back of her van.

I yell to Dad that I'll be there in a minute then cut back across the lawn, this time toward the beach.

Looking down from the top of the breakwater, the footprints on the sand go on forever. So many of them are Simon's and mine. I jump down and dig a hole quickly, deep enough to feel water, packing my fingernails with ashy grey sand. Heike's garbage goes in first, then the springs and screws.

Dad calls my name again, his voice getting louder, closer. I kick sand over the hole and stamp it down with my feet.

Simon's footprints are just a little bigger than mine; I find one easily. With two hands, I lift the wrinkled sand and let it crumple slowly into the empty baggie.

# Black River

**A**fter what happened to Jed, Lorna broke down and called Alex at the number he left for the Black River Peace Center in the foresty part of western Michigan. The young woman who finally answered said that Alex was in the middle of a "solo," and unless it was an emergency, could she please respect his wishes not to be disturbed? Feeling herself start to vibrate, Lorna said, "Well, I'm afraid this news is very disturbing." Then the woman, who sounded no more than twenty, asked, "Has someone died?" And Lorna said, "No, Alex's son dropped acid at the school's Run for AIDS and grabbed the new German teacher's ... backside." The woman said, "*Well*," as though evaluating whether or not this qualified as an emergency, as if it were up to her. "Tell Alex we're coming," Lorna said.

The first three days of Jed's two-week long suspension from school wasn't, in Lorna's view, punishment at all. More like a luxury of time to sleep, play with his Sega, masturbate. Lorna had to do something drastic.

When Alex phoned back, he said that a visit would be very "destabilizing." "I've been making progress," he said.

"He's your responsibility, too." Lorna felt like she was playing the role of a mother in a very bad high school production. Alex often made Lorna feel that way. Like her requests were vaguely hysterical.

Alex sighed. "It's awfully quiet here," he said. "Not a lot of fun for a teenager."

"Terrific."

"There's a real vibe here, Lorna, a real vibe that people work hard at. You can't just bring all your outer circle issues in and disrupt everyone."

Lorna's reply got caught in her throat. She wrapped the phone cord around and around her wrist. "This is your child, Alex," she said eventually. "There's nothing more inner circle."

There was a long pause. "I'll have to speak to our mentor about it. It's not something that can just happen."

Lorna clenched her teeth into a hard underbite. "I'm not asking permission."

The conversation ended with Lorna agreeing to bring down a couple of cans of corned beef. "It's a strict macrobiotic diet," Alex explained. "That won't mean much to you, Lorna, but Jed will appreciate having the option when he's here."

"Sure," Lorna answered, a mean spasm of satisfaction running through her, because the corned beef was clearly not just for Jed.

The drive could take six hours, more with stops. The plan was for her and Cara to spend the night and to leave Jed for the remainder of his suspension. Was it crazy to drop your kid off at a commune? (Not that Alex called it a commune. He called it "collective living," "a place of "harmony," a "spiritual retreat.") Maybe it was a little crazy, but Lorna was fed up. Fed up with Jed and all of his bullshit, but even more fed up with Alex, who was making her cope with it all on her own.

Alex had been at Black River for nearly a year now. After

losing his job at the bank, he moved to his mother's run-down lake house with grand plans to insulate, renovate, and sell the place—"soul work," he called it—but by Labour Day, nothing had been started, and it was getting cold. Over that summer of pretending to work, he'd become involved in something called "The Church of Remaking," which he described as not a physical structure but a movement of people seeking community, simplicity, and spirituality. They met regularly in someone's living room and had guest speakers, one of whom was from a centre called Black River. When Alex was back through the city at Thanksgiving, he told Lorna he was going to try a season in "collective living."

"What I'd like to do," Alex told her, "is centre myself."

"And how much will this cost you?" Lorna asked.

"Whatever I'm able to contribute."

"Which is nothing. You have no money. Will you make any money?"

Alex took a moment. "Not in the traditional sense. Not for a little while."

"So you'll be making non-traditional money?"

Alex crinkled his face into a look of pity for her small mindedness. She knew that look well. Just thinking of it made her crazy. "It's a season, Lorna."

A season. What an airy way to describe time.

"I need to sort out some issues," he told her.

Always Alex and his issues. Did he think that a bunch of meditation and stretching would make him rise above his problems? Alex had always had a woo-woo side, a grand faith that something was out there, something that he could find and unwrap, that could make his life better, that could make him the man he wanted to be. When they lived together, he would bring home crystals, meditation cassettes, Tibetan cookbooks.

Looking back, Lorna felt she should never have signed off on this collective living idea. But at the time, she was feeling a little sorry for Alex. He'd enjoyed his job at the bank and losing it was a blow. He'd also, in that Thanksgiving conversation, offered her a surprisingly large check from the sale of his Firebird. His baby. The car he bought at nineteen when he was making money as an actor and thought that one show under his belt meant a lifetime of celebrity or, at the very least, never having to look for a job. Beginner's luck had a tragic side. Lorna took the check. It was just a season.

Lorna followed the directions Alex sent her, staying clear of the freeway wherever she could. Since Debbie's accident she'd developed a fear of the freeway, a complete lack of trust in it. Still, if she had to drive at high speeds, something about having her children in the car comforted her. Their quiet trust, their confidence that she wouldn't harm them, kept her from total panic.

Cara sat up with Lorna, looking out the window, listening to her Walkman. She pretended that Lorna's "adult contemp"—Genesis and Richard Marx—could actually make her carsick. Lorna offered to put on one of Cara's cassettes, but Cara said she was good.

A slow-moving truck in front of Lorna had a bumper sticker that said, "TAKE YOUR COUNTRY BACK: PEROT FOR PRESIDENT!" She shifted her position on the seat. All of this tension everywhere! She was suffering a terrible bout of hemorrhoids. In her purse, she carried a small traveller's pack of ibuprofen and some bullet-shaped suppositories, but none of it was having much effect. She'd been snappy with Cara all morning simply for wanting information like how long the drive would be and if she'd have any time to do her homework at "the Church." It wasn't fair to make Cara feel bad.

Lorna pulled into the oncoming lane and passed the truck. Time to be brave. She looked over at Cara, but her daughter showed no signs of being impressed. She was staring down at her suede clogs and workman's socks, mouthing the lyrics to whatever was stuck in her ears.

Jed was the reason for the trip, but it was also an opportunity for Cara and Lorna. Lorna couldn't help but feel that her daughter was lost. Recently, Cara had been talking about quitting tennis lessons. On the one hand, it was a relief. She wasn't as good as she used to be, and Lorna understood the dangers in pinning too much expectation on something you were good at while you were young. But at the same time, if tennis wasn't going to give Cara something to aim for, what was there? Her daughter didn't appear to have any sense of self, any special interests. She seemed, finally, to have a circle of friends at school, but when she talked with them on the phone, it sounded like they did all the talking. Cara just seemed to cling at the edges of their lives. She got low Bs and watched a hell of a lot of television. And Lorna didn't want Cara to learn that Jed's style of behaviour was the only way to stand out, although it seemed that being noticed was the last thing Cara wanted. Even the way Cara walked seemed intended to achieve invisibility: shoulders in, arms crossed, like she didn't want to be looked at. Like she might prefer to just disappear, even from her own mother. When Lorna was fourteen years old, just starting the high school swim team, she had liked to think of herself as the big, shining quarter in a fountain full of pennies. But Cara was so buttoned up, and so unnervingly private. She hadn't even told Lorna when she got her period. Instead, Lorna had to find Cara's "lost" swimsuit, stained and hidden at the bottom of the bathroom garbage bin. Lorna hadn't found the moment to say anything about it, had no idea what to say, but she was hurt. The week Lorna started junior high in 1968, she found a sanitary napkin kit under her bed and taught herself to use it. She had wanted her daughter's experience to be different, but Cara made it all so difficult.

Punished and Walkman-less in the backseat, Jed slept easily. Peering at him in the rear-view, Lorna could see a large rosy splotch on his cheek, the way his face would always go when he was tired as a little boy. Baby Jed had been as fair and puffy-haired as a baby chick, and she and Alex called him Garfunkel. *Off he goes,* they'd say as he ambled unsteadily in his bib overalls. *Off he goes to Scarborough Fair.* Now Jed's hair was long and sweaty. He wore a plaid lumber jacket all day, every day, with the ragged cuffs of his shirts poking out. He made no effort whatsoever, but he was good looking and he knew it. It infuriated her how he ignored girls' phone calls: too lazy to check the messages, didn't notice or care, let their voices fill up the answering tape. Lorna didn't know who Jed's friends were anymore or how he spent his time. The acid was a shock, though she understood from the school guidance counsellor that the drug had recently become trendy again. A kind of resurgent hippie fashion among middle-class white kids, probably safer and easier on the allowance than the coke of the 1980s. Though frankly, at this point, Lorna was more concerned about Jed becoming an asshole than a drug addict. He'd woken up briefly at the border, handed over his passport, and re-closed his eyes, causing the border guard to knock on the window and say, "I'd appreciate you taking this seriously, young man." Then the guard glared at Lorna as though her disgraceful son was all her fault, which...well maybe so. The thing was, Jed's eyes always seemed partially closed. She'd given up trying to keep his eyes open. But as the guard waved them through, Lorna was hit with the realization that Jed was already sixteen. In a year he could get himself arrested for this behaviour. Did he understand that? Did she, truly?

Another thing: Lorna thought this road trip with her children might be a chance to take her mind off Ian, but as they drove thick into the country, through small, sweet towns with independent hardware stores and pumpkin displays, Lorna's mind turned with him. For the last year, he'd been living at his country home, taking a leave of absence to work on a book about demographic trends in voting. He'd made that unexpected decision within weeks of their kiss in the office, and she assumed the suddenness of the plan was at least a little to do with her. Of course she'd thought about him frequently in the last year, but two weeks ago, she'd had a letter from him out of nowhere: a personal letter to her home address. He said he'd like to see her—specifically, he said that *she* could come out and see *him*. He surprised her. The handful of times he'd been into the office for meetings, their conversations were brief, polite, always led by him and mostly about his book. She was never sure how warm to be, how much to smile or in what way, and afterwards she felt lost and stupid for days.

But now, Lorna's near certainty that Ian was inviting her to sleep with him, a scenario that would have been unimaginable just over a year ago, gave her a sexy kind of shock that sprang out like a firework from her lower gut. She imagined the two of them in rubber boots, taking a walk through foggy wet fields, making tea, and then fucking, eventually, by a fireplace: all images, it occurred to her, from a British TV movie she'd once watched. But she was torn about how to answer his letter. The career dangers of sleeping with one's boss were well established. And lately, with Ian out of the office, Lorna had reached a professional high point. She was leading all of OpinioNation's focus groups herself; clients praised her all the time, and she didn't want to risk that. But was she any better off turning him down?

While ambivalent, and likely screwed either way, Lorna found that she relished the control that indecision gave her. What happened next between them was in her hands, and this was big. Once she replied, control would shift back to Ian. If her reply made Ian feel guilty or rejected—the two likely outcomes—he would make her believe that this whole chapter between them was small, unimportant, and mostly the product of her imagination. He was frighteningly good at making people question their beliefs and change how they saw things. That was his grand talent; it was how he built his career and how he dealt with the world.

When the kids announced they were hungry, Lorna stopped for lunch at a restaurant next to a gas station, which, to the kids' disappointment, did not have a deep fryer. A fan whirred needlessly above their table and a muttering old woman with a wet, shuddering cough was the only other person in the place. The kids didn't appear to take much notice, but Lorna, who had the woman in her direct line of sight, found her deeply disturbing. She poured salt onto her burger before every bite. She spasmed nearly every time she lifted the burger to her mouth, toppings cascading down to her lap. How did this happen to her? Why did no one intervene? Where was her family?

"How much further?" Cara asked.

"Don't talk with food in your mouth."

"I didn't."

"An hour."

"Is there a phone we can use there?"

"I doubt it."

Neither of the children had asked her very much about Black River. Lorna wasn't involved in the talk Alex had with them, though she'd cautioned him against saying he "needed a break from it all," as he'd told her, worried this kind of language would make the kids feel they were a burden. Alex believed it was healthy for the kids to know that adults are fallible, that sometimes they need redirection, too. His fixation on honesty was frustrating to Lorna. He thought being honest was so virtuous that it released him from having to care about the effect of what he said or did on other people's feelings.

The landscape approaching Black River was a stretch of old highway lined with deep ditches. Every mile or so, a cluster of beige doublewides would sprout up like fungus across fields of yellow-brown grass, each lawn scattered with plastic toys, dogs on chains, more support for Bush than Clinton. Not the sort of place that felt ripe for a commune. A brown shingle reading private residence marked the turn that Lorna missed the first time. The road to the centre was narrow and overgrown. Branches pushed and scraped against the station wagon as Lorna, bent nervously over the wheel, drove over two bridges, past a netless tennis court, and then a weathered pioneer-style hut with a sign on the door that said DAY OF REST.

They arrived at an abrupt clearing of grass surrounded by woods. A spiral path of stones wound its way up to a large converted barn that looked neither old nor new, maybe something from the 1960s. A smaller brown lodge with a sloped roof and wood-shingled porch stood a few feet away.

Alex had clearly been waiting, and he was out the door as soon as Lorna's car pulled up. He wore a white nightgown-style garment with flouncy white trousers that fluttered to the grass. His feet were bare, but it wasn't warm. He looked skinny. Why did Alex get to be so skinny? Lorna felt a surge of envy. Skinny, free place to live, no kids' guidance counsellor to deal with. How was it fair that Alex got to have all of this?

Alex folded his hands together and bowed from the waist as Lorna and the kids got out of the car. He approached the kids first, pants swishing. Cara hugged her father but Jed held back, his hands rammed in his pockets. You could hear the river hiss somewhere behind the barn.

"Why did you grow your hair like that?" Cara asked. Alex's hair was almost as long as Jed's now but thinning substantially at the top. Lorna could see the pink dome of his scalp when the wispy strands lifted in the wind.

Alex ignored the question and put a hand on Jed's shoulder, pulling him in for a side hug. Lorna envied Alex's ease in touching Jed. She hadn't dared touch her son in so long.

"I gotta piss," Jed said.

Alex took the bags Lorna was unloading. Up close he smelled like cloves and something not fresh, maybe lamb stew. "Welcome." He squeezed Lorna's upper arm. It made her feel fat.

Inside the barn, Alex said that BRPC was once a Boy Scout camp that their "mentor," a man by the name of Neel Joshi, bought in the late 1970s. Neel Joshi — born Neil Johnston from Detroit — had trained in spiritual techniques in India and Nepal. According to Alex, Neel was truly gifted and really committed to his ideals, "not at all like the hacks they profile on *60 Minutes*." Alex spoke quickly as he showed them around. He said that at Black River, people came and went as they pleased. There was no true hierarchy. No forced rules. Everyone fell into harmony in their routines, even in their very personal quest for oneness.

"So where is everyone?" Jed asked.

"Meditation," Alex answered. "All thirty-three." His eyes went starry, the way they would after three too many drinks. "It's a beautiful thing. You'll see."

"How does it get paid for?" Lorna asked. "This whole... set-up?"

"There are many different ways of organizing the world," Alex said, mostly to the children, who didn't appear to be listening.

Lorna sighed and gave in. "And what's this Neel Joshi's way?"

"We're self-maintaining!" Alex grinned broadly.

"I see."

Alex explained that BRPC was sustained by donations as well as revenue from the gift and fresh veg market, which operated out of the little pioneer hut they'd passed on the drive in. Lorna couldn't come up with any idea of who was stopping to buy gifts. Beyond that, Alex said, the residents ran everything themselves: cooking, cleaning, general maintenance. "Our mentor has built a little ecosystem," Alex said. "A new order."

"Sounds like an *ego*system," Lorna said.

"You'll meet Neel," Alex said. "You'll see."

The barn contained the dining hall, a common room, and the women's dormitories. Each dorm room had four to six beds, but Lorna and Cara were given a special guest room—just two single beds with blaringly white sheets. A shared bathroom was down a long corridor. Rooms had switches on the wall, but no light bulbs. Alex showed them a drawer with a package of white candles and cheap terra cotta lanterns. Electricity was only connected to the bathrooms, kitchen, and dining hall. "We rise to greet the sun," Alex explained. Lorna glanced at Jed who was leaning against the doorframe. He generally rose after one in the afternoon. He gave no reaction.

"Then what?" Cara asked.

"We do meditation first thing," Alex said. "Then work practice."

"What's work practice?" Cara asked this in a way that made Lorna smile. She felt proud that Cara seemed to instantly recognize the silliness of the phrase: *Do you practise working? Do adults here actually do anything?* It was very easy for Lorna to understand what Alex liked about this place. He could go weeks without making a single decision. He didn't need to open bills or visit the laundromat or negotiate when to see his children. His day was set out for him: meditation, chanting, staying in one place, and thinking endlessly about himself. No pressure to do anything at all.

"We harvest vegetables, cook, dredge the pond," he said. What on earth was Alex doing dredging a pond? And cooking? When they all lived together, Alex made french toast with cinnamon on top about four times a year and expected everyone to fall off their chairs with praise. Otherwise he had always been terrible in the kitchen, timidly backing away from any assignment. "You do it all so well," he'd say to Lorna, as though flattery could conceal his laziness. Any task she gave him, she ended up snatching back.

"I generally work in the vegetable and gift market," Alex said, mostly addressing Lorna. "It's sort of a senior position." Hadn't he just told her there was no hierarchy here?

"Where will Jed work practice?" Cara asked.

"Everywhere," Alex said, rubbing Cara's shoulder and then glancing at Jed a few feet away. "He's going to feel connected to himself. Feel connected to the people around him. Feel conse-quences." Lorna wanted to laugh, but it wasn't worth the earnest, perplexed look that Alex would put on in return.

While Alex took Jed across to the men's lodge, Lorna and Cara dropped their bags off in their room. Lorna wasn't sure where to start with Cara. She found herself asking, "So what do you think?" in an eerily chipper tone.

"It's OK," Cara said. "I don't think Jed will like it."

"No?" Lorna's curiosity was painfully intense, but she needed to tread lightly or Cara would clam right up. "Why not?"

Cara shrugged and stretched out on the bed with her Walk-man.

In the bathroom, Lorna used another suppository. There was no place to throw out the foil wrapping, so she jammed it in her pocket. Through the bathroom window, she saw a sundial in the middle of the lawn. Someone was pinning white clothes to a line that hung heavy and still. She wished she could know what Cara was seeing. She supposed it really wasn't so menacing, was it? Alex seemed cheerful, happy to see the kids. She headed back to the room, dropping the foil in a plastic bucket in the hall.

...

They all met Neel Joshi at four thirty, before what Alex called the daily sermon, which took place in a room that reminded Lorna of a church parish hall with its white walls, linoleum floors, and royal blue industrial drapes. Two triangular west-facing windows, like two halves of a sail, let in the last of the day's light. Men and women were drifting in, also dressed in white, hair mostly long. Ages were mixed, but Lorna, having hit an age where she'd become obsessed with determining the age of others, figured most were in their mid-twenties. Quite a few residents did not look much older than Jed.

The room hushed as Neel strode in. He was tall and sinewy with a bit of a swagger. He had an olive complexion — though not precisely Indian, she didn't think — and he looked young, but you could tell he wasn't really, approaching fifty but possibly older. His hair was much longer and much healthier looking than Alex's.

"I'd like you to meet my family," Alex said, interrupting Neel's stride. Lorna wasn't sure whom Alex was addressing, whether "family" referred to her and the kids or to Neel and his disciples. Alex seemed nervous. He was speaking too quickly.

The man bowed. "Namaste," he said. His voice was deep and echoing. He smiled at Lorna with perfect white teeth. But there was something reptilian about his face, a jutting prominence in the lower jaw.

"My son," Alex said, steering Jed forward. "He will be with us a few days."

Neel touched the sleeve of Jed's shirt. His fingernails were long and curly. "You brought white clothes to wear, Jed?"

It was amazing. Jed actually looked a little frightened of Neel.

"Nope. Sorry," he said, but he looked away, immediately aware this was not going to fly.

"No white tracksuit?" Alex asked desperately, as if a white tracksuit was something Jed would ever wear.

Neel looked down at Jed's feet. "Slippers? Sandals?"

Jed shook his head.

"We dress in harmony here." Neel looked at Alex. "There's a five-and-dime twenty miles out of town in the Belmont Plaza. You may go tomorrow." Then he touched Cara's chin with his shocking fingernails and carried on to the front of the room.

Alex turned to Jed. "I told you to bring something white."

Jed shrugged.

"No," Alex said, looking, actually, very *uncentred*. "You do not ignore me."

Lorna noticed Cara glance at her sideways. Her upper lip was stretched over her teeth; she was either afraid or trying to stop from laughing.

"Did you hear me?" Alex said.

"Yeah, got it." Jed jerked his hair from his eyes and looked up at his father.

"All right." Alex looked at them all. "I'm going to sit up near the front." It was clear from the way he said it that they weren't to join him.

Lorna's butt hurt when she sat on the floor, so she leaned against the back wall at the edge of the room. She watched everyone lay down their mats and settle cross-legged like kindergarteners at story time. Neel looked out over the crowd, scanning the rows in front of him. He approached the front row and bent down to speak into Alex's ear. Alex stood up, moved back one row, then another, until Neel lowered his hands for Alex to stop and sit down. Was Alex being punished? Humiliated in front of his family because Jed wasn't wearing white? Lorna felt a scratch of pity in her throat.

Neel's hour-long sermon seemed to have something to do with pain. He spoke in balanced sentences, needlessly repeating certain words. "Life is suffering. Suffering is life. Life is not avoidance of suffering." His voice had a deep, rich quality, and he took long self-important pauses to allow his listeners to absorb the columns of wisdom. Occasionally, though, he would crunch down hard on certain words. *Wounds* was one of the harsh ones. He said it like it hurt his mouth. "We are born with wounds. Wounds tell of our suffering. Wounds give us courage." Lorna shifted the weight on her ass.

Neel extended his palm, holding out something silver. Lorna squinted. Was it a quarter? "Drugs disconnect us from suffering. Disconnect us from our courage," Neel said. He flicked the thing to his feet; it skittered across the floor with unsatisfying heft. The suppository foil. This, too, was almost certainly connected to Alex's punishment.

Neel let out a long, loud breath. "Let us set our attention to today's closing."

Lorna looked at Alex's back: stiller, straighter than everyone else. Did he want so badly to be teacher's pet? To be loved? Sometimes friends asked Lorna about Alex. To make a point, she would say things like, "How's Alex? I wouldn't know. He's off being a hippie on some farm." But even saying this, she still thought she knew. And yet she'd underestimated him. What he'd become involved in. This place wasn't the hippie colony she imagined. There were no naked, wild-haired children. No blanket tosses or tie-dye. She'd been dreading all that, but this was all so serious, so spartan. Where was the fun in it?

After a long period of quiet, and with no obvious introduction, Neel started to purr. He sat still, serene to the point of apparent indifference. Like Jed, his eyes were partially closed. Seemingly on some sort of cue, a young man began to drum on the overturned white bin that Lorna had assumed was trash two hours earlier. Accompanied by the beat, Neel shifted into a halting chant. One by one the congregation began to rise and dance. You would have guessed that there were thirty-three separate rhythms occurring at once. Some members swayed, some jiggled in place, some spun round and round with arms open, *Sound of Music* style. One scrawny young man danced with his chest poking out, his neck extending in and out like a peacock until he fell to the floor and slithered around. And then there was Alex. Spinning in place with his chin tilted up to the window's last strands of sun. It was the look on Alex's face that made Lorna turn away in embarrassment. A closed-eyed expression of rapture that seemed like it ought to be private. No, she didn't really recognize him.

Jed and Cara seemed bored for most of the bizarre sermon, but now they watched the dancing with rapt attention. Could they still see their father in this dancing, pyjama-wearing man? How sad, how lonely, to witness your father behaving like a nutter. Lorna was never especially close with her own dad, but she'd respected him. At the very least, she'd always wanted to please him. Lorna was glad the kids weren't killing themselves to win Alex's affection, but she didn't want them to dismiss him completely. If there was a part of her that wanted Jed and Cara to see their father's selfishness here in order to appreciate her own loyalty and steadiness, she regretted it now.

A girl, no older than twenty, sashayed in front of the three of them. She smiled in a vacant, wide-eyed way, like there was something very beautiful and transcendent going on just inches above their heads.

"You're joining us, I hear," she said to Jed.

The girl was very pretty. Long blond hair fell into ringlets just past her shoulders. Maybe a little greasy, but the effect was more whimsical than neglected looking. She wore a full white peasant skirt with a tight leotard top. Lorna, and presumably everyone else, could see the dimpled texture of her nipples.

"Just for a few days," Lorna cut in. "Visiting his father."

"We'll need a name for you," she said.

"Yeah? What's your name?" Jed was leaning back against the wall, looking up with arms crossed. He was flirting. Lorna hated that he was so sexually at ease. She'd seen condoms at home. Unlike his sister, he made no effort to conceal his rites of passage at the bottom of the garbage bin. In the girls' bathroom on her visit to the school guidance counsellor, Lorna had been unlucky enough to pee across from a prickly cactus graffitied on a stall door with the caption *JK's got a BIG one!* Of course there could be other JKs, but Lorna knew.

The girl pointed to her chest. "Peony." She swayed in front of him. "Will you dance with us?"

"Depends. What's your real name?" Jed smirked.

The girl laughed. "You're so much like Sparrow!"

...

In the half-hour "rest period" before dinner, Jed and Cara went back to their rooms. Lorna followed Alex to the dining room, where he began to set up folding tables for Breaking Bread, the name they used for dinner at Black River. The smell of cinnamon and ginger drifted in from the kitchen.

"So this is a day in the life," Lorna said with forced lightness.

"It's incredible, isn't it? I'm glad you're seeing this. It's a hard thing to describe." Alex wiped his forehead with his wrist, still sweaty from the dancing.

"So they call you Swallow?"

"Sparrow," he said, seriously.

"Sparrow, OK."

"You know, I have to apologize to you, Loo. I wasn't too sure at first, but I think the routine's going to be great for Jed." Alex righted a table and slid a few chairs underneath.

"You do?" What on earth about the last few hours could have made him feel that way?

"Routines will change everything. It's amazingly healing, Lorna. Since I've been here, I've felt my chaos lift." He raised his hands slowly, wiggling his fingertips. His nails, she noted, had also grown long. "Everything motivating Jed's behaviour right now, it's just cravings and fears. He'll learn to quiet those influences. Remove those impulses. Just be."

"Well," Lorna said, looking away. "I've been thinking about that." She felt her heartbeat jump up a tick. "I'm not sure this is a good idea anymore."

Alex stopped what he was doing.

"For openers," Lorna continued. "There's a woman here trying to sleep with him."

"What? No." Alex laughed, rocking back on his heels.

"Peony?"

"Trust me." Alex chuckled again and shook his head. "Peony will absolutely not try to sleep with Jed."

"What makes you so certain? Are you sleeping with her?"

"Come on, Lorna, no. I just know."

"He sleeps with people, in case you're curious."

Alex looked around. A few other helpers were coming in. He motioned for her to follow him to more tables at the back of the room. He spoke quietly. "We sign a contract, Lorna. No one here is having sex."

"You're forbidden from sex?"

"Well," Alex said, "it's terms we agree to. No caffeine, no meat, no alcohol, no sex. *Forbidden* suggests that we're forced. We're not forced to do anything. All of us here, we want to recreate our lives." He wrinkled his forehead with such sincerity that Lorna had to look away from his face. She thought about all those muscled young bodies swaying to the music. Why weren't they having sex? Why weren't they finding apartments, going to college, getting jobs? What would happen to them? Would they just grow old here without ever growing up?

"What's this business about needing permission to go out shopping?" Lorna asked.

Alex bent to unfold another table. "I don't need permission."

Lorna bit her bottom lip. "I think you do, Alex. And I think that's crazy."

Alex straightened. "This may not be your scene, Lorna, but it's not crazy. Do you really have no ability to uncouple things that are new to you from 'crazy'?" He made quotes like little doe ears with his fingers.

"Whatever, Alex." Lorna held up her palms. "What I'm telling you is that I'm not comfortable with —" she swept her arm out in front of her " — any of this."

"That's your work, Lorna."

"That's my *work*?"

"You see the world so negatively," Alex said. "You should work on that." He patted her upper arm again.

"Work on that how? Should I spend a year on a commune, too? I'd love that, Alex, but where would that leave our children?"

Alex's eyes darted around the room, evidently panicked about who could be overhearing the rise in her voice.

Lorna shook her head. "You know what? I'm taking Jed home."

Alex pinched his lower lip with his fingers. "You have to understand," he spoke softly. "I've imposed on this community. I asked a special favour to allow Jed to stay here." He picked up Lorna's hand. His was a little clammy. "If I throw that generosity away...well."

Lorna stared into Alex's worried face. She felt she did understand something. Alex may have felt stronger, but it wasn't real strength. He was afraid. And Lorna understood that if she took Jed away tonight, if they all turned their backs, they might lose Alex. He would go on and recreate his life without them. He would fail his children, and in the long run that could fuck Jed up even more.

At Breaking Bread, the dining area filled with the happy clatter of a high school cafeteria. It was the first normal thing to happen since arriving. The four of them sat at a separate table that Alex heaped with bowls of food: seaweed salad, brown rice with steamed vegetables, chickpeas. "All of the vegetables are grown here," Alex said.

"Where do you grow the seaweed?" Jed picked at his food. The smell of cigarettes came off his hair and jacket.

Lorna didn't make eye contact with Alex, and he didn't continue on the farming. He asked questions about school that only Cara bothered to answer. While mashing chickpeas with her fork, she described a social studies project using a frightening number of *like*s and *I don't know*s: "We just, I don't know, we cut things out in the newspaper and paste them in a scrapbook. Like free trade or what's happening with Sinead O'Connor. There's no, like, point." Normally Lorna would challenge this sort of laziness, but tonight she didn't have the energy. At least someone was talking.

"That's something," Alex said after such a long pause to chew his food that Lorna wasn't sure if he was still referring to the scrapbook or something else entirely.

Cara shrugged. "When are you coming back?"

Alex served her more chickpeas. "I'm part of something here," he said. "Like an ecosystem, remember? Who would take care of the shop if I went away?"

"What about for a weekend?"

"We'll see."

"Who's we? Who decides?" This was Jed now, leaning back on the two legs of his chair. "Jim Jones gives you a hall pass, or...?"

Alex looked accusingly at Lorna. "I think a certain level of respect is missing there, Jed."

"Who's Jim Jones?" Cara asked.

"Some fucking psycho preacher who killed like nine hundred of his followers with Kool-Aid," Jed said.

Alex turned to Cara. "You don't need to worry about any of that, OK? This is a healing place. Everyone here is happy."

Cara looked at Lorna. "I thought Jed was here for a punishment."

Alex put down his fork. Lorna cleared her throat. It was falling to her to redirect this disastrous conversation. "So!" She noticed how the brightness of her voice made Jed flinch across the table. "Tell us about some of your friends here, Alex. Who do you like to spend time with?"

"They're all friends, Lorna. Family, as a matter of fact." Lorna tried to dagger him with her eyes, but he was staring off in that new dreamy way. "I've never had anything like it before."

Couldn't he hear what he was saying? Lorna wanted to reach over and halt her daughter's dumbly nodding head. *You don't have to agree with that: you're his family.* She wanted to hurl the gummy seaweed at the wall. Instead she put down her napkin. "Well, it was a long drive. I'm ready for bed."

"You're going to bed now?" Jed flared his nostrils like he'd never smelt a bigger loser in his whole life.

"You guys go," Alex said. "Jed and I will clean up."


As a small child, Cara always begged Lorna to stay with her until she fell asleep. And it wasn't so long ago that Cara would drag her sleeping bag into Jed's room, or to the foot of Lorna's bed, after seeing something scary on TV. Any small thing could frighten Cara, and as much as Lorna believed in independence, she couldn't stand the idea of her daughter being alone with her fear.

Tonight, Cara changed in the bathroom, in private, and got into bed with just the quietest "Night." Lorna listened to her shift under the thin, papery sheets, heard her yawn. When her children were babies, Lorna was both relieved and terrified by their sleep. Several times a night, she would walk into the dark, hushed nursery room and listen for their breathing. She put a palm down on their narrow little chests. They were so helpless; she was so young. She had an urge to get up now and wrap herself around her daughter. When had she stopped touching her children? "Everything OK?" Lorna whispered.

"Yeah."

"Comfy?"

"Not exactly."

"I'm not sure what we can do about that." Lorna wasn't entirely sure what made her tone so sharp. But she knew she hated being so inept, so incapable of fixing things for her children. It was easier when they were little.

"Don't worry about it." Worse, it seemed like Cara didn't want or expect much comfort from Lorna. Perhaps she'd forgotten that her mother had ever done things that could make her feel safe.

Lorna wished she knew what could get Cara to talk to her like the mothers and daughters on TV. In focus groups, she used open-ended questions to get people talking, but these often seemed to irritate her kids. "What was the best part of the day?" she tried.

"Lunch, probably." She heard Cara's legs kick around. "I don't know. I'm really tired, Mom."

Lorna breathed out her disappointment. "OK, sweetie."

The river was easier to hear at night, or maybe it was distant cars. Lorna closed her eyes, listening to the rhythm. Lately, she'd been having trouble falling asleep. For Lorna, bedtime had become too much of a reminder of time itself: how much more of it was gone. At the end of the day, Lorna only ever felt older:

no wiser, no more interesting or accomplished. She thought of herself at Cara's age, fourteen, standing at the rim of a pool, so clear on what she ought to do.

When Lorna woke, she was sure she hadn't been asleep long. It took her a moment to orient herself. She was in a room with her daughter at the Black River Peace Center: not a place she'd ever imagined finding any of them. Next to her, Lorna heard shuffling, moving. Bare feet on linoleum. She rolled her head slightly and saw Cara crossing the small room and watched as she moved back and forth, from the wardrobe to the window, tapping each one. When she was younger, Cara was known to sleepwalk, usually when she was overtired. She never got very far, but once Alex found her curled up on top of the dryer.

"Cara," Lorna whispered. "What are you doing?"

Cara stopped, her fingertips on the window glass, but she didn't say anything.

"Do you need the bathroom?"

"No."

"I think you might be sleepwalking, honey."

Cara sank down on her bed.

"Try to fall back asleep. OK?"

"OK."

Lorna lay back, listening to Cara settle into her bed. What was keeping her daughter from sound sleep? Her long-haired father? Her brother's stories about Jim Jones? If Cara was afraid of something, Lorna wished she'd tell her. Closing her eyes again, Lorna let the day's faces and weird lines of conversation blur through her thoughts. Then, on the brink of sleep, she heard the slight yield of Cara's mattress again. Cara's feet hit the floor. There was a quiet tap, another tap. Lorna flipped around to say something, but just as quickly, Cara hopped back into bed. Lorna waited but there was nothing more. She'd have to remember to ask about this pacing in the morning. Sleep was important now. The last thing this family needed was a car accident tomorrow.

Lorna woke to the sound of distant music — the recorder? The flute? — she lit the terra-cotta lantern and checked her watch: 5:17 a.m. Cara was a mound under the sheets.

Alex was waiting for them in the foyer. He gave Cara a long hug and spoke quietly to Lorna over their daughter's head. "Jed'll be good here. You'll see."

"Sure. OK." She smiled at Alex, but there was a dropping feeling in her chest. As she watched his thin white figure pad silently down the long hallway, it seemed possible that he could disappear right into the walls.

Jed turned up as Lorna and Cara were loading the car. He was wearing his jeans and ratty long-sleeve shirt. None of this white pyjama business, not yet. He held a terra-cotta candle, though it was nearly light.

Lorna unlocked the car.

"Do I have to dance?" Jed said

Lorna turned around. "Dance?"

Jed looked at Cara and started to gyrate his hips, his arms waving in the air, tongue hanging from his mouth. Cara laughed, a white breathy puff of air. She glanced quickly at her mother, uncertain. Lorna smiled back: it was OK.

"Not if you don't want to." She put her hand on Jed's shoulder. He didn't move. Oh, how she wanted to keep her hand there. "Ten days," she said. "That's it."

Jed jerked the hair from his face and regarded her. Lorna could see that he thought she'd give in. He was waiting for her to say, "All right, you're right. This is crazy. Get your stuff and get in the car." But Jed was being brave; he wouldn't ask her to take him home. If he did, she might agree. She wanted her children to ask her for things. But Alex was lost here, and he needed Jed more than she did. He needed to remember who depended on him. As for Jed, no matter how embarrassing Alex looked in those white pyjamas or what absurd things he'd say in the coming days, a son should know his father gave a shit.

"I'm freezing," Cara said. She was opening the passenger door.

Lorna let go of Jed's shoulder. "We'll see you soon."

Jed held the lantern up to his chin. "Soon. Again. Again. Soon." He bowed his head like Neel. Cara laughed again.

Once they were in the car, Cara set her pillow up against the window and tucked her fists into the sleeves of her sweatshirt. Lorna thought of Cara's strange behaviour the night before, but it had been a strange day. Better not to ask Cara questions that would embarrass her. Everyone needed to feel OK now.

Lorna watched Jed in the rear-view as she drove away. A buttery smear of candlelight crossed his chin. She recalled that when Jed was a toddler, he was terrified of candles. Neither Lorna nor Alex understood where the fear came from. At his second birthday party, he worked himself into a frenzy over the lighted cake: dark pink face, gulping tears, his body shaking like a tiny engine. Then there was the night the power went out. Heart thumping, Lorna pulled two-year-old Jed from the tub and carried his slippery little body through darkness to the kitchen. She'd been impossibly young, terrified of electrical fires, masked men in the closet, god knows what else. She wasn't thinking when she took a candle from the kitchen drawer and struck the match, the flash of light spreading across Jed's betrayed, terror-stricken face. "Oh, Jed!" she said, her hand flying to her mouth. "I'm so sorry." But he didn't cry. Somehow, he knew she needed him not to. He looked at the beam of light on his naked chest and opened his hands to hold it.

# Shiva
SPRING, 1993

There's good food everywhere in the Grossmans' house: glass bowls of egg and tuna salad, pretty plates of twisty apricot cookies, mini-bagels, sliced fruit. No one is eating, though. People just bunch together with their little white cups. No one bunches with me. I'm practically the only young person, minus a few cousins. I wish we'd leave, but Mom just poured herself a whole new glass of water with drowned mint leaves.

On the drive over, Mom warned me not to expect much conversation. If the family wants to talk, she said, I should think of a couple nice stories to share. I was like, "What stories?" She just kept her eyes on the road. "We're here for the family. If you can't think of anything, just say you're sorry for their loss."

I stand at the very back of the living room by the open patio doors. A few feet away from me, Violet, the cleaning lady, is sitting alone with a plate of food on her lap. I look away before she can catch my eye. I haven't had an attack of the hell-thoughts in a long time. It would be the worst day for them to start up again.

Where I'm standing, I can hear a radio playing at a neighbour's house: "Warm temperatures will continue until Monday..." Somewhere else, a sprinkler tick-ticks like a rattlesnake. For most people, it's just a normal day.

"Some of you might know Samantha Grossman," Mr. Morris said in homeroom last Thursday, rolling chalk between his fingers. Everyone knew Sam: she was the fat girl. Sam wore basketball shorts every day until late October. In winter, she switched to a black velvet dress with a zipper that zigzagged up her wide back.

Mr. Morris wrote the word *meningitis* on the blackboard. "It's a freak case," he said. "We're trying to trace it." Elliott Culver in the back row actually laughed. "Freak case," he repeated. "Go figure." I wanted to turn around and glare at him, but I was frozen. I felt exactly like I did when I was four years old and someone at the cottage let me float too far from the beach on an inflatable mat. Holding hard to the surface of my desk, it seemed like everything and everyone in the room was fading away from me, and I couldn't do a thing to help myself.

The public health nurse who came to school said anyone who'd had exposure to Sam — shared a sip of her juice box, was her example — should leave school immediately. I'm pretty sure no one shared a juice box with Sam, but everyone loved panicking about it anyway. My best friend Ash pretended to have used the same pipette in bio so she could miss school for a week. No one cared that Sam was dead.

I watch a few people smoke cigarettes outside. It was back there that Sam and I tried smoking for the first time while her parents were out watching *Ghost*. We were so paranoid about the smell after that we brushed our teeth for ten minutes and ate pinches of curly parsley.

In the reflection of the glass doors, I see Ruthie walking toward me. My heart jumps. I was relieved we didn't see her when we got here. I figured she might be upstairs crying her eyes out; no one would blame her. When we first got the news, Mom was pretty much on the floor worrying about Ruthie and how she'd ever make it through this. But here she is.

"It's good to see you." Her hand on the back of my neck is damp.

It's my turn to talk, but I can't think of anything to say. I can't say it's good to see her, too. Sam's dead, and that's the only reason I'm here. I nod at our reflections. Ruthie was Miss Teen Winnipeg in 1970 and 1971; pictures in the basement prove it. She's pretty compared to a lot of moms, with thick dark hair that always reminds me of chocolate cake batter rippling from a bowl. She looks good even today. Even without makeup.

"You go ahead and call if you ever want to swim," she says.

I nod again. I can't turn and look at her. I feel sweaty and knotted up inside, the worst kind of liar.

"I mean it."

"I'm sorry for your loss." It comes out too muffled and rushed.

"Pardon?"

I really, really don't want to say it again, but I don't have to because a bearded man taps Ruthie's shoulder at the same time.

"Sweet girl," she says. "You come say goodbye before you go." Then she turns to speak to the bearded guy.

The last time I saw Ruthie was at Soul Bakery a few months ago. I was with Ash and we'd just finished a Matinée Slims Menthol, which I'm pretty sure Ruthie could smell when she kissed my ear, all "*Mwa!*" She tapped the glass display case of cakes and pastries and said, "Now. Remind me, Cara. Which does Sammy like best?"

Ash talked when I didn't say anything. "Everyone likes black-out cake."

Ruthie didn't even look at Ash; her eyes went straight back to me. "We'd love to have you over for Sam's birthday next week. Give us a call." She ordered a zucchini loaf, definitely not one of Sam's favourites.

When Ash asked who Sammy was, I said *he* was a family friend. I made up this story about a funny, strange kid who probably had a crush on me. I went on and on. It was actually pretty easy to lie.

A few days later, Ruthie called Mom herself. I heard her voice through the cordless. "I think the girls have been cooking something up!"

"We're in grade nine," I told Mom as soon as she got off the phone. "Who still gets their parents to arrange a sleepover?"

Mom seemed nervous. "So you want me to call back and say you can't go?"

"Yes, please."

Mom sat down at the table across from me. "It's Sam's birthday. I think she probably misses you, sweetie."

"Have you seen her lately? She's kind of a weirdo."

Mom didn't seem that mad. "Sam's always been a bit of an odd duck. It never bothered you before."

I look over at Mom now, but she's busy helping an old woman clean a spill in the kitchen. A couple of days ago, Mom tried to talk to me about her dead friend Debbie. She asked if I remembered the time at Mandarin Mansion when she couldn't stop crying over her. I didn't remember and had no idea what she was talking about, but her point was that it's OK to feel strange at first about a tragedy. The sadness may just hit you later, it can happen anytime. The conversation made me feel worse. I don't think I really have the right to cry over this. I wasn't nice to Sam. Most of this year, I actually wanted to erase ever knowing her at all.

I step out the glass doors and onto the terrace. I don't have my coat, but it's been warm all day and it's not yet dark. There's one man left smoking at the patio table, so I take a few steps into the garden and pretend to be totally absorbed by Ruthie's flowerbed: a mound of dirt with a few pale green leaves poking up like rabbit ears. I imagine for a second that Sam is buried under that curved mound, her pale skin dissolving from her bones. I try to kick the thought out of my mind.

I hear the man's voice behind me. "Were you a friend of Samantha's?"

I don't know how to answer him. I make my head do a mix between a nod and a side-to-side head shake.

The guy flicks his ashes onto the flowerbed. "You two knew each other a long time?"

"Since we were babies, pretty much."

"Ah. I'm sorry."

"That's OK."

"It's not OK." He puts his hand on his chest. "Pinchus. Well, Mr. Leftin to her."

So this is Lefty, Sam's Hebrew school teacher. She had a crush on him, or at least she pretended to.

"You go to College Heights?" he asks.

"Yeah."

Lefty has one of those smiles that turns down like a frown. He's a little bit cute, probably less than thirty. "Good school."

This was the first year that Sam and I were in the same

school. We were supposed to go to middle school together, but her parents moved to Israel for the two years instead. I cried when I found out they were leaving. I had always pictured us making friends and getting boyfriends as a team together. Ruthie made macramé bracelets for Sam and me that said "Best Friends 4-Ever" in the weave.

Lefty crushes his cigarette into an ashtray on the patio table. "Nice that you're here, kiddo." He winks like we have a secret.

I have a secret about Lefty. The time Sam made us french kiss, I had to pretend to be him. I didn't know what he was like, so I put on a fake deep voice: *Hey, hey, hey!* She said to take off my shirt but leave my jeans on, like those guys that jump out of cakes on birthday cards. I stood half-naked like that, getting cold while she put on eye shadow and stuffed her shirt with both sides of a pantyhose egg. The whole thing makes me feel kind of icky. It's probably not the best memory to have at a funeral.

It was weird after the Grossmans left because I didn't miss Sam at all once school started. It was sort of a relief, in a way, not to always have to call her back. Not to do what she said. By the end of eighth grade, before she came home, I was already getting nervous about mixing her in with Ash and my new friends once high school started. For one thing, Sam liked to tell really long stories. With Ash and them, you have to get your story out in one minute or less if you want anyone to keep listening. Also, if Sam ever suggested playing one of her messed-up games, like Jewish refugees or runaway teenage strippers, I would pretty much die. I wasn't into that kind of stuff anymore; no one I know now was ever into that stuff.

I cross the yard and open the gate to the Grossmans' pool, which is covered over for winter in a saggy black tarp. Old leaves and brown pine needles float in a puddle on top. My reflection on the surface is a faded moon, my hair slicing down at the water. It's just April now, but it's hard to believe the Grossmans will bother opening the pool this season. Sam and I were basically the only ones who ever used it. We dove for Smurfs, swam under each other's legs, had tea parties, and screamed out bubbles. Sometimes we practised lifesaving: one of us the victim, the other the rescuer. We took turns flipping and dragging each other out of the pool, checking pulses, doing fake mouth-to-mouth on the deck. Sometimes Sam would pretend to be dead and just lie with her eyes open, all rigid and unmoving until I'd get mad and threaten to go home.

When the Grossmans got back from Israel in August, I came over with my bikini under my clothes. It was about a million degrees out, and Ash and Lacey were going to see *Sister Act* at the mall. I wanted to go with them, but Ruthie had already left two messages to say they were home and I could drop by anytime.

"You look the same," Sam said when she answered the door. I had no idea what to say because she didn't look the same at all. She was big. Tall and puffed up. Her hair was huge too, a little like a clown wig. She wore boys' basketball shorts that fluttered down to new, hulking calves.

I followed her into the frigid air conditioning, into the familiar lime smell of the Grossmans' clean house. She opened the storage cupboard and stabbed the plastic on a new tray of Cokes with her long dirty fingernails. "Have as many as you want," she said, and took two warm cans up to her bedroom.

Sam's room was in the middle of being painted. One wall had a new black coat, but you could still see the old pink underneath. She used to have a bunk bed — me on top, her on bottom — but it had been replaced by a futon with a dark red comforter. Her lace curtains were in a puddle on the floor, and posters of scary looking punk bands I had never heard of were on the wall. All of Sam's stuffed animals were gone.

I tried asking questions. *How was Israel?* Hated it. *How's your mom?* Fake. *Want to swim?* You can if you want to. Her face looked like it had been inflated with a bicycle pump. If she suggested one of her freaky games, I'd already decided to laugh like it was a joke. But she didn't suggest anything. She just turned on *Divorce Court.*

When I left Sam's house, I saw Ruthie on the driveway. Because of how fat and weird looking Sam got in Israel, it surprised me that Ruthie could look so totally the same: skinny and tanned. She was hauling big bags of lawn feed out of her trunk, and I helped her bring them around to the backyard. She told me she really liked my hair, but it wasn't cut in any special way. She asked if I'd done my back-to-school shopping yet. I told her yes, all done, and I was grateful she didn't offer the annual trip to Yorkdale Mall. She thanked me about ten thousand times for the help. I figured that Sam probably didn't help with anything.

The whole week before school started, I was freaking out about Sam. I knew for sure that I couldn't combine her with my new friends. The problem wasn't just what Sam looked like now. She was a whole different person, almost like a dead person: a fat, black cloud. I wanted her to disappear. It took me a few days to figure out that I didn't actually have to stay friends with her. Nobody could force us, and it wasn't like she was phoning me.

Out on the Grossmans' pool deck, the sun is slipping behind the backyard fence. It's getting cold without the light. We've been at shiva for more than an hour, as long as Mom said we'd stay. Tomorrow's a parent-teacher conference day at school, and tonight Ash is having a sleepover at her dad's place downtown. If I get there too late, I'll miss the Chinese food.

I pull my sweater down over my hands and walk around to the pool cabana. The door swings right open and I walk inside, breathing the old towel smell. The cabana was always a good place to hide out. Today it's dark and creepy inside, but somehow that feels right.

Most of the interior space is taken up by pool equipment and Styrofoam float toys, but I find a spot on the bench across from an old poster Sam made: "Grossmans' Pool: Don't be Gross, man (that means pee or spit)." Sam could be funny, I guess.

I check under the bench for her parents' copy of the *Joy of Sex*. We used to hide it back here and flip through the pages to decide on the things we'd do with our boyfriends and the things we'd save just for husbands. It's not there and I wonder how it got back inside. Did Ruthie bring it in? Did she know Sam was a perv? I stretch my legs out and lean my head against a flutter board. Sam and I camped out in here once at a sleepover until we got too cold and scared about murderers and had to move inside. We also tried tampons in here for the first time, stolen out of Ruthie's medicine cabinet. I can picture Sam squatting down on the AstroTurf floor, her bathing suit stretched to the side. I don't think she even had any pubic hair. I blink my eyes a few times, wanting to clear the picture. I should really try harder to think of nicer memories.

Through a moon-shaped cut-out on the cabana wall, I can see lights in the Grossmans' windows. Their house always looked like this on shabbat: warm and yellowy, filled with people. I used to wish it were my house. For a moment, I try to imagine that it's not Sam's shiva, but a regular Friday in fifth grade. At the end of dinner, Sam and I would always wait for Ruthie to read our fortunes from the bottom of empty cups of cocoa. "I see your names in lights," she'd say, tilting a cup forward and back. "I see a very special friendship."

When we started high school last September, Sam didn't cling or even try to talk to me. I could go a long time without thinking about her, but sometimes I felt her staring in the hall. Once after exams, before the Christmas holidays, she found me alone at the bus stop. Her big cheeks were all red from the cold. "I got you a present in Israel," she said, digging out this mash of pink tissue paper from her backpack. "You probably don't even want it, but my Mom said to give it to you." I hoped no one was watching us. That was pretty much all I cared about. We sat next to each other on the bus, but I faked an orthodontist appointment and got off four stops early. At home I flushed the tissue paper without even looking inside. I felt guilty, but I thought it would be worse if I just left it hanging around in my room.

Sam's second floor window is the only one in the house that isn't lit. I try to imagine her bedroom window the way it used to be: her lace curtains, the god's eye we made with yarn and popsicle sticks, her collection of crystal animals that lined the ledge and sparkled when the sun came through. Everything is gone, I tell myself. *It's so sad.* But I'm not even close to crying.

There's a clackety-clack of heels on the terrace outside and then Mom's voice. "I saw her come out."

"Who?" It sounds like Lefty. He must be smoking non-stop.

"My daughter. She didn't have her coat. She's an old friend of Sam's."

I can't hear what they say next, it's too muffled. Then Lefty says, "If she's not back..."

"Just send her in if you see her."

The pool gate whines open and I hear Mom's shoes circling the deck. I wonder if she's remembering the hottest day of sixth grade when she came over to swim laps while Sam and I did handstands in the shallow end. Ruthie sat in a lawn chair wearing a yellow floppy hat. She said to Mom, "I'd kill for your shoulders." I thought, *Kill who?* But I was proud that Mom was good at something and everyone could see it. It felt sometimes like Ruthie wanted me to wish that she were my mom instead.

The pool gate slams shut again, and I'm glad Mom didn't find me. I don't want to go back in. Ruthie's rib-crushing hugs, her calling me a sweet girl, it's too much. The best plan is to sneak out along the side of the house and meet Mom at the car. I get on my knees to watch through the moon shape as Mom crosses the yard and back to the living room. What would she do if I died of meningitis? If I were the freak accident? Would she be nice to Sam at my funeral? She's probably the only one who would be.

The tears that come out next don't feel like normal tears. They're hard and hot like the last drops out of a dishrag after twisting and squeezing. But it's not Sam I'm crying for. I bet Ruthie didn't like what Sam did to her room or her hair this year, either. Maybe she called Mom about the birthday party because she knew Sam wouldn't call me. Sam and I were ready to stop being friends; Ruthie just wasn't. In a few years, I'm sure she would have gotten used to me being out of the picture. Probably Sam would have switched schools, found lots of new friends that were weird and pervy like her, and Ruthie would have figured out the truth and moved on. But that hadn't happened yet. It doesn't get to happen now. What did happen, for sure, is that Sam and I were best friends once. There's more than one truth, and Ruthie should get to remember whatever part she wants.

Lefty's by the pool gate now, and he smiles as I come out of the cabana, leaning back with his hands in his pockets. My own hands are shaky.

"See you around," he says. But he won't, so I don't say anything back. People like us have no reason to come together again.

I pass the pool and brush the cabana dust off the back of my pants, getting ready to head inside and say goodbye to Ruthie.

# The Favour

FALL, 1993

**L**orna peered through the gap in her office door. Edwina Needham looked nothing like her father. Too tentative, too pink-faced. Ian had poise; Ian had melanin.

Sitting in reception, Edwina's gaze was planted on the restrooms across the lobby. Her shoulders were forward, her purse hung, unzipped, from her wrist. The jean skirt was the strangest part by far. Edwina looked like she was waiting for a bus, not a job interview.

Not that this was an interview in any true sense. Marcus wanted to give the girl a starter job, a favour to her mother, and of course it fell to Lorna to set everything up. Lorna was nervous, though she told herself not to be. Edwina was just a girl, a little older than Cara, who'd had tough luck. Lorna checked her breath before leaving her office and wiped her palms down the length of her skirt.

Edwina's head turned instantly when Lorna entered the lobby. She didn't stand the way most applicants did; she just stared up.

Lorna smiled and strode toward her, hand outstretched. "I'm Lorna Kedzie. Do I call you Edwina, or ...?" Edie was the name she'd heard Ian use, the name etched in plaster on the tiny

"Happy Father's Day" footprint that hung on his office wall, but she didn't say it.

"Ed-wee-na," the young woman said, standing slowly. "You say it like wean a baby, not win a prize." Her handshake was moist. Her blouse stretched and gaped at the breasts, and Lorna could see the ridge of a beige bra and a *V* of patchy, pink skin. Lorna had calculated Edwina's age at roughly twenty-three, but she looked younger. Her makeup was ill chosen and ineptly applied: the work of a girl in a rush or without much space or light. The sort of over-pencilled eyebrows and peach-tinted pimples you'd expect to see emerge from a bus station bathroom.

"Well, it's a pleasure." Lorna renewed her smile and led Edwina across the lobby and into her office. She gestured at the seat across from her desk.

Edwina put her bag down and sat carefully in the leather chair, smoothing her jean skirt underneath her. She wiped a hand under her nose; it was not a straight nose like Ian's, but slightly warped at the tip. Perhaps a sports injury? Lorna scanned the resumé on her desk. There were no extracurricular activities of note, although surely Edwina had grown up with summer camps, ski trips, riding lessons. Lorna really knew very little about Ian's only child. In general, she'd appreciated how infrequently Ian talked about his family because she couldn't stand bragging fathers, especially the ones who, like Ian, spent so little time at home. Once, Lorna remembered, Ian had described Edwina as "rudderless," but his tone was not unkind, as though rudderlessness was part of the romance of being a university student. To be honest, the description reassured Lorna. She wondered if Cara might share that same adrift quality, and if it was fine enough for Ian's daughter, maybe Cara wasn't doomed after all. Although, according to Edwina's resumé, she never graduated from university.

"I want you to know how very sorry I am for your loss, Edwina," Lorna said, after they'd both settled into their spots. "Your father and I worked together a long time."

"I know," Edwina said. Lorna nodded, hoping it might encourage Edwina to say more about what she knew. Had Ian talked about his colleagues at home? She was quite sure her own children wouldn't be able to name a single one of the people she worked with.

"We were good friends," Lorna said.

Edwina looked out into the hallway. "His office had a view of the lake," she said. "It was nicer than this one. I used to come in with him sometimes when I was little, before you worked here. We could see sailboats as far as . . . I don't know. Far."

Lorna nodded. Ian's office was still empty

"Is this his desk you're sitting at?" The young woman's face flushed hard pink as she turned back to Lorna.

"Oh." Lorna put a protective hand on the polished teak surface. She tried and failed to catch Edwina's eye. "It used to be, yes. It's a beautiful piece, isn't it? I always admired it." *He would have wanted me to have it* was what Lorna didn't say, though she felt accused. She'd also taken his Montblanc pen and his crystal shot glass of mint toothpicks.

Edwina wiped her palm across the desktop, leaving a quickly vanishing smear of moisture. The edges of her fingertips were raw and peeled looking. "So weren't you, like, his secretary?"

"I'm a researcher," Lorna said. "And I manage all our client relations."

"My Dad said client service is like being a hooker. The people who hire you know you're involved with other clients, but they don't want any evidence."

"I've heard him say that as well."

"So you took care of that part?"

"What part?"

"I don't know. Keeping everything separate."

Lorna offered a third smile, not sure how else to respond. "Sounds like your Dad taught you a thing or two about the biz."

Edwina shrugged. Smiles did not seem to attach to her. "He left his focus group tapes in the car sometimes. When I was a kid, we used to listen to them on the way home from the farm."

"Ah." Lorna nodded. Ian always said his best insights came to him while driving. "That's an education."

"They put me to sleep."

"Yes, I imagine they would."

"Have you been to our farm?"

"No," Lorna said quickly. "I'm sure it's a special place." She leaned back into her chair and laced her fingers together with both elbows up on her desk; she wanted to project confidence and nonchalance. "So what do you think? Do you think you'd like to join us here?"

Edwina scratched her neck and left two pink lines. "Seems nice."

"I'm just curious if there is an area that especially interests you? Anything you'd like to learn. We're looking for someone to help with reception, focus groups, paperwork..."

Edwina picked up a highlighter on the desk. "I don't really like paperwork."

Lorna's first temp job at OpinioNation was all paperwork. At her own chair against the side of Ian's desk, she spent the summer of 1987 coding survey responses on every topic from cough syrup to overfishing. Ian hummed Lionel Ritchie while he worked, taking frequent breaks at the window to watch the sailboat races on Lake Ontario. His eyes crinkled against the blaze of the four o'clock sun. She'd been thirty-one then; he was forty-five.

Lorna bobbed her head from side to side. "Well. Some paperwork is always part of the job."

"Yeah. I know."

Was Edwina like this all the time? Twitchy? Defensive? Maybe Marcus hadn't actually met Edwina; if he had, how could he possibly think that hiring her was a good idea? She would make clients nervous. But maybe her prickliness wasn't her fault. Ian was off the wagon through her early childhood, and it was common for the kids of alcoholics to lack confidence. Still, Ian himself had always been charming with strangers; it was important to him to be liked. It made Lorna sad that Ian, with his confident shoulders and facility with words, would not be proud of his daughter's performance now.

"But anyway," Lorna continued. "With the computers we have these days, paperwork isn't what it used to be in this industry. So that's a bonus. Do you have any computer experience?"

"Depends what you mean." Edwina was looking around the office, seeming to conduct a mental inventory of Lorna's things. She tapped the base of the highlighter on Lorna's desk. It was unnerving.

"Well, walk me through this." Lorna slid Edwina's sparse resumé across the table. "Tell me what kind of experience you do have."

Edwina looked down at the paper as though it confused her. She swatted the bangs off her forehead, revealing an angry constellation of acne. "What do you want to know?"

In a way, it was a good question. What did Lorna want to know about Edie? Did she look like Ian? No. Did she have his sense of humour? Seemingly not. Was she damaged?

"It looks like you have two years of university," Lorna said. "What did you study?"

"Psych. Wasn't really the right call though."

"OK."

"But I'm doing a college course at night now." She paused for a moment and tilted her head to the side like this might help her remember the name of it. "Like business."

"Great!" Lorna tilted her head to meet Edwina's angle. Focus groups occurred at night. If Edwina was busy nights, it was a wonderful excuse not to hire her. Still, Lorna wanted to help Ian's daughter, give her a little more experience with a basic job interview. "What would you say are some of your best skills?"

Edwina scrunched her lips: a show of thinking. In focus groups, Ian had referred to inexpressive people like this as potatoes. Either Edwina had turned out to be a potato, or she really didn't care about the job. It occurred to Lorna that perhaps Edwina was also just enduring this interview as a favour to her mother. In all likelihood, Cara or Jed wouldn't have any genuine interest in a job that Lorna encouraged. And yet, Lorna felt certain that even at fifteen, Cara would put on a better show than this: she would understand what not to wear, that it was a no-no to touch anything that wasn't hers—wouldn't she?

"Your resumé says you've worked at Pharmasave," Lorna tried.

"My son works at a drugstore as well. Did you work in checkout or...?"

"Determination."

"Pardon me?"

"My skill. You asked about my best skill."

"Oh, right!" Lorna widened her eyes to display interest. "That's a good one."

"Because when I want to get something done, I usually do."

"How about a specific example?"

Lorna wondered, worried—for Ian's sake —what on earth Edwina would do out in the world, if not this job. It was hard enough for a grown-up, normal-seeming person with experience to get an interview and find a job in this economy. Alex, for example, was having a hell of a time getting back on his feet since returning from Black River three months ago.

Edwina pulled a strand of hair in front of her face. "I asked for a kitten every day for ten years, and I got one. My Dad's allergic, I mean he *was* allergic, but he still bought one for me."

"I didn't know he was allergic." Lorna said.

"But you were such good friends." Edwina smiled with sarcasm. It was probably normal for the family of the deceased to resent the assertion that a stranger was a "good friend." Lorna recalled feeling something similar at her father's funeral nearly eighteen years ago.

"Well," Lorna said in the most pleasant way she could muster. "No cats here, I suppose, so it never came up. But what I'm hearing from you is that you're persistent."

"Yeah."

As a researcher, people said Ian Needham was relentless, like a dog with a bone. When it came to Lorna though, he'd waffled. In the end, there was really just the one kiss in the office over two years ago. It began with closed lips, non-committal, two goldfish bumping together. It was Lorna who'd been prepared to take risks. It was Lorna who finally touched his face, pulling him closer, meaning business. But then he more or less disappeared until last fall.

After returning from the trip to Black River and feeling that, like Alex, she too deserved to recreate some aspect of her life, Lorna responded to Ian's invitation to visit his country house: the farm. Up in the stands at Cara's last-ever tennis tournament, while other parents watched the courts, gripped their knees, and fretted, Lorna wrote to Ian that she wasn't sorry about the kiss the year before and had been glad to get his letter. But she'd also written, in glowing terms — terms that embarrassed her now — about his steadiness, something she'd always admired and which made her reluctant to take lightly a trip out to see him. She asked for more clarity about that what he wanted. Boldly, she asked what the situation now was between him and Libby. She said she didn't want any responsibility in wrecking his life or his family. Privately, though, she imagined Ian as part of her family – a positive weekend influence, taking Jed fly-fishing, helping Cara with an argument piece for the student newspaper. She never considered the role Edwina could play in these scenes. Ian's daughter seemed to her to be older, irrelevant.

Edwina was talking now, finally, about her job at Pharmasave. She talked with her hands, large-knuckled hands that Lorna recognized. She said something about a thick skin. She said, "A lot of folks find the idea of dealing with everyday people too stressful. But you should see the stuff I've seen."

Lorna leaned in. "What kind of stuff?"

"Just. Weird."

"I believe you."

"But I bet you want a specific example?"

"Why not?" Lorna said good-naturedly. She checked the small clock on her desk; fewer than ten minutes had gone by.

Ian responded to Lorna's letter with a call from the Sutton Place Hotel a week or so later. He didn't explain what he was doing back in town, or at a hotel. She bought a pink dress on markdown at Eaton's and little beige kitten heels on the way over. In the mirrored elevator, she decided she looked like she was dressed for a First Communion.

A football game blared on TV from behind the door of Ian's suite. It took four or five knocks for him to answer, and he greeted her with a heavy hug that left too much wetness on her cheek. He had aged in the last year: more jowly, watery-eyed, his hair thinner. He wore a white Ralph Lauren button-down and seersucker shorts—inappropriate for October—and it was the first and last time Lorna saw his bare, unexpectedly thin and hairy legs. A plate of melting ice sat next to half a lime and a plastic knife on the minibar. The room was dim and stuffy. She crossed to the window, pretending to stare with interest at the view: grey government buildings, the dark green circle of Queen's Park. She watched a harried family in the hotel drop-off zone, a boy aiming his water gun at a passing stroller. Behind her, Ian lashed out at the TV, declaring his team—Lorna couldn't recall which one now; she hadn't known he liked football—"stunned cunts." Lorna sat in a leather desk chair next to the bed, not sure what else to do with herself. When the game went to commercial, Ian gave her a spacey smile and patted the mattress. Lorna asked if he wanted to go get a bite to eat, thinking this might even him out. He responded that she should sit on his face. Lorna laughed uncertainly, said she'd get more ice from down the hall. When she returned, which she wasn't sure she would, Ian was flat on his back and snoring, his shorts unzipped to white underwear. It was easy now to think of the decision to leave the hotel then as the right decision, but for days, Lorna wondered if she'd made a mistake. She thought of calling in the weeks that followed, but what was there to say?

The next news of Ian came just after Halloween. Marcus called Lorna at home on a Sunday night to tell her that Ian had hit his head in the swimming pool after drinking a bottle of Aquavit. (The latter detail was only disclosed when Lorna, as her first response, wondered out loud what the pool was doing open in late October.) Marcus asked that Lorna omit the cause of death in her note to clients and staff, as if she didn't already know better. The funeral, a year ago now, was small and private. Only Marcus attended from the office, and Lorna arranged the bouquet: *From Ian's family at OpinioNation.* A while after the funeral, she'd driven out to the address he'd given her for the Needham farm and parked five minutes away, by a field that stunk of sheep shit. She walked until she could see the modern grey house, which was nothing like she pictured, and then sobbed so hard she thought her ribs would crack.

"And one time," Edwina was saying, "this woman at the drug-store didn't have enough money to buy pads, but I couldn't give them away for free, right? So she took her used maxi right out of her pants and slammed it on the counter." Edwina slapped her fingertips hard on the edge of the desk.

"Geez," Lorna said.

Edwina drummed her fingers on the table. "Anything crazy like that ever happen here?"

"No." Lorna shook her head. "Not that I can think of."

"But you get weirdoes in focus groups sometimes, right? The 'great unwashed.'" It was Ian's expression. It gave Lorna pause to hear it from Edwina.

"We screen our participants. That usually weeds out serious trouble."

"That would be my job?"

"Does that interest you?"

"I don't know."

The phone rang then. Lorna looked at Edwina, "Do you mind?" She picked up, happy for a break. "Lorna Kedzie."

"It's me," Cara said dully.

Lorna was disappointed that it wasn't a business call. She had the feeling Edwina didn't take her seriously. She glanced at Edwina and gestured with her finger: *just a sec*. "Can I call you back in a minute? I'm in the middle of something."

"So why did you pick up then?" Lorna heard the crack and hiss of a pop can on the other end of the line. "I just want to know if I can stay at Dad's tonight."

"Tonight?"

Lorna had never asked for specifics, but she assumed Alex's new apartment, located across from a women's shelter downtown, was a gloomy place with a lava lamp to do your homework by and a beanbag chair to sleep on. She didn't love the kids staying there, had no clue what Alex fed them.

"That's what I just said. Tonight."

"Was that his suggestion or your idea? "

Lorna tread carefully. She was never entirely comfortable that Alex wouldn't casually disappoint her kids again. Last month, Lorna overheard Cara telling her friend Ash that Alex had been brainwashed at Black River, as if the whole episode were some psychedelic trance, totally out of his hands. She wasn't sure if Alex had fed Cara that explanation or if she'd made it up on her own. Lorna, on the other hand, knew that Alex might well still be living in Guru Neel's nuthouse if the place hadn't been raided for its marijuana farm and Neel himself hadn't been charged with eight counts of sexual assault, but she hadn't raised these details with the kids. For now they had their own versions of the truth that suited them better. Their capacity to excuse, even ignore, Alex's absence over the last two years impressed her, but it also perplexed her.

On the other side of the desk, Edwina was looking at a framed photo of Lorna and the kids from a Halloween ten years ago. All three of them were dressed like cowboys with wide hats, ruffled shirts, and tall boots. Edwina's fingers were all over the glass on the frame.

"Listen, I'll think about it. Let me call you back, sweetie, OK?" Lorna put the phone back down, cutting Cara off. She looked at Edwina, at the photo in her hands. "Sorry about that."

"These them? These your kids?" Edwina asked, not looking up. "The boy looks like you. But the girl just has the same eyelids. How do you call that?"

"I'm not sure I know what you mean."

"Hooded, isn't it?" Edwina brought the picture closer to her face and then glanced quickly back at Lorna. "Like, not really there."

Lorna didn't say anything. Was this what disappointing fathers produced? Girls like Edwina? Lorna felt the familiar shiver of guilt about Ian. She should have seen what was happening, her own role in it. But surely becoming this strange must have been a longer project for Edwina, not *just* the consequence of Ian's ridiculous death.

"What are they going as for Halloween?" Edwina asked.

"Oh," Lorna said. "They're teenagers now. Seventeen and fifteen."

"So what? I'm going as a butterfly." Edwina batted her lashes.

Lorna let out an uneasy chuckle. "That's a neat idea."

"Do you have pictures of your husband?" Edwina asked.

Lorna looked at her. "I'm not married."

"That's what I thought. But I didn't know for sure." Edwina's eyes rose up to meet Lorna's. It no longer made her blush to say bold things.

Lorna felt the tendons tighten in her neck. She rolled her chair back on the rug. Edwina knew something. "Edwina," Lorna said. "Do you have any questions about our work here?"

Edwina smirked. She put her fingertips on her resumé and clawed it messily to her chest. "You think I would actually work for you, Lorna?" She said the name in a mocking way. "My dad's secretary. How cheap can you get?"

"I'm not sure exactly what you're saying." Lorna's voice came out surprisingly calm — surprising because she was, in fact, sure what Edwina was saying. She wanted to correct Edwina on her title again but thought it was better to stay within the big picture.

"For your information, he was never seriously interested in you."

Lorna swallowed. What was this girl's information? That ridiculous letter from the tennis stands? Did all men keep such letters in cigar boxes at the top of their wardrobes? She would have expected more from Ian.

Edwina picked up the cowboy picture again. "You're lucky you have kids, you know." Her voice sped up. "Because I know people who could really fuck with you. They aren't afraid of shit."

Lorna realized that she hadn't checked who else was in the office before beginning the interview. What was Edwina threatening? Would she call a mobster to come break Lorna's fingers? She scanned the room for possible articles of defense in case Edwina was seriously unstable: keys, an umbrella, a toothpick? She had scissors somewhere, a letter opener. But come on. "Edwina, honestly I—"

"Please don't lie to me," Edwina said. She shut her eyes the way parents often did to show exasperation toward their children. "Just don't even talk. It's a question of respect."

Lorna managed to nod through the stiffness in her neck and throat. When she took a breath, she was sure that the rattling sound in her lungs was audible. She steadied her hands, pressing them firmly under the table.

"I wanted to meet you," Edwina said, standing now, "to see what you had to say for yourself." She reached down to her purse and pulled out a small paper bag, the kind used in penny candy stores. "But now I find I don't give a fuck." Her eyes shone. She placed the paper bag on the desk like it was evidence in a TV courtroom drama. "You can have this back."

Lorna eyed the bag, which obviously contained the letter. In a way, the request not to speak was a relief. She had nothing to say, nor did she want to prolong this meeting. The fact that she never actually slept with Ian seemed an unimportant technicality. Lorna wasn't guiltless, and Edwina was clearly driven to prove it. Like so many women in these situations, Edwina wanted to show that she wasn't a fool. Though Lorna couldn't help but wonder for whose sake. Just her own? Her mother's?

As Edwina swept her purse up off the floor, a cheap plastic hairbrush flew out onto the carpet. The moment was so inelegant that Lorna felt more pity for Edwina than anything else. She bent toward the brush but Edwina pounced, snapping it up first with her skinny, wily energy. One of her blouse sleeves was rolled way up and the other pulled down. Her face, when she glared at Lorna, had the patchy texture of raw ground beef. "We're done," she said.

Not wanting to set Edwina loose in the hallways, Lorna followed her nervously through the clean, empty lobby to the elevator bay, hoping to hell they wouldn't run into anyone. How in the world would she summarize this meeting for Marcus?

In front of the elevators at last, Edwina stabbed the down button and they waited, Lorna standing a few feet back. When the doors whooshed open, Edwina stepped inside and only then turned to face Lorna. The shininess in her eyes was gone. She had, suddenly, the wan look of someone who'd just finished a long exam, one for which she'd been up all night studying. Then she was gone. Sucked down the throat of the elevator.

Crossing back to her office, Lorna felt wobbly on her feet. The perspiration was damp and cool under her blouse. She closed her door, straightened the photo on her desk, and put the highlighter back in its cup. She sat down in front of the crumpled paper bag. Lorna pressed her palm down on top of it—immediately it was clear there was no letter inside. What Lorna could feel instead was something hard and thin through the paper: a metal ring of some sort. Lorna turned the bag over, and a small silver bracelet dumped out onto her desk. When she pulled apart the hook and eye, she saw the silver engraving on the inside of the bangle: *To LK love Mom*.

Lorna's initials, but not Lorna's bracelet.

Lorna returned the bracelet to the bag. She seldom wore jewellery and was allergic to most silver. It came to her without needing to think. The bangle belonged to Lizbeth Kotsakos. There was no other answer.

Lorna stood then, her body twanging with adrenaline. She had an urge to rush back to the elevators, to chase Edwina down, to tell her exactly whose goddamn bracelet this was. No, Lorna had not torn apart Edwina's family; she was not responsible for Edwina flunking out of university or for whatever mess she was making of her life as a result. Lorna looked at her reflection in the darkening window. She flinched at her arrogance. In the end, Ian's death had nothing to do with her.

Lorna's phone began to light up and ring again. She let four, five, six flashes go by before reaching shakily for the receiver.

"Lorna Kedzie."

"Jesus. Mom, it's just me again."

Lorna felt a fresh bolt of alarm. Why was Cara calling again? Had Edwina done something completely deranged? Left a bag of dead mice outside the apartment door? "Sweetheart? Is everything OK?"

"Um, yeah. You're the one who pretty much hung up on me." Cara sighed. "I just need to know if you care if I stay at Dad's tonight?"

Lorna glanced down at her watch. Edwina struck her as one

of those zigzagging, inattentive fast-walkers. If she rushed, would it still be possible to track Edwina down now?

"It's game five," Cara said. "You are aware it's the World Series, right? Dad wants to watch with me."

"Did you eat dinner?"

"He'll boil hot dogs."

Out the window, Lorna heard the bright eruption of a siren. An ordinary downtown sound, but she approached the glass to look. On the sidewalk across the street, a gathering of people had stopped to face her building. Lorna drew in her breath. She could see it happen: Edwina, blind with rage, stepping right into traffic. Maybe she even put herself there on purpose. Fucking Ian. Fucking Lizbeth.

But not Lorna's fault.

"Helloooo?" Cara said.

Lorna stood on her tiptoes, but from the sixteenth floor, and with a foot of radiator in front of the window, she couldn't see directly below her. She slipped out of her shoes and stepped up on the rad, the cheap metal yielding under her weight. The phone jerked and tumbled over the edge of the desk, the black console twisting like a bass on a fishing line.

"What's that random noise?" Cara asked.

Lorna put her face right against the glass.

"Somebody's hurt," Lorna said. The glass fogged when she spoke.

"Who?"

"No one you know."

"But who though?"

Lorna looked down at the crowd of people. She was glad that what she said was true, glad that her daughter didn't know

Edwina, and glad that she would never know about Edwina, or Ian, or any of the stupid things that Lorna had wasted too much energy on. Not letting Cara become like Edwina, not ruining her children with her own selfishness, should clearly be the point of every decision she made.

Lorna drew a line through the fog. "Cara," Lorna said, "what would you say is your best skill?"

"What. At school?"

"Sure."

"French," Cara answered without hesitation. "I have, like, an 86 now. Why?"

"Eighty-six. That's very good."

Of course there was Alex, and Lorna couldn't control his imprint, but could a kid be all that damaged if she still liked watching baseball with her parents?

As the siren shut off, the crowd across the street began to break up. Squinting through the early evening, Lorna could just make out Edwina's stooping shape, not moving with the crowd, not lying in a puddle of her own blood, but steadily watching someone else's disaster.

Edwina was safe; Lorna could likely catch up to her. But what could she really say? What would it change? Her dad was gone. Like Cara and her brainwashing story, the girl needed someone or something to blame. She was hurt, and she didn't want to believe it was her father who hurt her.

Lorna stepped off the windowsill. She returned her phone to the spot on her desk and slid the bracelet back in the bag.

"I'm coming now, sweetie," Lorna said quietly into the phone. "Just wait and I'll drive you over."

# Clutch

The night before the test, Dad takes me to dinner on the Fatso's patio overlooking the Don Valley Parkway. We sit facing the sun, eating our burgers, watching tiny cars bubble up from downtown and shoot off to the suburbs.

Dad stretches his legs and crosses one ankle over the other. "What's the first thing you're going to do, Care Bear?" he says. "First thing when you get your license?"

"We'll come here."

"No way," Dad says, his eyes on the passing traffic. "The first day of your license is a memory you make on your own." He crunches the paper wrapper from his burger. "What I'd do? Stick on *Gimme Shelter*, crank it, drive the parkway the whole way along."

I hate driving on any kind of highway, but I let him keep on imagining whatever he's imagining until he slides the keys across the table and it's time to go.

I've been meeting Dad for driving lessons every Friday for the last two months. We get together at Suds laundry where he drops off his clothes, and then we just drive until dark. He brings the tapes he wants me to hear — really hear, like Pink Floyd and the Who — and he tells me everything you could ever want to know about any car on the road. It works out well, Dad teaching me. Mom is the most uptight driver you've ever seen. We did a couple of practices in the parking lot together, but she couldn't let go of the holy shit grip and it started stressing me out, too. After that she sent me to Nolan from Safety-First, whose car smelled like apple cores. He was always swallowing for no good reason and telling me to keep my eyes on the road when obviously I wasn't about to look at him. I did my twenty hours with him and everything, but Dad's the one I learn from.

Back in the car, Dad cranks his seat all the way back, and I ease us onto the road. He just trusts me.

"What time again tomorrow?" he asks.

"Nine is good." That gives us a full hour before the test. You have to give Dad the extra time.

"You feel OK about it? Not too nervous?"

"Were you nervous before you got your license?"

Dad scratches under his ponytail. It's a weird look he has going on because his hair is all soft and wispy on top like a baby, but the ponytail bit is dark and stringy. "Can't remember, Care Bear. You know that." Dad has the worst memory, and it used to drive Mom crazy. Mom remembers everything. These days she's constantly getting watery-eyed over old stuff. Even on a regular weekday morning, she'll be in her bathrobe, scraping her spoon inside an empty yogurt container all, "Remember your first window plant? Remember how big it grew?" I'll lie and tell her I have no idea what she's talking about sometimes, just so she'll get over it. You can't just sit around remembering things all the livelong day.

Driving west toward downtown, the sky spreads out all grape-fruity pink over the lake, like a postcard from California. Dad lowers the sunshade and wriggles down in his seat. The warm wind coming through the window blows my hair to one side, and I feel like a girl in a music video, like I'm on some cool road trip, even if it's just with Dad. He's mellow, tapping his fingers on his thigh like there's a beat somewhere I can't hear. That's one thing about Dad since he came back from Black River: Mr. Relax-o. He even has this new slow way of speaking like he's been in the sun too long. "Let's go somewhere," I say.

"Let's do it. Get on the expressway."

The reason I hate the expressway is you can't trust yourself on it. At those speeds you can kill someone before you even finish thinking about it. One quick jerk and it's all over. How can you know you won't do it? "Expressway's not on the test," I say. "I only have to drive fifty."

As we drive past the expressway entrance, Dad sighs and rolls his head toward me. "You shouldn't be afraid of it."

"I'm not."

"You don't want to end up scared of life like your mother."

I can feel his eyes right on me when he says that. I shake my head because I don't want Dad to think I'm like Mom at all. I want to be the kind of daughter he would have had with a more easygoing chick, the kind of woman I'll bet he wishes he'd hooked up with instead of Mom back in the seventies. The real problem between Mom and Dad was that Mom's a total tight ass. "I just like regular streets," I say. "With people and stores and stuff."

"How is she?"

I glance at Dad. "Mom? She has this new short haircut. She thinks she looks like Lady Di."

"Does she?"

"No. She looks weird."

"She dating at all?"

"Yeah, right."

Dad bites the edge of his thumbnail. "When I met your mother, I thought she was the most confident woman on earth. She knew exactly what she wanted."

I consider what he means by confident. I picture some New York lady shouting at her home renovators from a car phone.

"I hope you make her laugh sometimes," he says.

"*Seinfeld* does."

"Don't let her get too old."

Mom is thirty-eight, same as Dad. It's different for women, though. I don't know when it happens, but at some point women start getting older than men. Even with Dad's disappearing hair, Mom seems, like, ten years older. "We'll go somewhere on the expressway next time," I say. "I have plans tonight. I just forgot about them."

"If you're ever going to visit, you need to drive at highway speeds."

"Visit who?" But the second I say it, I know.

"Shari's invited me to live with her."

After Dad quit Black River, he told us about Shari. They quit together. She lives up north near Barrie somewhere, and I met her once when she came down to Fatso's just to have a banana and a plastic bag of pistachios, brought from home, with us. She showed me a picture of her twin daughters: little blond girls in life jackets with their hair all blown back. I asked who took care of them when she was at Black River. Dad shot me a disappointed look, but Shari said, "That's fine, sweetie. Ask me anything." But somehow she didn't actually answer the question.

When I don't say anything Dad says, "Great skiing near Shari."

"It's summer."

"Sure it is, now."

"You only just got home," I say. "Plus how well do you even know Shari?"

Dad lets out a long breath. "Well enough. You need to take risks sometimes."

"Most people snowboard these days, by the way. Only people from the seventies ski."

"OK, Cara." I glance over, and notice his eyes are closed, a curtain on the conversation.

I make the car jerk at the red light. Dad's eyes open, but his attention drifts to a teal convertible in the next lane and a girl's freckled legs dangling out the back window. "A 1982 Honda Prelude," he says. "Cool colour, huh?"

"It's weird," I say.

"Cara, weird is a pretty irritating expression. Judgmental. I know where you get it from, but I expect more of you."

When I turn right, I stall the car for the first time in over a month. Dad's whole body rattles, and some punk chick on a bike gives me the finger and smacks the side of the car. "Ugly bitch," I say.

"Cara," Dad says, in that dazed new voice, "is cursing really the best way to handle that?"

"Yes."

Dad knows I'm pissed so he suggests stopping by the car-wash. When I was little, going with Dad to the car wash was my favourite. I loved being all snug in the car against the downpour of soap, the wet slap of blue noodles, and the hairy pompoms.

Today, though, I just remind him that I said I have plans, and we drive the rest of the way home in silence. I've been quiet in the car with Dad before, but this is the first time it feels lonely.

Mom's watching *Seinfeld* when I get home. We finally got cable a month ago and she's the one who uses it most. Dad's right about her complete lack of a life. She twists right around at the sound of the door. "How did the driving go?"

"Fine."

"How's your dad?"

That question is Mom's most annoying. She's happy not to be my driving teacher, but I know it makes her nervous whenever I'm out with Dad. I know she distrusts him, like she thinks he's going to turn me into some New Age freak. I usually go out of my way to talk about how Dad lives like a normal person now and has a normal job at TravelWorld, but I don't bother today because who knows, maybe that's all going to change. So I just say, "Same."

"What all did you talk about?"

"Different stuff." I go to the kitchen for a snack.

"Feeling good about tomorrow?" she yells.

Extra loud, I yell back, "Yes! I know how to drive."

When I pass by the TV again, Mom is still all cranked around and wanting to talk more, like she's been waiting all day for a conversation. Her hair is flat and still a little wet from her old people swim practice at the Y. "It's OK to be nervous," she says. "Driving is serious business."

"Yep." And of course that message is loud and clear because

right on top of the TV is that picture of Mom's friend Debbie who was killed in a car accident. What happened to Debbie is sad, but I don't see why we have to be reminded all the time. If Debbie were still alive, she and mom might not even be friends anymore. As far as I can tell, Mom only has friends at work, and they never come over. What would she and Debbie even do together?

"Why don't you put those crackers on a plate with some cheese?" Mom smiles and pats the seat next to her. "We can watch Wimbledon instead if you want."

"Nah."

I used to like tennis. At least, I liked being good at it. In the summer of grade seven, I got to play with a junior competitive team. I could hit the ball hard, but I never had much of a game plan. I was never able to think fast enough, and I did lots of stupid things. All the pressure made my head go wild. I couldn't serve without thinking something bad would happen if my serve didn't go in, like I'd fail grade eight or Mom would have a heart attack or something. Anyway, it's depressing that I'll probably never get close to being really great at anything else. I'm already sixteen. When Mom was my age, everyone thought she would make the Olympics for swimming. She hurt her knee in some accident—another reason that driving is "serious business"—or else maybe she'd have really been famous. Now she competes against other old people on Saturday mornings, and then they go out for pancakes at the Golden Griddle. This is the highlight of her week, pathetically enough.

I start toward my room, but Mom's still watching me. In the pale TV light, her skin looks like a bulletin board with one million tiny holes. It's not great to look at, and it makes me sad enough to sit down next to her. Shari's not exactly young, maybe thirty, but she's skinny with long hair and smooth, shiny skin.

The morning of the test, Mom's at her most aggravating. She just stands in her swimsuit and bathrobe, a shadow over my cereal bowl, being all *Do you feel relaxed? Are you sure about no socks? When's your Dad getting here?* I tell her to take a chill pill because we still have a ton of time, but I'm kind of panicked myself because there's just under forty minutes. Mom gives me her wrinkly *really?* face and checks the calendar for the three hundredth time.

"I should take you there myself," she says. "I don't want you to be rushed." Mom thinks rushing is the worst possible situation.

"Don't you have a very important swim competition?"

She rubs her thumbnail against her teeth. "Well, if you miss your appointment, you'll have to wait another month."

"I appreciate your concern."

Mom looks at her watch and then at the intercom. "Come on, Alex," she mutters.

"Go stress out somewhere else, please."

Mom clears the breakfast table while I'm still eating, like if she just starts moving, everyone else will. I wonder if Dad forgot. Maybe he's at home listening to *Gimme Shelter* and packing for up north where everyone has layered hair and frosted lipstick, except maybe Shari who is "nonconformist" like him, which as far as I can tell basically means not caring about your family.

Sometimes it makes me feel better to just let Mom go off on Dad, so I say, "Do you know Dad's moving to Barrie?"

Mom stops with the clearing and leans her back against the counter. "Oh." She pushes the sleeves up on her bathrobe. "He mentioned the possibility." She already knew. She's probably happy about it even.

"Well doesn't that seem, like, incredibly far away?"

"Your father's restless," she says. "You know that."

"You could have told me."

"I'm sure he preferred to tell you himself."

"I expect more of you," I say. I get up from the table and grab my shoulder bag with my driving permit and all of Dad's tapes that I'm going to return immediately.

Five minutes later I'm on the concrete steps in front of our building. I try to wiggle each of my toes one at a time. If I can get each one to bend by itself without triggering any of the others, Dad will be on time and I'll pass the test. I start on the right and make it all the way to the fourth toe on the left, but then I screw up and have to start again from the beginning.

I'm about to go back in and try Dad's number when Mom's crappy green Chevette pulls up. She honks the horn and then reaches across to roll down the passenger window. "Come on! Let me take you!" she yells.

"Did Dad call?"

"I don't want you to be late."

"I'm fine."

Mom stays parked in front of me; I look past the car, watching down the street for Dad. A few minutes go by and then Mom honks the horn three times like some leather-jacketed teenager picking up his girlfriend on *Happy Days*.

"You sound crazy," I say. I've never heard her use the horn.

"It's 9:40," she says. "It's come with me now or no test."

I know she's right. My appointment is in twenty minutes and the testing centre is at least that far away.

When I get in, all I can smell is Mom's warmed-up cherry deodorant, her usual panic smell.

"You wanna drive?" She asks.

"Nope." I've spent my whole life being a passenger in Mom's car, but I don't have a lot of experience driving it. The last time was in the parking lot.

"You know, it's a good day for this," Mom says as she pulls away from the curb. Her voice is so bright it actually makes me close my eyes. "No rain, not too sunny either."

I shrug and roll up the passenger window; I get cold when I'm nervous.

"I was freaked out for my test," Mom says. "My father wasn't an easy man to share a car with. Even after I got my licence, Dad checked the car for scrapes and updated the mileage in a little notebook every time I came home."

Mom doesn't talk much about stuff that happened in her life growing up. When I used to ask her about being a kid, she was just like, "All I ever did was swim." Both her parents were dead before Jed was born. I hardly know anything about her dad except that he liked to grow vegetables on sticks or something.

"Sounds like kind of a dick move."

She nods her head from side to side. "Just an odd way of showing his concern."

"So we both had dicks for dads."

Mom looks at me. "The 400 is murder in the morning. I'm sure that's all this delay is about."

"If he's on the 400 then you're basically saying he lives in Barrie already."

"I assume he spends a few nights there."

"Gross."

I look out the window at all the drivers alone in their cars—scratching their ears, tapping the steering wheel, leaning elbows against the window all casual. How are they so relaxed? How do they know they're not about to kill someone?

Mom drives in short jerky movements. Her seat is way upright and she holds her hands straight out on the wheel at ten and two.

"You drive like Frankenstein, you know that?" I tell her.

She peers at the windshield with a constipated look on her face. "Well, this Frankenstein has driven you to school, to tennis, to the orthodontist three hundred times. But just think! When you get your licence, you'll never have to drive with me again." She flashes me one of those sarcastic, rectangular smiles. Her teeth are not the greatest colour. I should get her those whitening trays for Christmas. "Just remember that the clutch is a little stiffer on this car, especially going into reverse," she says. "So take it easy."

"I know." But I don't remember what she's talking about and her last minute tip tears open a bag of butterflies in my stomach.

"Sometimes it lurches a little when you give it too much gas all at once."

"OK," I say. "I get it."

I try to stick Dad's Black Crowes tape into the player but Mom's *More Dirty Dancing* cassette is lodged in there; I swear it's been there six months. I pound the eject button. "Have you ever really tried to get this out?"

Mom glances down at the cassette player. "Sure, I've tried. It doesn't really bother me though."

"So you just listen to the same songs over and over. You're just like totally OK with that?"

"Mostly I don't listen to anything."

"When was the last time you even bought a new tape?"

"I don't know," she says. "Why?"

"Maybe because there's actually lots of good music around, Mom."

"You're probably right."

"You shouldn't be so scared of life."

Mom looks at me, but I look out the window to avoid her face. She doesn't say anything for a minute, and then she says, "What makes you think I'm scared of life?"

"It just seems like you are."

"Compared to who?"

"I don't know. People."

"People," she repeats. She slides her pack of Nicorette gum off the dashboard and pops a piece out. "Well, I'll buy a new tape if it's important to you."

"Don't worry about it."

Mom takes a big breath in and out. She doesn't say anything else. At the intersection by the testing centre, she stops and turns her left blinker on. Cars zip past like angry bees and my skin feels like it's tightening up all the way to the top of my head.

"I'm sure your Dad is sorry to be missing this," she says as we turn into the place.

"If I fail, he'll have to keep practising with me anyway, so ..."

"You'll do fine." Mom pats my arm. I don't like it when she just touches me like that. Her hands are always sort of cold and wet.

Next to our parking space, another mom is hopping around taking pictures of her son in front of a beige station wagon. "Jingle your keys, sweetie," the mom says. "Show us who's in the driver's seat now!" The kid shifts on his skinny red-haired legs, blushing so bad it looks like he might actually be choking. This mom's going to rush to the drugstore with that film, put her son's picture in a colourful frame on top of the TV, and maybe even cry about it. She'll be one of those moms who jokes, "My kid's on the road, everyone stay home, *ha ha ha*!" You can tell this is her big thrill of the month, maybe the year. It's kind of sad.

I follow Mom's fast walk inside the testing centre, which is crowded and over air-conditioned. A smell like new plastic snags my nostrils and makes me feel like throwing up. I breathe through my mouth.

"You're late," the acne-faced appointment lady says.

I look at Mom. She tightens her lips. "My fault," she says. "Cara here's all set."

The woman rolls her eyes and types a bunch. "Really gums up the works when people don't keep their appointments."

"Traffic," Mom says.

The woman ignores her and returns my permit. "Drive round back and wait for your examiner," she says. I look at Mom. "Go!" the woman says.

Out in the parking lot, I get into the driver's seat of Mom's car and immediately stall it. "Go easy," she says. She puts her hand over mine on the clutch.

I jerk her hand away. "Don't touch me!" I say. "Please. *Ever*."

Mom folds both her hands on her lap. "All right."

Nothing about this day is how it's supposed to be. "Let's just go home," I say.

"If you think you'd like to be better prepared . . . "

"So you think I'm not ready? You think I'm going to fail?"

"No one thinks you're going to fail. You just seem a little . . . hyper."

"I'm not hyper." I hate the word *hyper*. It makes me think of third-graders who eat too many Oreos. What's wrong with me is something different. I feel sort of like a skeleton: hollow, shaky, gutless.

Mom looks straight ahead. "OK," she says. "If you're going to do this test, Cara, you need to calm down, and you need drive around to the back right now."

"Fine." I jerk the car into first and drive, fear inflating my skeleton chest.

Two vehicles are ahead of us, thank Jesus Christ. A skinny guy with a thin brown moustache comes out the automatic doors and goes straight for the first van. He looks like the grade seven tennis coach who made me puke once from running too hard. Afterwards he was like, "And you thought you were so tough." It was so shitty because I never ever thought I was tough.

"That guy's the worst case scenario," I say.

"You know, maybe I should leave you alone," Mom says.

"Whatever you want." But my voice is tiny, and Mom doesn't leave.

The next examiner to come out is a white-haired Santa-looking guy whose uniform barely does up over his belly. "That one looks friendly," Mom says.

"But someone else is getting him."

I wipe the sweat off my hands onto my thighs. I shouldn't have worn shorts. I don't like the way my legs squish out all pink and white on the car seat. I wish I had Dad's skin, its cool light brownness, and not Mom's splotch. I wiggle each of my toes again. *Please let me pass. Please let me pass. Please let me pass.* When I look up, I see the Worst Case Scenario coming straight toward our car. How could the other van have failed so fast? I turn to Mom, who is actually smiling at him.

The Worst Case Scenario waves me forward and motions for me to roll down the window.

"All righty," the guy says, taking off his sunglasses and staring down into my window. "I'm George. Let's take a look at your paperwork." I hand him my stuff, feeling even emptier than a skeleton now, more like a ghost. My hands don't feel connected to my wrists; my wrists don't feel connected to my brain.

George chews his lip while he studies my permit. "OK, Ms. Ketchum. Your passenger can get out now."

I turn to Mom, and she crinkles up her face in a look of pity. It bothers me that George will see this, that it might make him question how confident I am.

When Mom's gone, George makes me show him the brake lights, the windshield wipers, the turn signals, and then he moves right into Mom's spot and clicks on his seatbelt. "'K," he says. "I'm going to ask you to do a few maneuvers, and you go ahead and do them when you think it's safe."

With slippery hands, I wiggle the car into first and George directs us out of the parking lot. Amazingly, I don't stall.

At our first stop sign, George smacks his lips. "Watch the stopping distance," he says.

"Sure." I feel myself going red.

"Naw, naw. I mean move up." He waves his thick hands in front of him. "You're like a mile behind that limit line."

I crawl ahead, remembering to go easy on the clutch. He

scratches something down on his clipboard. "When it's safe, make a right-hand turn."

I push the flicker up, look to the left, and see a bicycle farther down the road. George watches me closely, tapping his pencil while I wait for it to pass. When I finally turn, after there are at least four cars behind me, George groans and rubs his eyes under his glasses. "Practically needed a telescope to see that bike." He hates me; I know it. "Straight ahead, first left."

My leg wobbles as it comes off the clutch. I make the left, feeling every rumble of the road under my feet.

"Change lanes to the right."

I look that way, it's clear, but I don't move. It's like I've forgotten how. I swallow a few times like Nolan from SafetyFirst, but my throat gets all constricted, like I can't actually breathe. It's happening: I'm going to fail.

George puts down his pencil.

"I'm sorry." I sound like a five year-old.

I feel his eyes on the side of my face. "Turn onto that little street and pull over."

Somehow I manage to signal, do a fake look to the right, and move to the side street. There's no way he can't hear my heartbeat.

When I stop the car, George puts his clipboard down on his lap. "Listen, kiddo," he says. "You gotta relax."

I look away and nod. On the driveway across from us, two little girls get out of the backseat of a car. They're probably the same age as Shari's daughters. Maybe Dad will teach Shari's girls to drive one day.

"All you need to do is show me you can drive safe," George continues. "You don't need to be perfect. Everyone makes mistakes."

"I was supposed to drive my Dad's car."

One of the girls looks over at us. I stare back, my fingers shaking on the steering wheel. I wish I could switch places with her, just be, like, eight. What's so great about getting older, getting a licence? Where do I even want to go?

"I can tell you're a cautious driver," George says. "Just take a deep breath. When you feel ready, drive us back into traffic."

I try to wiggle my toes again but my feet are too slippery inside my shoes. There's no time to count. I take the breath he wants, curl my left hand around the wheel, and shift us back into gear.

For the next few hazy minutes, George directs me in circles around the neighbourhood. Everything I do, he notes with the loudest writing I've ever heard. When we're back at the testing centre, I reverse into a parking space the way Dad taught me: slow car, fast hands.

George sets his clipboard down on his lap. If I fail, it won't be so bad. It's the summer, so no one at school even needs to know. Mom can drive me home, and Dad's not here to argue with anyone about it or think I'm not confident. He'll understand that I just failed because of Mom's car. And now that I have the test route down, Dad and I can go through it over and over on Friday nights until I get it right. No matter how long it takes.

"Number one is you gotta keep those eyes moving," George says.

I move my eyes across the parking lot, wondering if Dad did actually show up. There's a line of people out the door of the testing centre, but no Dad. Mom is sitting on a bench outside, looking across at the cars turning in on the other side.

"Hey," George says. "I'm talking to you." But when I look at him, he's smiling. He unclips my papers and hands them to me. "Number two is you gotta relax." There's a happy face drawn at the top of the papers. "You'll do that for me?"

"Sure." I can taste the sun on my chin through the windshield.

"Make it official." George nods in the direction of the testing centre and then opens his door.

I cross the bright parking lot with George's papers, watching my reflection ripple past on the parked cars. I feel like I have my body back, but it also feels a little like Boxing Day, like everything I waited for is over and wasn't quite how I wanted it. I look around and try to make my own memory like Dad said I should: the shiny black pavement, the hedge trimmer whining at the side of the building, the pink and white plaid of Mom's shirt in the distance. I have no idea what I want to do first thing now that I have my licence.

Mom is still staring off in the wrong direction, but I'm close enough to see her red Kodak camera dangling from her wrist. She always closes the wrong eye when she tries to use it. The thought makes my chest muscles tighten. I squash the keys in my fist and blink up at the snappy blue sky, my mouth twisting in every direction to stop myself from crying.

Then Mom's right there, walking toward me, the camera swinging back and forth. She wraps her arms around my shoulders, and I hide my face in her armpit. "I'm sorry," I say.

"Oh, honey, it's your first time," she says. "We'll come back."

My tears press into the soft cotton of her shirt. Part of me wants to tell her the truth right away, make her laugh. But there's a big lineup for the testing centre, and people get held longer when they're sad.

# Arrangements

WINTER, 1995

Lorna decided to walk to Ballantyne's. She had an hour and
half to kill, and she hated the sound of an empty apartment.
It was also a pretty night for walking, the kind of snowy city
evening that could get you humming "Silver Bells" under your
breath, even though Christmas three weeks earlier had been
muddy and warm. Tonight, a light flurry turned under street
lamps, and the wet road cast back a slick honey glow. Parked
cars were dusted like pastry. Lorna could take the slow walk
through the reservoir.

Lorna was going to meet Alex. He'd called her office earlier
that week to say he had a small part in a TV pilot and was getting
a free Friday night at the Delta Hotel. He said it might be nice
to grab a drink. It was interesting because Lorna had planned to
call Alex herself right after New Year's, but as time marched into
the second week of January, she'd still not done it. She agreed
immediately to the drink, but spent the next few days in a quiet
panic. Alex was first on her list.

Lorna walked carefully up the winding path to the reservoir,
her hands jammed in the pockets of her coat. Once she'd avoided
the park after dark for fear of rapists and muggers, but getting
cancer and getting assaulted in the same month seemed unlikely.

Besides, the only people she could see on the path were a couple of teenagers, hunched under the weight of oversized backpacks. There was a time when kids like that might have intimidated her, when she would have worried about what they carried. Spray paint? Butterfly knives? What was a butterfly knife, again? All these things she still hadn't really learned.

But the backpacks were just security blankets. Cara wore one everywhere. Always a backpack, never a purse. She and her friends looked like a deflated platoon under the weight of those things, whose secrets she knew now were only notebooks, broken makeup, the occasional bottles of fruity beer wrapped up tightly in a sweater. They dragged themselves around food courts, parks, coffee shops. Bored seeming but with an undercurrent of snappish energy, ready for some unplanned excitement that could happen anytime.

The wind picked up at the top of the path where the reservoir stretched out into one great plain. Lorna shivered under the worn grey fabric of her coat, thinking she ought to be keeping warmer than this, should have looked around for her ski jacket. She inhaled deeply, trying to focus instead on the sharp clean air. The moon was almost full, just a little nick off its chin. A mother was coming her way, dragging a small crying child on a wagon. Lorna smiled at the woman's squished red face. Fine that the woman didn't smile back. Just because Lorna was sick didn't mean everyone else had to drop everything and appreciate life. This concern weighed on her with the kids, especially. Cara acted prickly and sullen these days, but Lorna didn't mind so much for her own sake. The bad part, for Lorna, was knowing that Cara might look back and hate herself for it one day. If Cara wanted to be rude to her mother, like any teenager, Lorna wanted her to have that. And then, of course, there was Jed.

But the kids were second on her list. The pressing issue now was to make arrangements with Alex about the surgery. In nine days, Dr. Kim would remove Lorna's reproductive organs: ovaries, uterus, tubes, and whatever else was in there. All of it would be excised, his word, in an effort to "nab it all." Lorna thought Alex could come down for a couple of days while she was in hospital. It didn't seem like too much to ask, though this news about an audition showed her how little she knew about Alex's time. Last they'd spoken he was happily working as the manager of an outdoor store. He and Shari lived in a new subdivision with her two daughters.

Lorna stopped at the hockey rink and leaned against a lamp-post, wiggling her frozen toes and catching her breath. She bent to fix a pant leg that had become stuck in the back of her boot and felt her dinner rise and burn her throat. Was that a symptom? She shouldn't have eaten the potpie so quickly, but it was just what happened now. Cara ate mechanically, moved rapidly away from Lorna to the next thing, even if the next thing was homework. The question of what to make for dinner was on Lorna's mind by eight a.m. every day, but she had long stopped thinking of eating alone with Cara as an event.

In front of the rink, a scatter of parents stood with their hands around Styrofoam cups and thermoses, watching a game between a red team and a grey team. Lorna imagined for a minute that Jed was one of the boys on the ice. She chose number eleven in grey: a tall, tentative player like her son had been. In the darkest days of single parenting, Lorna felt like she was doing something right when she took Jed to hockey practice. Even the smell of the car—humid skate liners and clothes damp with sprayed ice—gave her a twinge of pride. Boys in this climate were meant to play hockey, and she could do at least that for her son.

"Which one is yours?"

Lorna turned to the grinning middle-aged man behind her. He had a broad, handsome face, like a Kennedy.

"Oh. My son used to play. He's in university now." Lorna jammed her hands deep into the pockets of her coat and swung her arms forward to show she was a person on the move, not some weirdo who stood around in parks on Friday nights in January. "I'm just passing by."

The man shook his head almost violently, like a dog drying off from a swim. "You have a son in university!"

As a matter of fact, Lorna didn't have a son in university. She had a son who should be in university, but he had dropped out in his second week. He left her a voicemail with the news once he'd made it over the border. He said he was sorry, but not that sorry, because he had to do this thing now or he never would. This thing he planned to do, instead of university, was ride his bike the whole damn way to California. Why California? She had no idea. Maybe because Alex had gone there at his age. Maybe because it was the furthest he could get away from his mother with a bicycle.

The man pointed to a cluster of boys tussling at the north net. "Christopher," he said. "Number seven."

Lorna peered at the rink as the puck broke away across the ice. Number seven hammered hard toward it. "He's fast."

"What position did your son play?"

"Goalie." That had been true for about a month. She couldn't remember the names of the other positions. He quit after eighth grade.

"A man after my own heart. That was my position."

They both stood quietly for a moment. She watched the game but could feel the man watching her. Women her age complained about their invisibility, but at thirty-nine, Lorna was beginning to feel that she stood out in a new way: she looked good for her age. She'd lost fifteen pounds in the last year and could easily pass for thirty-two. She was a real adult woman, and men like this didn't feel ashamed to ask her out. Still, she rarely went on dates. After what happened with Ian, she didn't trust herself not to get tangled up in the wrong kind of relationships. The few times she'd been set up on dates, it had been the wrong kind of men — men who talked too long about car engines or their mother's scalloped potatoes — and then she'd still be too gentle with them, continue seeing them for five or six weeks. She had sex out of compassion or politeness: because dinner had been so expensive, because it was raining out and the roads could be slippery. It was a character flaw, a lack of heart or nerve. There were plenty of men she found attractive out there, but the attractive ones made her unsure of herself. Too eager to please, too nervous to make eye contact or smile with her teeth. Too on edge. She didn't like the person she became.

"Are you off somewhere fun?"

Lorna looked back at the man. Was this a reasonable thing to ask? She scanned the parents around her, but no one was watching them or offering her warning looks. Perhaps he was just friendly.

The man seemed to sense her discomfort and made a dismissive gesture. "Ignore me. I'm being nosy."

"No, that's fine," Lorna said quickly, immediately feeling guilty for the hesitation. Couldn't anyone just be friendly anymore? Or maybe kindness was the very thing that got her into trouble.

"I was only thinking, wow, kid in university, it's like getting your life back." He grinned all the way to his molars.

"I'm just meeting a girlfriend at Ballantyne's Bar. Do you know it?" Perhaps now she was overcompensating.

"That's not so close."

"I like to walk."

"It shows!"

Lorna felt herself blush.

The man stuck out his hand. "Bruce Lawson."

"Lorna."

Out on the ice, the ref blew his whistle. The boys stopped and number seven yanked off his helmet. He looked about fourteen. Bruce leaned forward. "Shit. Who won?"

"I think you did."

"Doubt it." He gave his son a two-finger salute then turned back to Lorna. "Do you want a lift? I could give you a lift, if you want."

"Oh, no." Lorna shook her head. "I wouldn't want to put you out. Thank you, though."

"It's no trouble. And it's cold. You're not even wearing a hat."

Lorna touched her hair. It was like touching a wet spider web. Her mascara was probably ruined, too.

"We'll just be five, ten minutes," Bruce said. "It's up to you."

There was gentleness in his manner, warmth in the way he motioned toward her with open palms.

The boys on the ice were filing into two lines to shake hands. *Good game, good game, good game.*

Lorna sat in the front seat of Bruce's Lexus while Christopher flipped through a magazine in the back. Jazz music, the kind that played in the lobbies of fancy hotels, came through the speakers. Bruce had taken off his hat, revealing coarse, curly hair. His fingers wrapped around the steering wheel were rugged but well groomed. If a younger version of herself were watching a movie of her future, this scene—and the assumptions underpinning it—would certainly be pleasing.

"I haven't been to Ballantyne's in years," Bruce said. "Kind of a student's place, isn't it?"

Was it? Lorna hadn't been in years, either. But as a student, she remembered feeling out of place among serious artists and journalists. She shrugged in a friendly way. "A drink anywhere will be nice. It's been a tough week." Lorna had no idea why she said that. She had no interest in discussing her week.

"I'm sorry," Bruce said.

"I think it was just hard to watch my son go back to school," Lorna said quickly. "You know, after the holidays?"

Snow was spiralling onto the windshield and sticking to the road. Bruce squinted as he drove, and she could see the fine chevron creases at the corners of his eyes.

"What's he studying?"

"Film."

"Sounds like a lot of fun."

Lorna imagined she was part of Bruce's family, part of this

calm, gliding car. She imagined their house: one of those narrow Victorians with large, textured paintings on the walls and big shadows from the poplar trees lining the street. She pictured a living room with high ceilings and stained glass windows, a cat on a Persian carpet next to her mother's piano. Thinking about Bruce's house made the world seem like a marvellous place.

The CD skipped. Bruce pushed a button to spit it out. "Anything you want to listen to?"

"Whatever's fine." Lorna smiled, but not right at him. Questions of music made her self-conscious. It's not that she didn't like music, but she had trouble cataloguing what she liked in a way that was easy to repeat to someone else. She was always either too broad or too specific. It was a question you ought to practise, like rehearsing your smile in the mirror. Looking out at the road, Lorna found herself contemplating the possibility that she could die not knowing exactly what kind of music she liked.

As they drove, Lorna watched the buildings slip by out the window. Soon they would pass Goodyear Billiards. After their five-minute dinner tonight, Cara had taken off for "Goody's" again, giving Lorna her usual short-tempered answers about what went on there. Lorna had seen grown men go in and out of the place. She didn't like it, but if other parents weren't saying no, how could she? Lorna squinted as they passed but couldn't see beyond the amber light of Goody's second-storey windows. She thought of Cara inside in the blue smoke, hunched in her backpack, waiting, waiting her turn to be found cute or interesting by some boy, waiting for a signal that life was really starting. She should tell her daughter it didn't work that way. You were always waiting for life to start, even after you had a boyfriend, after you were married, after you had a good job and a house—perhaps especially then. And next thing you knew, you were thirty-nine, your abdomen swelled like a four-month pregnancy, the first sign that life doesn't just start, it ends. And still you could find yourself in a stranger's car, wondering how long it would be until you were as much of an adult as he was. But what should Cara do instead? What was Lorna's great wisdom? Maybe Jed had the right idea, just checking out.

"I don't have a lot of new stuff." Bruce clicked open a middle console with a row of CDs. "I used to follow the trends, but ..."

Christopher snorted in the back seat. "Yeah, Dad. Like when Meatloaf came out with *Bat Out of Hell*."

Bruce gave Lorna a sideways smile. "As a matter of fact, Christopher, I happen to know Meatloaf has a new album."

"Sure, we'll pretend that album's new. Brand new." But the boy's tone was friendly. Lorna could tell he liked his father. She wondered about Christopher's mom. Was she dead? Out of the picture? Or was this simply Bruce's night?

At the red light, Lorna noticed Bruce looking at her again. "You get out to concerts much?" he asked.

"Me? Almost never."

"It's terrible. No time, is there?"

Lorna nodded. But it wasn't true; there was plenty of time. Time was infinite. People—she and Bruce—weren't.

"You like this one?" Bruce was passing her *Van Morrison's Greatest Hits*.

"Of course." Was she supposed to put it in? She opened the case and the CD flew down to her feet. "Shoot, I'm sorry."

Bruce shook his head. "It's been through worse."

Lorna bent down to retrieve the disc from the slush around her boots, wiping it on her thigh.

"Uhm, you just passed VideoLab," Christopher said.

"We'll go after we've dropped off our guest." Lorna saw Bruce look at Christopher in the rear-view before turning back to her. "Got any movies to recommend, Lorna?"

Lorna disliked this question almost as much as the one about music. "My daughter and I liked *Jurassic Park*," she said, figuring it was best not to seem completely without opinions.

"Seen it," Christopher said. "It's pretty good."

"You have a daughter, too?" Bruce asked.

"Yes, sixteen."

"What does she like to do?"

Lorna sighed and raised her shoulders. "I don't know. Blend in."

Bruce looked at Lorna and smiled as if this were a joke. But it wasn't a joke. Cara appeared to have resolved, some time ago, that the safest way to get by in high school was to disappear into a tide of girls, second-hand jeans, Body Shop perfume, and cigarette smoke. She wanted desperately to be normal, to fit in. Lorna wondered if this was somehow her fault, if a broken home had left Cara more needy for a group. But even as a very little child, Cara had desperately needed peer acceptance. Lorna remembered the time Cara came home in first grade after trading away all of the stickers in her album—all her precious scratch-and-sniffs and even the glittery, full-page unicorn that Lorna had given her for her birthday. Cara cried when Lorna found out they were gone, said she didn't know why she traded them all for nothing. But Lorna knew. Cara didn't want to have things that made her stand out. She wanted to be the same as everyone else, wanted people to like her.

Did she know that her mother liked her? Did she care?

But it was good for Cara to have so many people around. If Lorna didn't make it much longer, at least Cara would have a crowd to fall into. It wasn't so long ago that Cara spent too much time alone. She remembered how it troubled and even annoyed her that Cara seemed to lack social skill, that she preferred to spend her spare time beating a tennis ball against the wall. But now, she pictured Cara earlier that evening, getting ready to meet her friends, carefully applying her grape Chapstick in the hall mirror: taller than Lorna, but still drowning in her trendy corduroy overalls. She'd forgotten her hat and gloves on the way out the door. It was always so urgent to get back to the friends she'd spent all day with, all week with. Lorna never thought she would long for her lonely, tennis ball–beating girl. Why hadn't she spent more time with her daughter when she'd had the chance?

Lorna turned the CD over and slid it in. She did her best to smile at Bruce. She tried to think of something interesting to say, something she'd read about in a magazine or heard on the radio.

"Can we get Eddie Murphy?" Christopher asked.

Bruce turned slightly. "Again?"

Lorna felt an odd twinge of longing for a time she'd never really lived. At fourteen, Jed wouldn't have been caught dead renting a movie with her on a Friday night, much less the same movie twice. But what, in life, could possibly be more wonderful? She breathed in the damp, wintry smell of the car the way a resort vacationer inhales a sea breeze. She looked back at Christopher. "Your skates smell good."

Christopher crinkled his forehead. "My skates?"

Bruce coughed. Did they think she was crazy? Lorna felt her face flush; she was glad for the dark car.

"You ever skate yourself, Lorna?" Bruce asked.

Although the truth was that she'd never been much of a skater, there was one memory that burned bright: Elaine Harbell's skating party in seventh grade. Lorna and Elaine's lockers were next to each other, but the party invitation was a total shock because Elaine was far more popular than Lorna. Talking to Elaine often made Lorna feel nervous. When Lorna turned up at the rink on the Friday night, she was instantly concerned that Elaine would not remember inviting her, but Elaine waved her over. The boys at the rink chased after the girls and tried to kiss them. The girls all screamed "polio" when a boy got too close. That was back when polio was the only disease you worried about getting. Though Lorna hadn't been kissed that night, she could still see herself skating hard on the ice, spinning fast and shrieking with the prettiest girls in seventh grade. At school the next week, Lorna had been shy around Elaine again, and a few months later Elaine moved away, so they never really became friends. It was interesting, Lorna thought now, how the memories that stuck out most were the times you got to feel cooler, bolder, more liked than you imagined yourself.

"Sure, I skated as a kid. But I'm more of a swimmer," Lorna said.

"Competitive?"

"Yes." Lorna hadn't competed seriously in years, but it would feel good to show this man how fast she could swim.

"Huh." He grinned her way and Lorna relaxed, sensing his appreciation.

They were approaching Ballantyne's now. Lorna could see its vertical sign; Bruce was already slowing the car. She wanted to keep going, keep breathing this warm pocket of Bruce's life a little longer.

Bruce pulled up. "Well. Here we are."

The bar did look a little studentish with Christmas lights hanging loosely around the window frames. "Look Alive '95!" was frost-sprayed across the biggest pane of glass.

"That was fast."

Bruce pulled his wallet from his inner coat pocket and handed Lorna a card from inside. "I agree."

Lorna took the card; Bruce's hand brushed against hers. She kept her seatbelt on.

Bruce swallowed, glanced at the back seat, and gave Lorna an apologetic smile. "Listen, I don't know what your situation is," he said. "But I enjoyed meeting you." His cheeks had the slightest dimples. She had an urge to touch the dented, bristly skin.

"Me, too." Lorna wanted to say more, but she was afraid that anything she'd say might be too intense. She turned around. "Bye, Christopher."

Christopher looked up from his magazine. "Nice to meet you." Lorna was surprised, touched. Teenaged boys weren't usually that polite.

Lorna thanked Bruce again and got out. When she pulled open the door at Ballantyne's and looked back, the car was still there. Warm and humming.

Ballantyne's was crowded, though most people were bunched into the back where a young man was setting up equipment for some kind of performance. Lorna found two stools at the bar.

Fifteen minutes until Alex was due. She looked at Bruce's card: Bruce Lawson, Partner, Audit and Assurance, CFA, CA. She didn't recognize the name of the firm.

Lorna looked up for someone to serve her. A blond, ponytailed bartender, not much older than Cara, was wiping the daily specials off the chalkboard behind the bar. "Friday" vanished into a left-tilting smear. Lorna wondered if the ritual of erasing days became depressing.

"What can I get you?" the girl asked, over her shoulder.

"Rum and Coke, please."

"Pepsi OK?"

"Yes, fine. Someone else is joining me in a minute." Not generally the type to drink alone in a bar, Lorna was self-conscious and wondered what the bartender thought of her. Lorna often felt sorry for people alone at bars and restaurants, especially old people. She was sure she wasn't that old, but certainly there'd been a point in her life—this girl's age, likely—when she'd have considered thirty-nine to be *older*. The sound of the number could still take Lorna's breath away. She'd read somewhere that a North American woman's life expectancy was seventy-eight. Thirty-nine was halfway there.

The bartender had a small tattoo of a butterfly at the top of her spine. Jed had gotten a tattoo—the cursive words *Carpe Diem*, of all things—right on his neck. When he asked what she thought, she said she always figured that the sort of people who got neck tattoos didn't know they had a future.

As Lorna sipped her drink, she started to play the little game that now preoccupied her whenever she had a minute or two of downtime on the streetcar or at the doctor's office. She let her life flash before her eyes.

The first time Lorna tried this, it was a little like putting a quarter in a jukebox. She shuffled through years of images, but she couldn't quite find where she wanted to stop and linger. The expected bits of nostalgia — the kids' bowling parties, nativity plays, Easter egg hunts — didn't make the meat below her ribs ache in that strange, sudden way that a whiff of Swedish tanning oil on the escalator could, taking her back to hot concrete pool decks and to Debbie. Maybe it was morbid, but when Lorna's final minutes came, she didn't want to flounder. She wanted a reel of her life's greatest hits. More memories like the skating party.

The music paused and the doors chimed. Lorna turned, but it was just a couple leaving the bar. Still, she began to feel nervous. Alex would be here any minute and she wasn't ready. She hadn't thought of a way to begin the conversation. He had a new life now; her sickness was the last thing he needed. He'd want to know, but wouldn't ask, what would happen *if.* She knew nothing of the arrangements that had to be made. All the deaths in her life had been quick: her mother after a weekend of postpartum septicaemia, her father of a stroke, Debbie at the side of the road. Lorna had never imagined her own death as a process, one with catheters and visitors and foil-topped cups of apple juice. Death, when it came, would come suddenly to an older, wiser Lorna, a woman who found the time to go for walks and knew the names of birds, a woman who could speak a second language or properly load wine glasses into the dishwasher. She had never really imagined the when or the how of death. She never imagined anything but time. Lorna's hands were shaking and she put down her glass.

Across the bar, the young guitar player was introducing his set. Lorna flipped Bruce's card over on the counter. She wondered how long he would wait for her to call. She hoped he wouldn't be disappointed with her, or worse, with himself, if she didn't. But perhaps he'd never notice. Maybe he gave out a thousand business cards every night of the week. He was a friendly, square-jawed man with a lot of initials after his name. What could she do for him?

The young man up front was singing something about sandstorms and hard times. Couples swayed with their arms around each other, eyes half-closed, like there was nothing more romantic than hard times. Lorna glanced over her shoulder at the door. The street outside looked empty and boring, but you could see in the trees that the wind was stronger. A thin film of snow swept across the dark road like a tide rolling in. No sign of Alex. Relieved, Lorna took a large swallow of her drink. What she would do is tell Alex exactly what Dr. Kim said: that there was no reason not to be optimistic about surgery. And, if they couldn't "nab it all," patients usually did well with chemotherapy. Lorna understood that "do well" didn't mean "get cured," but it didn't not mean that. It was an easy thing to say. No one had a problem with doing well.

"Would you like another?"

Lorna looked down at her nearly empty glass. Why not get a little tipsy? It had already been a strange evening. "All right."

When the door chimed again, Lorna found herself thinking, *It's Bruce*. The hope was so strong that she couldn't bring herself to look away from the guitar player. It wasn't such a crazy idea. He could easily pull over, tell Christopher to hang on a minute, walk into Ballantyne's with snowflakes in his eyebrows. But it was a group of young men crowding through the door. They huddled up at the bar, all cold leather and cigarettes. One of them knocked

Lorna's chair and said sorry. She turned and smiled, "I've been through worse." Then she saw Alex coming up behind the boys, his face red from the wind.

Alex hugged Lorna's shoulders. "How are you, Loo?" The old nickname felt like warm hands on her face, and it made her throat tighten. She hadn't cried once since December — only almost, very unexpectedly, when the dentist asked if she wanted to book her next cleaning, because six months out was a long time, and who knew where she'd be then.

Alex slapped his toque down on the counter. His hair was cropped very short.

"You cut your hair!"

Alex ran a hand over his head. "Yeah, well. I had to face certain realities."

"It looks good."

He settled into the stool next to her and Lorna waited while he ordered a gin and tonic. With Cara able to drive out to her father's on her own now, Lorna rarely saw Alex in person. He looked handsome: cheeks ruddy, eyes glossy from the cold. Had he always been handsome like this? Had she forgotten?

"So you're acting!" Her voice sounded loud and false in her ears. She didn't mean it that way.

Alex knocked the wedge of lemon into his drink and pushed it down with his straw. "It was Shari's idea. She says I miss it. Maybe I do."

"What's the show?"

"I don't know what you'd call it. Sort of a college drama? I've got a couple scenes as a professor. Kind of funny, when you think about it."

She picked up her glass. "I think you'd make a great professor."

He smiled. "If only I'd done what you said, Loo. Finished *To the Bleak House*."

"*Lighthouse*."

"I know."

Lorna tried to make her voice casual. "Speaking of not finishing things, have you heard from our son?"

"Nothing in a while." In November, Alex got a postcard from Jed that said: *Guy in Lincoln selling that Wrangler you want. $1000 US. Runs good.* There was a number, but no answer from the guy with the Wrangler. Lorna tried at least ten times.

"When I got back from Renata's brunch on the twenty-sixth, there was one of those long hang ups on the machine," Lorna said.

Alex clicked his tongue. "I'll bet you that was him."

Lorna looked at Alex. She could tell he was humouring her by the way he avoided eye contact, shifting on his stool to stare at the band. Jed's whereabouts weren't a good topic. They didn't feel the same way about it. Alex acted like he had some kind of encoded male understanding of Jed's choices, and Lorna was tired of his admiration for Jed's restless spirit. When she'd expressed hurt and disappointment back in September, Alex was quick to tell her not to take it personally, that Jed would be back to real life in no time. Lorna thought she knew Jed better: he wasn't the same as Alex had been at that age. Jed was much more intense, uncompromising. Sure, Lorna had wanted university for Jed, but what upset her now was that Jed hadn't told her what he wanted. To Lorna, it felt like Jed had run away from her and may never come back.

Alex stretched his arms out on the table and then turned to Lorna with a shy sort of grin. "Actually, I have other news."

"You do?" Lorna put down her glass. "I suppose I do, too. But you go first."

"Well." Alex rubbed his palm across his shorn head again. The bar was silent between songs. "Shari and I are getting married. I'm going to marry Shari."

Part of her was expecting this when he said he had news, and although Lorna felt fine about it, she was at a loss over how to respond. Alex seemed to detect this and carried on. "I just figured, what the hell, you know? What do we have to lose?"

Lorna made a low whistling sound. "I hope you said something more romantic to her."

"Nah. She knows what she's getting into."

Lorna held up her glass. "Well. Congratulations, Alex."

Lorna had met Shari just a few times. She was a children's librarian with a side business selling crystals and numerology readings. Lorna hoped Shari did know what she was getting into, but where Alex was concerned, she could no longer define what that was.

He looked down at his hands. "We're excited. The girls are over the moon."

"Her girls, yes? You haven't told Cara?"

"God, no." Alex took a loud sip. "I wanted to ask you about that. You think she'll take it OK?"

*Good luck*, Lorna thought, but she nodded her head from side to side as though there were many ways this could go. "Don't let her spoil any of it for you."

Alex bobbed the lemon a few more times, chasing it around the glass. "Yeah. I probably deserve a little flak. Anyway, I don't deserve to be this happy. The universe likes to balance things out."

"Maybe."

"How is our discontented daughter?" He did an exaggerated duck, wincing slightly in anticipation.

Lorna felt a defensive shudder down her spine. "She's not so unhappy."

"Maybe not."

"She's a teenager—"

"Yep."

Lorna forced a smile. "She probably didn't tell you, but her French teacher suggested an exchange program in Montreal next year. Apparently Cara understands enough to do something like that." This was all true, but there was no way that Cara would go, no matter how good at French she was. Her grade twelve year with Ash and that other girl was too precious.

"Huh." Alex wiped the bottom of his glass.

"I think she might turn out fine," Lorna said.

"Better than fine, I hope," Alex said.

"Right." Lorna could tell he was about to turn the conversation back to her. It was too soon, though. "So," she rushed in. "When are you thinking of having the wedding?"

Alex steepled his fingers. "Well, that's the thing. Maybe soon. City hall has an opening in two Saturdays."

Lorna sucked in her breath. "It doesn't give Cara a lot of time to get used to the idea."

Alex dipped his straw back in the glass, but the lemon had given up and sunk to the bottom. He put the end of the straw in his mouth. "I thought about that, but how's the wait going to make it better? It's not like Shari and I don't already live together. She's used to us."

"What about Jed. Best man?"

"At one time I might have hoped that, but fuck it!" Alex slapped his hands down on the bar. Bruce's business card blew off the table. Lorna watched it land and stick on the wet floor underneath Alex's stool. "We don't want to wait. It's not a crime."

Lorna tried to smile again but was distracted by the card on the floor, getting stained.

Alex leaned into her. "So what do you think, Loo?"

"I—"

"I know. It's sudden. I know." Alex chuckled. "I should let you digest."

Lorna slid off her seat. "It's...no. Just give me a sec."

"You OK?"

"Yeah, I just need to..." Lorna bent down to pick up the card. There was no heartburn this time. She wiped brown grit off the back. When she sat back down, a little breathless, it seemed like Alex's smile had grown even bigger. "Sorry about that," she said. She brushed the hair away from her face.

"Anyway," Alex rolled his hand toward her. "You said you had news, too."

Lorna shook her head, her thumb and forefinger clamped hard on Bruce's card under the bar. "It wasn't anything, really." Lorna tucked the card in her boot, pretending to wipe at a salt stain on the leather. The moment she'd had with Bruce tonight did not give her the same floaty feeling as her first kiss with Kenneth at the Christmas athletic banquet. It didn't bring the same pride she'd felt watching her children care for a tiny, red-eared turtle. Bruce's touch didn't make her heart leap the way her daughter had earlier that year, grasping Lorna's hand so naturally in the climax of *Jurassic Park*. Tonight's meeting with Bruce might not be anything, really, but Lorna wanted it. For the reel. Just for this moment.

"Come on, Loo."

Lorna took a sip of her drink. "Everything's fine." She patted her bangs into place and smiled at Alex. "I've met someone, too."

# Freedom

You would think St. Bart's would be off in a meadow somewhere with chirping robins and rolling streams, but nope: it's a concrete box, webbed with scaffolding, at the corner of two busy streets. Not happy busy, but sad busy: whizzing rush hour cars, a parking garage on one side, a construction pit on the other, and no shops except a first floor "deli" that sells pale sandwiches in plastic wrap. St. Barf's. All you can hear inside is *Jeopardy* on TV combined with *Coughing's Greatest Hits: Volumes Wet and Dry*. It's like the place was especially conceived to make life look grey and miserable, which I guess is considerate: everyone here is on their way out.

Mom moved here in July. Cancer in the lymph nodes and spleen now, so no point in being anywhere but St. Barf's. She didn't tell me she was going until the last minute, but she made a big fuss over my birthday party in the last week of school. I told her I didn't want to do a whole big thing, but she invited Ash and Lacey anyway and made lasagne and chocolate cake. Her hands shook when she lit the candles. Seventeen of them: it just went on and on. Ash and Lacey stared at the edge of the table until it was done. After that major awkwardness, we went to my bedroom and they gave me a Zippo lighter with my initials and a hash pipe in the shape of a mushroom. Later we went to Goody's.

I typically won't go into St. Barf's until someone with dark hair comes out first. It's this thing that I started for luck, for Mom, and I don't want to risk not doing it. It normally doesn't take too long to spot someone, but because it's raining today and I'm later than usual, I let a dude wearing a Blackhawks cap be enough.

I'm supposed to sign-in at the front desk, but the receptionist never calls me on it; she just pity smiles at me as I head to the elevators. The elevators are old and creepy with buttons set so deep in the wall that pressing them feels almost private, like sticking your finger into a stranger's bellybutton.

Mom's bed isn't in her room when I get there. Someone probably just wheeled her out for tests or something, but I'm worried anyway that I should have waited for actual dark hair. No more slacking off. I promise myself that next time — *please let there be one, please let there be one, please let there be one, please let there be one, please let there be one, please let there be one, please let there be one* — I'll wait for seven dark-haired people. Mom's name is still outside the door: Lorna Kedzie. The disposable paper name card is terrible looking. No one is even pretending that patients will be here for long. The paper says: this is a name that will expire.

I sit in the chair by the window, resting against a heart-shaped pillow that someone from Mom's swim team gave her, someone who obviously doesn't know that Mom hates cheap crap.

If Mom were dead already, probably someone would have called the school, but you really never know with these nurses.

They miss stuff. For example, sometimes they forget to take the foil off Mom's apple juice cups and she basically has to wait for me to arrive before drinking anything. If I didn't show up, would they just take the juice away while she's asleep? Let her get dehydrated? They also speak to Mom like she's five years old. When I visit, they're always like, "Oh, Lorna! Look who's here! Aren't we lucky?" It's embarrassing. Sometimes they show me her arts and crafts projects—like this church she made out of sugar cubes—and talk like it's the greatest thing she's ever accomplished, but it's totally depressing because Mom doesn't like arts and crafts. Do they even know she was practically an Olympian?

On Mom's bedside table, next to a family photo from a very long ago Halloween, is an open roll of wine gums. I count nine grooves in the foil and eat two to bring the number down to seven. When Mom got cancer, she switched from Nicorette to wine gums, and packs of the gummies were everywhere: the kitchen drawers, the bathroom, and every purse. Once I ate her last one in the car without realizing, and she lost her shit. I told her they tasted like sour leather and she shouldn't be so obsessed. She said they only tasted that way to a thief. I felt bad for stealing her candy but actually worse for ruining her whole concept of a treat when she's dying.

The expiry date on the wrapper is January 1997. It's fucked up that this stuff will outlast Mom. A week ago, the doctor on the floor told Dad and me that Mom had about three months. Then he said, "But these estimates can mean anything." I rip the dated part of the wine-gum wrapper so she'll never have to think about dates.

After a while of sitting in silence, I finally hear the thrum of wheels on the hospital tile. A blond nurse brings Mom's bed through the open door. She holds a finger to her lips, and I let go of the breath that I didn't know I was holding. Mom is propped up on the bed, but she is sound asleep. Her wrists dangle over the sides, and her hands are bluish pink, the exact colour of frozen turkey. Her mouth is hanging open, and I think of that old kids' song about an old lady who swallowed a fly. No one knows why she swallowed the fly, but perhaps she'll die.

Mom is wearing her swim team sweatshirt. If you can believe it, her swim team name is the Brown Beavers. These middle-aged women actually go around in public with that name blaring on their shirts. It's so awful. Seriously, Mom's face could have been on milk cartons and cereal boxes. Now she's going to die with her Brown Beavers sweatshirt on.

I get a paper out of my backpack and write: *Cara wuz here. Stop avoiding me. It's rainy, the worst. Later Christian Slater.* It's not like I want all this credit exactly, but I want Mom to know that someone came to see her. I pause for a moment, and then I write: *P.S. Lee's back.*

Ash called on Wednesday to say she saw Lee at CanPharm, the drugstore where Lee and Jed used to work as bike couriers. Actually, what she said was, "Jesus rose again and he's playing at Drifters on Thursday." Ash has been obsessed with Lee since grade nine. He looks slightly like the Jesus in paintings: long greasy hair, almond-shaped eyes, skinny but muscular. Still, it's completely lame to call someone that. The only reason I care about Ash's update, and think that Mom will, is because Lee and Jed left together on that stupid bike trip to California last year and no one's heard from him since before Christmas. No phone calls, anyway. I want Dad to hire a PI, but Dad says hunting Jed down is not our job and he'll come home when he's ready. Sometime after Mom got sick, Jed's status in this family went from deadbeat runaway to bohemian hero. I guess it makes Mom and Dad feel better to pretend Jed is bravely living his life to the fullest or something. The truth is he's a selfish ass.

Because Mom's asleep, I do the rounds of her room before leaving, tapping each window and the door seven times. It's just an old habit at this point. It probably doesn't make a difference, but it can't do any harm, and now is not the time to really test things. But when I'm done the sevens, I don't leave. I sit for a while and watch Mom breathe, making sure her chest is moving up and down. When Jed and I were babies, Mom said she did this, too: stood over our cribs and stared at our chests. Until grade two, at least, I made Mom sit on the end of my bed until I fell asleep. I think about that now: that cozy, safe feeling of having her so close by, mixed with the anxiety of knowing she would slip away again once my eyes were closed long enough.

The streetlights come on and the bottoms of Mom's sheets flood with yellow light. The woman in the next room turns off her TV. I look back at my note and tear off the PS. Maybe it's cruel to get her hopes up. I shut the heavy blue drapes on the window and squeeze Mom's blanketed foot on the way out.


On Thursday night, Ash, Lacey, and I sit at a table at the back of Drifters waiting for Freedom Horses, Lee's new band. I recognize a few other people Jed used to hang out with, but I don't know any of them well enough to talk to. I always feel idiotic, or at least act that way, around my brother's friends. I spoke to Lee exactly once last year when he was in our kitchen, stirring some kind of special drug tea. I told him the tea looked like piss. He said, "No problem for me, so long as it's not." Then I said the lamest thing in the world. I said, "It's snot?"

Since the beginning of the school year, Ash has been dressing all 90210 prep: spaghetti straps, chunky high heels, boot-cut jeans. But tonight, for Lee's sake, she's wearing last year's full on hippie-gear: clay beads, bandana, bell-bottoms. Real hippies, like Dad's girlfriend Shari, don't use deodorant or cut their hair. Ash, on the other hand, is pretty much the vainest person I know. Even now she's staring at her reflection in the blacktopped table.

When Freedom Horses come on, everyone goes nuts. A few kids bounce around and bash into each other near the stage like they're too excited to stay contained within their own bodies. I normally can't stand live music if I don't know the songs, but this is OK. Along with the usual stuff, Freedom Horses has a trumpet, a trombone, and tambourines. Lee just plays guitar. He looks more skinny and bearded than I remember him, and his hair is knotted into a half ponytail, like a girl's. I glance at Ash, but she's in some fake sort of trance, biting her lower lip and shaking her hair to the music.

When the first set is done, a waiter not much older than us asks what we're having.

"Just draft for me," Ash says.

"And you two?"

"Kahlua?" Lacey sits up tall in her chair.

"Kahlua," the guy repeats. "Like a shot, or . . . ?"

"Um, just like a glass?" She glances at Ash. Lacey cuts her hair identical to Ash and went on the pill the exact same day, though neither of them is actually screwing anyone. Ash blew

Stu Maynard once in her basement, but they didn't go all the way. And I'm pretty sure that even I've fooled around more than Lacey has. I took my shirt off for a private school guy at a party three weeks ago and probably would have gone further, but then he barfed up, like, two litres of vodka and OJ.

The waiter guy looks from Lacey to Ash. It's easy to see what's going on here. He knows we're underage, but he thinks Ash is hot. Her hotness can be useful. "A glass of Kahlua," he repeats. "Look, I can't serve that, exactly."

"No problem." Ash sticks out her chin and smiles, showing off her shiny white teeth. "We'll all have draft."

When the waiter leaves, I swear Lacey's about to cry from embarrassment. She starts apologizing and Ash goes, "Being sorry is not really the point." I'm hardly listening, though, because the set's over and Lee is hopping down from the stage. A girl with thick dreads grabs him around the waist, and they have this drawn out, slow-dancey hug. If Ash weren't so mesmerized by her own lecture, she'd see that Lee probably has a girlfriend.

As Lee makes his way to the bar, I get down from my stool. "I'm going to talk to him."

Ash narrows her eyes at me. "You're just going to go up to him?"

"Yep."

The courage that got me out of my chair drains completely as I cross the room. I know Ash and Lacey are staring. I squeeze next to Lee, close enough to feel heat coming off his skin. My heart feels like it will gallop right out of my chest, but I cross my arms all casual and say, "So. You're back."

He turns toward me and pulls a cigarette from behind his ear. "What?"

"Unless you have an evil twin."

He packs the smoke on top of the bar. "Who are you again?"

"Jed Ketchum's sister."

"Right on."

I don't think he recognizes me. I'm always remembering people who don't remember me. "How is he?"

Lee squints out at the crowd. "Jed's Jed."

I don't think anyone would ever describe me as Cara's Cara. That wouldn't mean anything. For Jed, it's obvious. Jed just does his thing, which is whatever he wants. Fuck other people's feelings. If he hurts anyone doing his thing, he basically thinks it's their problem for not being as freewheeling and independent as he is. He loves being this way, considers it a special gift. "Do you know how to get ahold of him?" I ask.

"Not really, man."

"So you don't have a number or anything?"

"No, man, I don't."

I wish he'd stop calling me man. I bet he wouldn't call Ash man. I should have brought her over. He glances at the stage again like he's looking for an excuse to blow off this conversation.

"Well, is he alive at least?"

"Last I heard."

"Good for him," I say. "His mom's dying."

Lee looks hard at me for a second like he's trying to decide if someone would joke about this. The light from behind the bar shows ridges of scarred skin at the sides of his face. I bet if I touched his cheekbone, it would feel like zucchini peel. He slides one hand under his armpit and lets out a beery sigh. I think how much Ash would want that beer breath all over her face. "You want a drink?"

I guess this is his way of saying sorry. Sorry for being a jerk, or sorry for my mom dying. "I'll have a bottle of draft," I say.

"A bottle of draft?" He tilts his head.

"If that's OK."

"Whatever you say." Lee holds up an empty bottle and flashes two fingers at the bartender. I really want to look back at Ash.

"Your brother and I split ways in San Luis Obispo," he says. "We ran out of cash, but you know Jed."

"Did he make it to California?"

"That's where SLO's at."

Jed made it. Mom would probably like that.

Lee motions for a pen from the girl behind the bar. When she hands it to him, I can tell from her face that she's thinking: *Of all the chicks in here, why would you want her number?* He slides me the pen and the back of a coaster. "I'll tell you if I hear anything. I'm just saying that dude's pretty nomadic, so I probably won't." I write down my number and take my beer. "Thanks."

Back at the table, Ash is losing her shit wanting to know what we talked about and whether Lee paid for my beer. I light a cigarette, squint, and tell her that Jed and Lee split ways in SLO, and that's all I wanted to know from the guy. I love that she doesn't know where SLO is, but she doesn't ask.


I'm not tired when I get home from the Freedom Horses gig, so I pour myself a bowl of cereal. Somehow I manage to knock it off the counter, and Dad comes running in like there's a major emergency, practically giving me a heart attack. Dad stays here with me Sunday to Wednesday, but he goes back to Shari, the twins, and his job at the outdoor store on weekends. I get to stay here because everyone agreed that would be least "disruptive." Dad and Shari are planning a wedding, but it's on hold right now, presumably until Mom dies.

"Doing a little drinking tonight, Care Bear?" He looks pleased with himself for knowing this and it annoys me. "A school night?"

"No. I was actually seeing a band."

"Uh huh. Where?"

"Don't worry about it. You won't know the place."

He bends down to the floor and starts picking up Cheerios. "You know, your mother and I used to go out lots around here."

"Great."

"Superb little bar scene back in the seventies. Jed was born because of a date at that little place on—"

"Ballantyne's. Please Dad, I know." I hold up my hand. I just can't think of Mom right now without seeing her frozen turkey hands. I don't need to think of frozen turkey sex.

"There was a rainstorm that night."

I've heard the story before, pictured the scene a thousand times. I know the world must have been as bright then as it is now, all the same colours and everything, but when I imagine Mom and Dad in the seventies, all I can see is faded beiges, rusts, and browns, like old furniture. There's this great photo of Mom in her freshman yearbook from 1975 with her hair all feathered; she's standing next to some tall guy in front of a tree of dripping tinsel and the text along the bottom says "Seasons Greetings Athletes!" She's wide-eyed and seems surprised at being caught by the camera, but happy, too. Happy and surprised is not a combo I'm used to seeing on Mom's face.

Dad stands up, wipes the fallen Cheerios into the sink, and pours me a new bowl. I know what Dad looked like at that same age because of the dumb dog show he was on. He had thicker hair and was way fitter in his twenties, but I guess people still think he's sort of good looking, or at least a teacher told me that once. Still, his acting career is pretty much in the toilet. In the last two years he's been in one yogurt drink commercial and one scene in a show that got cancelled before it even aired. I guess neither Mom or Dad really became the people they thought they would.

"I know the whole story," I say. "How it was raining and you made Mom invite you in. I bet she wishes it never happened."

Dad leans against the counter. I can tell he's staring at me, but I don't look at his face. "Is that what you think?"

"I don't know. Probably."

"Well, I'm not sure that's exactly how she'd feel."

"Really? You cheated on her." Mom's never exactly said that to me, but I'm pretty sure it's true. This time I look at Dad. He's staring up at the track lights with tired, sagging eyes. He could use some sleep instead of staying up spying on me.

"I knew this was coming."

I think about Mom listening to rainstorms alone in her tiny St. Barf's room. A crackle of anger shudders up my spine. "So what's your answer then?"

"I never wanted it to end up that way. Trust me."

"What, you got forced into cheating?"

Dad's eyelids flutter when he closes them. "Don't try to hurt me now, Cara. It won't change anything."

"All I'm saying is that if I were Mom, and I could go back in time, I'd stay home for every rainstorm forever."

"Well, then, you'd never exist." Dad never gets mad, and it's a little bit exciting to hear the edge in his voice. The reality is,

Freedom **287**

if it weren't for that rainstorm night, it's Jed who wouldn't exist. I only exist because of Jed. If Mom hadn't gotten pregnant and ended up having Jed because of that night, I seriously doubt Mom and Dad would have become a real couple. She's a much better person than him when you think about it.

"Maybe that would be best for everyone," I say. "Because that way you could just be at Shari's right now, talking all you want about the stupid rain or your wedding, and there wouldn't be the hassle of having to think about me."

I look over at him, but he's smiling and shaking his head. "Shut up, Cara."


A week after the Freedom Horses thing, Lee still hasn't called. I'm sure he forgot to even think about me. I consider looking up his number, but I don't want to have some humiliating conversation where I need to explain who I am and what I want all over again. Instead, I start going to CanPharm after school.

I see Lee on my fourth visit, unlocking his lime-green bike outside. He gives me a funny smile when I come out the automatic doors like he was expecting to see me. "Little Ketchum."

I try to act like this is all very surprising. "Oh, you work here?"

He ignores my question and looks down at my plastic shopping bag. "Get anything good?"

"Chapstick."

"Can I have some?"

"Chapstick?"

"That's what we're talking about, right?"

When he ties his hair back into a ponytail, I can see the sweat stains in his armpits. Out of nowhere I have an urge to put my mouth on them. It's like getting an urge to throw yourself off a balcony when you're up really high. You know you won't really do it, but the idea is just there poking at you over and over. I hand over the Chapstick.

"So I think Jed's staying with a woman," Lee says. "Down in LA."

"What woman?"

"Her name's P." He wheels the Chapstick all the way up and sniffs the waxy finger.

"P?"

"Don't ask me. I have no idea what it stands for. What is this? Cherry?"

"I don't know."

"She's older," Lee continues. "Pretty old, actually."

"How old?"

"Thirty-five, maybe? She liked Jed a lot."

I'm not really sure where to go with this information. LA is obviously huge, and *P* can be the start of a million names. But I just stand there, hoping this is the beginning of a longer story.

"She worked at this bar in SLO. I could probably find the number." He smears on the Chapstick and smacks his lips together.

"OK."

"If you want to wait, I should be done this delivery in half an hour."

"Sure. Yeah."

I feel a little bad because I was supposed to go to St. Barf's, but waiting for Lee for info is probably better for Mom in the long run.

While I'm looking at my French homework on a bench outside, I hear a car door slam, followed by the sound of jangling keys and high heels on concrete. My automatic feeling is that it's Mom. When I look up, there's just a twentyish woman crossing the sidewalk. She pushes her sunglasses into her hair and jangles her way into the pharmacy. The slam and click-clack of groceries coming home, of getting picked up from somewhere — those aren't Mom's sounds anymore. They won't ever be again. All of that is already gone.

We don't talk on the walk to Lee's place. He pushes his bike ahead of me and whistles to himself like he's alone. He walks fast, and I need to take a double step every few seconds. I fantasize about Ash running into the two of us together. Sure, she'd act pouty and betrayed all week, but it would be worth it.

Lee lives a few blocks from our old house on a dark, leafy street of mostly duplexes. It's warm for the end of September and people are still acting summery. I can smell the smoke from a backyard grill, and kids play on driveways while their parents garden or whatever out front. I think of Mom's sad planters on our balcony. Also how I'm an asshole because I haven't done a thing with her plants since she left for St. Barf's.

"I used to live near here," I say to Lee.

He doesn't care, doesn't turn around.

There's never much reason to ever come back to this neighbourhood, even though I think about our old house pretty often. When I'm trying to calm myself down, sometimes I close my eyes and walk through the house room by room, trying to remember all the little details, like the exact number of cupboards and drawers in the kitchen and what we kept inside each. Sometimes

I call our old number. I know the number probably belongs to someone else now in some entirely other place, but no one ever picks up, and I like imagining the ring filling up the old rooms, searching for us.

When we get to Lee's house, he rolls his bike up the driveway to the back gate. I stand on the sidewalk, not sure whether to follow or wait for him to find the phone number for me. He turns and looks at me. "Coming?"

At the back of the house, Lee's kitchen is small and dark. He gets two beers from the fridge and opens them under the handle of a silverware drawer, leaving the caps wherever they skitter to the floor.

"One bottle of draft." He hands me a beer, and I try my best to take a sip in a not-losery way, like drinking beers on a Wednesday after school is a totally normal activity.

Lee continues to the living room where he flops onto a corduroy beanbag chair, shaking off his Birkenstocks. Pairs of shoes are spread everywhere in the room. He picks his guitar up off the floor and starts strumming in this casual, absent sort of way, making a low humming sound. I'm not sure if I'm supposed to sit and watch this performance or ignore it, so I just stand there and shift my attention between him and the rest of the room. Every surface is heaped with papers held in place by cups and mugs. The window ledge is lined with small cheap-looking toys, the kind of gifts you might find at the back of a convenience store — a Ms. Pac-Man eraser, a bendy Santa Claus — but also one of those brightly painted, bowling-pin dolls that hides other dolls inside it. Shelves climb most of the wall space, but they have more magazines than books squeezed into them. There's one blown-up photograph of two blond boys with tennis racquets in a plastic frame. Other than that, I don't see anything really personal or decorative. No plants or pottery. No posters or other artwork except a framed ink sketch, propped against the wall, of about a hundred eyes — all different sizes and shapes, staring off in different directions. It looks like it was done by a twelve-year-old.

After a few minutes, Lee looks up at me and tilts his head like there's some sort of question I still haven't answered. "Jesus," he says eventually. "Do you need an invitation to sit down?"

"No." Like some kind of obedient dog, I rush too quickly to the low couch across from him. I cross my legs and then uncross them, wondering which position looks more natural.

"They say chicks who pick at their bottle labels are sexually frustrated."

There's a neat white scratch through the logo of my bottle. I stare at it for too long a time, trying to think of the right thing to say back.

"That's Fever," Lee says. "You're in his spot."

I look down at a hairy orange cat staring up at me from the middle of the floor. The cat arches his back and shudders.

"Should I move?"

"Nope." Lee reaches his bare foot out to run up and down Fever's tail.

I pick up the bowling-pin doll and twist it apart, unpacking the smaller, identical dolls stacked inside. Six in total. We had one just like this in the kindergarten room at school. I used to think of myself as the baby — the hard little nugget deep inside — and Mom was the shell. I guess now I'm something in the middle.

"Russian," Lee says.

"Yeah," I say, though I didn't know that.

Lee lights a cigarette with a Redbird StrikeAnywhere. He looks like he's concentrating really hard when he takes the first drag.

"You can smoke in here?"

"Nobody here but me. My mom's checking things out in Chechnya."

I know I've heard of Chechnya, like there's a hurricane or a war or something there, but I didn't exactly absorb the details. "Cool."

"Sure. She's a professor."

"Cool."

"Right. So *cool*." Lee's making fun of me. He makes his lips thin and holds the cigarette between them. He narrows his eyes and stares.

"What?" I say.

"Fuck, I don't know. Tell me something, Ketchum."

"Like what?"

"Like what kind of music do you like?"

I know there's a right answer, but I don't know what it is. "Different stuff."

"Different stuff. Like what? Like Alanis? You like her?"

"No." I think through the music in Jed's room, trying to remember something I actually like, but I'm taking too long to answer. "Smashing Pumpkins."

"Smashing Pumpkins. OK. Everyone likes them."

"I know."

"I bet you like Porno for Pyros, too."

"Yeah."

"And the Trousers?"

"Sure."

"They don't exist." Lee tucks his hair behind an ear. "But I'm glad you like them. That's what I want to name my next band."

In his eyes, I am definitely a total loser, but I don't want to act impressed by him either, so I just shrug and pretend to look at a spot on my fingernail.

"You know what I'm really into?" he asks.

"No."

"Ancient Greek music. I mean, the stuff we know about." He turns his guitar around like a cello and plucks out three aggressive, springy notes. "It's heavy metal, basically, but without amp. A lot more simple. Totally Zen, if you're into that."

I don't want to be embarrassed again for pretending I know something I don't. "Who's Zen?"

For a second, Lee looks like he might answer me, but he just shakes his head and makes a clicking noise out the side of his mouth. "Man."

"Weird eye picture," I say, changing the subject.

Lee stops strumming. "By the way, Ketchum, who told you about my brother?"

"What brother?"

"You said something about it at Drifters." He looks at me for a long moment.

"No. I asked about my brother."

"Yes. But also..." He nods at the bookshelf, and I look again at the photo of the blond boys holding tennis racquets. I remember, then, saying that weird thing about an evil twin at the bar. As soon as I think the worst, Lee says, "Take it easy. He's not dead or anything."

"Is he here?"

"Fuck, no. You ever see the music video for that song 'Jeremy'?"

I know the video. A little kid snaps and kills a bunch of people at school, splattering their white shirts with blood. I change the channel when it comes on. Videos like that on TV, even commercials for horror movies, still give me scary thoughts that follow me around forever. If I want to stay normal, I can't look at things like that. Some days I don't even look at the knife holder in the kitchen. I'm afraid that if I see it, I'll snap and kill someone in their sleep. I'm pretty sure I could never actually do it, but it's the thinking that's bad. The thought will go around and around for weeks sometimes.

"He's like that kid," Lee goes on. "He's never hurt anyone or anything yet, but he needs to live in this very specific way."

"Scary."

"Just the way it happened, man."

I want to say I'm sorry, that I obviously didn't know he actually had an evil twin, but I also don't want to talk about it anymore.

Lee nods at the eye sketch. "He did that."

"It's interesting." Except that now I'm noticing that a single, mean-looking slit is pointed right at me. I turn to look more directly at Lee.

"No, you're right. It's totally messed." Lee stops playing for a second and pinches the bridge of his nose. "The last time I visited my brother, he said he was going to pick my eyeballs out with the corner of a Post-it note." When Lee starts strumming again he laughs a little bit. "Jed doesn't seem so bad now, right?"

"Your brother sounds sick, maybe. Jed's just selfish."

Lee puts his guitar down and pulls Fever up onto his lap. He looks like a truck mechanic with his cigarette hanging off his lower lip. "Jed's a pretty little stray and the world wants to feed him. Plus it's not like he knows your mom's dying."

"He could call."

"You don't get it. We slept under tarps on the side of high-ways. We ate leftovers off all-you-can-eat breakfast plates at the Holiday Inn. We showered, like, every seventeen days. We were totally incompatible with society."

"That's gross."

"If freedom is gross, I'll take it."

It doesn't sound like freedom; it sounds like being broke and stupid and selfish. "So why did you come back then?"

"Other shit I want to do."

"The band?"

"I've got school in January, looks like." This surprises me but also gives me a hopeful sort of feeling about Jed, for Mom's sake. Mom was so proud of Jed for getting into school. The summer before he took off, she talked on and on to him about being in university in the seventies as if this were relevant information. She took him to the bookstore in August and spent, like, two hundred dollars on school supplies. It makes me so mad that she wasted her money on him like that. She probably won't be around when it's my turn to go to school. She won't be around for any of the things I'm supposed to do with my life, and he just totally abused her time.

"Where are you going to school?" I ask.

"Montreal. You know I was born there?"

"Do you even speak French?"

"Nope. Moved here with my mom when I was two. *Divor-ciados*."

"That's not French."

He drops the smoke into his beer bottle and swishes it around. "Close enough."

"Do you think Jed will go back to school?"

"Probably not. Jed already knows everything, right?" Lee winks at me.

"Do you even like Jed?"

"Sure. I thought you didn't."

"Maybe that's true." Do I like my brother? It's a weird thing not to know. I pick at my beer label then stop because Lee's watching me.

After a long pause Lee says, "The thing is, the two of you are really different."

I make a face like I have no idea what he's talking about. It's obvious we're different, but I want to know how it looks to someone else. Specifics.

He leans in like he needs to get a better look at me. "You're sort of weird and nervous." His eyes move up and down. "The weird part's not bad. But you're definitely afraid of me."

"No." I make a snorting noise, but it's too sudden and totally unconvincing.

He gestures to the spot next to me on the couch and cocks his head. "May I?" I shrug and slide to one side, my face and armpits getting warm. For a second I'm afraid Lee isn't Lee at all. That Lee is still off with Jed somewhere and this is his no-name evil twin. But I'm also pretty sure that I don't really think that: it's my brain making up a reason for feeling so nervous. It does that.

Lee crosses the floor and drops down next to me. I smell his greasy hair and warm, sour breath. I notice his right hand has one long, dirty thumbnail. It feels like this is some kind of test, his sitting next to me. Lee doesn't want to help me unless I'm cool enough, but I don't know how I'm supposed to act. He rolls his head back and looks up at the ceiling. I stretch my legs out in front of me and try to look totally relaxed.

"Jed didn't talk much about his family."

"I'm not surprised." But part of me is surprised. What did they talk about all that time? Mom probably thinks about him a thousand times a day. Worried herself into getting cancer.

"Gotta go meet some people." Lee claps my knee suddenly and it makes me jump. It could have been funny, but Lee looks totally surprised and even sorry to have startled me. "Shit, man. Did you forget I was here?"

I stand up then, feeling like an extreme reject and just wanting to go. "No. Thanks for the beer."

"Hang on." Lee gets up, too, and goes to the bookshelf and pulls out a chubby pink paperback. "Read this sometime." He tosses it to me and, thank god, I catch it. The cover says *Zen and the Art of Motorcycle Maintenance.* "Get educated, all right?"

I leave Lee's house with the book and walk through the tree-lined streets, out of my old neighbourhood and back to our apartment. We never looked for the phone number.


The next time I visit St. Barf's, Mom is awake and reading a giant book: *Don Quixote.* She has a bunch of big books like that at the hospital. She says she's trying to make up for lost time, but what's the point of reading a bunch of stories and information that you won't ever get to use or think about in your actual life? Anyway, she puts the book down and asks me to get the cards from the bin beside her bed.

"How's everything settling at school?" she asks.

I stack the cards up on the little table. "Fine, I guess."

"Any tests coming up?"

"Nope." I wish Mom didn't still annoy me. Why would she ask me about tests? Would she rather I just go home and study for tests instead of hanging out?

"You're lucky you don't have SATs. I still have nightmares about them," Mom says. "Can you believe that?"

"It's believable."

"It's funny," she says. "I can be any age when I'm dreaming. Does that happen to you yet?"

"I'm not sure."

Mom shakes her head. "Maybe you're too young. I don't know. You get to be my age and every time you wake up, it takes a little while to catch up with who you are. How old you are, everything that's happened. I'm always saying, *Relax, Lorna. High school was a million years ago.* And that's when I really freak out." She smiles. "Because it hits me exactly *how* long ago that was."

I shuffle the cards quickly, the breeze lifting the hair on my arms. "You're not that old." It doesn't sound like the right thing to say to someone who is dying.

"It's always a shock anyway. You run through all the years since you were seventeen, twenty. You think, where did all that time go? What's there to show for it? You'll see."

My whole entire life happened since Mom was about twenty. That's something, but I don't mention it.

"Do you ever dream about our old house?" I ask.

"On Mowers?"

"Yeah. Do the Sokolovs still live there?"

"I heard they moved West."

"Maybe one day I'll buy it back."

She glances up at me from her cards. "Yeah? It wasn't a perfect house. The roof leaked and the kitchen was too small."

"So you didn't even like the house?"

"Not especially."

I look at the Halloween picture on the bedside table with Mom, Jed, and me in cowboy costumes. People get sappy about the past because everyone's always smiling in pictures. I'm sure everything sucked as much then as it does now. I bet I wanted to be Strawberry Shortcake or something that Halloween, not some stupid cowgirl. Jed was the one obsessed with the Wild West. He had that lame talking knocker on his bedroom door: "Dodge, Kansas. Leave your guns at the door." I should tell Lee about it, see how cool Jed looks after that.

"What do you like dreaming about then?" I ask.

"I dream about water," she says.

I figure she'll start talking about almost going pro, but instead she says, "Remember in the summers when I'd take you guys to the dock after the sun went down? You were the brave one, just diving in. Jed was more of a chicken." Mom closes her eyes and starts singing the old song that would get us to jump off the dock, her voice all crackly like an imitation of a dying person on TV: "Two little ducks, sitting on the bank. One swam off and the other one sank..."

I look over at the door, but no one is listening. "Yeah, I remember."

"You told me once that you wanted to swim right down to the bottom of the lake and push the sun back up again. Remember that?"

"No."

"It was sweet. My summer baby. You wanted everything to last." She turns her head a little toward the window. The street lights are coming on; every day they're a little earlier. "How's your Dad?"

I want to go back to talking about those nights when I was little. "How come you never swam with us at night?"

Mom looks at me. "Didn't I?"

"You never taught us to swim like you."

"Is that what you wanted? I'm sorry." And she actually looks sad about it, though I didn't say it to make her feel bad. "I always thought you two had your own things you were interested in," Mom says. "Tennis. Stuff like that."

"Yeah." And I guess I don't remember ever wishing that she'd teach me, exactly. It just strikes me now that it's a little weird she didn't. Did she think we wouldn't be good, or did she just want to keep it to herself?

"I suppose I always wished my mom could have taught me piano," she says.

"But your Mom died, so she couldn't."

After I say that completely stupid thing, Mom takes a slow, shaky sip of juice and for once I'm glad this requires enough concentration to stop talking. I reshuffle the cards. When she puts the cup down, she says, "You should get to do the things *you* want. You and Jed both." Her face is sad again, and I wonder if I'm the reason for it. I feel guilty for not having done anything cool or interesting by this point in my life. It would be better if she could die knowing I was talented or something.

Mom reaches for the roll of wine gums on the bedside table and kicks them toward me with her fingertips. "Take these, will you? They don't taste right to me anymore. My teeth are shot."

"Thanks." I put the pack in my jacket pocket.

"Payback for watching the plants," she says. "How are they holding up?"

"Fine."

"Herbert?" Shame punches around in my stomach. Herbert is Mom's old ficus tree. After Jed left, she moved Herbert to his room for the best sun. By now, I'm sure he's a dry stump, brown leaves everywhere. I just forgot about him. I don't know what my problem is sometimes.

"Uh huh." I count the cards out loud, like she's interrupting my dealing.

"Watering him?"

"Yes!"

"Not too much; not too little."

"I know, I know." It's highly unlikely she'll ever be in a position to catch me in my lie, and I feel guilty for the relief this gives me.

Mom's staring directly at me when I finally look up again. Her skin is getting see-through near the temples, but her eyes look the way they always have: the same deep, rich colour of apple seeds. They're prettier than most brown eyes, prettier than mine, and I'm glad to notice this now, but I'm sad, too, because I don't think I've ever noticed before.

Mom shifts in her bed. "You and your brother used to love to plant things. I thought you'd grow up to care about gardening."

Our supposed obsession with plants lasted exactly one spring when Jed was trying to get a Scout badge in agriculture. We saved our apple seeds and plum pits all winter and tried to grow fruit in the yard. Nothing ever worked, probably because Mom's fruit was genetically engineered Frankenfood from the Discount Ranch. That same year, though, Dad came home with a paper pack of grape seeds on Mother's Day, and we planted them in the hard strip of earth that ran along the fence out front. Dad said the grapes would be leaping up the fence by fall, but nothing grew. Still, thinking about those seeds, my little hands in that gritty, cold earth, opens up a tender spot below my ribs. It's probably dumb, but I wish Mom liked our old house.

"You can bring Herbert here if you won't miss him," Mom says.

I organize the suits in my hand. "Yeah, maybe. I usually come straight from school though, so..."

"Just a thought."

"OK." I can hear the noise of the *Golden Girls* blaring in from the room next door. Mom used to call it the crazy old lady show. It's an episode I've seen before where the four grannies go to Hollywood to star on a game show. Mom will never be an old lady. Like a true old lady. I know a lot of people say that they never want to be old. They say things like, "Kill me before I get that old!" But come on, would they seriously rather be Mom?

"How's your Dad?" she asks again.

"The same."

"Any roles?"

"Doubt it." What I really want to do ask is, "Why do you care? Why would you think about Dad when you have barely any time left to think about anything?" I could win the game if I take her discard, but I don't.

Mom spreads her hand out in front of me. "Gin."

"Cool."

Mom side-eyes me like she knows I let her win. "You know," she says, sweeping the cards back into a pile. "You really don't need to come here every day."

"I don't come every day."

"You have a life." Mom knows exactly what kind of life I have: come home from school, microwave some popcorn, listen to Ash on the phone. She hasn't been gone that long. "Your friends are important. And I realize this isn't exactly a whale of a time."

"It's fine."

"*Fine*!" Mom chuckles. "Remember when that was your answer for everything. Clear the table — *fine*! There's a stain on your shirt — *fine*!"

She tries to shuffle the cards, but her fingers are too stiff and it looks awful. I take the cards from her.

"Your life should be better than fine," she says. "Have you thought about that Montreal exchange thingy?"

"No."

"I wish you would. Are you still good at French?"

"Oui."

I actually have thought about Montreal, but those kids leave in a couple months, and I'm not about to just take off. Does Mom realize I actually care what happens to her?

"I'm very proud of you," she says. "Learning another language so well. I always wanted to do that."

I can see Mom's trying to make me feel good about myself today, but I don't know why exactly. "I'm not that good," I say.

"I bet I couldn't learn it."

"Les cartes." I hold up the deck and start dealing a new hand. We're technically playing, but every few minutes her eyelids close for a long moment. When she opens them again, she sort of fakes like the closing never happened, and it's hard to watch someone pretend something like that for too long. I figure now that she probably wasn't reading that book before I showed up. It was just a show, maybe entirely for me.

By the time I put the cards away and have my jacket on, Mom's actually asleep. I kiss her on the forehead, which feels cool and waxy. I don't think I have ever kissed my mother when she was sleeping. I wonder how old she is in her dream.

The next time I hear from Lee it's after two o'clock in the morning. Dad and I get the phone at the same time and, of course, we both think it's about Mom. I'm tapping the closet already when Lee says in his slow, rolling way, "Sketchum?"

"Jed?" I can hear the hope in Dad's voice even though Lee sounds nothing like Jed.

"No, Dad. It's for me."

"It's late," Dad says. I know he's disappointed because this wouldn't normally bother him. He totally prides himself on being cool about things like late night phone calls, not that I've ever gotten one before.

"Can you just please get off?"

Once we hear the click, Lee asks, "Does Jed still have my Trans-X album?" He's talking loud for late at night, like maybe he's drunk.

"I don't know what that is."

"French-Canadian synth-pop? Jesus. You're sleeping so close to one of the world's best singles, and you don't even know it."

"I thought you were into Ancient Greek music." For some reason, it's easier to act cool and sarcastic in the dark, on the phone.

"Can you check? I really feel like listening to it."

"You want me to look now?"

"If it's all the same to you."

I lay the receiver on my pillow.

I haven't been in Jed's room in six months or more. I expect it to be messy, but Mom must have cleaned up because the bed is made and the CDs have been put away in neat lines on his bookshelf. Only Herbert looks terrible, just like I thought: gnarled and brittle, like some cheesy hand coming up out of the earth. I can barely look. Suggesting I bring him over is pretty much the only thing Mom's asked from me since she got sick.

On the carpet by Jed's shelf, I notice an old Band-Aid—the small circular kind Mom used to have on her arm after blood draws, a brown dot in the center of the gauze. I imagine Mom with her annoyingly slow, careful movements, coming in here every day with the watering can, trying to keep Herbert going. What did she think the last time she was in here? Did she think of it at as the last time? Did she lie down on Jed's bed and smell his pillow? Did she lie down on mine? The idea is too much and I have to close my eyes for a second.

I'm expecting Lee to have fallen asleep or hung up or something, but he's still on the phone when I come back. "Yep. I have it."

"Can you put it on?"

"Right now?"

"Jesus."

I slide the CD into my stereo and sit next to it, cross-legged on the carpet. My life is so different than it was last year. I'm on the phone with a guy at two thirty a.m.

The music has this bright, fast sound—it's artificial-seeming, like fireworks—not at all like the stuff I've heard Lee play before. "Why is this so urgent?"

Lee exhales like this is the world's most boring question. "French people just do shit cooler," he says. "They're ahead. If I want to get gigs in Montreal, I gotta make some changes."

"Isn't this pretty unrecent?"

"Timeless, Sketchum. You should hear the French version."

"I speak French, you know." I squish the sides of Mom's Band-Aid together.

"Yeah? Good for you. You want to teach me?"

I open and close the CD cover, wondering if Lee's question is real. "Are you going to help me find Jed?"

There's a long pause on the line. "Look, I talked to a buddy who knows P."

My heart speeds up. "What did he say?"

"Jed's not with her. They say he's on a ranch somewhere."

I wind the phone around my wrist. "In California?"

"I assume."

"A ranch? That's pretty hard to picture."

"Is it? I don't know what else to tell you."

We don't have much to say after that. I agree to return Lee's CDs tomorrow and we hang up. I fall asleep wondering how long he knew all this about Jed and P and the ranch and why he waited to tell me.

...

I start going to Lee's house pretty often after school. I tell Dad I'm visiting Mom, or sometimes tutoring, which is sort of true because Lee did ask me to teach him French. Dad reminds me that Mom was his tutor ten thousand years ago.

"Don't you think it's sort of weird to be having all these memories about Mom when you're about to get married to someone else?" We're sitting on the balcony eating subs on dirty plastic furniture. If the point of Dad being here is to look after me, he's definitely failing in the cooking and cleaning departments.

Dad crosses one leg over the other and his pant leg lifts up so that I can see his neon sock. The words "Best Dad" are printed around the ankle. I know the socks didn't come from Jed or me.

"Lots of things make me think of your mom," he says. "The smell of chlorine on a hot day will do it."

"Romantic."

He cracks his fingers all nervous-seeming. "What about you, Care Bear? What are some of your nice memories?"

It's hard to watch him. It's like he just finished a book on talking to kids about death. "I'm good."

"See her today?"

I narrow my eyes at him. "Did you?"

"Look," Dad says. "Your mother will always have a place in my heart." I think of Dad's heart like an apartment building. Shari and her girls, Juli and Lesley-Ann, have the penthouse.

It's like Dad knows what I'm thinking because he says, "Given any thought to coming out to Barrie this weekend?"

"I can't."

"Shari would love to see you. We're taking the girls to an indoor water park."

"Yeah, no." Running after Shari's kids in my bathing suit in front of Dad and Shari is pretty much the worst Saturday I can imagine.

"All right." Dad turns and looks out at the elementary school across the street. "Your choice." It's kind of surprising Mom ever had the guts to kick Dad out. When he's disappointed, he's so helpless and pouty. I don't think I could take it.

"Thanks for asking," I say.

After a moment, Dad goes, "Your bedroom in Barrie is always there for you. You know that Care Bear, right?"

"Uh huh." My bedroom in Barrie is just the guest room. Shari's sewing machine and a dozen garbage bags of her fabrics are in there. The truth is it's just too late for Dad to bring me into the penthouse now. When Mom dies, I'll be like Lee. Rattle around in my own space.

I have no idea how to teach French, but it turns out Lee actually wants to learn. When I go over there, he and I start by putting labels on things in the living room: *le Guitar, la chaise, la poupée russe*. The sketch of the eyes becomes *le dessin fucked*. We listen to some Trans-X and then to his mom's Serge Gainsbourg records, and after a while he rolls a joint and we smoke it. Pot makes my lungs itch, but it also makes me less nervous, makes everything around me feel less sharp and easier to blend into. I learn some things about Lee's family, like that his brother Ben weighs nearly three hundred pounds now. Apparently the guy just draws and eats and almost never says anything. Lee's Dad is a dentistry professor; he lives somewhere close to the brother and takes care of him. His mom's pretty checked out of that whole situation, and possibly every situation, but we don't talk about her much. We don't talk about Jed, either.

The second time I come over for tutoring, I bring a French movie from VideoLab. Then I just start doing that every few days. I know French movies are meant to be sort of sexual, so I deliberately go for ones that look innocent, like the one about a little kid who grew up in the wild without human contact. That turns out to be a good one for Lee because there's more acting than talking to follow along with. He gets twitchier than normal during the violent parts, and I wonder if he's thinking of his brother. I try other movies with kids, because maybe they're easier to understand, but it feels kind of depressing watching G movies and smoking up at the same time.

Once I misjudge the description and accidentally pick a movie with no real plot and a very long scene of a grimacing man doing it to a redheaded woman from behind. The man makes low grunting sounds and just keeps whomping the woman back and forth, her mouth in this big wide *O*. Lee and I watch the whole scene with Fever between us. When I get up to go to the bathroom, my underwear is damp.

I get the sense from Lee that our French lessons are a secret, though I don't know who exactly decided that. Lee's always taking off afterward to meet friends or to play music somewhere, but he never invites me to come along. I don't tell Ash or Lacey about him either: there'd be too much explaining, and Ash would find a way to make me feel dumb about it.


On Thanksgiving weekend, Dad goes back to Barrie. He wants me to come, of course, but Ash got a flyer for a warehouse dance party downtown. Someone from another high school rented the place, and there's going to be kegs and bands and stuff. I tell him I promised Mom I would spend most of the weekend with her.

Ash wants to dye her hair platinum blond for the party, so we go to CanPharm after school for Nice'n'Easy. I act casual when we see Lee across the store. I want him to hug me in front of Ash the way he hugged the girl at Drifter's that night, but he doesn't do anything except watch us come toward him.

"What's happening, ladies?" His voice is different than normal, more smiley.

"We're just getting some shit for a party tomorrow," I say. For some reason I'm embarrassed to look him in the eye.

"Legal shit? Sudafed's down there. Mix it with espresso or a can of Jolt."

"We want hair dye," Ash says. She can't be left out of a conversation. It's weird that she doesn't just automatically know that Lee probably thinks hair dye is girly and superficial.

Lee looks at her. "Why? Your hair's awesome the way it is."

Ash blushes and I don't like the way his eyes move over her dumb denim dress that she knows makes her look exactly like Jennifer Aniston.

"Whose party?" he asks.

"Warehouse dance thing," Ash says. Lee looks at me. He angles his head like *really?* "You should come," Ash says, bold now that Lee actually talked to her. She glances at me: *see what I can do.*

"Not my scene." Lee glances at the pharmacy counter. "But if you want better provisions—Ritalin, Diazepam, 3s—she has my number." He nods vaguely in my direction.

"We'll definitely do that," Ash says.

Ash decides not to buy any dye at all. I get a box of some house brand described as "Rousse Mouse" with a picture of a redhead with giant tits on the box.

When we leave CanPharm, Ash is giddy about her one-second conversation with Lee. I want to tell her that she doesn't know anything, that Lee gave me a pink book—a book just for me about some Greek god—and that we talk on the phone late at night. I don't, though. It feels like Ash could just make the power of it all disappear. Ash asks me over to her place as we're leaving, but I tell her I have to visit Mom because it's Thanksgiving weekend. She gives me this big hug at the door and is all, "*Awwww*. I hope your Mom's OKeeee!" It's just a show for Lee, so that she'll seem like a sweet person. When I hug her back, she steps away. "You're, like, the weirdest hugger," she says. "Someone needs to teach you how to hug."

Instead of the hospital, I just kind of find myself in front of Lee's house. His shift isn't over for another two hours, but the kitchen door is always unlocked. I let myself in and take the last beer from the fridge. Fever hops down from the counter and weaves around my shins.

The living room is a mess like always. I clear Lee's guitar and music binders off the beanbag chair for a place to sit. Fever marches around my legs and then curls himself into my lap. Everything feels hushed and kind of eerie. I can't see the eye picture behind me, but I feel it staring.

A bowl of crusted cereal sits next to me on a stack of about fifty music magazines. I pick one up and flip through shots of sweaty guys playing guitar. An article on Rush is folded over, but I get bored after the first couple of paragraphs. Jed still gets magazines like this in the mail. No one reads them, but no one throws them away, either.

On the bookshelf, I can't tell which kid in the tennis photo is Lee. Both boys wear blue shorts with white stripes and white T-shirts and have the same stubby Prince tennis racquet. The tennis court behind them is busy with kids, all out of focus. I wish I knew Lee when we were little. I think it must mean something that we both played tennis and that we both have messed up brothers.

I press play on the tape deck and bob my head to the low beat, watching my reflection in the window across, sipping the beer. I'm acting like someone's spying on me and finding out that I'm this super chill girl. I'm acting like the person I want to be: cooler.

Fever, so warm on my legs, purrs deeply, and I realize he's asleep. The sunlight tilts through the blinds onto my face and my eyelids get heavy. I put down the magazine and curl up on the beanbag, too.

It's the bang of the kitchen door that wakes me up. Fever hops down from my lap, and I hear Lee greet him in the kitchen: "Hey, Johnny Fever. Hey, kitty cat." His backpack smacks down on the floor. "You hungry?" The cupboard doors open and slam closed. The electric can opener whirrs. "There you go, guy." If Lee and I lived together in this house, this is what every day would sound like. The fridge opens and closes and I hear Lee gulping. Then his footsteps start toward the living room.

Milk sloshes out the top of Lee's glass and onto the wood floor when he sees me. His shirt is off and his naked pale chest is a smatter of freckles.

"Scared *you* this time!" I say.

Lee's face goes from frightened to kind of stony. "Jesus, Ketchum. What are you doing here?"

"You drink milk?"

"What?"

The photo is still next to me on the beanbag. "I thought we could play tennis."

"I thought you were going to the hospital." He disperses the spilt milk with his foot on the floor.

I sit up slightly, feeling a little too low with him standing over me. "I used to be a junior champion. Or almost. Did you know that?" I really do want to play tennis now. It would be good to be out in sharp air, just to pound the ball back and forth. "Do you have a racquet some place? Actually, we'll need two," I say.

"I'm not playing fucking tennis. I have shit to do." He puts the glass down. He's clutching a clementine in his fist. "Don't you have a kiddie party to get ready for?"

"Whatever. My friends are lame."

"Cute and lame." He has a dumb smile on his face that feels like an elbow in my chest.

"I actually just came around to get the provisions," I say.

He looks at me like I'm not making any sense.

"At the pharmacy you said . . . "

He nods, understanding. "I only have mushrooms here."

"We probably can't afford the other stuff, so . . . " I'm standing up now, talking fast. The window shows how boring I look: jeans, T-shirt, lumber jacket. My hair is in a dull brown ponytail. No one would go out of their way to tell me my hair's awesome.

Lee sinks his thumbnail into the clementine skin. "Just tell me where you and your friend will be. I'll hook it up, my treat."

"The mushrooms are good. I don't want anything else."

"Whatever you say."

I follow Lee to the kitchen. Immediately he finds his shirt and tugs it on. He opens the freezer door and digs out a sandwich bag of squiggly brown mushrooms and tosses it on the counter. "They're old."

I have no idea how to take mushrooms, but I don't ask. It's like we're both mad.

Lee leans against the fridge, crosses his arms, and taps his heel like he just wants me to go. For some reason, I keep staying. After a while he says, "How's your mom?"

"Good, I guess."

He twists his hair back with a vegetable elastic from off the counter. "You don't have to act like it's no big deal."

I make a face like my mom's none of his business, which she isn't.

"She's still dying right?"

"Yeah."

He rips off a piece of clementine and shakes his head. "Crazy." For some reason, it annoys me when he says it.

"Not really. People die all the time," I say. "It's a pretty basic thing about being alive."

Lee looks at me with squinted eyes. "That doesn't make it, like, a neutral occurrence."

I shrug and look out the kitchen window at the backyard which is a mat of wet brown leaves. "Did you ever figure out what's happening with that ranch?"

Clementine juice hits my chin. "Give it up, Ketchum."

I look back at him, a loud rushing sound in my ears.

"Seriously," he says, swallowing. "Your mom's going to die. She's never going to have to think about her shitty son again. Jed has to live with being shitty." He eats while he talks. "You don't want to spend your life feeling like an asshole, too."

"Why am I an asshole now?"

"Maybe because you wasted your mom's last months on earth obsessed with Jed and not with her?"

I look at the calendar on his kitchen wall. It's still flipped to March. My voice is dry and empty. "No, I haven't."

"When was the last time you saw her?"

"She wants me to have a life, OK?"

"OK," Lee says. "So then have one. Why are you here all the fucking time?" He chucks the peel into the sink.

I stare down at Lee's socks. A sharp, sucking feeling in my chest makes it hurt to breathe. All those times I charged up his front steps with videos, thinking we both liked this stupid secret, thinking we were friends. My throat aches, and I'm so close to crying that it's better not to speak, but still I say, "You should rake your fucking lawn," before picking the mushrooms up off the counter and letting myself out the back door.

At home, in the shower, the piss smell of the hair dye stings my nostrils and scalp. Thin streams of red dye roll down my chest and thighs and swirl down the drain.

My hair comes out a dark purple-red, staining the white bath towels, but I feel like I'm starting to look like someone else, someone older and maybe French. I go to Mom's room looking for something to wear. Her clothes are just hanging in the closet exactly the way she left them, a few blouses and skirts still in their clingy plastic dry cleaning bags. The cool smell of lavender potpourri is everywhere. It feels wrong to touch or move anything.

The one thing I do take is a pair of green pumps from the Goodwill box on her closet floor, shoes I remember seeing exactly once. I was on my way home from a school trip to the planetarium, and I saw her out the bus window on the street, walking with some tall guy and looking all breezy and important, like someone from that movie *Working Girl*. She looked way cooler than she ever did at home, way cooler than the shorthaired juice-box moms on the bus. I liked seeing her in those secret shoes, not boring loafers or Keds. I never told Mom I saw her. I could tell her now, but it's not even a story. It doesn't have a point, but I feel suddenly afraid that if I hadn't seen the shoes in the closet just now, the whole memory of that afternoon would have disappeared.

Back in my own room, I put on a short black skirt that I bought last month with Ash at a store in Kensington Market and a pair of pink star earrings that look good but turn my ear holes green if I accidentally keep them in overnight. While I wait for Ash and Lacey to come over, I try dialling my old phone number, picturing the beige Touch-Tone phone that was mounted to our kitchen wall. It rings once and then picks up for the first time: *The number you are calling is out of service. Please hang up and try your call again.* I try again, but same thing. Why does the operator have to sound so angry?

When Ash and Lacey show up, the first thing Ash says is, "Are we calling Lee?" She doesn't even say anything about my shoes or hair. I tell her I already got the stuff and point to the defrosted baggie on the kitchen table.

Ash scratches her neck. "I thought he was coming though." She has this way of looking right at you, like she can see all your deceit right through your skin.

"I was passing his house anyway."

Ash pulls her cigarettes out of her fun-fur purse and just lights up. She would freak out if I did that at her house, but I let it go.

We eat the limp mushrooms on saltines in the living room, sharing one of Dad's beers. For a long time nothing happens. Ash pouts and smokes, Lacey does her hair, and I just sit thinking about Lee and whether I'll ever talk to him again, whether I even want to. He never helped with anything, anyway.

I turn on the TV to a TLC music video. I'm the only one watching at first, but after a while I guess we're bored of ignoring each other because we get in position, copying T-Boz and Left Eye and the pretty one. It's totally clear that we've all watched the video before, though we're supposed to be way cooler than TLC. It feels like we're friends again: a trio. The three of us work on Lacey's hair, weaving tinsel between her braids and chucking it around the room like an indoor rainstorm. We put glitter on our faces and drink a few more of Dad's beers.

Eventually Ash tells me she loves my red hair. I want to kiss her. I love my hair, too. The colour makes my eyes bright blue, like the ink in Lee's brother's sketches, like my eyes have been scribbled in. I turn to Ash, "Do my eyes look scribbled in?"

Ash looks at me with mean slits. "What are you talking about?"

I turn to Lacey. "What color are my eyes?" Lacey just looks back at Ash.

When I go back to my room to get my purse, I scream when I see the bloody towels on the floor. Did I kill my brother? Is that why he disappeared? Ash and Lacey scream back from the living room. I lean against the closet frame, my heart beating at four hundred miles an hour. "It's nothing!" I yell.

Ash has her hands on her hips when I get back. "Was that a joke?"

"Kind of."

Ash rolls her eyes. "Normal."

"Are you OK?" Lacey says. "Your face is, like, extremely green."

"As green as that wack footwear," Ash says, looking down at my feet. "Uh, 1983 called. They want their shoes back."

"Are you wearing those for serious?" Lacey asks.

"Maybe." I look down, too.

"Just come on," Ash says.

As we're leaving, I tap the door a few times after locking it, my nerves still shrieking under my skin.

"Do you have a thing," Lacey says, "where you need to touch the doors a million times?"

"I just wanted to make sure it was closed."

"You do it all the time," Ash says. She looks at Lacey. "It's part of her psycho routine." I pretend to laugh, like it's all a dumb joke, but they don't laugh back. Ash gives Lacey a look like, *See, she's even more brutal than we discussed.*

On the ride downtown, people on the subway stare at the three of us. I'm nervous and sweaty like I've had too much coffee. As we roar past the ravine, I swear that I can see Mom's face in the window. Turning to grab Lacey's arm, my heart pinging against my throat, I realize that it's just another woman standing behind us. A tired looking woman in a long raincoat, even though it's dry and warm out for the early fall.

We follow Ash's instructions to a line of kids, curled into a damp alleyway. Everyone puffs on cigarettes, talks too loud. People are all wearing glitter and shiny stuff, but I'm the only one in high heels. We stand against the back of a building, breathing leaky garbage bags and feeling the thump of music straight up through our feet.

"These mushrooms aren't working," Ash says.

"I think they are," Lacey says. "Just look at that light for five seconds. It kind of goes out of focus then..."

"Lee should have come over."

Hot since the subway, I peel off my lumber jacket. There's sweat on my forearms and clavicle. "I thought you wanted drugs. I got them for us."

Ash looks at Lacey. "That wasn't really the point." Her voice sounds far away.

"It wasn't," Lacey says. "Ash has liked Jesus for a long time and you're hoarding him just because he knows your brother."

"His name's not Jesus. And he doesn't even like me." My throat catches on that last part. I could tell her about the whole last month and really piss her off, but it wouldn't be worth anything because Lee's probably done hanging out with me. He'd probably say this was the most boring month in his whole life.

Ash turns away so that she's only talking to Lacey, her voice getting more and more distant. I reach out to touch her arm, just to make sure she's still there. She yanks it back. "Don't touch me, psycho!"

A remixed ABBA song drifts into the alley, one that Mom and Dad used to play when we lived on Mowers. I don't think

I've heard either of them play ABBA separately. I move my body a little to the music and pretend I don't care that I don't have any friends. I think it would be cool if every time you heard a song, you could travel back to the first time you ever heard it. That tender spot opens up between my ribs again. Where would I go if I could go anywhere back in time? Maybe the Halloween from Mom's bedside table wouldn't be so bad: Mom, Jed, and me, an actual family trio. I wonder where Mom would choose to go. I hope she'd still go out in the rainstorm.

As we move closer to the warehouse door, a zitty guy in a ponytail starts frisking the front of the line. "No drugs, no weapons."

I look at the guy straight in the face. "Dodge, Kansas," I say. "Leave your guns at the door."

He looks at me. "Pardon, sweet tits?"

"She hasn't made any sense," Ash says. "For a really long time."

But everything makes total sense, and I tell Ash and Lacey I have to go. Suddenly I'm running toward the subway station, my fists balled and my heels rubbing hard inside Mom's shoes. As I bust through the turnstiles, I feel powerful, like I'm strutting into a western saloon with an important message. Everyone stares at the sound of my heels.

Lee hears me coming up the steps; I don't even need to knock. The door opens and he says, "Cara?" It's the first time he looks surprised to see me. The first time I've heard him actually say my first name.

"Jed's ranch is in Kansas!" I blurt this through chattering teeth, before he even lets me in. "Jed's in Dodge City, isn't he?"

I realize the second I'm done how stupid this sounds.

Lee tells me to just come in. I take off Mom's shoes and cross to the centre of the living room, trying not to look at his brother's eye sketch and trying not to cry from humiliation. There is blood at the backs of my heels. He brings me a glass of water and a towel that he drapes over my shoulders like a blanket. "You're freezing."

"I'm actually hot."

"You're coming down."

"I like ABBA," I tell him. "ABBA is my favourite music."

He lights a cigarette and offers me a drag. "Nice hair, Sketch."

My whole body rattles under the towel. Lee puts the cigarette down and rubs my arms. "Get warm."

We stand for a long time with him behind me. Every few seconds, it feels like he moves in a little closer. Or maybe I push back. It goes that way for a while, until I start to feel his heartbeat in my spine. His voice itches my ear tunnel when he asks if I want to go upstairs and lie down. I nod yes, but I'm afraid to look right at his face. I'm not sure what face I'm supposed to make. I've never been upstairs in Lee's house before.

Lee's bedroom turns out to be small with a slanted ceiling. The bed is rammed up against the window, held open a third of the way with a beer bottle. He kneels on the mattress, the streetlight hitting him square on his crotch. I go and kneel across from him, and for a second it's like we're two little kids in front of a campfire or something, waiting for the excitement to happen. He pulls the elastic out of his ponytail and shakes out his hair. Then he hooks his hands around my jaw and pulls my face into his. His lips are warm and chapped.

When Lee takes off his shirt, the smell of wet dishrag lifts from his chest. He presses me down against the bed, and I feel something like a tube of Rolos in his front pocket. Everything around us seems to be vibrating. My skirt zipper snags the soft skin below my ribs. After my clothes are gone, he crosses the room and picks Fever gently off his desk. He searches a drawer, and I watch the bending vertebrae in his thin, white back.

Lee kneels back on the bed and tears the condom with his teeth. I read somewhere that people shouldn't do that, that it could make holes, but I don't say anything, just watch him turn away to put it on. The first few jabs don't go in. I slide up to meet him, bend my knees back farther and jam my eyes shut against whatever's coming. I'm thinking of the sketches in the Grossmans' *Joy of Sex*, the woman's legs curled up like a roast chicken. When it doesn't seem to be working, I reach down there myself and stuff him inside. It feels like cutting. I grab the edge of his mattress and turn my face away from Lee's curtain of smoky hair. Part of the slanted ceiling is stickered with glow-in-the-dark stars and planets. I concentrate on the yellow-green constellations, trying to breathe quietly without whimpering.

Afterwards, Lee and I lay shoulder to shoulder, my arm crossed over my chest. I've never been completely naked in front of anyone. Not even a girl.

"Do you need to go home?" Lee's voice is hoarse.

"My Dad's at his girlfriend's."

He turns onto his shoulder and tucks his hair behind his ears. "We can do it again then. If you want to."

"Maybe later."

"Sure. You want to sleep here?"

"Peut-être."

He squints at me. He hasn't learned any French at all.

"I may be going to Montreal, too," I say. I touch a few strands of his hair and then withdraw my hand because it just feels uncool.

"Non sequitur." He flips onto his back. "Why? What for?" I wish he didn't sound annoyed.

"Exchange. I have an 88 in French." I find my underwear and then pull the thin comforter up to my chin.

Falling asleep, I try to stay on my side of the bed by the wall, but his body is so much warmer and when I wake up, I notice that I've sucked myself right up against the heat from his crotch. The clock radio says 5:21 a.m. Carefully, I climb over Lee's hot, snoring body and find my clothes on the floor.

My lips look like one big red smear in the bathroom mirror, and my chin is scratched and scaly. I turn the butterflies gently at the back of my earrings and feel an itchy, crunchy feeling.

It burns when I pee, but there's hardly any blood. I wet a mound of toilet paper and pat gently at the swollen place between my legs. Downstairs, I wrap Lee's towel around my shoulders and take his cigarettes before leaving through the kitchen door with Mom's shoes in my hand. Fever brushes his head up against my ankles, and I reach down to pet him under the chin.

Lee's block is mainly dark under the cover of trees, but as I walk toward what used to be our part of the neighbourhood, pale banners of yellow and orange light are spreading up into the sky. I light a cigarette and the jogger headed toward me crosses the street. I'm not a kid anymore: it doesn't alarm adults to see me smoking or walking around at dawn on my own. Maybe I make them a little on edge. I walk faster, finishing the cigarette and then lighting another right off it.

When I reach our old street, even the sidewalk feels familiar under my feet; I wonder if the cement recognizes the pressure of my footsteps in the same way I remember its slants and cracks. The houses look like they always did, but some of the cars are different. Our old house pokes out from its usual spot, two in from the end of the block, with its same exact face: wide-set windows for eyes, frowning red door, black awning moustache. The house belonged to us, to me. I could just walk right in and put my fingers on everything. I could climb onto the roof from the back fence. We have garden tools in a knotted plastic bag at home, still crusted with the yard's dirt. But today I'm not allowed any closer than the sidewalk. This house is a stranger now.

A light flicks on in the kitchen of the house next door. I know it's the kitchen because the Costa family lived there once, though now a red pickup is in the driveway with a bumper sticker that says, "I'd hit you but shit splatters!" Mrs. Costa went to church all the time, so it seems pretty likely that they've moved, too. Elena Costa used to paint my nails when she babysat. Now she's probably twenty-five or more. Maybe married. I saw her at the Body Shop last Christmas and was too embarrassed to say hi. When I was a little kid, I watched her and her boyfriend washing a blue sports car in their jean shorts and sunglasses on the driveway. I wanted so bad to be a teenager, to finally be pretty and cool. It's hard to believe that I'm already seventeen. And the truth is, Lee would never wash a car with me, not like that.

I'm looking hard at the house. We were happy here, I tell myself. *We were happy then.* What I want to do is make myself cry. I want to cry like I did when I figured out the Sokolovs were moving in, but I just feel cold and awkward standing here now, staring down this house that Mom never liked in the first place.

A car slows behind me. I swivel around, but it's just a guy delivering the *Star*. The roll of newspaper slams into the fence along the side of the house, making a sprawl of wide green leaves shake. I think I'll steal the paper as a souvenir from this whole weird morning, the morning after I lost my virginity, but when I get closer to the fence, I notice purplish clumps peeking out between the leaves. Our Mother's Day grapes. I sink my hands into the vine, grabbing and ripping the fruit and dropping handfuls into the towel.

When I unlock the door to the apartment, the first thing I see is Dad standing at the kitchen counter. Right away, I know.

He turns toward me, a mug of coffee in his hands. He looks so tired. "Hey, Cara." A dry ache tunnels down my throat. I didn't see Mom yesterday, not all week. Why didn't I go? The last seven days flash through my brain: not one thing I did instead seems at all important.

Dad puts down his coffee. My hand is still on the doorknob. I want to walk back out, tap a few times, and try to do this over again.

"We just got in," Dad continues. "I tried to call you first…" He crosses to a chair across from the door and folds a grey fleece puddled on the seat, a perfect cigarette burn punched into the cuff. "He got the redeye from Los Angeles."

I say this back to myself. *He got the redeye from Los Angeles. He got the redeye from Los Angeles.*

"Get some sleep. In a few hours we'll go see your mom."

"Where is she?"

Dad looks confused. "St. Bart's. Same as always."

I should be relieved, and I guess I am, but it's like I can't breathe. I lean back against the door.

Dad bunches his eyebrows. "You OK, Care Bear?"

I nod and try to say something halfway normal, but getting the air in is difficult: each sip sounds high-pitched. My jaw wobbles and I bring the towel up to my mouth, letting the grapes dump onto the floor and roll off in every direction.

Dad takes a step toward me, but I hold my hand up. I don't want to be touched or even looked at.

He stops. He must think I'm totally drunk or high or something, but he doesn't ask where I've been or why I'm carrying a ratty towel. "Get some sleep. You'll feel OK in the morning." He says this even though it's already morning. Then he says, "I like your hair."

Dad's footsteps fade down the hallway. I hear him run the tap in Mom's bathroom, turn on the TV, and lower the volume. *You'll feel OK in the morning*, I repeat to myself. Maybe not tomorrow's morning, maybe not the morning after, but at least *this* morning. I bend for the grapes, wrapping them gently in the towel to take back to my room. They're not Herbert, I know, but she should have them.

A pair of trashed leather sandals sits outside Jed's door, the soles about ten shades darker than the straps. Maybe he'll call Lee in the morning and they'll go get high somewhere. Maybe I'll go along and smoke with them. Maybe Jed and I will actually hang out now.

The vertical blinds rattle where I left my bedroom window open. I toss Mom's green pumps into my bedroom closet and tap it seven times. Outside, I hear the cheep of an automatic car lock and someone calls out the name Rita twice. I slip under the sheets in my clothes, like an exhausted person, but my body is tense and shivery. I get up to close the window and then again to bury my too-loud alarm clock in the closet. I do seven taps of the closet door before getting back into bed each time. Maybe it's psycho, but isn't it working?

The wine gums from St. Bart's are on the windowsill, and I mash a blackberry gum into my back teeth. I thought I would keep this wrapper forever: the last thing Mom ever gave to me. Now I wonder if that's a mistake, if I'll find the wrapper in ten years and just feel awkward again trying to get emotional over something Mom didn't care much about. But for now I stuff it in the drawer of my bedside table, hidden with my old birthday cards.

I curl my legs up and try to read the first page of Lee's book, but the words blur together. I put my face against the page and inhale. A tickly feeling wraps tight around my stomach. I had sex with Jesus.

Sleep won't catch on when I close my eyes. I try to do the mental walk-through the old house, but my heart's not in it.

When I was a little kid, listening to Jed's breathing could calm me down. I slide up against the cool stucco wall that Jed and I share, listening for the sound from my brother's lungs: up and down, in and out, like water boiling softly. I close my eyes again, but my hands on my pillow smell like rubber, and the muffled tick-tocking across the room is so much slower than my heart.

Three chapters have appeared in other publications in different forms. "Wise" was published in *White Wall Review*, "Ernie Breaks" was published in the *Bristol Short Story Prize Anthology*, "Catch My Drift" was published in the *New Quarterly*.

My greatest appreciation to all the wonderful women who made this book happen: my editor, Bethany Gibson; my agent, Stephanie Sinclair; and my thesis adviser, Nancy Lee. Cordelia Strube, thank you for giving me the confidence to push beyond the earliest drafts. Emma Richardson, Carly Dunster, and Lindsay Bell—your kindness, hilarious anecdotes, and support helped enormously from beginning to end.

Thank you also to the many peers who braved early drafts of this manuscript (and early experiments in general) and offered such thoughtful and generous guidance, especially Todd Light and the Imperial gang. I'm especially grateful to my family, particularly my parents, who have stood by my wide-ranging and often unpredictable professional choices, and who understand more than anyone that writing this novel was the right place for me to land. Finally, thank you, Jesse, for always believing in me and in Cara.

Genevieve Scott is a graduate of the University of British Columbia's Creative Writing MFA. Her short fiction has been published in literary journals in Canada and the United Kingdom, including the *New Quarterly*, the *White Wall Review*, and the *Bristol Short Story Prize Anthology*, among others. Genevieve Scott grew up in Toronto and currently lives in Southern California with her husband and son. *Catch My Drift* is her debut novel.